FANTASTIC TALES OF TERROR

EDITED BY
EUGENE JOHNSON

**Let the world know:
#IGotMyCLPBook!**

**Crystal Lake Publishing
www.CrystalLakePub.com**

Cover and Interior Art:
Luke Spooner—http://carrionhouse.com/home-page

Interior Layout:
Lori Michelle—www.theauthorsalley.com

Proofread by:
Paula Limbaugh
Kat Nava
Tere Fredericks
Jessie Gulmire

WELCOME TO ANOTHER CRYSTAL LAKE PUBLISHING CREATION.

Thank you for supporting independent publishing and small presses. You rock, and hopefully you'll quickly realize why we've become one of the world's leading publishers of Dark and Speculative Fiction. We have some of the world's best fans for a reason, and hopefully we'll be able to add you to that list really soon. Be sure to sign up for our newsletter to receive two free eBooks, as well as info on new releases, special offers, and so much more. To follow us behind the scenes while supporting independent publishing and our authors, be sure to follow us on Patreon.

You can also subscribe to Crystal Lake Classics where you'll receive fortnightly info on all our books, starting all the way back at the beginning, with personal notes on every release.

Welcome to Crystal Lake Publishing—Tales from the Darkest Depths.

**Tales from the
Darkest
Depths**

Dedicated to my partner in life Angela and my four wonderful children for standing by my side. My family. My grandparents, who raised me by nurturing my creativity. To God. My great friend Luke Styer, for always standing by me. To all the authors and artists for their belief in this great project and their support.

Special thanks to my friends and mentors Scott, Paul, Taylor, Joe, Doug, Michael, Lisa, Jonathan, Elizabeth, and Angela for all the help and guidance working on this project and more.

To my publisher, friend, mentor, Joe Mynhardt for believing in me, and this anthology.

Eugene "Gene" Johnson, June 25, 2018

COPYRIGHT ACKNOWLEDGEMENTS

TABLE OF CONTENTS

INTRODUCTION

WHEN I WAS a child, the internet did not exist. There were only three channels on TV. The local movie house had only two screens. During the long summer afternoons, there were only two havens for a boy with an active imagination.

The drug store and the library.

The drug store was tricky if you didn't have any money. And believe me, I did not. I can't begin to count the number of times I hunkered in the back aisle reading comic books and hoping the cashier was too busy or too lazy to notice. On a good day, I'd get through a few. On a bad day, I'd barely get through the door.

That left the library. It didn't have comic books, but it had two things no amount of money could replace. Air conditioning and books. For a poor kid living in an even poorer neighborhood in Hartford, Connecticut, it was paradise. Countless worlds to explore and countless thrilling adventures were at my fingertips and I accepted every challenge.

Whether they were tales of soldiers going to war, astronauts discovering distant worlds, scientists battling sea monsters or simple stories of love lost and regained, I read them. So many aspects of life in

Hartford were difficult and if it were not for my Aunt's unconditional love and my love of tales and stories, my life would be quite different today.

That is why I am writing this now. *Fantastic Tales of Terror* is an anthology steeped in unbridled imagination. An electric stew of fanciful *what if* scenarios. Historical figures thrust into the world of the supernatural. Speaking as an actor, these hypothetical situations are our manna.

Actors thrive on reinterpretation and reinvention. It is the foundation of my first love, theater.

Every actor does their best to bring something new and unique to the beloved roles and productions people have been attending all of their lives. I had the honor and privilege of originating the title role in August Wilson's play *King Hedley II*. It was one of most satisfying experiences of my professional life, but as much pleasure that experience brought me, I gain even greater satisfaction from watching other actors interpret the character. Art has an organic life of its own and creativity should have no limitations.

Which brings me back to the book you are holding. This collection of wild *what ifs* takes the reader to the darkest sides of alternate histories and timelines. Ever wonder what would happen if Teddy Roosevelt decided to hunt werewolves? What if Annie Oakley squared off against Native American demons? Or perhaps Bela Lugosi was actually a vampire? And what reader could resist a tale of an elderly Elvis Presley doing battle with an ancient Egyptian mummy?

All of these dark imaginings and many more await you. Each author brings their unique voice to these twisted, bloody and sometimes surprisingly humorous stories. From my roles in *Night of the Living Dead* to *Candyman* to *Final Destination*, I am no stranger to good horror and the horror stories in this anthology are a good as they get.

So without further ado, the stage is set, the lights are low and the curtain is rising . . .

I hope you're not afraid of the dark.

Love and peace,

Tony Todd

THE DEEP DELIGHT OF BLOOD

TIM WAGGONER

MIKE HOLLAND STOOD in the cramped gas station restroom. It had one toilet, one sink, and one very dead body lying on the floor. The body had blood all over it, and there was blood on the floor, the walls, and both the toilet and sink. The mirror above the sink was splattered red, and—somehow—the ceiling was stippled with it. And, of course, it was all over Mike. He was fucking *drenched* in the stuff. His face was a slick crimson mask, his hair a matted mess, and his clothes—army jacket, *Lost Boys* T-shirt, jeans, sneakers—were sodden with gore. He looked as if he'd just come in from a torrential downpour, except blood had been falling from the sky instead of rain. In his right hand he held a butcher knife, blade dripping red.

The body belonged to Kari Owen, a barista in her early twenties that Mike had picked out when he'd stopped by Starbucks for a white chocolate mocha earlier that week. He'd staked out the Starbucks for three days, waiting for Kari—he knew her first name from the nametag she wore at work—to walk out of the store when her shift was over and head home. He'd followed her for three days, driving his piece of shit

Chevy Malibu, hoping for an opportunity to approach her. It had finally come tonight when she'd stopped for gas on her way home. He'd stopped too, parked, and followed her inside. She paid and then had gone to the restroom. Knowing his chance had come, he'd followed her in, drew his blade from an inside coat pocket, grabbed her from behind, and slit her throat from ear to ear before she could make a sound.

He had never cut anyone's throat before, and he hadn't expected so much goddamned blood to shoot from her wound like water from a fucking sprinkler. She'd pulled away from him and spun around and around, arms flailing, mouth gawping like a fish, eyes filled with terror and confusion. He'd been so surprised that he'd only stood and watched as she painted the bathroom—and him—crimson, finally collapsing to the floor when the blood jetting from her wound became a trickle and then stopped.

She lay in a fetal position, like a bug that curls in on itself when it dies. He'd found her pretty. Brunette hair up in a bun, black-framed glasses that highlighted her blue-gray eyes. But now she looked like a drowned rat . . . if that rat had been drowned in a vat of blood, that is.

"Are you fucking kidding me?"

The voice—heavily accented—came from directly behind Mike. He didn't jump at the sound, and he didn't immediately turn to face the speaker.

"I did the best I could," Mike said. "You know I don't have fangs yet."

He hated how defensive and whiny he sounded, but he couldn't help it.

"Have you ever given thought to working in a slaughterhouse? I think you'd do quite well there."

THE DEEP DELIGHT OF BLOOD

Mike turned to face his companion. The man was tall and handsome in an old-world fashion, with a noble bearing beneath which lay a smoldering intensity. His midnight-black hair was short and swept back, each strand perfectly in place. It tapered to a light widow's peak over his forehead, the style giving him a hint of satanic sinisterness. His eyes were arresting, almost mesmeric, and his lips were full and red-tinted. His skin was almost chalk-white, making him look as if he'd been carved from marble. He was dressed in old-fashioned formal evening wear, complete with a long, flare-collared black cape.

Béla Ferenc Dezsö Blaskó—better known by his stage name of Bela Lugosi—looked at Mike as if he were a puppy that had just vomited, pissed, and shit all over an extremely expensive antique rug.

"It's only to be expected that you'd spill some blood during your first attempt. But that is no excuse for turning this lavatory into a fucking abattoir."

Bela didn't have so much as a single drop of Kari's blood on him. No surprise. His clothing was always immaculate, no matter the situation.

Mike glanced over his shoulder at Kari's body.

"I didn't expect there would be so much. Blood, I mean."

Bela sighed. "The amount of blood in the human body is approximately seven percent of body weight. The girl is short and thin, so I estimate she had a gallon of blood in her. Perhaps a bit less." He glanced around the room. "And it looks like you got out every last goddamned drop." He shook his head in disgust. "And have you given any thought as to how you will escape? It's not as if you can assume the form of a bat and fly out of here or turn to mist and simply drift away."

The restroom was located inside the gas station, and there was no direct exit to the outside.

"Maybe there's a back door I can use?" Mike ventured.

"Perhaps. But it will surely have a security camera keeping watch on it, just as other cameras observe the interior and exterior of the station. Bad enough that you were recorded when you entered. Far worse to be recorded leaving the scene of a murder drenched in your victim's blood."

Fuck! He hadn't thought about cameras!

"But you can worry about that in a few moments," Bela said. "First you must do what you came here for."

Mike nodded, feeling both excited and terrified, exactly as he had the first time he'd had sex, with Lucy Vargas during his junior year of high school. At least this time he didn't have a partner to disappoint—not a living one, anyway—and that took off some of the pressure. But performing in front of his overly critical mentor just put that pressure right back.

He turned away from Bela and started to crouch down next to Kari, but his foot slipped on the blood-slick floor and he landed on his ass with a wet smack.

Bela rolled his eyes.

"Fuck," Mike whispered, his face burning with embarrassment. He raised his hands and saw the palms were coated with blood. He looked at them for a moment, then moved them toward his face, intending to lick them clean.

"The *neck* for Christ's sake. Don't humiliate yourself further, boy."

Bela was right. If you were going to do something, you should do it properly. Mike wiped his hands on

Kari's jeans, then got on his knees and bent forward until his mouth pressed against the wide wound in her throat. He thought Bela would insist that he use his teeth to make new holes, but the man said nothing, so Mike went to work.

He tried sucking, like the vampires in his beloved movies did, but he couldn't latch onto an open vein or artery, so all he managed to do was make loud slurping sounds as he drew in the blood pooled in her wound. He'd prepared for this first by drinking the blood left over in packages of meat, and then by cutting himself and sipping from the wounds. He liked his steaks rare—when he could afford them—but he'd still expected drinking his victims' blood would take some getting used to. But the metallic taste and sickening thick texture nauseated him from the start, and now as Kari's still warm blood filled his mouth, coated his tongue and slid down his throat like copper-flavored mucus, his stomach cramped in rebellion.

The restroom door opened then, and Mike drew back from Kari's throat and turned to see who it was, gore dribbling down his chin.

A heavy-set blond woman wearing a violet-colored sweater and blue slacks—in addition to far too much eyeshadow, Mike thought—took one look at the horrific scene before her, drew in a deep breath, and screamed like a banshee on fire.

Bela sighed heavily. "You forgot to lock the fucking door, didn't you?"

Mike's only response was to open his mouth wide and expel the contents of his stomach.

It took three showers for Mike to get most of the blood

off his body. His ruined clothes were stuffed into a plastic trash bag and hidden under his bed. He planned to dispose of them in a dumpster far away from his apartment. He wasn't sure what to do about his car, though. He'd gotten blood on the seat, the steering wheel, the door, and who knew where else. Maybe he could take it to one of those do-it-yourself car washes and see if he could scrub out the stains. Then again, the station's security cameras had probably filmed his car. He wasn't too worried about the police being able to identify him from the security footage, though. He didn't have a police record, and Kari's blood covering his face and matting down his hair had acted like a makeshift disguise. Still, he probably should do something about his car. Maybe he should drive it somewhere, remove the plates, and torch it.

He'd never imagined that becoming a vampire would be so damn complicated. In the movies, vampires stalked their prey, attacked swiftly, fed, and then departed as quickly as they'd come, leaving nothing behind—except the slowly cooling corpses of their victims, of course. They didn't have to worry about stupid things like evidence and witnesses and police.

Getting out of the gas station had been a nightmare. He'd knocked down the blond woman—who screamed even louder when she hit the floor—and then made a dash for the front exit, too rattled to think about searching for a rear door. He left a trail of bloody footprints behind him, and once the clerk behind the counter got a look at the blood-covered lunatic running through his store, Mike was certain he called

911 immediately. Mike managed to reach his Chevy and get the hell out of there before any cops showed up, but he couldn't decide whether to go straight home or drive around for a while to make sure he wasn't being followed. Although precisely who he thought might be following him, he wasn't sure. In the end, he'd parked at a McDonald's—well away from any other cars—and sat shaking for twenty minutes before finally heading home to his apartment. At least Bela hadn't ridden home with him. He didn't think he could've taken listening to the man bitch about how badly he'd fucked up.

Thankfully, he'd managed to hold onto the butcher knife as he'd fled the gas station. As soon as he was home, he'd tossed it in the sink, poured an entire bottle of bleach over it, and then put it in the garbage bag with the rest of the evidence he planned to dispose of.

He got out of the shower, but he let the water run a bit more to wash away whatever blood might remain in the stall. He'd need to buy some more bleach to clean it out thoroughly. He dried himself and then examined the towel for bloodstains. It looked fine, but he decided to throw it away with his bloody clothes, just in case. He stuffed the towel into the garbage bag, shoved it back under the bed, and started to get dressed.

His bedroom only had one window, but he kept the blinds closed during the day. He wasn't a real vampire yet, but he figured he might as well start getting used to avoiding sunlight. That way, he'd be less likely to slip up and expose himself to the sun's deadly rays once he officially joined the ranks of the undead.

The walls of his bedroom were covered with

posters of women who'd starred in vampire movies. Ingrid Pitt from *The Vampire Lovers*, Catherine Deneuve from *The Hunger,* Sharon Tate from *The Fearless Vampire Killers*, Jamie Gertz from *The Lost Boys*, Kate Beckinsale from *Underworld*, and the queen of them all, Gloria Holden from *Dracula's Daughter*. He was too embarrassed by his fuck-up at the gas station to meet what he imagined to be their disappointed, almost contemptuous gazes. He hurriedly put on a fresh T-shirt—this one featuring Johnny Depp as Barnabas Collins from Tim Burton's version of *Dark Shadows*—and jeans, and then headed for the living room, closing the door behind him, as if to shield himself from the women's disapproval.

Not that it helped much, considering the rest of his apartment was decorated with posters from other vampire movies. *From Dusk Till Dawn, Near Dark, Blacula, Love at First Bite, Martin, Fright Night, Innocent Blood,* and more. And then there were posters of the best actors to portray the legendary Count himself: John Carradine, Christopher Lee, Gary Oldman, Frank Langella, and the greatest of them all, Bela Lugosi. He didn't want to face any of them right now, either, so he got an Orange Crush from the fridge in the hope it would wash the lingering taste of blood and vomit from his mouth. He then selected a Blu-ray from his voluminous collection, popped it into the player, and sat down on his worn, secondhand couch as *Queen of the Damned* began playing.

"This film is a piece of shit."

Bela sat on the couch next to Mike, cape off, legs stretched out, his polished leather shoes resting on the old orange crate that served as a coffee table. Mike had no idea where Bela's cape was. Sometimes he wore it when he appeared, other times he didn't.

Mike didn't acknowledge Bela's presence right away. He took another sip of his soda and tried to concentrate on the movie. Bela went on.

"This is cheap, garish entertainment, more about fucking than anything else."

"It's a metaphor," Mike said.

"Metaphor, my ass. Fucking is fucking."

Mike tried to change the subject. "Want an Orange Crush?"

Bela shook his head. "I never drink . . . soda."

Bela had first visited Mike one night at work. Mike had been behind the counter at Second Run, a small store that sold used movies, going through a box of DVDs someone had brought in to sell and calculating how much he could offer them. He was hunched over the counter, jotting figures on a small yellow pad when he sensed someone standing at the counter—which was weird because he hadn't heard anyone approach. He glanced up and standing there, looking as if he'd somehow been transported from a 1930's movie set, was Bela Fucking Lugosi in full Dracula regalia. He told himself it couldn't be the real Bela, of course. The actor had died in 1956, and if by some miracle he was still alive, he'd be at least 130 years old, and the man in front of him looked to be in his late thirties, early forties at most.

The movie on top of the stack to Mike's right was, coincidentally enough, one of Lugosi's: *The Devil Bat*. The man dressed like Bela looked at the movie and then tapped the case with a perfectly manicured index finger.

"I hated making this one. The stuffed giant bat they used looked like a teddy bear with VD."

There was something in the man's voice—aside from his European accent—and in his bearing that told Mike this wasn't some random cosplayer who'd wandered into the store. Somehow, amazingly, this was the real deal. Mike was too flabbergasted to say anything, and Bela soon turned and walked away. Mike watched him leave the store and head west down the sidewalk. When the man was out of sight, Mike's paralysis broke, and he ran to the front of the store, where his coworker Tiffany Barnes stood behind the register, looking bored. She had long black hair and a dull glaze over her eyes, as if she were on the verge of falling asleep. Normally, he wouldn't have bothered her. There were often lulls in activity at the store, and it wasn't uncommon for the staff to space out when nothing was going on. But he was too excited to keep quiet.

"Did you see him?"

He spoke so loud that Tiffany jumped, eyes wide with alarm. Once her gaze focused on him, she relaxed.

"Saw who?" she said, sounding completely uninterested.

He answered without thinking. "Bela Lugosi."

Her eyes narrowed and she cocked her head slightly.

"Are you on crack or is this some kind of dumbass attempt at a joke? I know you're a big vampire fan and all. Hell, I love 'em too, but if you're starting to hallucinate dead horror actors, maybe you should find yourself another hobby."

Her words stung.

THE DEEP DELIGHT OF BLOOD

Tiffany perpetually dressed in black, always looked slightly malnourished, and possessed pale skin and puffy dark patches beneath her eyes. She was exactly his type, but although he'd tried flirting with her, had even asked her out—with no luck—he hadn't been able to catch her interest. Still, he had hopes of hooking up with her one day, so to try and redeem himself in her eyes, he said, "I mean I saw a guy who *resembled* Lugosi, that's all."

She looked at him for a moment, as if trying to discern if he was lying.

"I've been at the register for the last hour," she said. "I haven't left, not even to pee. If someone—regardless of which old-time movie star they looked like—had come in and then gone, I would've seen them. And I didn't see any Belas. The only customer we've had in the last hour is the dude who brought in those movies for you to make an offer on."

She nodded to the man, who was browsing the Action-Adventure section while waiting for his offer to be ready. The guy was in his early twenties and of Indian descent. As Tiffany had said, no Bela.

"I saw what I saw," Mike said, sounding more defensive than he liked. Without waiting for Tiffany to reply, he turned and headed back to the buy counter.

The next time he saw Bela was when he went to a small arthouse theater in town that was showing Werner Herzog's *Nosferatu*, starring Klaus Kinski. It was a late afternoon showing on a weekday, so Mike was the only one in the audience—until Bela walked in and sat down next to him.

"This one is not so bad," Bela said. "Although I

prefer the original. Vampires are more frightening in black and white."

Normally, Mike loathed people who talked during movies, but as they were the only two present—and this *was* Bela Lugosi—Mike figured he could make an exception.

"I don't mean to sound disrespectful," he began, "but why are you here? I mean, you're . . . "

"Dead?" Bela sounded amused. "As long as my films survive, as long as they are viewed, I endure. But as to why I am here sitting next to you right now, I have come to teach you. When did you first realize you wanted to be a vampire?"

Mike was shocked at first. He'd never told anyone about that, not ever. His first impulse was to deny it, to insist that just because he loved vampire films, it didn't mean he actually wanted to *be* a vampire. After all, vampires were make-believe monsters that were fun to read about or watch on the screen, but nothing more. But he couldn't lie. Not to Bela.

"I guess it started when I was a kid. I was watching *Dracula*—your *Dracula*—on TV, and when you said 'The blood is the life, Mr. Renfield,' you said it with such conviction, such *passion* . . . I wanted to feel that passion too. I wanted to feel that alive."

"Did you know that when I first played Dracula on the stage, I spoke very little English and had to learn my lines phonetically? I barely had any idea what the fuck I was saying."

"That's a showbiz legend," Mike said. "By the time you starred in *Dracula* you knew English. Well enough to get by, anyway."

Bela gave him a sidelong look before speaking again.

"You wish to become a vampire. I have come to teach you how to do so."

"Are . . . you going to bite me?"

Bela burst out laughing.

"Why the hell would I want to do that? That is nothing but movie bullshit. You do not become a vampire by catching a supernatural version of the clap. You must *become* a vampire. It is a matter of personal evolution, a profound transformation, not unlike the way actors learn to immerse ourselves in a part. To surrender to it, our identity becoming totally subsumed."

And that's how it began.

Mike never doubted for a moment that Bela was real. He didn't know if he was a ghost or if he had somehow literally become Dracula. He'd asked Bela about it once, and the man had said some method acting bullshit about how *true* actors—ones who were willing to do the arduous mental and emotional work their craft demanded—ultimately became their parts, and in return, their parts became *them*. Mike didn't really care about the specifics, though. All that mattered was that his dream—of power, of strength, of transcending mere humanity and becoming something more, something *better*—was now within grasp.

Bela spoke once more. "A true vampire does not focus on sex." He paused, then added, "Not *only* sex. The soul of any great vampire story is romance. That is what lies at the heart of *my* Dracula. He is an immortal creature, cut off from a world that has passed him by. He wishes to see the modern world, to be a part of it. And he longs for a connection to a living woman who embodies her age."

"Mina," Mike said, almost reverently.

Bela nodded.

"No more butchering anonymous women in gas stations. You must find your own Mina and make her yours. You must *seduce* her. Do you have a Mina in your life?"

Mike smiled.

"I do."

Tiffany was scheduled to close on Tuesday night, so Mike called off sick—mightily pissing off his manager in the process—and took up a position in the alley across the street where he could keep watch on Second Run's entrance. He knew Tiffany lived downtown and walked to work, and tonight he intended to follow her and, as Bela had said, make her his.

It was chilly out, and Mike—who wore only a dark blue windbreaker—was freezing. He hadn't wanted to wear a heavier coat because real vampires didn't feel the cold. Besides, a hooded parka was hardly a cool look for a vampire. He regretted his sartorial choice now, though, and he kept his hands balled into fists in his pockets and periodically stomped his feet in an ineffective effort to warm himself.

Wish I had a cape, he thought. *I could pull it around me like a blanket and it would still look cool.*

Bela wasn't present. Mike wished he was, if for no other reason than he'd be company. But it seemed the old vampire was too smart to waste time hanging out in a cold alley with his student.

Second Run closed at ten p.m. every night, but there were always a few things left to do before anyone could leave, and it was close to 10:30 by the time

14

Tiffany walked out of the store. She wore a black knit cap, a black leather jacket, and a pair of black gloves. She didn't exactly look toasty, but she looked a hell of a lot warmer than he was.

He left the alley and followed, keeping to his side of the street and doing his best to stay in the shadows. He felt the cold metal of the knife he carried tucked into his left sock—concealed beneath his pants leg, of course—and he experienced a pang of shame. It was a smaller knife than the one he'd used on Kari the barista. The larger knife remained in the garbage bag with his bloody clothes beneath his bed, which he still hadn't gotten around to getting rid of. He knew Bela wouldn't approve of him using another blade, but until he sported fangs, he'd have to keep making do.

Block after block went by, and he began wondering just how far from work Tiffany lived. If they kept walking like this, they'd end up on the other side of town before long, and by then his testicles would probably have frozen off. But she eventually took a left turn and disappeared from his view. He stopped at the corner and waited a few moments before hurrying across the street and continuing after her. He quickly caught sight of her once more and felt a wave of relief. Bad enough that he'd made a mess killing Kari, but if he lost Tiffany, he was sure Bela would never let him hear the end of it.

Mike doubted this situation was exactly what Bela had in mind. This was more like stalking than romantic pursuit. But it *was* exciting. His pulse thrummed in his ears, and all of his senses were clear and sharp. He felt an electric thrill of anticipation in the base of his chest, adrenaline building for what was to come. This might not be as classy or dignified as Bela would like, but he did feel alive in a way that he never had before, a way that up to this point, he'd only imagined. Killing Kari had been rushed, sloppy, and ultimately unsatisfying. But this . . . this was what it was all about—the hunt and the anticipation of its culmination. He was surprised to find himself actually looking forward to tasting Tiffany's blood. He bet it would be different than Kari's, more like fine wine.

There was yet another layer to his excitement. He had a feeling that if all went well tonight—and right now he was confident it would—he might complete his transformation and at last become his truest, darkest self.

He couldn't wait.

The road sloped downward toward a poorly illuminated underpass, and he knew that would be the place where he'd make his move. It wasn't a bedroom where a woman in a diaphanous nightgown lay beneath silk sheets, head back and neck bared, waiting for her vampire lover to materialize by her bedside and penetrate her tender flesh with his sharp, rigid fangs. But Mike no longer gave a shit. Fuck Bela and fuck his advice. This was *his* hunt, and he'd conduct it any way he liked. To hell with Bela's old-world bullshit. This was the twenty-first fucking century, and if you wanted something, you took it, and screw everything else.

He picked up his pace to decrease the distance between them. He wanted to be close enough to Tiffany by the time she reached the underpass so she wouldn't be able to escape him. He paused, bent down, and drew the knife from his sock. He gripped it tight and began walking once more. He no longer felt the cold, no longer felt anything except a burgeoning need deep inside the core of his being. A need that could only be called *hunger*.

He was less than six feet behind Tiffany when she entered the shadowy gloom of the underpass. Traffic passed back and forth on the road above, engines humming, tires whispering across asphalt. But when he stepped into the underpass, the sounds of moving vehicles died away, and all became silent. He was so focused on Tiffany—on his *prey*—that he scarcely noticed.

When she was halfway through the underpass, he glanced quickly forward and back to make sure no cars were approaching from either direction. When he saw none, he raised his knife and sprinted toward Tiffany. He was almost upon her when she spun around and grinned at him, displaying a pair of long ivory-white incisors.

"Hey, Mike," she said, and then opened her mouth wide and came at him.

***

Bela watched as Tiffany crouched over Mike's body, face pressed against his neck as she drank. He sighed.

"I thought he showed promise."

Bela wasn't alone. Standing next to him was a tall man wearing similar clothes—cape included—but his were plainer, less ornate, with the sole exception of his cape, which had a striking red inner lining. He had a serious, patrician mien, and his eyes—threaded with small crimson veins—gazed upon Tiffany as well.

"You shouldn't blame yourself," the other man said in a British accent. "I had better material to work with, that's all."

17

"I suppose you are right." Bela looked upon his failed protégé one last time, and then he smiled at Christopher. "Until we meet again."

The other man gave him a measure nod, and Bela's body began to fold in upon itself. Seconds later a large black bat resembling a teddy bear with VD flew out from beneath the underpass and rose into the night sky.

UNPRETTY MONSTER

MERCEDES M. YARDLEY

THE TITANIC WAS a grand ship, full of beautiful things and people. There were fine ladies and handsome gentlemen dressed in their best. Men and women with gowns and furs and threadbare knickers and skirts. There were children with scrubbed faces and perfectly brushed hair, and other children who wore their poverty like dirt on their faces. They were perfect in every way for what she and her sisters needed.

She met a human man on this ship. He had a strong, white smile and brown eyes that didn't shy away from her. She realized her gait was awkward and her fingers were too long, almost otherworldly. She wrapped them around the railing of the ship and looked out to the sea, which called to her bones in a way that made her breath catch.

"Are you all right?" this man asked. He put his hand on the small of her back, kindly, protectively, an easy gesture that had been bred into him from years of impressive schools. She automatically tensed up under his touch, but then tried to remember the ways of humans.

"I don't mean any harm," he said, and drew his hand away.

She smiled demurely, careful not to show her teeth. "No harm. I'm simply a bit . . . unsteady."

His hand jumped to her back again. "Shall we sit down? Please, let's do that. My name is William. Will you tell me yours?"

She had a name centuries ago, long and deliciously difficult, but that was a more complex time. It was a time where gods left thunderous footsteps on top of the mountains, and monsters openly vaulted against the sky. They didn't need to hide or blend in or secret themselves away. They didn't don the skins and trappings of their prey and move amongst them. Things were simple now. There was no grandeur or nuance in the way that things were. The earth belonged to artless creatures, and she had also let her wondrous name slip away.

"Call me Nim," she said, and she liked the way he tasted her new name in his mouth like the finest fish in the sea.

"It is unusual," he said, and nodded. "Where are you from? I can't quite place your accent."

She started. "My accent? Do I not speak just like you? Do I not use the same words?"

He was quick to placate. "The same words, certainly. You speak beautifully. But the way you pronounce your words are unique. Quite lovely. I'm certain I've never heard such an accent, but at the same time it sounds utterly familiar." He blushed, a strangely human thing, and Nim wanted to reach up and feel the tips of his red ears to see if they were indeed as hot as they looked, but she kept her strange fingers to herself.

"English is not natural to me," she said, and

shrugged. It felt good to sit, to tuck her legs under her as easily as she would have tucked her tail. "I spoke many things first. Greek was what I remember most, I think. After a while they all run together."

His attention was starting to drift, his pupils dilating at the sound of her voice, the cadence of her words, and she didn't want to lose him yet to the siren's curse. She cleared her throat.

"What about you? What can you tell me about this ship?"

She tapped her foot sharply on the deck, and his eyes focused.

"I . . . what? Oh, the ship. Yes. Well, it's very new. Very special. Unsinkable, they say, and filled to the brim with the nicest things."

"Like what?" she asked him. "What do you consider nice things?"

He hesitated. "Well, it's not what I consider nice, I suppose. It's what they consider nice."

"Who are they?"

"You know. They. The ones who make the decisions."

"Like your king, then? King of the humans?"

He blinked at her.

"I suppose I never understand the concept of they. Others telling you what to do. Then again, I never listened to the gods themselves," she said, and smiled. This time she forgot herself and showed all of her teeth. They were sharp and pointed at the ends. "This has been both my freedom and my bane."

Her smile was unlovely, she knew. She was always the homeliest of her sisters, the unpretty siren, but it wasn't about appearances, was it? It was about the song. The desire. The raw need that she and her kind tapped into.

She quickly covered her mouth with her hand, hiding her teeth. She wanted to talk more, to ask questions, and more than that, to actually speak. To talk about sailors breaking against the rocks and the taste of men's blood, certainly, but to speak of other things, too. Of her lost brothers, of sea foam, of the wonders far below the waves that so few humans had the chance to see. There were horrors and terrors and so much beauty their souls would ache.

She couldn't speak of these things, of course. She couldn't speak of anything, because opening her mouth for more than a few sentences would seduce anyone who listened, would drive them mad, and while she would be expressing her love for the sea or her fascination at the birds who float above it in their own ocean of stars, they would be slitting their own throats or throwing themselves from their bows in order to quiet the madness inside of their heads.

A siren is meant to sing, but must silence herself in order to not be a monster.

"Do you find me to be a monster, William?" she asked, but his fingers were already walking themselves to his throat, ready to thrust themselves inside and suffocate him with his own flesh.

She took his hands in hers, firmly, and held them until his fingers stopped twitching. His brows furrowed and he blinked rapidly.

"I'm sorry," he said, and his words were slightly slurred. "I can't recall what we were talking about. Perhaps it is too much sun."

She nodded, and released his hands. She missed

the feel of them, strong and warm with bones and blood. She heard his heart beat. A single heart, such a simple organism. Her three hearts were a perfect percussion in her body. Too ornate. Too intricate.

"The ship," she nudged, and his eyes refocused.

"Ah, yes. Let us go inside and we'll explore, you and I."

There was a grand staircase made of polished wood. It reminded her of the ships of old, where the wooden figureheads were polished and painted, shining like the sun until they were worn down by the salt of the sea.

"Show me more, please," Nim said, and William showed her different tables and dishes, with beautiful cloths and silverware. He showed her how the joints of the ship were fitted tightly together, and, most of all, he showed her how the people walked around in wonder.

The humans! They had dry skin and bright smiles and walked so smoothly on their stilted shoes. Children ran around, chasing each other and not caring when they bumped into her.

"S'cuse me, Miss," one called before scurrying away. Nim eyed him hungrily.

"They can be little terrors," William said apologetically.

Nim shook her head. "Little wonders, you mean. We have no children at home. They're so difficult to come by. They're like tiny breaths of spring."

"No children? But where do you—"

William was interrupted by the long, low sound of the ship's fog horn. Nim was relieved. His questions were getting a bit too close.

"Let's watch more people, shall we?" she chirped. She followed a woman with a feathered hat, and reached out to touch it, cooing with delight.

Men were for eating. Their bones were sharpened and used for tools sometimes, but other than that, they were for nourishment and perhaps a few hours of fancy. But human women? They were rare. They weren't allowed on ships at first, angering the gods and cursing the sailors. They were exquisite, their skin dewy, and their dresses were both ridiculous and magical. Nim looked down at her own dusky gown, pilfered from an unattended piece of luggage. It was better than the human rags she was wearing previously, tattered and full of salt. She wanted to fit in, just for a day, in order to see something different. That was all. Was it really too much to ask?

"I wish I could stay with you all forever," Nim told William. Her eyes were full of lights, she could feel them, but she couldn't shut them off even if she wanted to. She was far too happy. "This is where I want to be."

"Why can't you?" he asked, puzzled, but then his eyes unfocused again. Something dark and deadly swam across his irises, and Nim gasped.

"No," she said, and picked up her unfamiliar, heavy skirts. She burst through the doors and ran outside to the railing of the ship.

The beautiful, hellacious voice of her sisters rang from the sea. They were hungry. They were so lonely. Wouldn't somebody join them and keep them company? Wouldn't somebody offer their delicious souls, their toothsome sorrows, the firm meat of their body to satiate their hunger?

"Not this ship," Nim shouted, but her voice was only one of many, lost in the swirl of sound.

"Nim?" William asked. He had come up from behind her, his face pale and sweating despite the cold air. He looked into the water below.

"Don't look. Don't listen," Nim said, and grabbed his face between her hands. "They will kill you. They have no love for you, do you understand?"

Join us. The waves themselves seemed to echo the song. Forget your troubles. Be free.

"I wish to be free," William murmured. Nim held him fast.

"It isn't freedom. It's death," she said, and was surprised to find her face wet. It must be the sea spray, she thought. Tears were for humans.

"So beautiful," a woman next to her said. Her dark eyes swam with madness. She pointed into the sea. "Look."

Nim knew what she would see. Her sister's faces rose from the ocean as they swam easily alongside the ship. They were stunning, their mouths open in song. Long hair wound around them like seaweed, moving in the water luxuriously. Now it covered their nakedness, now it demurely hid it. They splashed their tails and reached longingly toward the ship.

Join us. Please. We are ever so hungry.

The woman beside them nodded once. She removed her fine hat and slid her dress over her head.

"No, please," Nim said, but she didn't dare let go of William.

The woman slipped silently over the railing. There was a quiet splash and then the water frothed. Nim's sisters sliced the water with their tails and ripped their prey apart with pointed teeth. The sea bloomed red.

"Let me go," William said dreamily, and stretched his hand towards the sea. "I need to go. They're so lonely."

"They're hungry, William. There's a difference. A terrible difference."

The siren's song increased in volume and urgency.

Come. Join us. Jump to your deaths. Impale yourself on our teeth and claws. Let us wrap our tails around your throats until you are dead. Oh, so wonderful! Oh, so wanton!

William's muscles bunched as he pushed Nim away. But she refused to let go. She, too, was a monster of the deep, and she, too, knew how to get what she wanted.

She captured his eyes with hers and opened her mouth.

Stay with me, she sang. Her teeth were sharp and white and glorious. There is nowhere but here, no one but me. Stay.

William struggled, his fingers reaching for the railing even as he seemed to go boneless in Nim's arms. She nodded and covered his mouth with hers.

The kiss was final. He would never heed another siren's voice again. He belonged to her.

There was a scraping and a great groaning as the ship listed violently to one side. Nim stumbled and William grabbed her, pulling her safely to the railing.

"What was that?" she asked.

William's eyes were full of Nim's lights, but his voice was clear enough. "I think we ran into something. What would we possibly run into out here?"

The sisters in the water laughed triumphantly.

Not this ship, Nim sang down to them. Any others, but I told you to leave this one alone.

Who are you to tell us anything, weak one? They answered back, fangs glinting. Nim had been on the receiving end of them more than once. We lust, little ugly one. We feel greed. There are so many on board, and soon they will be in the water. We will feast on their hands and their hearts and their eyes . . .

Stop it.

. . . and we will especially enjoy the one you cling to now. He will scream your name as we tear him apart. He will beg you for help, but what will you be able to do about it? You will do nothing but watch him perish.

Their ugly laughter was the worst part. It always was.

Yelling filled the night. Crew ran this way and that, inspecting the sides of the boat and the equipment. Nim could taste their terror, their franticness.

"We are going to sink," she said.

William smiled at her. "Impossible. This ship is unsinkable, after all."

Sweet human. Trying so hard to calm her terror even as he was realizing the true horror of it all. Was this the way of man? Is this what humans did?

She took his hand and held his fingers to her lips. "You will not be allowed to live," she said simply, and turned away.

He pulled her back. "What do you mean?"

She felt the sadness in her smile. Oh, she wanted this kind person to survive, to marry and have more little humans and tell them the stories of his childhood, and perhaps even stories of her. But that wasn't to be. He had heard her call and would never fully be free from it. He could live in the desert but would long for the sea, crawling on hands and knees through the dunes until he could make his way to the coastline. He would look for her all of his life, forgetting to eat and drink and sleep until his body gave up. Even then, his soul would be trapped if she didn't come for him.

"I'll do what I can for you. I think you're a good man."

She stepped away and fell backward over the railing. She heard William scream her name and closed her eyes so she wouldn't see his horrified face. She hit the water and took a deep breath. The sea caressed her skin more gently than any lover ever had. She twisted free from the binding human dress and her awkward legs became a graceful tail once more.

"We brought the entire ship down," her sister said. She swam around Nim with glee. "All we need to do is wait. We'll have them all in the end."

It was what sirens did. It was what they have always done. It was a curse and a gift, this craven desire, this jubilation for carnage, but Nim had grown tired. History repeated and repeated and repeated. The gods had died and forgotten them. They were simply more predators in the sea, sharks with higher senses of self-importance.

She watched the ship break in half. The lights went out and the screaming onboard increased. She thought of the beautiful staircase, of the marvels of human creation, and felt empty sorrow when the bodies plummeted into the sea en mass.

Her sisters began their feeding frenzy. Tails

whipped the surface and churned the water into foam. They feasted on those in the water and beat at the windows to get to the terrified passengers inside. Their seductive songs ceased as they filled their bellies.

After a few hours, there was an aching silence. The screams and chatter died down, and the sirens, fat and lazy, sank to the bottom of the sea to rest. Nim swam quietly to and fro in the dark.

She found William clinging to a floating barrel, listless and barely moving in the cold. The hollows of his cheeks stuck out pitifully. Nim looked closer and saw a gash on his head. His soul oozed illness and pain.

"My friend," she said, and was surprised at how relieved she was to find him.

"Nim?" His voice quivered in the dark. "Is that you? You're alive."

"I am. I'm so glad I found you. You're terribly hurt, aren't you?"

"I think my back is broken, Nim. Something hit me on the deck. But the water is so cold that I can't feel much. That's a blessing."

He was so dear, this brave man. She swam closer and pushed his hair out of his face.

"Look at me, William."

His eyelids fluttered but he managed to meet her eyes. His face lit up and a smile rested on his lips.

"May I sing you a song, my human? It will make everything go away."

He nodded as best he could, and Nim pulled him to her. He released his grip on the barrel and tangled his fingers in her hair. She touched her forehead to his and sang him a song of freedom, of peace, of love and desire, as she pulled him down to the beautiful depths below.

THE TELL-TALE MIND

KEVIN J. ANDERSON

THE CRAMPED, CLUTTERED offices of Inspector Dupin were less impressive than the Richmond chief of police warranted. The window was so narrow and fly-specked that he had to light a kerosene lamp on his desk so he could read his handwritten case ledgers. The inspector himself needed a shave and a bath, and his dark blue uniform was dotted with stains that had been brushed off but not washed.

But Edgar Allan Poe was not one to cast judgment. He cut an even less impressive figure, bedraggled and desperate, but he had to make his report. He had to expose the terrible crimes he had seen in his mind. Poe could only hope that his strident wavering voice conveyed urgency rather than irrational agitation.

"I assure you, Inspector Dupin, I am not mad. You must believe me. I am not mad!" Poe placed both of his palms against his high forehead, stroked back his unruly raven locks of hair in a demonstration of abject misery. "Reginald Usher has murdered three people that I know of. I've seen it."

Inspector Dupin had initially taken the young writer seriously when Poe barged into his office, slapping the side of his head as if to scatter buzzing bees from his thoughts. Dupin leaned forward at his desk and rubbed his weary eyes. "Has the police department not heard your accusations before, Mr. Poe? And have they not always turned out to be false?"

"Not false! *Unproven*—as yet. I am not mad. You must believe me."

Poe realized that he came across as entirely the opposite. His eyes were bloodshot and red-rimmed from far too much drinking. It was the only way he could silence, or at least quiet, the haunting, yammering voices that barged through his head. "I am not mad," he whispered as if unsure he could convince even himself. "I *know* Usher committed the murders. My senses are heightened. My powers of observation keen."

How could he explain that he often heard the feverish thoughts of others in his own mind?

Dupin poised with a quill pen in hand, the ink pot open, the page of his case ledger still blank. "As a writer and a poet, no doubt you believe in your understanding of human nature, but your claims are preposterous. Reginald Usher is a man of high social standing, a wealthy benefactor of the town's orphanage. He prints the most reliable newspaper in Richmond, *The Epitaph*." The inspector narrowed his eyes. "Until recently were you not in the employ of Mr. Usher, writing articles and literary criticism for *The Epitaph*?"

Poe looked away. "That job proved to be . . . untenable. The things I saw there, the thoughts I heard."

Dupin raised his eyebrows. "The *thoughts* you heard, Mr. Poe?"

"I am not mad," Poe insisted again.

He recalled the time he had gathered the nerve to face Usher in his newspaper office, a finely appointed room that was more a private library than a business office. Reginald Usher had many shelves of fine books, classics of Greek and Roman literature, the plays of Socrates, the lives of Ovid, the histories of Plutarch, the works of William Shakespeare, and hundreds of unmarked journals of ancient philosophers. As a philanthropist, Usher made his wealth of information available to *Epitaph* reporters should they need to look up a fact or verify a quote, and also to scholars and seekers of truth in general, but few took him up on the invitation.

With his fascination for literature, having published his own volume of poems in 1827, Poe aspired to make his living by writing. He had accepted the position with the Richmond *Epitaph*, vowing to become an important reporter. Poe had not expected such a devastating experience when he entered the editor's office, though. Instead of a quiet sanctuary of books, he found the room *loud* with Reginald Usher's violent, unshielded thoughts that rang throughout his sensitive mind. He witnessed what the man had done, heard the screams of victims, felt the blood, and experienced the sheer joy he drew from it.

"He has killed at least three people," Poe said again, resting his clenched fists on the inspector's desk. "I am here to report a crime."

"Who are these three victims? No bodies have been found, no one reported missing."

Poe wished he had a drink as he sat sweating, shuddering, trying to get his thoughts under control.

He adjusted his cravat, swallowed hard. "One is an old man . . . I don't know the name. He was a boarder with a vulture-like eye, a lazy eye. It obsessed Usher so much that one night he killed the old man, smothered him with a pillow. Then he cut up the body into pieces and buried it under the floorboards. You can find the body still there in Usher's home, if you look. Even his wife does not know about it."

The inspector did not look sufficiently horrified, nor convinced. "I can't send police to tear up a man's floor because you've had a nightmare." He narrowed his eyes. "Or because you are at odds with your former employer."

Not wishing to explain, not yet, Poe pushed on. "The second victim was a business rival. A wealthy man from Atlanta who made a fortune in tobacco. Malcolm . . . " He struggled for the name. He'd only caught a flash in Usher's thoughts, drowned out by the hatred and smug satisfaction. "Malcolm *Fortunato*. They knew each other, disliked each other. Fortunato came to Virginia with plans to start a new newspaper that would have ruined Usher."

Poe was breathing hard, the memories as vivid inside him as if he had committed the murders himself. "Usher pretended to be jovial, invited the man to a private dinner at his home, just the two of them. He got Fortunato drunk on expensive sherry, and when the man was unconscious, Usher chained him to a wall in the cellar. He bricked Fortunato up, leaving him there to starve in the darkness, his screams unheard." His voice dropped to a whisper. "But Usher often returned to listen, pressing his ear against the fresh-laid bricks."

THE TELL-TALE MIND

"Your imagination is horrific, Mr. Poe." Inspector Dupin placed the cap on the bottle of ink and set aside the quill, upset that his time was being wasted. "Again you have yet to offer a shred of proof. How do you know these things?"

Poe struggled to put the horrors into words. He tugged at the collar of his shirt. The cravat seemed constricting. "Is there no air in here, man?" The fumes of the kerosene lamp were stifling. Dupin unlatched the leaded glass window and swung it open, although the breezes did little to help. The ringing in Poe's head changed to a different, higher pitch.

He continued doggedly, "The third murder was his cousin Berenice, a beautiful young girl with perfect white teeth, like pearls. Usher was obsessed with them just as he was obsessed with the vulture eye of the old man. He and his wife took Berenice as their young ward, but the girl is gone now. You can verify that much."

"The man killed his niece because of her teeth?" Dupin asked with a long, dubious sigh.

"Because he wanted the teeth, he *needed* the teeth. He broke them out of her jaw and kept them in a jar. I think . . . I think he wanted to make a necklace of them."

Dupin was repulsed. "You have tried my patience enough, Mr. Poe."

"These things can be checked. Find what happened to Malcolm Fortunato. And the old man, his boarder. And the girl Berenice. Where are they? Surely the great Richmond police inspector can solve the crime."

"I am not convinced there is any crime," the inspector said.

"Then prove to me there isn't! If these people have indeed disappeared, will that not be enough to raise questions?"

Dupin was at least partially swayed by the writer's earnestness. "I do appreciate solving a crime." He rose from his desk and went to the office door, calling out into the busy main room. "In the meantime I shall have you wait in a place where you'll be safe, although not comfortable. You need it for your own good." He scratched the stubble on his face. "If your assertions turn out to be false, there will also be consequences."

The nightmarish visions continued to plague him, the murders he had witnessed through the thoughts of a killer. "They are true. You'll see."

The inspector addressed the two waiting officers. "Take Mr. Poe to the holding cell. He may be drunk or disoriented. At the very least he could use a good, long rest."

Poe was alarmed and infuriated as the policemen took him by the arms. "Look into the matter and you'll see, Inspector! I will wait to be vindicated, and then I will see Reginald Usher pay for what he's done."

With a rattle of keys in the lock, the iron bars swung open, and Poe groggily rose from the hard, narrow cot. He had slept poorly in the jail cell, hearing the muddled thoughts of another drunk in the next cell. Worse, he also overheard the violent recollections of a policeman in the corridor, a man who enforced the law while he was in uniform but went home to beat his wife because he liked her when she was terrified of him. The shuddery memories rang in his head, and Poe squeezed his eyes shut.

The frown on Dupin's face held questions, even uncertainty. Poe recognized the change, heard the doubt in the inspector's thoughts. "You've seen it!" He stepped toward the open cell door, trying to gather his composure. His body smelled of sweat, his mouth tasted of sour old wine. He looked a disgrace.

"It is enough to make me wonder, Mr. Poe. I investigated the matter, as you requested. Malcolm Fortunato is no longer in Richmond, and he has not been seen for two weeks."

Poe felt a shiver. In his mind he saw the images of the man hanging in manacles in the dark space behind the cellar wall, while Usher used trowel and mortar, brick by brick, to seal him alive. "Because he is entombed alive behind a brick wall."

Dupin said, "Fortunato apparently boarded a ship to England, where he has other business interests. He is not expected to return."

"But you can't prove that," Poe said.

"Now you're the one who asks for proof?" The inspector extended another finger. "Then there is the old man you spoke of. Some remember a boarder at the Usher's house, and one person even remarked about the man's oddly staring eye. But he has moved on, a transient—as boarders often are."

"Again, that is no proof! He is buried under the floorboards, I tell you. Tear them up, and you'll see."

Dupin was singularly unruffled. "As for the cousin Berenice, the young girl was a ward of the Ushers, but has been sent off to a boarding school in Baltimore."

"No, she is dead. Send a rider to Baltimore," Poe insisted. "You will find that the girl is not there."

"The reasoning is thin to send a courier on such an

arduous journey. Rather, I'll send a letter by post, just to investigate all possibilities. That will be sufficient."

Though not satisfied, Poe couldn't force the inspector to do more. "So I'm free to go then?" Trying to regain his composure, he shuffled out of the cell and down the corridor.

Following, Dupin scolded him. "In the meantime, you are not to besmirch the honor of Reginald Usher. You'll only find yourself thrown back in jail." The inspector spoke wearily as if he knew his words would not be heeded.

When they reached the front office, a gentleman and lady entered the Richmond police station, both of them finely dressed, both looking indignant. Poe reeled back clutching Inspector Dupin's arm for support. "Reginald Usher!"

The newspaperman had a dark goatee, heavy eyebrows, and a stare like obsidian. Poe could not have described a more evil man in his most overwrought short story. Usher had a frock coat, a top hat, and a perfectly knotted purple cravat held in place with a diamond stickpin. Their eyes locked like daggers drawn.

Usher's voice boomed, "Poe, you spread vile rumors about me, and I'll have none of it! You were fired from your position for cause, and this is just some disgruntled revenge."

But Poe's gaze locked on the woman accompanying him, slightly plump with a powdered face, red hair done up in tight curls, a green velvet dress. And a necklace of perfect white, polished pearls, a string set off against her creamy throat.

Poe heard the horrified screams of victims in his

mind. "The teeth. Berenice's teeth! That's what you did with them, you monster!" He broke free of Dupin's grasp and lunged forward. As Mrs. Usher shrieked and clung to her husband, Poe fell upon her. He grabbed at the necklace, yanking it free. He felt the hard white objects in the palm of his hand, broke the strand, and they clattered and bounced on the floor of the station.

The inspector grabbed him, while other policemen rushed to help. Usher raised his walking stick and struck Poe on the shoulders. "Leave my wife alone."

"They are teeth. Berenice's teeth!" Poe howled.

As the necklace broke, the round white objects spread apart, rattling on the floor. Just pearls . . . ordinary, beautiful pearls.

"Accusing me of heinous murder, assaulting my wife! This man should be in a madhouse." Usher glared at Poe. "I gave you a chance, young man. I thought I saw talent in you, but you are a menace."

As Mrs. Usher found a seat and fanned herself, and the policemen collected the valuable pearls from the floor, Dupin dragged Poe to the side of the room, as far as possible from the newspaperman.

Usher continued, seething. "Have you looked into this man's life, his character, Inspector? Edgar Allan Poe is a disgrace to everyone who has tried to help him. He was ejected from the University of Virginia due to excessive drinking and gambling, estranged from his foster father because of enormous debts, discharged from the United States Army under questionable circumstances. I could go on at length."

Unable to deny any of it, Poe hung his head. His hand clenched, as if longing to hold a bottle of wine so he could drink himself into a stupor.

THE TELL-TALE MIND

The inspector's expression changed, becoming disappointed, even disgusted. Poe didn't have to listen in on Dupin's thoughts, and he doubted the inspector would even write a letter to the boarding school to verify the whereabouts of Berenice.

"I have seen enough. You are dismissed, Mr. Poe." Dupin looked up at the newspaper owner. "Unless you wish to press charges, sir?"

"Poe is pathetic, and he hasn't a penny to his name. I'd waste no further time on him, although if he continues to sully my good character with his wild accusations, I shall be forced to respond with all the force of the law."

Usher turned with his lady, and they left the station. The policemen waited a sufficient length of time before throwing Poe out into the streets.

<hr>

Even drunk enough to blot out his conscious thoughts, Poe could not entirely escape from the resounding thought-echoes buzzing around him. At night the taverns, the dancing halls, and the gambling dens were a maelstrom of shouting minds that sucked him down. Poe had spent his last few coins on a bottle of cheap grog which had only dulled the uproar by a small amount.

Now he staggered through the dark streets of Richmond, leaning against the brick walls of houses, keeping himself up by holding the rough bark of a stately elm. Feeling too exposed, he walked between buildings, seeking shelter in the shadows of an alley.

Poe could not go home, not in this condition. Even with the misery and heartache he had given his aunt Maria, she would still fawn over him . . . or his lovely young cousin Virginia, of whom he was quite fond, would want to mother him, though she was just a child. They both knew of Poe's illness, his passion, the clamor in his mind, but for some odd reason they excused it as the workings of a great creative mind. They knew his muse was so insistent it drove him to the verge of irrational behavior.

Poe's parents had been actors, and the spirit of drama surely lived within him. Young Virginia adored him when he told her stories, even the horrific ones that he dredged out of his nightmares. But he couldn't share all of his pain and misery, not the true horrors he had seen in the hearts of even respectable men like Reginald Usher. Neither Aunt Marie nor sweet young Virginia deserved that.

Poe didn't deserve it either, but he had been cursed with a special acuity. All his life the ringing and droning had ricocheted through his head. Guilty memories, dark unintended confessions sloshed out of other minds like the foam from an overfilled mug of beer. He had heard the ghosts of lost loved ones, the violence of past crimes. The only way he could get a modicum of peace was by drowning those mental echoes with brandy, wine, or even cheap grog.

Lurching down the alley, he took another swig from the dark bottle. He turned into another dark street, lost and uncaring.

At the police station, Usher had deprecated him, and the man's belittlement was all true. Poe was a failure in every aspect of his life, not through lack of talent but through a weakness in his character. How could a man lead a normal life when his very existence was an inner battle with tortuous thoughts that rose like a miasma from the crowd of humanity? Poe knew the dark secrets of even the most nondescript man in the crowd. He had to live with the guilt of every sin on which he eavesdropped. How could any man be strong enough for that?

He drained the last of the grog and tossed the empty bottle aside. The breaking glass masked the sound of other footsteps, and Poe blearily made out the burly shapes of three men at the other end of the alley. He had come here hoping to find silence from all the clamorous thoughts in the city, but now he heard a roar of violent anticipation boiling from the men. These were thugs focused on hurting him, with no subtlety whatsoever. They did not even have thoughts of robbing him, although Poe would have been a disappointing mark for any cutpurse.

He tried to flee, but his body was too clumsy from the drink, and two big men were upon him in a moment. He realized the third man was a different sort altogether. His thoughts were sharper, more dangerous and black, like the wings of a raven.

"Hold him," said the voice. "Hurt him."

One thug dutifully grabbed Poe by the collar and hauled him against the alley wall. The other man pummeled him hard in the face and again in his gut. As Poe collapsed, retching, the thoughts of the third man became more distinct. Even though he couldn't see through the shadows, pain, and alcohol, he knew this man. Reginald Usher.

Poe managed to croak, "You'll kill me now, like the others?" He meant to sound defiant and challenging, but he convulsed and spewed vomit on the ground.

"You are a madman, and your accusations are

maddening." Usher leaned close, grimacing at the stink of vomit and whiskey. "I should have these men cut you open and tie you with your own entrails." He paused and grinned, showing white pearly teeth that must surely have been as noteworthy as Berenice's. "Better yet, I should just bury you alive in an unmarked grave. No one would ever find you, and you would suffocate slowly, slowly. Ah, that would be fitting."

In the resonance of Usher's murderous thoughts, Poe knew that he meant to do it.

"But first you will tell me how you know." He shook Poe by the shoulders, slamming his head against the alley wall. "Were you watching? What did you see? How is that possible?"

"I saw because you saw," Poe said. "And *you* can't stop thinking about it." He laughed. "The teeth . . . the teeth were so hard and white, but you didn't expect all the blood when you used the hammer to bash them out of her lifeless face, did you?"

Usher recoiled.

"And the old man with the staring eye! You could hear his heart beating, couldn't you? Even after he was dead, pounding in your head, pounding . . . "

Usher kicked him in the ribs, but it was more a reflex with little strength behind it. The two thugs, though, beat him harder. Poe kept laughing as he stared up at Usher's animal eyes, saw even deeper into his mind. "I see Fortunato on the chains, sloppily begging for his life. You may be a powerful businessman, Mr. Usher, but you're a bad bricklayer."

The man was horrified and infuriated. "You can't know! You have no proof."

Poe chucked and then spat blood. "I have your guilt."

Usher stepped away, disgusted but clearly shaken.

"Should we kill him?" asked one of the thugs.

Usher shook his head. "The police know of my connection to him. If he died now, too many people might question me." He clearly hated his conclusion. "But no one will take him seriously. He's disgraced and clearly deranged."

Even through his fog of alcohol, blood, and pain, Poe found that amusing. "I am deranged? You murder people on a whim . . . and *I* am deranged?"

"Let his own demons punish him," Usher sneered, then considered. "But in the meantime, you can make him hurt."

The thugs kicked and pummeled Poe, but before he fell into unconsciousness, he was smiling. He had seen even deeper into Usher's mind and found exactly what he needed.

The annoyed policemen tried to prevent Poe from seeing Inspector Dupin. He tried to break free of their tight grip, and the struggle only exacerbated the pain of his countless bruises, his cracked ribs, his split lip. His black eye was so swollen he could barely see. "I must speak with the inspector! It is a matter of utmost importance."

Dupin emerged from his dingy office and regarded the battered man with grave disappointment, though he showed a small amount of sympathy at seeing his injuries. "I see your words have gotten you into even more trouble, Mr. Poe."

Poe yanked his arms free of the policemen. "Not

my words, sir—it is what I *know* that makes Usher fear me."

One of the policemen interjected sharply, "He was obviously beaten and robbed while he was in a drunken stupor."

"Do you intend to blame this on Reginald Usher?" Dupin asked.

"It was his ruffians, but he will deny it." Poe tugged on the muddied remnants of his jacket, then stripped off the mangled cravat as a lost cause. "But this assault is insignificant when compared with the heinous murders he has committed."

The policeman groaned, and Inspector Dupin turned away. "Let me never see you again, Mr. Poe. I don't know why you bothered to come."

"Because I have proof! And I can show it to you. A full confession written in Reginald Usher's own hand."

Dupin paused and turned with a skeptical frown. "Usher was quite clear that if you made false accusations against him again, he would press charges. You will be ruined."

Poe straightened his shoulders and looked the inspector in the eye. "If you should find my claims insufficient, then you may arrest me. But you will arrest Usher instead when you read what he has written. I can show you."

The policeman who had been holding Poe looked upset. "Waste of time, sir."

Poe pushed past the pain of his injuries, heard the thoughts and unanswered questions in Dupin's mind, and took hope. "Surely there must be some question in your mind, Inspector?" His eyes pleaded. "We simply need to go to his newspaper office. It'll take only a moment, and you will take a murderer off the streets of Richmond."

"I will lock someone up before this day is done, that's for certain," grumbled Dupin. "This is your last chance."

When they arrived at the offices of the Richmond *Epitaph*, Reginald Usher rose from his great mahogany desk, clearly indignant. "Inspector Dupin, I had hoped never to see you again."

The newspaperman's office was appointed like a fine withdrawing room with its own fireplace, a small side table with a cut-crystal decanter of brandy, an overstuffed leather chair. The walls were covered with fine oak shelves filled with countless books of varying sizes, fat volumes, slender volumes with embossed spines and bound in shades of leather or cloth. The books were arranged haphazardly, giving no indication as to how the books were arranged, whether by subject, author, or language.

Two policemen entered behind Dupin and stood at attention by the door. Poe remained close as the inspector spoke in a formal voice, "Police business, sir. I hope to accept your invitation to make use of the resources in your library?" He glanced at the shelves filled with more books than any one man could read. "Might I avail upon your generosity to double-check a detail?"

Usher looked witheringly at Poe, wary. "Why have you brought this . . . creature? Did we not put an end to his ravings the other day?" He sniffed. "He appears to need medical attention—and a bath. Has he hurt himself?"

A flare of violent suspicions leaked out of Usher's mind, like smoke from a badly vented fireplace. He was on the edge of more violence, expecting Poe to accuse him of the assault, which he would merely laugh at.

But Poe was not so foolish. He also heard Dupin's doubts, the impatience, and his surprising dislike for Reginald Usher. Dupin was a keen inspector with an instinct for what was not right. Poe had explained what he needed from the newspaperman's office.

The inspector led the conversation. "No need to bother with that, sir. I merely need an item from your library. One quick verification, and then I can absolve you of all guilt. No one will ever give a second thought to Mr. Poe's wild stories."

"No one ever did," Usher said pointedly, then fashioned a magnanimous smile again. "I have always said that the learned men of Richmond may peruse my library. What is it you need, Inspector? A quote from Pliny the Elder? A Greek translation of the Holy Scriptures? Berlini's account of the red death in Italy?"

"Mr. Poe has a specific title in mind."

Usher frowned at the idea. "And what does he know of my library?" Poe sensed a flare of puzzlement, then unease rippling through the murderer's closely hidden thoughts. Something about the wild look on Poe's bruised expression gave him pause. "My books are very well cared for, some of them quite valuable . . . "

When Usher looked about to withdraw his invitation, Dupin quickly stepped in. Poe sensed the surprise and growing suspicion in the inspector's thoughts. "Sir, I am required to complete my investigation. Now, I would not dream of tearing up your floorboards or knocking down your brick walls in search of hidden bodies. But perusing a book from your library is not too much to ask, is it?"

Taking the initiative, Poe hurried over to the nearest library shelf. "It's here, I know it is!" He squinted with his one good eye to read the titles on the spines. He moved from volume to volume, trying to match what he had seen in a flash of Usher's memories the night before. One particular volume . . .

As a murderer, Usher was ruthless. He had hidden the bodies of his victims, but his greatest camouflage was to cloak himself in the guise of a respectable businessman, to hide himself in plain sight. He relished the violence he committed, and he felt frustrated that he couldn't share his bloody deeds with others who might appreciate them.

Poe scanned the next shelf, then the next, book after book, but nothing caught his attention. He didn't bother to pull any volume from its place, didn't open a single cover.

"How much longer must we endure this masquerade, Inspector?" Usher asked. "Arrest him and end this harassment." The two policemen at the door fidgeted, uncertain.

"You are a clever man," Poe muttered. "But your greatest failing is your arrogance. You simply could not resist boasting about what you had done, writing down every aspect of how you smothered the old man and then butchered his body, how you smashed out the teeth of your dear niece after you killed her, how you taunted your rival as he hung on manacles in your cellar." He glared at the newspaperman. "You wrote it all down."

Usher scoffed. "If I were guilty of such outrageous deeds, why the devil would I document them?"

"Because you were certain no one would ever find it." He ran his fingers along the volumes on the next shelf, saw Usher stiffen. Inspector Dupin looked on with keen interest.

Poe continued, "In your journal confessing to the crimes, you recorded every last violent and painful detail because you were confident in your hiding place. A perfect hiding place." He spotted several unmarked volumes in the second middle shelf, right at eye level. "If Inspector Dupin were to ransack your offices and your house looking for such a journal, he would rack his brain to find the cleverest hiding place. He would never find it, would he?"

Poe rested his finger on a drab, nondescript volume. When he smiled, his split lip ached. "But you chose to hide your bloody confession in plain sight, right here where anyone could see it, in your own personal library which you have made available to any scholar in Richmond." Triumphant, he seized the unmarked journal, a thin volume invisible among so many weightier tomes. "But why would anyone notice something like this?"

Poe held up the book and opened the cover for Dupin. "Here, Inspector, in Reginald Usher's own hand is the full account of his murders."

Dupin was fascinated by his monologue, and the two policemen pressed forward to read as Poe opened the pages to reveal a dense account in tightly efficient handwriting.

A wordless howl of inhuman rage startled him. Red faced, Usher seized the iron poker by the fireplace and rushed at him. His eyes looked like shattered glass. In that instant, Poe saw the bestial look that his other victims must have seen.

A loud shot rang out, the report from Dupin's pistol. The bullet struck Usher in the upper chest and hurled him back into his mahogany desk. The two policemen rushed forward, taken off guard. They had been prepared to grapple with *Poe*, and had never assumed the newspaperman might become violent.

"I always allow for possibilities, no matter how small," said Inspector Dupin.

Usher groaned, bleeding onto his fine desktop as the policemen seized him. Poe handed the nondescript journal to Dupin without reading it, because he already knew what the pages contained. He had witnessed the crimes themselves in the haunting thoughts of Reginald Usher.

Dupin blanched as he skimmed the first several pages. "You were right. You were right all along. This is . . . hideous."

"I can also show you where to find the bodies. I wager you'll be willing to knock down the bricks and tear up the floorboards now?"

The inspector was clearly shaken. "I do not doubt you anymore, Mr. Poe, but how could you know? How could you possibly know?"

"Guilty thoughts are loud and clear to those sensitive to them," he said.

The thin explanation was insufficient, but the inspector shook his head. "Whatever the reason, you have caught a killer. Usher will surely hang for it. You have done a great service, Mr. Poe."

He did not feel victorious, however. The guilty

thoughts, the miserable ghosts, the haunting crimes would continue to swirl around him. Every person had secrets, and Edgar Allan Poe could hear them, whether he wanted to or not. Even though Usher would harm no one else, countless other horrors continued to emanate from the crowds in the city, from strangers he met or, worse, from people he considered friends. The whispers and screams would never stop plaguing him.

His only respite from the ghoulish din was drinking himself into a stupor, but that was its own path of self-destruction. Usher himself had gained cold satisfaction by documenting what he had done, however, confessing to an invisible audience.

Poe himself was a writer. Maybe there was another way to purge the horrors that other people placed unwillingly in his mind. He might find some personal release if he captured those awful incidents using his gift of words.

He could write them down and publish them.

TOPSY-TURVY

ELIZABETH MASSIE

The carrots were nasty, but then again, I'd eaten plenty of nasty things so I didn't think much about it. I had no idea they were poisoned and that those idiots were determined to murder me.

Hindsight, right?

Barney told me, "Don't sweat it, Topsy, it's over."

But seriously. I should have suspected something. I mean, come on. Joe O'Malley, my more-often-than-not drunk handler there in Coney Island's Luna Park, was acting unusually sober and pleasant that morning. He opened the stable window to let in some fresh, brisk January air. He talked sweet as if he liked me. He scrubbed me with a broom on my belly where it can itch like the blazes. The other Luna elephants, tied up down the line, gave me the stink eye, wondering what was up.

I should have been wondering, too. But damn, that was one great belly scrub.

Then O'Malley held out a batch of bright orange carrots and wiggled them just so. "Mmm, yummy," he said. "A treat for you, big girl." I scooped them from his hand with my trunk and stuffed them into my mouth. The taste was bitter but then again, I wasn't used to good food. O'Malley crossed his arms and watched me closely, as if he was expecting something to happen. And yes, I admit, I started to feel a little light-headed.

"Good girl," O'Malley said. "Everything's gonna be all right." His voice squeaked a little and his lip hitched. He gave me another couple of nasty carrots and, of course, I ate those, too.

And began feeling a bit more woozy.

Carl Goliath entered the stable, wheeling a barrow in which were a lovely copper harness and several lengths of chain. Goliath was a gristly-bristly man with a hideous mustache and eternal frown. He'd been hired as an elephant "expert," but trust me, he was no better than O'Malley. They were both bums. O'Malley and Goliath used step stools to secure the harness onto my head and then attach lengths of chain, which hung down my sides like a hula skirt. In my less than clear-headed state, I thought perhaps I was going to lead a grand parade up and down Surf Avenue to help promote Luna Park. What with the lovely copper harness, jingling chains, and all.

Wrong.

Once adorned, the bums led me out of the stable while the other elephants watched. Jealous, maybe?

Not for long.

I lumbered along beside O'Malley and Goliath, across the backstretch of the park that was still under construction, past piles of boards, mounds of frozen mud, half-built food stands and trinket booths. My breath fogged the winter air. The bums shivered as they walked, swearing that they best get an extra day's wage for all this craziness.

We stopped at the edge of the park's large lagoon, Luna's central "masterpiece." In the middle of the lagoon was an island and on the island was the partially-constructed, soon-to-be 200-foot tall "Electric Tower," which, when the park opened in May, would shine so bright "the man on the moon will be able to see it" owner Frederic Thompson claimed. At the foot of the tower's frame stood Thompson and a handful of official-looking men in bowlers and tailored coats. Beside them was a large steam engine and numerous electric cables snaking along the ground.

I should have bolted then and there. I'm an elephant, for Heaven's sake. I'm the most powerful animal on Earth. But those stupid carrots . . . those stupid, nasty-tasting, poison-laced carrots.

"Quit obsessing," Barney told me, trying to bring me back to the present. "Let it go. Seriously, Topsy, if you were still alive you'd give yourself a heart attack." I ignored him.

A narrow wooden bridge spanned the ice-frosted lagoon to the island. O'Malley pulled out his bull hook and thumped me on the ribs. "Git," he said. "Over the bridge with you."

I don't do bridges. O'Malley thumped me again. Groggily, I shook my head and didn't budge. O'Malley didn't stick me a third time. He was well aware of my past. Sure, I've killed a couple people, but trust me, they deserved it. One man had stabbed me with a pitchfork. Another had burned my trunk with a lit cigarette. If they didn't deserve to be dashed and crushed, I don't know who does. And so O'Malley knew better than to get me upset. He called out, "She's not coming over, Mr. Thompson. We have to figure out something else."

"Make her!" shouted Thompson.

"No, sir, can't do it."

"What about you, Goliath?"

Goliath's hideous mustache twitched. "Not going to happen, Mr. Thompson."

Thompson threw out his arms. "Damn it all. All right."

It took a work crew quite a while to rig up the "something else." The cables and engine were hoisted onto dollies and brought across the bridge to where I stood. The official looking men in their tailored coats and bowlers followed the cables and engine across the bridge and huddled in bunches, looking at once both fascinated and impatient. Thompson came last, giving me the human stink eye, which is more deadly than an elephant stink eye.

As the crew made their attachments and adjustments for whatever spectacle they had planned, I glanced around. Though my vision had become blurry, I could see that in addition to the rich men in their rich coats there were men with a moving picture camera. And atop the solid wooden fence that separated Luna Park from the rest of Coney Island, were even more people. Poor people, these were, staring down at me with wide eyes. Okay, so there wasn't going to be a parade. There would be some sort of show, obviously, with me as the main attraction. I didn't dance like Thompson's monkeys, or turn flips like Thompson's seals, but I could pose real nice, trumpet, and make people clap and say, "Ah! How fine is that elephant!"

Ta-dah!

"Okay, Topsy," O'Malley said. "Time for your shoes."

Shoes?

O'Malley and Goliath coaxed me to lift one front foot and then one back foot so they could secure a wooden slipper on each. The slippers had metal studs protruding from the sides and they were terribly uncomfortable. I tried to shake them off. O'Malley said, "Hold on there, girl," and gave me another batch of carrots. Of course, I ate them. I'm an elephant. Very little impulse control. Even more woozy now, I stood docilely in place. Better for me had I been able to draw on my well-known temper and stampeded the hell away from there.

But no.

"Let it go," Barney repeated, a trace of annoyance in his voice now. "It's all in the past. You're dead."

But I couldn't let it go. I just couldn't.

Goliath fastened cables to the studs in the sides of my wooden shoes. O'Malley gathered the hula skirt chains up under me and attached them to yet another cable. Quite an ordeal it was. I kept thinking, "What the hell is going on?" but was too foggy to put two and two together. And so, like the most stupid elephant that ever lived on this wild green Earth, I just waited.

The rich men stepped closer to me. Thompson gave them a look of warning and waved them back. One man hesitated, though, angling his head and gazing at me with a pair of beady eyes and a most bizarre, satisfied grin. Then he ducked his face down into his cloak as if afraid someone would recognize him and he backed up to join the others.

That man.

That beady-eyed, grinning bastard.

I didn't know who you were then, Tommy-boy, but I know now. You couldn't stay away, could you? You had to be there to see the *pièce de résistance* at Luna Park, that final, most grand animal execution of all, so much more exciting than mere dogs or cats. You didn't want others to know you were there. Yet it was the company that bears your name that provided the current. It was the Edison Manufacturing Company that filmed the event for the entertainment of the masses, using a moving picture camera you helped invent.

Yes, that was you, hiding in your cloak.

The camera began rolling. I could hear its clickety-clickety-clicks. O'Malley gave me one final carrot. As I chewed, he and Goliath stepped back. Way back. Like they thought I was going to let out one huge elephant-sized carrot fart. As a matter of fact, I could feel a big, bitter carrot fart swelling in my bowels. Would that ever feel good once it moved down and out. Fart that shitty carrot gas out and maybe I wouldn't feel so awful, maybe I—

Then something enormous, crackling, and white-hot blasted through me, blowing up my insides, cooking me like a five-ton ham. My body locked. My trunk curled and my feet began to smoke. I didn't even have time to think, "What the Hell is going on?" before my eyes rolled back and my body crashed down, taking my mind with it.

"Topsy," said Barney.

Is that the way to treat such a fine creature as an elephant, I ask you?

TOPSY-TURVY

"Topsy!" said Barney.

I looked over at Barney, who was next to me in the white, ethereal clouds. He was an interesting little after-death spiritual guide, tall, skinny as a rail, with big brown eyes, a crooked nose, and a blue robe. I would have preferred an elephant guide, but Barney explained that there weren't a lot of those available and they were all currently occupied with other clients. So I got stuck with him. The two of us were floating in the space that Barney called the "In-Between." No angels, no heavenly lyres or choirs. Just clouds and light and a pleasant smelling mist. For those who don't know, the "In-Between" is where those who die come to make their final decisions on what they want to do now that they're dead. They can either go on into eternity or be reincarnated. They have up to a year to make the decision. Most decide in a matter of minutes. And then there are those like me, who have to weigh everything carefully.

"Topsy!" Barney repeated more forcefully.

"What?" I asked.

"You can waste your year fuming about what happened, or you can make some decisions. Seriously, I have other clients and you're driving me crazy. We've been at this way too long, my pachydermatous friend."

I snorted through my trunk. It wasn't really a trunk anymore, just a suggestion of a trunk. I was dead, I was in afterlife transition, don't forget. And I was stuck.

"I don't know what to do," I said. "You gave me all the information I needed. You filled in the blanks. I was executed in Luna Park for killing the people who hurt me, even though, damn it, they asked for it! You told me how I was killed—poisoned carrots and

59

electricity. You told me who was there to watch my demise, such as Tommy-boy Edison. You told me the film of my death was fascinating for a few months, and then people lost interest, as people usually do. You said it was my right to know all this, and that knowing it I should let it go."

Barney ran his fingers through his thinning hair and shook his head. "And my advice stands. Listen to me. Eternity is wonderful. Just do eternity, okay?"

"I feel like my life has been turned upside down."

"Your life's over, Topsy. Accept it. For both our sakes."

"I can't."

"Just forget everything I told you, okay? That'll make it easier to decide."

"Ever hear the old saying, 'an elephant never forgets?'"

"That's not true. Somebody just made that up."

"Maybe. Maybe not."

Barney rolled his eyes.

Then I said, "I think there's a third option you haven't mentioned."

Barney drew back a little.

"Am I right?"

"Well . . ."

"Come on. Answer me. Am I right?"

Barney nodded slowly.

"Good, then," I said. "I want to be a ghost. I want to haunt Tommy-boy Edison."

"Stop joking around."

"I mean it. I want to haunt the shit out of that brute."

And so it was that Barney gave me permission to

be a ghost. I had some of my year left to torment the man who had devised the electrocution of animals and had sneaked in to watch mine.

I've heard people say that revenge is a dish best served cold. And Tommy-boy was going to get a huge mouthful of cold.

Luckily for me, not all ghosts have to stay where they were killed. Some, like me, can travel to the source of their anguish and establish themselves there. Thomas Edison was a main source of my anguish. He had a home and laboratory in New Jersey. Not hard to find for a ghost, I just followed the man's arrogant stink. I set up housekeeping in his attic and made my plan. And then, when Mrs. Edison was gone for several weeks with a friend, Tommy was all mine.

It was late evening. He was seated in a plush chair in his plush library, reading a book of some sort, smoking a cigar, feet in slippers and propped up on a hassock. A lamp glowed on the chair-side table.

The first thing I did was blow frosty air on the back of Tommy-boy's neck. Just for starters, you know. Just to stir things up, a bit, put him on edge. Tommy rubbed his neck and kept on reading. I blew again, harder. Again, Tommy rubbed his neck and kept on reading. Again I blew on his neck. This time he took the cigar out of his mouth, frowned, and looked around for a breeze. There was none. Good start, Topsy. I retired to the attic and waited.

The next evening, as Tommy-boy sat in his chair in the library, another book in his lap and another cigar in his mouth, I used my ghostly trunk to flip over the page Tommy was reading. He flipped it back. I flipped.

ELIZABETH MASSIE

He flipped. I flipped. He grunted, slammed the book shut, and stubbed the cigar out in the ashtray beside him. He stood, turned around and around, cursed under his breath, then sat back down and continued reading. Yes, this was good.

The following evening, I went for the chair side lamp. It had one of Tommy's precious light bulbs screwed in it. I rocked the lamp back and forth. Tommy reached out and stopped it. I rocked it again. He stopped it again. "Damn it, what's going on?" he muttered. But he didn't seem completely frightened, which was what I was after. No problem. I had time. Over the next few nights I was going to unnerve him, then terrify him, then make him piss his pants, choke on his cigar, and die.

Simple as that.

And so I picked up the lamp, dangled it in front of Tommy, and slammed it to the floor. It didn't smash well, so I stepped on it. Right there on the Oriental carpeting. Crunch went the lamp frame! Smunch went the bulb!

Ha!

Tommy scrunched up in his chair. He nearly swallowed his cigar. "Okay, this is not normal," he stammered. "I'm a scientist. I'm a highly intelligent, rational human being. There is a reason for this."

I grinned.

But then his expression changed. He relaxed. "Ah, yes. I know what this is," he said. "And of course it's not ghosts, for there are no such things."

Wait . . . what? My grin died right there on my elephant lips.

Tommy unfolded in his chair and suddenly looked

quite at ease. "It's life units."

No ghosts? Au contraire, Tommy! And what the hell was a life unit?

It was time for some terrifying vocalizing. That should convince Tommy that ghosts were real and some of us meant business.

"Whoooooooooo hooooooooo boooooooooooo!" I howled. And as an elephant, even a ghost elephant, that's quite a loud and frightening sound.

Tommy took a puff on his cigar, tapped the ash off in the ashtray stand. "I hear you, life units. Where did you come from? Possibly from my parents, or friends who have died? I hear you. Don't worry, my dear ones. You will settle soon. You will come together into a new life form, and all will be well."

Settle soon? All will be well? Oh, I don't think so!

I knelt on my big fat ghostly elephant knees and leaned into Tommy's face. I howled with all my might "WHOOOOOOOOO HOOOOOOOOOO BOOOOOOOO!" Come on, Tommy, be scared! Come on Tommy, clutch your chest in fear!

Tommy didn't clutch his chest in fear. He merely waited 'til I'd run out of air, shook his head, picked his book up again, and started to read.

I retreated to the attic. I sat on an old trunk to think. I'd hoped to prolong the dread. I'd hoped to reduce him to a quivering, shivering blob of weeping humanity. And then I'd hoped to give him one final shock and watch him keel over, dead as a stone. But that hadn't happened. Tommy was one cool cucumber.

Time to release the Pachen.

The next evening, with Tommy settled yet again in his library, this time with a glass of wine as well as the cigar and a new lamp on the chair-side table, I drifted down and entered the room.

No more playing around, Mr. Moving Pictures. This time, you're going to die.

I hovered before the man, swung my trunk out to the side, then whipped it back again, slamming Tommy in the face hard enough to snap the man's neck.

Die, Tommy, die!

But my trunk went right through and out the other side with no effect on Tommy.

I tried again. I wrapped my trunk around Tommy's neck to lift him up and slam him down, just like I had the man with the pitchfork and the man with the lit cigarette. But I couldn't grasp him. It was like he was a ghost to my ghost, with no substance at all.

I bellowed, and then went for the bookshelf. At least ghosts can pick things up—that's one small thing in our favor. And what a nice, hefty bookshelf it was. I lifted it high, dumping books in a scatter, then hurled it at Tommy. Tommy, surprisingly quick for a man of fifty-six years, leapt out of the way. The bookshelf struck the floor and fell into three large pieces.

"No need for that," he said calmly, peeking around the room to see what might be next. "Time for peace, life units."

Next was the elegantly carved sideboard. Up in my trunk it went, sending glassware and a silver tray flying, and I flung with everything I had, right at old Tommy. Again, he ducked out of the way and it shattered on the far wall.

I grabbed his chair, threw it. Missed. Then a straight-backed chair. Tommy scurried into the hallway. I followed and threw a mirror from off the wall. Missed. Damn!

Tommy went outside. I couldn't follow him. His house had been my chosen place of haunting and so I could only watch through the window.

"I'm going into town," Tommy called back. "You life units best calm yourselves down or Mina and I will move to Florida until you do." Then he climbed into his Pierce Arrow and motored off into the darkness. I stood there, shaking with rage. I couldn't scare him. I couldn't kill him. And I couldn't follow him to Florida because as a ghost, I'd chosen Tommy's New Jersey house as my establishment.

Well, Hell's bells, as I used to hear O'Malley say.

I returned to the In-Between. Barney was there and oh, boy, did he look perturbed. "Didn't care for ghosting?" he asked.

"Why didn't you tell me I could move stuff around but couldn't move a person? I could smash a lamp but couldn't even choke Tommy?"

"You didn't ask."

"And why didn't you tell me Tommy was in good enough shape to dodge everything I threw at him?"

"You didn't ask."

"I couldn't even scare him! He doesn't believe in ghosts, did you know that? He just chalked it all up to 'life units.' Are you kidding me? What on Earth is a life unit?"

"It's his concept of what happens to life-energy after death. He believes it rearranges itself and then takes up residence in otherwise lifeless matter—or bodies—and that's how life continues on Earth."

"That's stupid."

"Maybe. Maybe not."

"Oh, just shut up! Being a ghost is worthless!"

"Ready to move on into eternity?"

"No! I've had no retaliation! My life units want to be reincarnated into someone who can carry out my revenge!"

"There are no such things as life units," said Barney.

"I don't care!"

We stared at each other for some very long moments there in the white clouds of the In-Between.

Then Barney said, "You do realize that when you reincarnate, you merge with the personality that is already there. You don't totally take over that person, right?"

"As long as I can have some control, I'll be fine!"

Barney held up his hand to shut me up. "Okay, Topsy. Your choice."

I smiled, triumphant.

"We'll have to look at the babies soon to be born so you can pick the best one."

"How will I know which one is best?"

"You'll have to figure that out on your own."

"Really? What kind of spiritual guide are you, anyway?"

"One who is ready to call it quits and take a vacation to Florida, thank you very much."

I considered several options for reincarnating. One was a baby to be named Jerome Lester Horwitz. But I had a feeling this one was going to be a lovable comedian of some sort, and not the revenge type.

There was a baby to be called Vladimir Horowitz, who reeked of music and ever since my time in amusement parks I wasn't crazy about music. Then I discovered a baby whose name would be John Herbert Dillinger. I got a good feel from this one. I told Barney of my choice. He nodded, and with a whoosh my spirit rushed down and merged with soon-to-be baby John's.

You may have heard of us. John and I grew up to kick some major ass, as the old saying goes. Though we never got to Tommy (that man was slippery as a trout), we blew away Joe O'Malley's second-cousin, William Patrick O'Malley, outside the First National Bank in East Chicago, Illinois. We bankrupted Carl Goliath's son and daughter-in-law, who had their life savings in a bank in Sioux Falls, South Dakota. We ruined the career of Frederic Thompson's nephew, who worked at the Crown Point Jail, when we planned and executed the best escape ever. Not total revenge, but we're still going strong.

We're heading to the theater tonight. A little R & R at the Biograph Theater in Chicago. We're going to see *Manhattan Melodrama* starring John's favorite actress, Myrna Loy. Should be a nice relaxing evening. We don't relax much.

Then we'll be back to taking care of business. There are lots more folks who can help pay the bill for what was done to me in Luna Park.

Ah, revenge.

And Barney thought reincarnating wasn't a good idea.

RAY AND THE MARTIAN

BEV VINCENT

A RESOUNDING BOOM shook Ray's bed, arousing him from a deep sleep. He pried open his eyes and tried to recall where he was. Then he heard his older brother snoring in the bunk above—Skip could sleep through anything—and he remembered. Still, the room felt unfamiliar—they'd only been in this house a few days.

His father had lost his job, so the whole Bradbury family had packed their belongings into a $20 Buick and headed southwest, their destination influenced by Leonard Bradbury's fascination with the American West. They had ended up in Roswell, New Mexico, where Mr. Bradbury was trying to find work. Ray missed his relatives and friends back in Waukegan, but his father had promised an adventure, and five-year-old Ray loved nothing more than an adventure.

It was just after midnight, but light flickered through the bedroom curtains. At first Ray thought it was lightning, but the color wasn't right and the sound had been more of a crash than a rumble. He threw back the covers, his head filled with images of cannon fire and natives on the warpath, like in the stories his father and his aunt read to him.

When he drew open the curtains—slowly to avoid waking his brother—it looked like the back yard was on fire, but that couldn't be. Unlike in Illinois, there was nothing here to burn. Only cactus and mesquite grew in the rocky ground, and even they struggled.

Ray threw on his clothes and ran downstairs to the kitchen, where his father was putting on his boots. "Keep the boys inside," he told Ray's mother.

Ray pressed his nose against the window and watched the flashlight beam bob and sway across the yard. The flames were dying down by the time his father reached the water trough. He was about to beg his mother to let him go out, but stopped. Easier to ask forgiveness than permission, he decided. While his mother busied herself making coffee, he stuck his feet into his shoes without tying the laces, eased open the back door and crept outside.

He pretended he was a cowboy tracking a wild animal, walking as quietly as possible to avoid detection. He closed his eyes and sniffed the air like he'd seen a man do in a Western movie. It took him a few seconds to figure out what was wrong: it was too quiet. Although there was a steady breeze, he couldn't hear the tall, rickety windmill that a previous owner had built to pump water to the cattle trough. In the few days since they'd arrived, he had grown accustomed to the way it creaked when the blades turned and squealed when the vane swung into the wind. He should have been able to hear it. He should have been able to see its silhouette in the moonlight, too.

Had lightning struck it? Ray crept closer, staying in the shadows and avoiding cactuses. He watched his father fill a bucket from the trough and carry it across the yard. The water hissed when he poured it on something. His father turned his flashlight on the steaming object, a misshapen, dark lump that came up nearly to his shoulders.

Ray had learned about meteorites, and he'd seen shooting stars in the night sky, but he'd never expected to see one up close. What bad luck that it had knocked down the windmill.

As he knelt behind a gnarled mesquite tree, he noticed something moving nearby. He also detected a strange odor, like one of the spices his grandmother used when baking. He peeked around the tree trunk and saw a dark figure. It crouched beside a cluster of prickly pear cactus, watching his father. A low rattle emanated from its throat—a growl, like a dog might make when defending its territory. Ray thought he saw claws at the end of its misshaped fingers. He'd read stories about ogres and trolls, but none of those tales featured anything like this.

A cloud passed over the moon. In the darkness, Ray sensed the creature creeping away. It seemed to be dragging one of its cornstalk legs. He tried to trail the shambling figure, but it eluded him. The strange aroma grew fainter and before long he was left with nothing to follow.

He heard footsteps approaching from the direction of the meteorite. He had to get back to the house ahead of his father or he'd be in big trouble! He scampered to the porch as quickly and quietly as possible, eased open the back door, kicked off his shoes and crept up to his room.

Skip was still asleep. Ray climbed into bed and listened for the sound of the door opening and closing.

When it did, he waited for his parents' voices, but they never came.

Later that night, the creature scratched at his bedroom window. It pressed its elongated face against the dust-covered glass. Its eyes were as large as goose eggs and as black as ebony. Its mouth was crooked and full of teeth that jutted every which way. After he awakened from this nightmare, covered in sweat, Ray clung to his blanket and slept fitfully until he heard the comforting sounds of his mother preparing breakfast.

Before descending, he looked out the window. The ground near the remains of the windmill was scorched black. Jagged pieces of wood extended from the windmill's base. The meteorite sat among the ruins like a dead elephant. It would be something to tell his new classmates about at "Show and Tell" next week, for sure.

His brother had already eaten breakfast and headed off in search of new friends by the time Ray went downstairs. Ray was eager to investigate, but he knew his parents would never let him go outside until he finished his breakfast. He put jam on a slice of toast and folded it in half, cramming the whole thing into his mouth at once.

His father pushed his chair back, drained the last of his coffee and took his dishes to the sink. "Got a lead on a job," the elder Bradbury said. "Wish me luck." He got a peck on the cheek from Ray's mother, and a muffled version of "Good luck" from Ray, who was having a hard time swallowing his toast.

After his father left, Ray helped his mother with the dishes, then put on his shoes and dashed out the back door. He stood on the top step and tried to remember everything that had happened during the night. The meteorite was over there, so that meant he had been over here, and the creature had gone . . . there, maybe? Or was it that way? The yard was unfamiliar, and everything looked different in the dark, anyway.

He looked up at the sky, wondering if other meteorites were about to plummet through the clouds and crash to the earth. What if one struck his father's car? Or the house, turning it into a smoking ruin. What if mother went out to hang the laundry and was eaten by that terrible, shambling creature? He shook his head. That couldn't have been real. Must have been a dream.

He was suddenly aware of someone standing beside him. A dark figure. His heart leapt—at first, he was sure it was the creature from his nightmare. Then he realized it was a person, and he calmed down a little.

The stranger wore a black shirt, a black coat, and black pants. He also had on an oddly shaped black hat. His face was clean shaved and his eyes were as dark as embers. Something about his demeanor made Ray consider running into the house to warn his mother, but he couldn't make his legs move.

The man tipped his hat. No one had ever done that to Ray before. "Good morning," he said.

"Morning," Ray said, wishing he had a hat to tip back.

The man looked around. "Quiet," he said. "Where is everyone?"

"Mom's inside," he said. "My father's away. Skip, too." He didn't know why he said all this. It seemed rude not to answer the man.

"Did you see what happened last night?"

"The meteorite?" Ray said. "Yessir."

The man frowned. "Is that what you think it is?"

Ray nodded. "They come from outer space. I learned about them from a book."

The stranger's eyes narrowed. A chill ran down Ray's spine. "Did you, now?" He took off his hat and sat on the topmost step, patting the spot next to him. "Sit yourself down," he said. "Tell me everything. Spare no detail."

Ray swallowed, took a deep breath, and told the man about how the meteorite had destroyed the windmill. How his father had poured water on it and how it had steamed. He didn't, however, mention what he'd seen near the mesquite tree.

The man leaned forward. "Did your father open it?"

"Open it?" Ray's eyes widened. "You mean, hit it with a sledgehammer or something?"

The man expelled a burst of air and leaned back. "If that thing gets out . . . " He seemed to be talking to himself, but the way Ray's eyes opened wide must have told him something. He grabbed Ray by the shoulder and leaned in close again. "What do you know, boy? Tell me now." Spit flew from his lips as he spoke.

Ray cringed, suddenly afraid of this stranger who smelled like a summer breeze and raged like a winter storm.

"What did you see?" The man relaxed a little, perhaps sensing the boy's fear. "The lives of everyone you know and love may depend on this. Show me now."

Ray led the stranger to the charred remains of the

windmill. The earth was grooved for dozens of yards, as if an enormous plow had been dragged through it. He saw several shards and chunks of what might have been molten glass or metal. The meteorite was dark, almost black, and rough, like a boulder. It was egg-shaped, nearly ten feet long and taller than he was.

The stranger held out a palm, warning Ray to stay back, but Ray ignored him. This man, whoever he was, wasn't his father. He had no right to boss him around. Ray's eyes were fixed on the black rock. As he got closer, he realized that the features on its rough surface were intricate carvings. Maybe even a kind of writing.

The stranger reached inside his coat and brought out something shiny. It had tubes and rods pointing in all directions. It might have been a weapon, but instead of a trigger it had several colored buttons made of a material unlike any Ray had ever seen. The man ran his hand over the rock, found something and pushed. The entire side of the meteorite glided upwards without a sound.

Ray gaped. The spicy aroma he had detected near the mesquite tree wafted out of the opening. Inside, he saw a depression that resembled the outline of the elongated creature he'd encountered. All around it, glassy circles of every imaginable color twinkled like stars. A flat panel glimmered with pale blue light at the tapered end of the rock, near where the creature's head would have been when it was nestled inside. Arcane characters and symbols streamed diagonally across it.

Ray could only stare. "Is it magic?" he asked. Ray loved magicians.

The stranger pointed his device at the opening. It beeped and trilled like an exotic bird. "To you, probably," the man replied. He stepped away from the object and examined the ground. Ray looked down, too. The hard soil didn't show any footprints. If the stranger intended to follow the creature's trail, he would need impressive tracking skills.

"I saw it over there," Ray said, pointing toward the mesquite bush. "I think it was hurt." He showed the man where he'd hidden. Here the ground was softer and the man had no trouble finding the creature's tracks.

"You followed it?" the man asked a few seconds later.

Ray nodded. "Tried to, anyway."

The stranger shook his head and sighed.

The footprints fascinated Ray. They were at least fourteen inches long but narrow. "Looks like he lost some toes," he said.

"Quiet, boy." The stranger held the beeping, blinking gadget out in front of him. "And stay where you are."

Ray heard a door slamming. He turned to see his father coming down the porch steps. "What's going on?" he demanded. "Who in tarnation are you and what are you doing with my boy?"

The stranger held up his empty hand to call for silence. Ray's father's face grew dark and pinched. He spun on his heel and went back inside. When he emerged a few seconds later, he was carrying a shotgun. "I asked what you were doing," he said.

The stranger ignored Ray's father, staring at the ground as he approached one of the taller mesquite trees in the yard. After scrutinizing the ground, he looked up.

Something dropped from a branch, pinning the man to the ground. The creature was even more horrific than in Ray's nightmare. Its gray-green body was a lumpy cylinder, and its head looked like an elongated pumpkin. Its arms were long and crooked. Its dark eyes were as big as saucers and its mouth gaped open to reveal dozens of needle-sharp teeth.

It knocked the stranger's gadget aside, grabbed the man by the shoulders with its long, gnarled fingers—only three on each hand, Ray observed—and bashed his head against the ground. It then arose from its crouch, swiveled and saw Ray, who was less than five feet away. It took three strides to reach the boy. Its arms may have been spindly, but they gripped Ray like a vise, crushing the very breath out of him. The spicy odor overwhelmed him. Ray closed his eyes, waiting for those terrible teeth to bite into his neck and chew off his head.

He was dimly aware of a ratcheting sound behind him—his father pumping a shell into the chamber. "Put him down," his father screamed. "Put him down."

The creature's grip intensified. Ray cried out in pain. His heart pounded as he struggled for air.

A shot rang out. Ray felt the creature flinch and loosen its grip. Then its smothering arms dropped away. Ray fell to the ground, knocking what little remaining breath he had left from him. Constellations of stars filled his head.

His father ratcheted the shotgun and fired again. This time the creature screamed—a terrible sound. Birds scattered from the branches of the mesquite trees. Ray heard a soft thud and managed a glance in that direction. The creature had collapsed two feet away. It wasn't moving.

After the gunshots and the horrible wailing and the

clamor of the birds, the world went quiet. Ray stayed still, catching his breath. His father rushed over and knelt by his side. "Are you all right?"

Ray nodded without speaking and took another deep breath before slowly getting to his feet.

The stranger regained consciousness after Ray's father splashed water onto his face. He shook off his injuries, brushed dust from his coat, and went to investigate the creature. Ray watched, his father at his side with an arm casually draped around Ray's shoulder. The stranger's gadget beeped and squawked. A few seconds later, he pronounced the creature dead.

Ray's mother emerged from the house and rushed to them. She shrieked when she saw the dead thing on the ground.

"What is it?" Ray asked the man.

The stranger arose from his crouch. "Mighty hard to explain. Something not from around here. Something nasty."

"You're not from around here, either, are you?" Ray's father said.

The man grinned. "Guess not. I'll be taking these with me," he said, nodding at the dead creature and the strange rock in the ruins of the windmill.

"You'll need help," Ray's father said.

The stranger shook his head. He raised his gadget and pushed a few buttons. He pointed it at the dead creature and then at the rock. A moment later, two beams of colored light descended from the sky and lifted the dead creature and the rocklike object into the air. Ray watched them go up and up and up until he could see them no more. His father uttered a soft curse and his mother almost swooned at the sight.

RAY AND THE MARTIAN

"Someone might come looking for him," the stranger said, indicating the spot on the ground where the creature's body had been only a few seconds before. "Not right away. Takes a while to get here. They may not land, but if they do, stay away from them. They aren't friendly, as you've seen."

"Who are you?" Ray asked, but before the words were out of his mouth, there was a pop as the air closed around where the stranger used to be, and then he was gone.

Ray told his brother about his adventure later that afternoon when Skip returned home. They wandered around the backyard, where Ray pointed out where everything had happened.

"Gosh," Skip said. "Sounds like a movie. And to think I missed it all. It's not fair!" He gave Ray a playful punch on the arm. "What do you think it was?"

"I think that big rock was some kind of flying machine. Maybe the creature inside it came from Mars."

"A Martian? For real?"

"In our backyard," Ray said. "Imagine that."

He looked up at the sky, which was cloud-filled and blue. Far beyond that, he pictured planets and stars. What would it be like to live on another planet? He remembered Waukegan—his family and friends who still lived there—and wondered if the man from Mars had a family back home who would miss him.

He thought all these things that afternoon, and in the following days when the family moved on to Tucson, and in the ensuing years when they returned to Waukegan and eventually moved to California. Ray claimed in later years he could recall his whole life, including the moment of his birth, but some memories were more vivid than others.

The day Ray met the man from Mars was the day the universe entered his imagination. He would never look at the world the same way again.

THE GIRL WITH THE DEATH MASK

STEPHANIE M. WYTOVICH

November 17, 1925
Mexico City

IT WAS EARLY Sunday morning when I woke to the sound of shuffling limbs. The sun had barely risen and the faint glow of its arrival had yet to grace my window. The quilt mother had wrapped me in was too hot, and I felt the sweat drip down my plaster-coated legs. The itch was unbearable, but the fear that wet my mouth kept me still.

Against the faint scent of dying vanilla orchids, shadows climbed my walls.

Were they back?

I tossed and turned, trying to keep my focus on the drapes. There were tapestries with blue flowers and deep green stems. On my good days, the warmth of the red felt romantic, reminded me of tequila-soaked kisses and girls with painted lips, but on the bad days—which were more and more frequent these past weeks—the coloring reminded me of the way the gasps and screams of the other passengers fell on my body like freshly sewn fabric, their skins a soft blanket to help sop up the blood. I don't remember the iron

handrail that pierced my abdomen, but when the doctors told me that my uterus was punctured, I felt the dream of children slip from my heart despite the nails that held my body together.

When I got on the bus that day, I had no idea that the face I wore was already painted with the brush of death, and sometimes when I closed my eyes, I could still smell the gold leaf in the air, the allure of fate fresh on my tongue. But what I haven't forgotten is his face, the portrait of the man dressed in teeth who tried to help me, the one I turned away when I begged for God.

Sometimes I think I imagined him, created him so I could face my death.

Other times, like when the day bleeds into night, I know it was real.

The whine of a floorboard filled the room.

"Hello? Is someone there?" I said.

Silence.

I propped myself up on the bed, the layer of pillows behind me like a fortress to cushion my shattered spine. Sweat lined my brows and dripped down my face.

"Frida? Are you awake?" asked my father, Guillermo. A photographer by nature, he, too, was always up with the sun.

"Unfortunately," I said. "Is there coffee, yet?"

"Si. Un momento, mi hija," he said, his accent still carrying a hint of German on the tongue.

I heard the clangs of pots and pans and tried to make myself comfortable amongst the noise and unease. At this pace, the whole family would be up soon, and father would never have time to work with Mama slinging out orders about our overgrown garden.

I swept the room with quick nods to the corners, the white-washed ceiling.

Empty. Alone. Safe.

For now.

"Gracias, Papa," I shouted, my voice catching as I hoped for a strong shot of caffeine to take with my painkiller cocktail.

I rubbed my eyes and swallowed hard while the mirror above my bed watched me, a constant companion to my pain.

When will this Hell end?

It had been two months since the trolley took my body from me, locked me in this plaster prison, and I've been painting to keep my hands busy and my mind sane. A week ago, father bought me some paints and canvas as room on my cast dwindled inside my ever-growing collage. Pink and yellow butterflies lined my breasts as dark smudges of skulls and tropical flowers trickled down my chest and navel. It was beautiful until it wasn't, and even then, the beauty only faded against the call of my nightmares.

I reveled in the smell of acrylic, the fresh cut of charcoal.

They helped tame the maelstrom that circled me, the storm of death and agony that positioned itself against the door to love and health while day in and day out, I lay here, a waking corpse amongst the living.

La chica con la mascara de muerte.

According to the mirror, I needed my braids redone as the black of my hair looked sullied, gray, my face dried out from the hands of sleep.

I reached to my bedside and dipped a washcloth in the tumbler of water Mama left out for me last night.

THE GIRL WITH THE DEATH MASK

It was lukewarm, but it felt cold on my face as I scrubbed and fluffed my eyebrows, cracked my neck.

In the corner of the room, something scuttled up the wall, disappeared into the ceiling.

My breath caught in the panic building in my throat.

Tantos diablos.

"Frida? Darling? Are you okay?" asked my father holding a tray of coffee, milk, and fruit.

"Yes. I mean no. I just—"

"Have you been sleeping? Taking your medicine?" he asked. "You look like you caught your death."

"Sometimes, father, I really think I did," I said.

<hr>

I took a forkful of grapefruit and savored the sweet-sour tang as I licked my lips. A chill crept into the room, the draft of November a cold kiss against my aching bones. I'd spent most of the afternoon writing, my diary a mixture of recorded fears and pressed flowers that soaked up my pain between pages.

Yesterday, I'd left off drawing a crushed-in skull with fresh roses in its eye sockets. The red was vibrant, bright, and I even had father crush up red petals in the paint for me, but the smell made me sick and I had to stop, my stomach churning, flipping.

Today, I added tears to its cheek, little blue specks salted with the water leaking from my own eyes. It bonded me with the skull, this skeletal rebirth.

It's strange to think that before the accident, I wouldn't have left the house without putting a dab of rose water on my wrists, but it had been weeks since I'd felt like myself, and the scent of roses made me nauseous now, filled my mouth with the taste of copper, the memory of blood and asphalt on my teeth.

No. No. No.

I picked up the tumbler of water and drank straight from its lip.

Easy now, easy. It's just a memory. It will fade.

The doctor was due to our house in a few hours, and his visits always left me with scars that not even he could treat. I didn't like the way mother choked back sobs when she stood in the corner watching, or how father stood tense, his muscles clenched, near ripping as my body was twisted and turned.

It's one thing to know you're disabled.

It's another thing completely to see it magnified in someone else's eyes.

That's why I couldn't tell them about the shadows, the presence of the little devils. They were in enough pain over the survival of my broken body. It would be too much for them to see the ghosts I bought back, too.

The room was dark, but the shadows were darker. I watched the walls take a breath while the pitter patter of hooves scraped against the wood, their footprints large, twice the size of a full-grown man. I froze, my body tight against the sheets as I tried not to breathe, but my heart beat howled, their growling deeper now, hungrier.

I watched the red in the drapery drip to the floor in splashes of hot fire. I saw the lights of the trolley in the distance, the screams of its passengers forever written on the inside of my eyelids. I had prayed to God that day, begged him to let me live, to survive the horror of my broken body, the desecration of my womb.

THE GIRL WITH THE DEATH MASK

But not tonight.

Not again.

I didn't know how many of them were in the room with me, but the smell of ash, of burning, crawled into my nose, the scales of a snake warm on my tongue. My jaw trembled as bile collected in my throat, but I swallowed it against the nails that held me together.

"I k-know you're here," I said, my voice shaking. "I'm wasn't ready before, but I-I am now."

Laughter filled the room, the air thick, heavy with surrender.

"And what has changed, little Frida?" said a voice from the darkness. "You didn't want me then. What's to make me think you're ready for me now?"

I saw myself haggard and withering away under my mother's quilt, my skin like parchment, dried, aged. I'd never walk again, never have children. I would know no love that wasn't in obligation. This body was my corpse, my grave. I had to leave it.

"Being like this? It's not worth it. I'm in the same Hell I tried to escape. I'd rather be dead than suffocate in this body another night."

A tall, thin man walked out from the corner of the room, his boots dragging against the floor as he came to my bedside. He had a cane made of femurs, his eyes two yellow moons under the expanse of a black top hat, fashioned with teeth.

"You taste different," he said, dragging a fingernail across my forehead, his tongue like sandpaper against my cheek. "But even still, I cannot take you. You made your choice that day on the street when you turned away my hand."

"I didn't know what I was doing. I didn't know what I was bargaining for."

The man smiled a toothy grin, his mouth a hospice of rotted teeth.

"Tantos diablos," he said. "My children have taken a liking to you."

A high-pitched screech filled the room.

The sound of a thousand footsteps ran towards my bed.

"Please," I whispered again. "Help me. Get me out of here. I'll do anything."

"I think you just might be telling the truth, little Frida."

I collected what strength I had, held firm against my fear.

"Name your price," I said.

The man pounded his cane three times against the floor and a child walked out from behind him, only it wasn't a child. A little girl in a pink dress and a ruffled white collar walked to my bedside, a sunflower in her hand. Her skull was polished and white, the color of lilies and grandmother's lace tablecloth. Chained to her foot was the head of a monster, a bleeding, decapitated ogre with bulging eyes and pinched ears.

"Take the flower and eat it. It will give you the sight you need to be able to walk, a reason to use your legs," said the man.

The little girl held out the sunflower and Frida took it, the taste of the Devil's garden on her tongue.

"In return, you owe me a soul," he said, handing her a piece of paper, the edges burned from where his fingertips touched it. "Bring me this man, this frog, *my little dove, and I will fill your world with fantasies beyond your wildest dreams."*

I nodded my head.

"You have my word."

Rain fell from the ceiling, his laugh a clash of thunder as I pulled teeth out of my hair. He sank back into the shadows, the white of his cane the last thing I remember before a hand reached down from my canopy and grabbed my throat.

"Frida, mi hija. The doctor is here," my father said as he knocked on my door.

I opened my eyes to the whitest light I'd ever seen and coughed so hard it turned into a gag. Cupping my mouth with my hand, I vomited, the bile scratching my throat raw as it came out in clumps.

What the—

In my hand were two molars and a crumbled piece of paper.

"Frida, did you hear me?" my father asked, his tone louder now, agitated.

"Just a minute, papa," I said.

Shaking, I opened the note:

You are your subject. And Diego Rivera is mine.
Stand tall, my dove. I'll see you burn yet.

"It was real," I said.

"As real as you and me," said a voice.

I looked to the canopy of my bed, watched how it sagged under the weight of a body. Leaves fell from the bed side as vines crept out from underneath my blankets, secured themselves around my neck. A figure crab walked out from under the bed, it's body naked and in labor. Horrified, I watched my face rip through its vaginal walls while an adult version of me tore out the creature's heart and then wore it around her neck as a prize.

All these versions of myself stood with me in the room, their reflections magnified in the mirrors that kept me company. They were my nightmares revisited, played out for me scene by scene. Self-portraits of pain.

This is how I get to him, how I seduce Diego.

I spun the teeth in circles in my palm. They reminded me of dice, rolls of fate. I had met Diego once, shortly before the accident, the communist pig. He was a brilliant muralist, a renowned misogynist, never faithful to one woman, but oh, could he paint. I used to find excuses to see him, teasing him while he worked on his piece, *Creation,* at the Bolívar Auditorium of the National Preparatory School in Mexico City. I even asked him if I could watch him work once, his wife, Lupe, ever jealous of my presence near her husband.

But I painted my demons, if I worked my Hell into my art, he'd never be able to deny me.

Not me, his little dove.

La chica con la mascara de muerte.

I slid the two teeth underneath the mattress.

"I'm ready," I said. "Please come in."

Both the doctor and my father walked in the room, his face a contortion of fear and concern as he looks at my body cast, the sweat dripping from my brows. My mother and sister walked in soon after, right as the doctor began to examine me.

THE GIRL WITH THE DEATH MASK

"How do you feel today, Frida?"

"I feel like I'm going to walk again," I said.

Nodding, the doctor smiled. "I think you may very well be right dear. After all, how else will the world see all the beautiful paintings you do?"

I smiled at this compliment while the eyes of the little devils watched me from shadows in the room.

"Beautiful, yes. But my painting carries with it the message of pain," I said. "And one day, every soul in Mexico City will know my name because of it."

The room fell silent, my promise hanging on the tips of their tongues.

"Now please, doctor, get me out of this cast," I said. "I have an appointment with a frog that I very much intend to keep."

ON A TRAIN BOUND FOR HOME

CHRISTOPHER GOLDEN

THE LATE AFTERNOON sunlight glinted off of the rooftops of Vienna, casting long September shadows onto the cobblestone streets. Harry Houdini sat in the back seat, twisted slightly to one side to make room for the travel cases beside him. In the front, his publicist on this trip, an enterprising young man named Ned McCarty, rode with the driver. Harry listened to Ned's easy banter, so confident at the age of twenty-two, and wondered if he had ever been as lighthearted as that. Ned spoke almost as little German as the driver did English, but somehow the two had struck up an easy camaraderie that Harry envied. When the driver pulled up to the train station, Harry was glad to have that particular journey over, even as he felt such dread about the one he and Ned were about to begin.

The auto had barely rattled to a halt before Harry unlatched his door and clambered out, closing it behind him. The sun had slid farther toward the horizon and dropped just behind the train station's roof, silhouetting the building with golden fire and casting the street where Harry stood into deep shadow.

Beyond the station, visible past the platform, the Orient Express awaited, hissing and smoking in preparation for departure, putting him in mind of a sleeping dragon. He took half a dozen steps toward that station and the platform and then hesitated, full of a trepidation he could not name.

Ned and the driver took the bags from the car and set them down. Harry glanced over in time to see Ned giving the man a tip and receiving a hearty pat on the back in return.

"Thank you," Harry said, touching the brim of his felt hat in a little salute.

The driver waved in reply and climbed into the car, which gave a full-throated roar as he started it up. A moment later it clattered away, a strange sight amidst the horse-drawn carriages and carts on the street. Harry turned his attention back to the train station, automobile and driver forgotten.

"You speak German," Ned said, frowning at him. "You couldn't bid him farewell in his own language?"

"I speak rotten German," Harry replied, "and not much of it. Besides, I'm an American. I speak English. We hired him to drive specifically because he spoke our language."

All during the exchange, Harry's gaze never strayed from the sight of the Orient Express, seething and steaming as it awaited them. He had admired machines and mechanisms of all kinds throughout his life—ingenuity intrigued him—and a machine as beautiful and powerful as this train impressed him. The handful of days he had spent in Vienna had been a pleasure thanks both to the loveliness of its architecture and to its near-constant gastronomic delights, particularly the tortes at Gerstner on Karntner Strasse. The night he had attended the opera with the city's mayor had been the one disappointment. The performance had bored him, and he had spent its duration wishing that he had been the one on the stage, playing to a packed house at the Wiener Hofoper. But it wasn't just the beauty of Vienna that made him reluctant to leave.

"Harry?" Ned said, nudging him.

"Hmm?" Harry glanced at him and realized that Ned had picked up his own valise and travel case and stood waiting, while Harry's own bags remained on the ground beside him.

"Do you want me to get a porter?"

"You're the publicist, kid. Do you want *the Great Houdini* to have his picture taken carrying his own bags?"

He smiled, just in case Ned hadn't caught the sarcasm. On stage he would always be the Great Houdini, and he played that up for the crowds on the streets and in the bars in order to feed his fame. But sometimes he grew tired from the effort it took to inhabit the role. Ned hadn't known him very long and he didn't want the kid who was supposed to be drumming up the Great Houdini's press to think that the Great Houdini *believed* his own press.

Ned studied him for a second or two, troubled and unsure. "You're right," he said. "Herr Diederich will have some journalists to see you off, for sure. Let me get the porter."

Harry shook his head and bent to hoist up his bags. "Forget it, kid. It's the Orient Express, first class. I won't have to lift a finger while we're on board unless it's to cut my steak. I can carry my own damn bags."

Weighed down with his cases, wishing he had packed fewer shirts, he started toward the front entrance of the station. He passed out of view of the platform and lost sight of the waiting train. A shiver went through him.

"You all right, Harry?" Ned asked as they approached the front doors, the people around them all in a hurry, whether they were arriving in Vienna or departing.

"Might be coming down with a cold," Harry replied.

"It's not that," Ned said. "You seem . . . well, I've never seen you nervous before. If I had to guess—"

Harry raised his chin a bit and gave the kid a hard look. "I'm fine."

An older man came out through the doors and was polite enough to hold one open for them.

"You know you don't have to do this," Ned said. "You're feeling ill, right? We can cancel."

Just inside the station, in the midst of echoing footfalls and the susurrus of voices, Harry paused to glare at him, using anger to hide the battle he was waging in his heart.

"How would that look? For Pete's sake, Ned, you're the damned publicist!"

For more than a decade, as he toured the world, Harry had been challenging local constabulary to lock him up in order to establish his reputation as an escape artist. In time he had begun to accept challenges from ordinary citizens. Most of them he ignored, because once he had publicly accepted such a challenge, anything other than success would be an embarrassment and a black mark on the image he had worked so hard to build. Sometimes, however, he simply could not resist.

Ned glanced around to make sure they were not being overheard and then shuffled toward a wall, tilting his head to indicate that Harry should join him.

"You're on edge," Ned whispered. "If it's not the escape that's got you worried, do you mind telling me what the hell it is? Take me into your confidence. It's the only way I can do my job properly."

Harry took a long breath, fighting the tension in his back and arms, forcing himself to exhale. He glanced past Ned and saw Herr Diederich across the station. The Vienna banker stood with several others whose clothing and bearing marked them as similarly wealthy. They were surrounded by a small gaggle of perhaps half a dozen reporters, all of them hanging on Diederich's every word, save for a smartly dressed young woman with her auburn hair caught up in a tightly knotted bun. Of them all, it was she who spotted Harry, and she gave him a small, knowing smile, as if to say she didn't blame him for hanging back and delaying his exposure to the small circus that awaited his arrival. That smile charmed him, even from thirty yards away.

He turned to Ned, studying the young man's earnest blue eyes and the neat little mustache he had grown to make himself look not quite so young but which had had precisely the opposite effect. A young man, but smart and loyal.

"The reporters are coming over," Harry said quietly. "They've seen me now and will be upon us in moments. But you deserve an answer, Ned, and it's a kind of confession, I guess. I lived in Appleton, Wisconsin as a kid—"

"I know that."

"—But I wasn't born there. My real name is Erik Weisz. That's Hungarian, my friend. I was born in Budapest and spent the first four years of my life there. I remember almost nothing of that period, of course. The Orient Express, the journey we're about to embark upon . . . for me it's boarding a train that's bound for home, and it makes me feel like a charlatan."

Ned gaped at him. "Wow, Harry, I had no idea."

"Now that you do, you won't speak a word of it to anyone. I'm no charlatan, Ned. I've worked as hard as I know how and nearly died a hundred times to get to where I am. But you wanted to know what's gotten under my skin, and so I told you. It's Budapest, kid. It haunts me."

"You could have refused to—"

"But I didn't," Harry interrupted. "And we're here now, so let's give 'em a show."

Before Ned could reply, the reporters descended upon them, firing off questions that Harry ignored with a magnanimous smile until Herr Diederich pushed through them with his rich friends in tow and put out a hand to shake.

"Mister Houdini, what a pleasure," Diederich said in thickly accented English. "The train is to depart soon. I was afraid you would not make it in time."

"Not make it?" scoffed a gray-bearded man with spectacles and a ruby pin in his lapel. "You thought Herr Houdini had decided to break his word, that the challenge had frightened him away?"

Bristling inside, Harry managed a smile. "Not at

all, my friends." He glanced at the charming woman with the auburn hair, saw the notepad and pencil in her hand and realized for the first time that she was one of the journalists. He liked that: a girl with pluck. "Just saying farewell to lovely Vienna, in case I never see her again."

The reporters exploded with excitement at this, as they always did whenever he dangled the possibility of his own death in front of them. The reaction never failed to elicit a strange combination of amusement and disgust in Harry. Only the lady journalist, in her smart suit with its buttons in a severe, slashing line down the front of both jacket and skirt, seemed to hang back, waiting for an opportunity to strike.

"Anna Carter of the Boston Globe, Mr. Houdini," she said in the first lull. "Do you mean to tell us that a challenge this dangerous, circumstances in which most men would face almost certain death, doesn't intimidate you at all?"

The question quieted them all as they awaited his answer. Harry directed it toward the lady who'd posed it.

"My dear Miss Carter," he said. "The Great Houdini is not '*most men.*'"

Harry enjoyed the rocking of thuisine e train and the way the candle on his table in the dining car seemed to stay still, only the flame wavering back and forth. The first class dinner menu had been extensive, but he had chosen the duck with traditional Austrian dumplings and cabbage. Ned had ordered wild boar and somehow managed to consume the entire dish. He had a prodigious appetite for so thin a man, and Harry envied him his youth.

"How do you find the duck, Mr. Houdini?" Anna Carter asked, over the rim of a glass of Piesporter she had been nursing for half an hour.

"Delicious, Miss Carter. And your veal?"

"Very tender," the reporter replied. "Honestly, I never expected to experience a meal so fine in such circumstances. The cuisine on board a train generally leaves much to be desired."

Harry smiled at her, but not only her—his gaze took in Ned as well as the four other journalists at the table. "Perhaps you ought to travel in better company."

Anna arched an eyebrow. "Duly noted."

One of the others—the gentleman from the *Times* of London—asked a question to which Harry only half paid attention. Ned jumped in to answer, giving Harry the opportunity to take a sip of water. He'd have preferred a whiskey, but drinking with his life on the line had never seemed a good idea. As it was, he had eaten perhaps more than he ought to have, in his effort to contribute to the convivial atmosphere at the table. Diederich and the others had gone along with Ned's request for them to dine with the reporters instead of their hosts, so he thought he ought to make the best impression he could muster. There was no point in having reporters around if he couldn't use them to the greatest advantage.

"So, Mr. Houdini—" began Herr Kraus of *Wiener Zeitung*, an Austrian paper.

"Harry, please."

"Harry," Herr Kraus went on, his accent thick but not impenetrable. "Tell us: The escape you will attempt tonight . . . is it really a challenge for you, or merely something arranged to keep your name in the papers?"

"Herr Kraus," Ned began, but Harry held up a hand to forestall any protest on the publicist's part.

"No, it's a fair question," he said, noting the spark of curiosity in Anna Carter's eyes. He glanced at Herr Kraus before addressing the entire table. "I'll admit that some of the challenges I've accepted have turned out to be simple enough for one of my abilities. But Herr Diederich and his confederates have gone to great lengths to make this more complicated than escaping from a jail cell. They've bolted a platform on top of this train. I'm to have manacles placed on my wrists and ankles, the chains looped through clamps that are welded to the platform. I will be blindfolded, hands behind my back. There is a tunnel forty miles or so outside of Istanbul whose ceiling is quite low—low enough, in fact, that if I am still on that platform when we reach the tunnel, I will surely be killed."

No one at the table spoke. For journalists, this was a small miracle. It took Harry a moment to realize the reason—he meant what he'd said and that startled them. Of course he had a dozen ways to escape the trap, had trained most of his life for just that sort of thing, but he had never done anything like this on top of a speeding train before.

"Aren't you afraid of dying?" asked the man from London, after another moment's pause.

"My good man," Harry replied. "I have no intention of dying, but if tonight is the night death comes for me, fear will hardly save me."

A waiter arrived, a swarthy, thinly-bearded man in wire-rimmed spectacles. He kept his dark eyes averted as he began to clear plates and glasses.

"Perhaps it's time to inspect the platform and the chains," Ned suggested.

Harry waved a hand. "I've done it already, while you were resting. We've an hour before the challenge begins. I recommend coffee and whatever pastries the chef has provided, though I myself must abstain in preparation."

Another waiter arrived to inquire as to whether they desired sweets or hot drinks. He had the dignified air shared by so many of the staff, that of one who found nobility in service, proud of his station. Something tickled the back of Harry's brain and he glanced around in search of the other man, the one who'd cleared their dishes. The dark-skinned man, of Middle Eastern descent he believed, had kept his eyes downcast in a conspicuously subservient manner, nothing like the others. And yet, hadn't there been just the hint of a smile on his face, as if he had taken some private amusement from the moment?

Harry spotted him farther along the car, where Diederich and the others who had funded the challenge sat, already enjoying dessert. The strange waiter delivered a small metal pot—perhaps of hot cocoa, a tradition in Austria—to the man beside Diederich, and then made his way toward the far door of the car, where the chef and his assistants were at work. As he passed through the door, the man gave a single glance backward, and Harry frowned deeply. Had he seen that face somewhere before, those dark eyes, the long, thin nose, the brows with their almost diabolical natural arch?

"Mr. Houdini?" a voice whispered beside him. "Harry?"

He turned to see that Anna had shifted her chair nearer to his. Ned had begun to pass after dinner cigars around to Herr Kraus and the reporters, who had all slid back from the table and begun a loud conversation about the most extraordinary stories they had ever covered for their respective papers—providing an opportunity for Ned to amplify just what an amazing feat they were to see that very night.

"You don't like cigars?" Harry asked Anna.

Her smile held a hint of admonition. "Why haven't you tried to seduce me?"

She said it so quietly that for a moment he thought he had misheard.

"I'm sorry?"

Anna's hazel eyes sparkled with a hint of green, the wavering candle flame throwing suggestive shadows upon her face.

"Oh, it's not an invitation, just a matter of curiosity. Every other man here has at least made overtures, but not so much as an inquisitive glance from you."

Harry inclined his head in a polite nod. "I never practice the art of seduction before ten p.m., I'm afraid. In any case, I reserve my earnest attentions for Mrs. Houdini."

The appreciative look she gave him held a distinctly American frankness.

"A happily married man, huh?" Anna said. "I figured them for a myth."

"Not a myth, Miss Carter, though perhaps very nearly extinct."

They were interrupted by much shuffling and murmuring as Diederich and his associates rose from their table and came along the car toward them.

"The time has come, Mr. Houdini," Diederich said in his wonderful accent.

"Now?" Ned said, brows knitted in consternation. "We're not scheduled to begin for three quarters of an hour, at least."

The imperiously mannered white-bearded gentleman to Diederich's left sniffed dismissively.

"Our speed is greater than anticipated," he said. "If you are to have the agreed-upon interval before we reach the tunnel, we must begin in twenty minutes. Thirty at most. Surely if we are willing to give you more time to avoid being smeared along the ceiling of that tunnel, you do not object?"

The journalists all laughed good-naturedly, though the white-bearded man had not so much as smiled. *And I thought it was the Germans who have no sense of humor*, Harry thought.

"By all means, sir," he said, rising from his chair with an affectionate glance toward Anna. "By all means."

The blindfold posed no problem. Harry had spent countless hours practicing his craft in the dark, sometimes upside down, inside a tank full of water, or both. The speed of the train did not trouble him either, but its swaying and juddering did offer a challenge. He had a lock pick secreted beneath his tongue and several others in the lining of his clothing, including the cuff of his left coat sleeve. His hands were shackled behind him and the chains had been drawn taut enough that he was on his knees on the platform. In truth, if not for the fact that he wanted his challengers to feel as if they'd gotten their money's worth, he could have escaped in under a minute. Instead, he struggled and strained against his bonds, testing the chains, purposely crashing onto his side as the train jerked around a curve, when actually he was simply trying to adapt to the unpredictable shimmy and shudder of the Orient Express.

As the wind whipped past him, buffeting his face and making his coat billow around him, Harry heard voices murmuring in a strange sort of rhythm. A frown creased his forehead. He knew he was not alone atop the train car; Diederich and his associates had installed three platforms instead of just one, with Harry shackled in the middle and delicately-carved wooden chairs bolted to the other two, four each, so that the financiers of this feat could watch from ahead and behind. In the dark, with only the bright moonlight to illuminate the showman, they would not be able to see the finer elements of his escape. If he could hide lock picks from a theatre audience, he could do it atop a speeding train in the dark.

The journalists had not been afforded seats. Instead, they had been told they were welcome to view the event but would have to take their chances. Only Herr Kraus and Anna Carter had dared spend so much time exposed atop the train without any way to anchor themselves. Harry admired their courage and wished them well. For his part, Ned had returned to the dining car for a drink with the other journalists. He would handle the questions during and after the escape but Harry did not want him to take any unnecessary risks.

Now, though . . . that chanting . . . what in God's name were they up to, these men? Trying to break his concentration? If so, it wasn't very sporting of them.

The voices grew louder, all rough, guttural syllables that sounded like gibberish to him, and he realized they were indeed hoping to throw him off his game. A ripple of anger went through Harry. This might have been all in good fun were it not for the fact that they were hurtling at top speed toward a tunnel whose low ceiling would turn him into a red streak along the train's roof. Diederich and Wagner and the others would abandon their seats and retreat safely down the iron rungs between train cars, never risking their own destruction. Would they leave him up there, if their nefarious chanting achieved its purpose of distraction? Ordinarily he would have said no, but these seemed the type who might actually enjoy the notoriety of having posed the challenge that killed Harry Houdini.

To hell with them, he thought.

Working quickly, he pulled his wrists taut against his shackles and twisted his right hand so that he could snag the cuff of his left coat sleeve with his fingers. In a heartbeat he'd plucked the lock pick free of the lining, careful to keep his hands turned so that those behind him would not glimpse a glint of moonlight on the pick. He shifted his head, tossing it as if attempting to free himself from the blindfold but really only drawing their attention away from his hands and toward his face.

With swift precision, he slid the pick into the lock on the manacles around his wrists. He heard Kraus ask about the purpose of the chanting, but it only grew louder. It occurred to him, just for a moment, that he had heard it before. In the back of his mind, a memory began to rise. Harry pushed the distraction away, tugging against his bonds, hearing the chains clank against the hooks to which they had been moored. But he had stopped listening to the sounds of the train, stopped paying attention to the rattle and judder of the cars ahead of him, and so was unprepared when their car suddenly shunted to the right, switching tracks.

His wrists clacked together, twisting the lock pick from his hand, and he lost it.

"Shit," he muttered under his breath, his anger growing.

A dozen options presented themselves in his head, various ways in which he could still manage his escape. Some required physical contortions that would likely tear his jacket, for which he had paid handsomely. The chanting—the familiar, rhythmic chanting—infuriated him both because it was irritating and because it had achieved its goal. The bastards had distracted him enough that he had not only dropped his first pick but he had lost track of time. How long, now, until they reached the tunnel? He wasn't sure.

He opted for the quickest escape, which would also be the most painful.

Bracing himself on the platform, knees apart, he shifted his upper body, took a deep breath and exhaled, and then thrust out his right shoulder, dislocating it completely. Harry bit back a roar, allowing only a grunt. Trembling, breath coming in hitching gasps, he raised both arms and brought them over the top of his head, back to front. The damnable chanting faltered for a moment.

With a twist of his arm and another small grunt of pain, he popped his shoulder back into the socket. His lips were stretched into a rictus grin to hide the pain. He'd dislocated both shoulders on occasion but had never learned to fully disguise the extent of his discomfort.

The chanting grew louder, but now Harry didn't care. On his knees, he rested a moment, shackled wrists hanging before him.

"Enough games," he muttered as he reached up to tear away his blindfold. The wind shearing across the top of the speeding train whipped at him and stung his eyes but he blinked them clear and then froze, shocked into paralysis by the scene that the moonlight revealed.

Diederich and two of his confederates sat on the chairs bolted to the platform ten feet ahead of him, along with a fourth observer—the swarthy waiter with the thin beard and wire spectacles. Confusion sparked in Harry's mind, but the others arrayed on the roof of the train ignited that confusion into a conflagration. In the space between his platform and the next, and arranged in a ring that encircled his position, were another dozen figures, cloaked and hooded in heavy black fabric run through with strands of moonlit silver. They were on their knees, palms upon the metal roof of the hurtling train, heads hung low so that their hoods hid any hint as to their identities. The chanting came from these hooded men, who it seemed had also hastily painted a scattering of arcane symbols on the roof around him.

Memory rushed in as if some barrier had been holding it back and now it flooded his mind. Two years past, on a visit to Egypt, he had endured a night of terror unlike anything else he had ever experienced. Lured beneath the sands, under the pyramids, he had been knocked unconscious and woken to find himself a captive, surrounded by creatures with human bodies but the heads of beasts, the intended sacrifice in a nightmare ritual that opened an aperture in the fabric of the world as some ancient, malignant presence— some dark god—attempted to slip through. Harry had escaped, of course. He had survived and immediately begun to obliterate the memory from his mind, doubting and undermining the experience, persuading himself that it had been a nightmare or some drug-induced phantasmagoria, the result of some malicious attack by the guide he had hired to bring him safely on a tour of Egypt's most ancient sites.

His guide. Abdul Reis el Drogman.

Harry snapped his gaze back toward the platform, staring at the swarthy man beside Diederich. Take away the spectacles and the beard, account for the passage of time . . . Harry knew him now. *Abdul Reis, here.*

Panic set in.

Abdul Reis saw the recognition in his eyes and offered a sinister smile as the others continued their chanting. Harry stared past him and Diederich and the others, watching the nighttime horizon. There were low hills around them and many ahead. How far to the tunnel? He had no idea.

"Son of a bitch," Harry hissed, glaring at Abdul Reis.

Shoulder throbbing, he went to work, shifting his tongue around to force out the thin lock pick he'd hidden in the corner of his mouth moments before they shackled him. His heart hammered in his chest; this was no longer a game. He took the pick from his mouth, listened for the jerking and rattling of the train car ahead of them and managed to keep his balance like a sailor getting his sea legs. Barely glancing at the cuffs, he picked the lock on his manacles and slipped them off, allowing them to drop to the platform with a heavy clank.

Diederich slid forward in his chair, gripping its arms, his eyes lit up with alarm.

"Stop—" he began, but Abdul Reis clamped a hand on his wrist and gave a silent shake of his head, and only then did Harry truly understand who had been the mastermind behind this madness.

Abdul Reis raised his other hand and gestured. Behind Harry there came a scuffling and a cry, and he thought that over the wind he could hear someone calling his name.

Even as he sat down on the platform, working the pick into the lock on his ankle shackles, he twisted round to look behind him. The rest of the circle of hooded acolytes looked identical to their fellows, but toward the rear of the car, Diederich's remaining confederates stood in front of their chairs, restraining a pair of captives.

"Make no further attempt to escape, Mr. Houdini!" Abdul Reis said, shouting to be heard over the wind. "Or they both die!"

Ned McCarty and Anna Carter struggled against the men who held them, but there was little they could do. Both had their hands bound behind their backs. Anna had been tightly gagged, but the gag on Ned had slipped down to his neck; he had been the one to shout Harry's name.

Anna had been stripped to her white underthings, baring her pale flesh to the moonlight. In the short time during which they had shackled Harry and he'd

110

been feigning difficulty with his escape—while he had been putting on a show for them—these chanting madmen had painted her skin with the same bizarre sigils that had been drawn onto the roof of the train. She hunched slightly, grimacing as if in pain, and he realized that her bucking against them was not an attempt to free herself but a series of paroxysms caused by crippling pain in her gut. Bright, bloody crimson lines showed where the flesh of her abdomen had been cut and the skin peeled open in folds like flower petals.

"Anna!" Harry shouted. "Ned, don't let them—"

Ned lunged forward, fighting his captors, and wrested himself free. He turned and drove himself at one of the cultists holding Anna, trying to knock the man from the speeding train. The cultist turned to defend himself, holding an ornate, curved dagger. Ned collided with him and they both went down. Harry felt a surge of hope, before the cultist tossed Ned aside, the dagger jutting from his chest. Harry screamed his friend's name. Wide-eyed, Ned stared pleadingly at Harry for a moment, all of the strength leaving him . . . and then his killer hurled him over the side of the moving train. His body tumbled off into the night and was left behind in the wake of the rattling locomotive.

Harry sneered at the killer, ignoring the hooded men and their benefactors, Abdul Reis forgotten. Ned was dead, and Harry understood that the only chance Anna had of surviving to see the sunrise was if he was free. He bent to unlock the shackles on his ankles and one of the cultists rushed at him. Harry swayed with the rhythm of the train and when the man leaped at him, he twisted aside, grabbed the man's wrist, and used his momentum against him. The man sprawled across the roof, slid and tried in vain to get a grip before he, too, fell over the side and into the dark. As another cultist moved in, Harry unlocked his ankle shackles. They clanked to the platform as he stood, facing Ned's murderer and his compatriots.

"Let her go!" he demanded, knowing even as the screaming wind stole his voice away that he could not intimidate them, not one man against so many.

Still, he intended to save her, whatever the cost.

Harry stepped off the platform, advancing toward the back of the train car, and two of the hooded acolytes that separated him from Anna and her captors glanced up, flinching at his approach. One of them was the Austrian journalist, Herr Kraus.

The other had the head of a tiger. Its black lips curled back from its fangs in a low growl as it began to rise.

Harry heard the ratcheting of the car ahead of theirs and braced himself as the train jerked to one side, following the tracks. Jostled, the tiger-headed man went back onto his hands and knees. Harry took two long strides and lunged between him and Kraus, landing just in front of the platform where Ned had just been murdered. The chanting increased in volume and speed.

He caught a few words on the wind and glanced back toward the front of the train. Abdul Reis had spoken.

"Not this time, Houdini," the Egyptian shouted. "This time, you will die."

Abdul Reis barked an order and the two men holding Anna drove her forward and shoved her at

Harry, who caught her even as the collision forced him backward. He fell with her wrapped in his arms, the two of them sprawling past the hooded ones and crashing to the platform atop the coiled chains Harry had just shed.

Anna's eyes were bright with pain and she screamed against her gag. He tugged the cloth down and her words flowed in a frenzied, anguished torrent.

"It hurts. Oh, Harry, it's tearing me apart inside."

Harry shushed her as he worked her free of her bonds. On his knees now, holding her, he turned to glare at Abdul Reis.

"What did you do to her, you monster?"

Abdul Reis only smiled and gestured to the others. The chanting grew louder still, the acolytes lowering their heads so far they could have kissed the metal roof. The words had changed, and so had that guttural rhythm. Their ritual had entered a new phase.

Anna screamed and thrashed against him.

"Damn you, take me! You wanted me for your sacrifice!" he roared at the Egyptian. "Take me!"

The smile vanished from the Egyptian's features, replaced by open loathing and malice.

"You misunderstand, Houdini," Abdul Reis called to him. "You *are* the sacrifice. You have always been the sacrifice. You have escaped death again and again, and each escape has made your life force more powerful, more radiant. Your death will be a beacon, sure to guide the Old Ones into the world."

"Then let Anna go!" Harry shouted.

"No, you fool," the Egyptian said. "You are the sacrifice, but she is the *door!*"

Anna cried out to God and threw her head back,

going rigid in Harry's arms as her eyes rolled up to their whites. She bucked, thrusting her abdomen upward, and he looked at her pale, smooth belly to see that a pulsing, bloodless slit had appeared there, a vertical mouth that began to open.

With a grunt of revulsion, Harry released her and tried to scramble away, but in the same moment a pair of thick tentacles slid from the pouting slit of her abdomen, probing the air like dogs seeking a scent. The chanting grew louder and Harry could hear the laughter of Abdul Reis as the hideous tendrils extruded further, joined now by a third.

Jerked forward by the things forcing themselves from within her—*no*, he thought, *not within her but somehow through her; she is only a door into this world from some vast, chaotic other*—Anna looked down at her naked, obscenely split belly and began to scream as madness took her. She whipped her head around, eyes wild and searching, and locked her gaze upon him.

"Harry," she whimpered. "Please, Harry."

He twisted around, scanning the tracks far ahead in search of that tunnel, wondering how long before it would smash all of them from the roof of the train. He saw that they were approaching a bridge that spanned a deep river gorge. Regret and guilt swept him as a terrible decision presented itself. Harry tensed, crouched on the roof, balancing himself with his hands.

With wet, sticky sucking noises, the tentacles shot further from Anna's belly and seized him, slithering and coiling around him like serpents. Harry tried to fight them but his struggles only caused them to tighten. The thick, mottled tendrils dragged Harry toward her even as the slit in her belly grew, splitting her breastbone so that it seemed the entirety of her was opening to him, trying to pull him *in*.

A noxious, stinking gas exuded from that hole, the stench of some hellish otherplace, and as he gazed inside of her, the moonlight revealed nightmare things that had never existed in this world, other shapes that made his mind scream with their impossible geometry.

"No," he grunted, as the chanting reached a fever pitch.

His hands wrapped around Anna's throat almost of their own volition. Her eyes rolled back again and she jerked in his grip. Harry felt her life pulsing in the veins of her throat and he knew he could end it, knew that he had to end it, not just to save himself but to prevent the abominable others from being birthed into the world through the vast womb that her body had become.

Yet he could not. He thought of Ned, barely more than a kid and now dead because he had joined Harry on this journey. And then he thought of Bess, his sweet Bess, his best friend and staunchest ally, the foundation of his life. He had to get home to her, and to keep the world unmarred by the unimaginable malignance of the Old Ones.

Tentacles squeezed him, crushing the air from him, and he felt his body pressed to the moist, stinking gap in Anna's belly like some obscene lover.

The train began to rattle across the bridge. Beyond it he could see a low, narrow tunnel cut into the rocky face of a hill. Time had run out.

Harry counted to four, prayed they were over the

river, embraced Anna Carter, and then pistoned his legs to hurl them both off the side of the train. He heard Abdul Reis scream in fury as they fell, and then he could hear nothing but the air whipping by his ears and the slippery squirming of the tentacles around him, pulling him into those sucking, wet folds.

The fall seemed to go on for eternity. Just before they struck the water he drew a ragged breath and held it, and then they plunged into the cold, deep river, the current carrying them swiftly away from the train bridge. Submerged, dragged along the river bottom, Harry fought against the tentacles and against Anna's flailing arms, but he did not strive for the surface. Instead, he struggled to stay down. The Great Houdini could hold his breath for a long, long time.

As they floated upward, he twisted in the water and kept her down, until at last Anna went slack in his arms and the tentacles loosened their hold and began to withdraw.

The river swept them into a shallow pool near its bank, scraping them against the rocks, and Harry dragged Anna up onto the shore. He could see the long slit that stretched from her groin to her throat, peeling her open. Nothing shifted in the dark, glistening cavity within her. He could see gray organs and pale bones, but whatever passage had opened inside of her, that door had closed with her death.

Harry wept into his hands, shaking with sorrow and fury.

When he could catch his breath, he lifted his gaze and stared upriver at the bridge spanning the gorge. The train would be far away by now. It would arrive in Istanbul without him. The homecoming he had imagined was not to be, and yet he had no intention of completing the journey. Home had taken on a new meaning for him, not his childhood home, or even the place he and Bess had made a home for themselves. He had caught a glimpse of what waited outside of his reality, and it had made him understand that the whole world was his home, and he would do anything to defend it. He would meet Abdul Reis el Drogman again. He would seek out every occultist and sorcerer, expose the charlatans and destroy the true practitioners, until he found Abdul Reis, and then he would kill the Egyptian.

For this had been no dream. He would never be able to persuade himself that it had been a nightmare, nor did he wish to. Anna's death demanded that he remember. More than that, he had seen the nameless things moving on the other side of the door that had opened inside her, and he knew those things could never be allowed to come through.

Harry Houdini sat bloody and bruised on the bank of an unknown river and pondered what would have to be his greatest escape. He understood now that he was still a prisoner, bound by a future whose chains would continue to tighten around him until at last either he or his enemy, the diabolical Abdul Reis, was dead.

Only then would he truly be free.

THE CUSTER FILES

RICHARD CHIZMAR

The handwritten letters, journal entries, and notes excerpted below are from the personal collection of esteemed historian Ronald Bakewell. The papers were discovered after Bakewell's recent death and assembled into the narrative that follows by Bakewell's longtime associate, Byron McClernan. They have not been made available to the public until now. In an effort to provide clarity, minor editing has been done to the language, and spelling and punctuation errors have been corrected.

———∼∼∼———

(Personal letter—Private George E. Adams, Seventh Cavalry—June 21, 1876)

```
Dear Father and Mother,
    I miss you both desperately but
believe you would be very proud of
your youngest son. I have learned
so much during my time here and the
men I ride with are of the finest
caliber. I am proud to serve by
their side and pray I will
distinguish myself in battle, as so
```

many others in the Seventh have done before me. Lieutenant Colonel Custer is a larger than life figure. He reminds me of Grandpa Frank at times, with his booming voice and ability to make the tallest of tales seem believable. The men admire and fear him in equal measure. Some believe him to be aloof, even cruel, but I find him charming and confident, and would follow him anywhere . . .

(Journal entry—Corporal John J. Callahan, Seventh Cavalry—June 21, 1876)

. . . and because of this strategy it has been long days of riding and short nights of rest. It is no wonder the men are so tired. Still, I have heard few complaints and witnessed even fewer moments of weakness amongst the men. We have been trained well and know the routine. I have little doubt the campaign will be successful.

Oh how I wish you were here with me, my darling Wanda, sitting beside me on this dark prairie, staring up at the magnificent night sky, counting the stars and playing our wishing game. My first wish upon a star tonight would be for our precious baby Genevieve to grow up to find happiness and good health. My second would be for you and me to build that cabin by the lake we always dreamed of, to grow old together, and watch our grandchildren play at our feet. One day, soon, I promise you . . .

(Personal letter—Private George Eiseman, Seventh Cavalry—June 22, 1876)

I hate it. The men are filthy. Fighting, cursing, farting, burping, shitting, pissing. They are no better than the horses that carry them. The officers offer meager improvement, bullies and barbarians to a man. The days are endless, the mess tastes like buffalo droppings, and there is not a single aspect of this dreadful land I can give praise to. I hate it here.

(Journal entry—Lt. Col. George Armstrong Custer, Seventh Cavalry—June 23, 1876)

. . . therefore I can only describe it as a feeling of being set free after a long imprisonment. Imagine an eagle taking flight for the first time after enduring a lengthy injury to one of its wings, a grizzly bear healed of its hindquarter wound and returning to the fast hunt. That is akin to what being on campaign feels like for me. I was born to lead men in the field. I was born to chase glory. I sit here on my cot inside my tent, writing by the light of a single lantern, and I am at absolute peace with but one corner of my heart left incomplete. I will return to your arms soon, my dearest Libbie, and we shall once again sit upon the porch at Fort Lincoln, sip your splendid tea, and doze to the setting sun. Sleep now, as shall I. More tomorrow, my Rosebud.

(Journal entry—Corporal John Foley, Seventh Cavalry—June 23, 1876)

I believe the men feel it, feel *something*, even if the officers continue to turn a blind eye. First, there was the missing food supplies. The cooking staff was publically scolded for being careless but the matter was never investigated further. Unusual to say the least. Reno is the most detail-oriented officer I have ever served under. Then there was the captured scout from two nights ago. Reno insisted that he was Lakota, while Tom Custer and Benteen argued that he was Cheyenne. Well, then why did my old friend Sergeant Perkins tell me confidentially that the scout was of neither tribe? That he was some new breed he had never seen before. Wild, feral, with the strangest markings on his pony Perkins had ever seen. Eyes the color of blackest night. Skin paler than many white men. And then there are the rumors of how the scout had bitten two men during his capture. Both soldiers now quarantined in Sick Hall. Finally, there is the matter of so many other men falling ill. Why so many? And why all the secrecy surrounding their illnesses? I am not a man of superstition, but it is beginning to feel as though this campaign has been cursed.

(Personal letter—Captain Thomas Custer, Seventh Cavalry—June 23, 1876)

. . . but I imagine we will just have to wait and see. Terry and Gibbon are out there if we need them. The same should be said of Crook, but I believe he would be a tad slow in coming to our aid, even if summoned. (That was a joke. I think. I hope.)

George is clear-headed and affable thus far into the march, if a bit more subdued than his usual nature. One of the Crow scouts asked me yesterday, a look of sincere concern etched across his brown face, why George had cut his long yellow hair. He was convinced that it was bad luck for him to have done so before battle. I could only chuckle when brother Boston chimed in and responded with that crooked grin of his, "Come now, haven't you ever heard of 'Custer Luck'? The only kind of luck George has is of the good variety. The man was practically born with a horse shoe up his rear end."

I will write again, old friend, when time and temperament allow. In the meantime, light a cigar for me next time you sit down at the chessboard. Tell Charlie I said to break a leg.

Yours truly,
Tom Custer

(Personal letter—Sergeant Robert H. Hughes, Seventh Cavalry—June 23, 1876)

Something is wrong here. It began as an underlying feeling of unease-the past few nights have been too quiet; where have the night creatures gone? Even the crickets and frogs remain silent-but it has since grown into something else entirely. I have the most dreadful feeling.

(Journal entry—Corporal George H. King, Seventh Cavalry—June 24, 1876)

I was on the way back from my morning smoke when I overheard Curley and Bloody Knife talking to some of the officers. The hairs on the back of my neck stood up as I listened to them report, "Big camp. Many lodges, many fires burning. Too many braves to count." I pulled Bloody Knife aside later in the day and asked for more details. His eyes told me everything else I needed to hear. "Must wait for more men. Bigger guns. Yellow Hair is brave but will not listen." Bloody Knife's voice was solemn, his eyes anxious. I have never seen him act in such a manner. He told me he is praying to the Great Spirit for a vision to be sent to Custer in his sleep. I'm not holding my breath. I'm not sure the bastard ever sleeps.

(Personal letter—Sergeant Jeremiah Finley, Seventh Cavalry—June 24, 1876)

We lost another two men last night. Their rifles and packs and horses remain, but they have otherwise vanished. This brings the total to nineteen missing. Desertions are rare for the Seventh, this level of frequency unheard of. Who leaves all of their personal belongings and sets off on foot in the middle of this inhospitable terrain? It makes little sense. We have doubled the guard and still no one has seen or heard anything out of the ordinary. To the contrary, the nights have been unnaturally quiet and still. We long-marched almost eighty miles today and with good reason, I figure. We better hurry and catch up with Crazy Horse or there won't be enough of us left to fight . . .

(Personal letter—Captain Thomas Custer, Seventh Cavalry—June 24, 1876)

. . . which is perhaps a stroke of profound good fortune, as we should be close enough to engage the enemy within a day, two at the most. Once again, George has managed to accomplish what many others before him could not. His unbridled energy this campaign is only matched by his fierce determination to defeat the legendary Crazy Horse on the field of battle. I asked him during this morning's ride if he would be satisfied with Crazy Horse's surrender. He appeared shocked and rather dismayed at such a proposition. His response? "Sitting Bull, yes. Crazy Horse, I want to destroy."

(Journal entry—Private William Moodie, Seventh Cavalry—June 24, 1876)

They're lying and for the life of me, I cannot figure out why. There is no way in hell I'm believing that Elmer deserted. And without his horse? His gun? His lucky squirrel tail? I don't believe it. He would just as soon run out of here without any trousers and boots on than leave without his lucky squirrel tail and carbine. Private Elmer Babcock is a lot of things-a

shitty poker player at the top of
that list-but he ain't no goddamn
deserter. You couldn't find a more
loyal soldier anywhere.

**(Journal entry—Private James Brightfield,
Seventh Cavalry—June 24, 1876)**

I know what I saw and I know what I
heard. I was standing guard post on
the northern perimeter of camp. It
was after midnight when I heard one
of the men crying out in the dark.
A quick, muffled bark, and then
silence. At first I thought maybe
my ears were playing tricks on me-
there shouldn't have been anyone
out there beyond the safety of the
firelight-but then I heard the
sucking sounds. A wet smacking,
slurping noise like a starved
animal feasting on its kill. It was
then I knew it wasn't an Indian.
They may be savages, but they move
like the wind. I mustered my
courage, and with my rifle pointed
in front of me, I went to
investigate. I freely admit that I
made as much noise as I could
manage with the hopes that whatever
was doing the feasting would soon
be frightened away by my approach.
Thirty or so yards outside of camp

I found a wide circle of blood. Splashed on the grass. Soaked into the dirt. And a scrap of bloodstained cloth that looked like it came from an undershirt. I stood there scanning the shadows and had the strangest sensation that I was being watched. Looking over my shoulder the entire time, I hurried back to camp and reported what I had found to my Sergeant. He thanked me and promised to relay the information to the Captain. It was only later that I realized something: Sarge hadn't looked the least bit surprised when I had told him my story. I find that rather unsettling. Sarge also made me swear not to repeat any of the details to the other men. Not that I would have anyway. Who would ever believe such a tale?

(Journal entry—Lt. Col. George Armstrong Custer, Seventh Cavalry—June 25, 1876)

The scouts have returned. Today is the day. I will not wait for Terry or Gibbon. I will not wait for more guns. We will surround and attack the village on my command. Reno will approach from the south,

Benteen on my far flank. The scouts are uneasy, as are many of the officers, but I remain supremely confident. I believe the savages will see our dust coming, will hear the thunder of our horses, and they will flee. There is not an enemy walking this earth that can defeat the Seventh.

(Personal letter—Captain Frederick Benteen, Seventh Cavalry—June 25, 1876)

The fool! It's already been decided: we attack today. No cannons, no Gatling guns, no reinforcements from General Terry. Custer, once again, the impatient fool. I dared to question the great one's decision to split up the regiment into three, and his only response was typical Custer arrogance: "You have your orders." The men are exhausted. Why not at least allow us another night's rest and to engage at dawn instead of midday? I'm sure we will emerge victorious, of course, but at what cost? Custer is without conscience. He cares only of the newspaper headlines and his own perverse sense of immortality . . .

RICHARD CHIZMAR

(Personal letter—Trumpeter Thomas J. Bucknell, Seventh Cavalry—June 25, 1876)

Dearest Court,

The orders came down just minutes ago. We will attack the village in an hour's time. I've heard rumors of almost a thousand Indians, perhaps more. Please know how much I love and cherish you if I am unable to make it home to your arms. Please know that I tried my very best.

With all my love,
Thomas

P.S. Give my momma a hug when you next see her.

(Journal entry—Private John Papp, Seventh Cavalry—June 25, 1876)

I overheard my sergeant talking about the camp this morning. Lodges as far as the eye could see. Too many ponies to count. We're all going to die in this valley. Every last one of us.

(Personal letter—Private Andrew J. Moore, Seventh Cavalry—June 25, 1876)

THE CUSTER FILES

I've never seen so many Indians.
May God have mercy on us all.

(Battlefield note dictated by Lt. Col. George Armstrong Custer to runner, Trumpeter John Martini—June 25, 1876)

Benteen.
   Come on. Big village. Be quick.
Bring packs.
   P.S. Bring packs.

(Personal letter—Corporal Henry M. Cody, Seventh Cavalry—June 25, 1876)

In the event that someone finds this upon my almost certain death . . .
   Bloody Knife is dead. Major Reno is incompetent. He ordered us to retreat and fight on foot in the timber and now we are trapped here and dying. I can hear the dull roar of gunfire in the distance, presumably Custer's companies engaging. We are badly outnumbered and have but one chance at escape. To ride through their lines. Otherwise it will be a massacre. Reno is no longer giving orders. God help us.

Regretfully,
Corp. Henry M. Cody

RICHARD CHIZMAR

(Battlefield note given to runner—written by Major Reno, Seventh Cavalry—June 25, 1876)

```
Need  reinforcements.  Ammunition.
Outnumbered  but  holding  timberline.
Something  wrong  with  these  savages.
Bullets  do  not  stop  them.  Men  are
being  eaten  alive.  Chaos.  Hurry.
```

(Personal letter—Captain Otto Hageman, Seventh Cavalry—June 25, 1876)

```
We  are  fighting  monsters.  How  do
you  kill  your  enemy  if  they  are
already  dead?  They  are  toying  with
us.  I  saw  Custer  fall  .  .  .
```

(Battlefield note given to runner—written by 1ˢᵗ Sergeant James Butler, Seventh Cavalry—June 25, 1876)

```
G.  Custer  is  gone.  Killed  in  the
first  moments  of  battle.  Heavy
casualties.  Send  men  and  guns.
Surrounded.
```

(Journal entry—Sergeant James T. Riley, Seventh Cavalry—July 1, 1876)

```
Strict  orders  have  been  given  by
General  Terry  not  to  speak  of  this
but  I  feel  as  though  I  must  record
```

my thoughts lest my head burst with the horrid reality of what I recently witnessed.

On June 28, my men and I were tasked with burying the bodies of the massacred Seventh Cavalry. It was a dreadful duty, as most of the bodies were bloated and blackened by the sun, and mutilated beyond recognition. Even poor Thomas Custer was not spared the indignity, as his head was crushed flat and he was only identifiable by the crude tattoo located on his left shoulder. As for the legendary George Custer, he was one of the very few that remained without disfigurement. Only his eardrums had been punctured. Perhaps most strangely, he died with a smile on his face, as if he knew his heroic death would cement his legacy once and for all.

As is usual procedure, a casualty count was completed, and it appeared as though many of the bodies were missing. Perhaps as many as three dozen with no explanation. When I questioned the other officers, I was greeted with backs turned, heads held close, and conspiratorial whispers. I am quite certain that one or more of these officers held the answer close to their lips but simply did not feel comfortable sharing that answer with me.

But yet that wasn't the worst of it. Amongst the gruesome mutilations we encountered on that field overlooking the Little Bighorn were crudely amputated arms and legs, disembowelment, sliced off noses and ears and penises, and of course missing scalps to a man. One body inexplicably held one-hundred-and-five arrows. Another was posed with the trooper's severed arms laid out in place of his missing legs, which were never found. But none of these travesties troubled me as deeply as the many throats I came upon that appeared to have been ripped open . . . no, that's not entirely accurate or truthful . . . they appeared to have been *chewed* open. And, still stranger, all of these particular corpses were as pale as a winter snowfall. Seemingly drained of every last drop of their blood. What kind of savage could inflict such a wound?

(Personal letter discovered after his death— Private Christopher Criddle, Seventh Cavalry—November 19, 1907)

THE CUSTER FILES

To Whom It May Concern,

   I pray this letter is duly noted upon my passing and its contents are taken in the spirit in which they were written-as my absolute truth and atonement.

Most here in Springdale know me only as an honest storekeeper. No spouse, no family, a handful of unremarkable details regarding my past. Just a solitary man in his later years who loves his books, root beer floats, and the striking of a fair bargain.

What they don't know-and what would certainly come as a shock to each and every one of them-is that in a former life and faraway place I was once a Private in George Custer's famed Seventh Cavalry. It was long ago and I was a very different man then. Young and angry and desperately in need of discipline and acceptance. In short order, the Seventh became my home, and I came to adore everything about this choice of life. Until the Little Bighorn, that is.

   Yes, I was with Custer at the Little Big Horn. I knelt no more than ten yards away from him when he was felled by a gunshot to his temple. Minutes later, his brother Thomas went down at my feet and followed George to whatever awaits us all after this world.

But how could this be, you ask? There were no survivors at the battle of the Little Bighorn. The newspapers claim it was a massacre. It was and I did. Survive, that is. Thanks to simple dumb luck and the unexpected aid of one generous soul-whom I will never mention, not even here in my final testimony-I not only was able to survive the battle with only a minor wound to my shoulder, I was also able to disappear, my body and mind after that day incapable of returning to a life of soldiering.

So, yes, I admit I am a deserter. A fugitive at large. Although I am quite certain that no one realizes this fact-not then, and not now. From what I have come to understand, many of my fellow troopers were missing from the field that day. Many others mutilated beyond recognition. Somewhere on that grassy knoll, I am certain there is a wooden cross with my name scrawled upon it.

I, alone, know the details of that day. I saw the Indians stream by the hundreds out of those hidden gullies. I heard a shocked Custer bark his orders and the bugles blow retreat. I was there when we realized we were cut off and surrounded, when we dismounted to make our final stand. Most of the men fell to arrows and spears and bullets at intermediate range, but as the battle raged, more and more resorted to taking their own lives. The air became filled with gun-smoke and screams. It was hard to hear if any further orders were being given, harder still to see clearly. That's when the creatures came. They crawled on their bellies through the high grass like snakes, their bloody teeth bared, their black eyes unblinking. I watched as trooper after trooper were dragged to the ground with incredible strength . . . their throats ripped open by razor-sharp teeth . . . and drained of their blood. I tried to kill the savages but my bullets had no effect on them.

For decades, I have never been able to find the proper words to put a name to the monsters I witnessed in that God-forsaken valley. And then, several years

ago, I heard about an Irish writer
by the name of Bram Stoker who had
recently published a
sensationalistic novel entitled
Dracula. The book told the story of
a night creature who drank the
blood of his victims and cursed
them to the eternal life of the
undead. These creatures were given
a name: *vampire*. I was able to
acquire a copy of this book a short
time ago from one of my contacts in
Boston. Stoker's tale was set
across the ocean in Europe, a far
cry from the dusty plains of the
American West, and there were of
course many other differences from
what I experienced at the Little
Bighorn. But there were also a
multitude of striking similarities,
enough so to convince me that
Stoker's book might not be merely
a work of fantastic fiction.

I've never spoken or written of
that fateful day at the Little
Bighorn until now, and I will never
make mention of it again. If only
it was as easy to erase it from my
conscience. I dream of them, you
see. With their dark, hungry eyes
and protruding, razor-sharp teeth.
Sometimes, I find myself sketching
their hideous faces on the backs of

bills of sale while standing at the counter in my store.

When I realize what I am doing, I inevitably crumble these drawings and toss them into the trash bin or watch them burn in the flames of my fireplace at home. But it doesn't matter. The faces always come back to me in my nightmares. I cannot ever forget them. So many mornings I wake up drenched in sweat and terror, my hands clutching my throat, protecting the soft flesh and holding in my screams. Then, I wash myself and dress, and head to the store, where I greet the townsfolk with a tired smile and a nod of my head and perhaps a few pleasantries. And each time the bell above the door rings, signaling the arrival of a new customer, I glance nervously from whatever task I am performing and pray that I don't see those strange, dark eyes or razor-sharp teeth, that whatever those creatures were, they haven't decided to journey East in their quest for fresh blood.

So, there you have it. My truth. I alone survived the Battle of the Little Bighorn. And on those long and lonely nights when their faces visit my dreams, I wish to God I hadn't.

Sincerely,
C. Criddle

(Personal letter discovered after his passing— Ronald Bakewell—February 9, 2018)

. . . and so I leave the final

decision in your worthy hands,
Byron. History is yours for the
changing. Or not. No one should
judge your either decision. Just
remember our old motto from
University days: nothing holds more
power than the truth.

> Yours in admiration and
> friendship,
> Ronald Bakewell

RED MOON

Michael Paul Gonzalez

"FELLAS. THAT'S THE MOON. The god-damned moon!"

"You keep saying that, Buzz."

"You're not impressed? You landed on a bigger moon you didn't tell me about, Neil?"

"When my wife bends over to fold the laundry," Armstrong retorted, bringing a nervous chuckle out of Collins.

"You're only saying that because she can't hear you right now," Aldrin giggled.

"You got that right."

"Just for that, I'm going first. We're all switching seats."

Collins spared a glance from his instrument panels out the side of the lunar orbiter.

"What do you think, Collins? You want to go down there, let me fly this thing around the moon instead?" After an uneasy silence, Aldrin asked. "What's gotten into you anyway? You've been pretty quiet."

"This is a special mission of national and international importance," Collins said, almost robotically.

"We know," Armstrong laughed. "Space rocks.

Research. Good of humanity. We're going down there to become god-damned legends."

"First men on the moon!" Aldrin shouted, slapping his thigh.

Collins let out a sigh. "No, it's . . . I'm supposed to wait until we're in lunar orbit to tell you this. There's no easy way to it, so I'll just say it. Aside from President Nixon and a handful of higher-ups in agencies that don't officially exist, you'll be the only ones with the knowledge I'm about to share. I'm supposed to swear you to secrecy, but I won't. Time's wasting and there's nobody in the world who will believe what I'm about to tell you." Collins locked in his trajectory and flipped down two switches, turning to face them. "Exploring the moon is not your primary objective. You're going down there to go hunting."

"Beg your pardon?" Armstrong said, sharing a glance with Aldrin.

"You won't be . . . you aren't the first men down there."

"Mike, come on . . . "

"Buzz, there are men down there. Sort of. Your job is to make sure you're the only men that come back. Gentlemen, your primary mission from this point forward is to locate and terminate three Soviet operatives. Cosmonauts." Collins paused and swallowed. "Werewolves."

Aldrin barked a short laugh, then choked it off, looking at Armstrong.

"You feeling okay, Mike?"

"We're on a controlled entry here, fellas. We have little time for explanation and no time for debate."

Collins reached under his seat and popped open a

small panel, pulling out a metal box. "This mission was compartmentalized. Need-to-know. Until now, you didn't need to know. You each have one of these boxes under your seat. Pull it out."

Collins opened his box to reveal a large metal wrist brace. Mounted to one side was a long barrel with a large cartridge box behind it.

"What the hell is that supposed to be?" Aldrin asked.

"What's it look like to you?" Collins replied.

"It looks like that prototype bolt driver they had us working with in case anything broke while we were down there."

"The very same. And now it's driven by a big pressurized gas canister. Brace your feet. Wait for your target to charge you. Let 'er rip," Collins stared at the two other men. "It's a gun."

"You're serious about—now just what in the deep blue hell is—" Armstrong's brow creased, his eyes meeting Collins' in the eerie silence. He flicked on the radio.

"Houston, Eagle. How do you read now?"

"Roger. Five by, Neil."

"Houston, we might have a situation on the CSM here. Collins is saying—"

"Collins, you started early?"

"Roger that, Houston."

"This was supposed to wait until dark side, Collins, and—"

"Pardon my French, Houston, but this is a lot of shit to dump on a couple of guys before they go to walk on the god-damned moon, and I need to get it done so I can get busy helping them land on said god-damned moon, and if you have a problem with the way I'm running the mission at this point, feel free to fire me and send up a replacement."

A long silence, punctuated by the occasional click and ping of metal.

"Copy that, commander. Aldrin. Armstrong. Collins has command. You don't have to like this situation. You don't have to believe a word of what he tells you. But you WILL do as he tells you. Copy?"

Armstrong and Aldrin looked at each other.

"Houston," Aldrin's voice cracked. "Houston—Jesus I hope this is off the national record—Collins is claiming there are . . . werewolves on the moon. Can you confirm—"

"Collins is incorrect. There's no such thing as werewolves. These are Soviet agents."

Aldrin sighed and looked at Armstrong. Houston broke in again.

"More accurately, these are Soviet Lupine Lunar Mutations."

"Is it April first?" Armstrong muttered.

"Handy of them to wait until after we did the TV shot to drop this on us," Aldrin said.

Collins flipped a switch and killed the radio. He opened a small panel in the box on his lap, withdrawing two slim pamphlets.

"We've got about twenty minutes until you need to go strap in the lander. My recommendations are to take ten of those minutes to read through those pamphlets, take the next five minutes to familiarize yourself with the guns, and take the last five minutes to pray to whatever god you hold dear."

Armstrong unbuckled from his seat and drifted

down towards the lunar lander module. Aldrin followed suit.

"You're staying up here to wait for us, right?" Armstrong asked.

"Of course."

"Why do you have a gun? You supposed to kill us if we say no?"

"If you don't come back, I don't come back," Collins said.

"You'd kill yourself if—"

"They'd change my course. I'd suffocate and die somewhere between here and Venus. I'd rather not have a slow death. I'd rather not hear the broadcasts they'd send up letting me know the ramifications of mission failure. I'd rather not hear my wife and your wife on the news crying over us. Neil," Collins said. "Get this done. Please."

Armstrong drifted down the hatch into the Eagle lander. Collins replaced the storage box below his seat and flicked on the internal comms.

"You copy this?"

"Yeah," Armstrong muttered.

"Fuck off, Mike," Aldrin said.

"Copy that," Collins said. "Everything you need to know is in that book, but I'll give you the nickel tour. If you have any questions, save them for the trip home. Now, just after WWII, Soviet commanders discovered a Nazi bunker buried in the ice in northern Russia. Nobody knows how long they'd been working there, but it was a full-on research facility. Captured Soviet soldiers were their lab rats. Typical Nazi shit, you know. Making men into supermen. They failed, obviously. Every man they tried it on died. But they made strides. There were corpses there. Huge muscles. Skeletal mutations. All of them dead. The Krauts left some promising notes. Jump ahead to 1957, when the Soviets placed a primate into successful earth orbit."

"Hold on. That never—we were the first to send—"

"What did I tell you about questions, Neil? They did it. Just take that as fact. They weren't testing the viability of launching a living thing into space, they were testing the formula they found in that Nazi base. Apparently the thing that hampered the serum's effectiveness on men was gravity. They shot that fuckin' monkey so full of Nazi dope that it would have killed him on Earth. In space . . . he grew. He turned into something. Something so strong and powerful that the capsule he was in couldn't contain him. He broke out, tore it open with his bare hands."

"And did he survive the fall?" Aldrin asked, rolling his eyes.

"We don't know," Collin said. "The safe bet says no. They estimate the vessel came down in the Pacific Northwest. There have been teams of US soldiers moving through the area to find evidence of its demise or terminate it on sight. No more questions. The Reds saw what they needed to see. Two years ago they started testing it on humans. Low-dose. Vladimir Mikhaylovich Komarov, that name ring a bell?"

"First man to die in a spaceflight. Killed on impact in a landing malfunction, right?"

"Yes and no. He was the first to get a full dose of their treatment in space. First to become superhuman. They just needed to verify it worked. Then they rigged the craft to kill him on impact so they could examine his remains."

Collins pitched the craft, bringing the moon's eerie light into the cabin.

"And now, sixteen days ago, they landed a craft on the moon. Three cosmonauts, fully dosed. We have a rough idea of their LZ. We're coming in about a hundred yards away."

"You're telling me they've been up here for over two weeks with no food or water? Or air for that matter?" Armstrong asked.

"They had the benefit of not needing to land with a reusable craft. They have rations, and their metabolisms work a little differently now. They're alive, as far as we know, and probably hungry. Just waiting for a ride home. They've been pushing to get us up here to stop that. Intelligence suggests we have a ten hour headstart on them. They're on our tail and time is short. If they land, if they're able to recover those soldiers and get them back to earth . . . god help us all."

"And what are we supposed to—"

"Just read the book, Buzz. Strap into your chairs, get the hatch set. I wish this was under better circumstances. You wanted to go to the moon, you're going to the moon. My job is to drive the bus and make sure you have a ride waiting after you get done. Your job is to get down there, pick up some space rocks so we have something to show and tell, and kill some god-damned commie werewolves."

"Jesus H—" Armstrong muttered, sliding into position in the Lunar Lander Module.

"What if we miss?" Aldrin muttered.

"Don't miss," Collins yelled back at them. "This is for America and the world, fellas. The whole shebang. You're not allowed to fail. That's it."

Collins secured the hatch to the Lunar Landing Module and moved back to the pilot's seat. A small pendant of St. Christopher hovered next to his ear in zero-grav, spinning like a tossed coin, the patron saint of travelers not knowing where to begin.

***

Aldrin and Armstrong sat in uneasy silence, staring out of the windows on the Lunar Landing Module, waiting. Aldrin's finger tapped a staccato rhythm on his thigh. He lifted the wrist gun to examine it more closely, set it down, then lifted it again. He opened the chamber and looked at the rounds in the magazine. Long like a rifle cartridge, but fat like a shotgun shell, each topped with a sharp, silver projectile.

Armstrong let out a long sigh. "Shit." He opened the pamphlet and scanned the information again. It was laid out simply as any good government dossier should be. Large text. Short sentences. Lots of diagrams. What he saw made no sense. Men, mutated, larger than life, coated in hair, their jaws distorted and misshapen, teeth jutting at odd angles. Heavy brows that hid their eyes, shoulders hunched so high their necks were no longer visible. The artist had helpfully drawn a large Soviet Flag behind the creature, as if this would spur some sort of patriotic sentiment to drive their mission forward. There were three names listed next to the drawing, presumably the three cosmonauts-turned-lab rats. The last names were spelled in heavy Cyrillic characters with an English translation to the right.

ВОЛКОВ: VOLKOV.
СОКОЛОВ: SOKOLOV.
ГОЛОВКИН: GOLOVKIN.

"What do we do here, Buzz? Volkov, Sokolov—"

"Blow their heads off. Neil, I—We do our jobs. Look, I personally think everyone's gone off the reservation here. I expect there's some kind of stress-related . . . I don't know, Neil! I don't know. Maybe we walk out there and nothing happens. We get some dirt, we plant a flag, we go home. We don't have any options here. This thing is landing on the moon, we're inside of it, that's that. We have to kill a . . . "

Aldrin's face creased up, a tear streaked out of one eye. He let out a strange barking howl. It took Neil a moment to realize he was laughing. The ridiculousness of the situation smothered him like a wave.

"We're werewolf hunting," Neil said, laughing.

"The very notion is . . . is . . . "

"More ridiculous than a man on the moon?" Armstrong asked.

They laughed again, because what else could they do? What else but strap experimental weapons to their wrists and prepare to die for their country?

"Six shots apiece," Aldrin said, shaking his head.

"And three of them."

"You think these things work?"

"They're designed and manufactured by the US Government," Neil said, followed by an uncomfortable silence.

"You think these things work?" Aldrin asked again.

<hr/>

They spent the rest of the descent alternating between nervous laughter and unbearable quiet. It had been a relatively smooth flight down. The feeling of the landing impact thudded through them like a heavy bass drum. They sat in silence, staring out the windows.

"Neil?"

"Yes?"

"We're on the moon, Neil."

Armstrong paused, holding his hands in front of him. "Yeah. You hear anything out there?"

"We're not going to."

"You see anything?"

"Nope."

The intercom crackled. "Eagle Houston, do you copy?"

"Houston Eagle, we're . . . we're here. You rolling cameras for air on this?"

"Public cameras stay off until your first job's done."

"But you have a private feed? Gonna enjoy watching us get torn to shreds?" Aldrin asked.

"What are you seeing out there?" Houston continued.

"We hit the mark. What are we looking for?"

"The area of concern was marked on your maps. We expect contact either inside of the Little West Crater or over its far ridge. Last intelligence received from . . . that the Sov . . . "

The comms went fuzzy. Armstrong looked at Aldrin. "Of course."

"All right. Quickest way to get this done is to get it done, right? You got that wrist rocket ready to go?"

"Yeah," Armstrong said. "You sure you don't wanna go first?"

"I'll be stuck behind the door until you get out of here. Soon as you clear, I'll follow you down. If the ground is solid I'll just drop in."

"Well. Since this isn't being recorded for posterity, I'd just like to say that it's an honor for America to be on the god-damned moon, and whoever thought of this mission without telling us can kiss my ass."

"They oughta put that on a plaque, Shakespeare."

"Let's go."

Armstrong felt the pop of the airlock door more than he heard it. As the hatch creaked open, brilliant white light flooded the cabin, reflected from the lunar surface.

"Wait until you see this, Buzz."

Armstrong leaned through the hatch cautiously, straining to check his peripheral vision through the bulky spacesuit. All was still and quiet. Now came the hard part. He turned his back on the moon and reached a leg out to the descent ladder.

"Still alive," Armstrong muttered.

"Copy that."

Armstrong descended one rung further. "Two rungs. Still alive."

"Copy that, Neil. Maybe reserve the comm batteries for important announcements."

"Me being alive is pretty fuckin' important Buzz. To me, anyway. Four steps to go. Still alive." Armstrong hustled down the remaining rungs and hovered above the final step. He turned as much as his suit would allow to survey the ground. Once he'd gotten the word he'd be going through the hatch first, he'd envisioned this moment, how to place the first footprint on the moon. And now, looking down, he saw the point was moot.

There were footprints there. That word lingered in his brain. Footprint. Not boots. Large, five-toed mammalian markings that were somewhat human save for what looked like a large opposable toe. Spaced about five feet apart. Left, right, some of them with divots in the soil that Armstrong assumed to be a handprint.

"How's it looking, Neil?"

"Clear for now. Collins wasn't lying. We're not alone."

"Coming down, clear the way."

Armstrong held his breath and pushed lightly back from the ladder, drifting down to the lunar soil like a feather. The land beneath him felt like soft sand over stone. Fine and powdery. He laughed, because he thought that's what it would be, but here he was . . .

A shadow drifted across his peripheral vision, Aldrin drifting down from the ladder. He hit the ground and strode past Armstrong, wrist-rocket aimed ahead. He swept the perimeter. "Wake up, moon man."

"Look around you, Buzz . . . "

"I know. I should be enjoying this. So should you. Damn commies."

"A-hunting we will go," Armstrong said, releasing the safety on his wrist-rocket.

"Is that uhhh . . . " Aldrin pointed at the strange footprints.

"That's them. That's our path."

"Sea of Tranquility my ass . . . " Aldrin said. "Cover me. Let's move."

They hopped ahead, thoroughly unsure of how to proceed. There was some basic military training that kicked in, how to watch the horizon, how to cover each other, but all of that was based on earth gravity, a full field of vision, and full range of motion. They had none of that.

"Little West Crater ahead," Armstrong said. "How do you want to handle this?"

Aldrin scanned the edge of the crater. "It's like standing in a god-damned oil painting. Nothing's moving."

"That's a good thing, right?"

As the words left Armstrong's mouth, a small puff of dust rose over the edge of the crater. An irregular shape, different from the surrounding rocks and dirt, this looked more like a large burlap sack covered in hair and rolled in soot.

"Feels like we got eyes on us," Armstrong said.

"We do."

They stopped, bobbing slightly as they watched the lip of the crater. Something was watching them, low to the ground, moving slowly. They had no way of judging its size. But there were two tiny, shining black pits, unmistakably eyes, watching them. The thing slithered slowly to their left, then lifted its head up to scream a soundless warning. It lowered itself down into the crater.

"Okay," Armstrong said. "Okay. Okay."

"Okay," Aldrin replied.

"Okay."

"Yeah," Aldrin said. "How are they breathing? Where are their suits? What do they—"

"Buzz, get back!"

Armstrong bounded to Aldrin and shoved him down as a jagged moonrock shot over their heads.

"Guess they know we're here, huh?" Aldrin said.

"Do we shoot?"

"Not from this distance."

Another puff of dust appeared over the ridge. A small scrap of uniform floated slowly over the hill, a shred of reinforced fabric with a torn hose connected to it. It spun before them like a disembodied internal organ. A hand rose slowly over the crater rim, palm facing them. Its fingers were blackened and purpled, the skin swollen over elongated bones. It rose higher, attached to a twisted forearm clothed in the tattered remains of a cosmonaut's spacesuit.

Slowly, it extended one finger, then pointed at the fabric floating in the space between them. Aldrin reached out to grab it. "You read Russian?"

"Cyrillic," Armstrong said. "And no. But that name stamped on the fabric is one of the ones from the pamphlet. Sokolov."

"Any ideas?" Aldrin asked. "He introducing himself?"

Armstrong shrugged his shoulders, then realized Aldrin probably wouldn't notice such a small gesture. "I'm gonna get closer."

"Wait!" Aldrin shouted.

The rim of the crater exploded as if a land mine had gone off beneath it, and a great, shadowy shape rocketed toward them.

"Shit. Shit shit shit!" Armstrong shouted, readying his wrist rocket.

The shape was on a beeline for Aldrin, and in zero-G, there was no way to react in time. The thing extended twisted hands for Aldrin, aiming claws for the visor of his helmet. Aldrin lifted his wrist rocket to fire. He depressed the button and felt a vibration at his wrist. A small plume exploded at the thing's shoulder, fluid spattering into globules that floated all around them. Still it charged. Aldrin cursed himself for firing too soon as he tried to ready a second shot.

The thing hadn't changed course, and it was too late. Aldrin saw its face, finally. It was a horrible stew of features lupine, simian, and human. Jaw distended, cheek skin frozen solid and cracked wide open from howling, eyelids flaking away. Snapped tendons and torn muscles flapped in the low grav as the thing's fingers extended, claws coming straight at Aldrin's face. The last thing he saw before squeezing his eyes closed was another name in Cyrillic he recognized from the pamphlet, VOLKOV. He closed his eyes.

A hard tap on the front of his visor sent him tumbling backward, cartwheeling and slamming twice into the lunar soil as he floated away from the impact. He assumed the worst, that his visor had shattered or his suit had been punctured, and waited for the cold vacuum of space to take him.

Through squinting eyes he saw the inside of his visor covered in sweat and spittle, but intact. He turned and dragged a foot along the soil to slow his momentum. He clambered to his feet, Armstrong fifty feet away, circling around a chaotic whirlwind of dust and debris.

Volkov, the thing that had come for him, was tangling with something else, something equally twisted. The new creature had Volkov pinned to the ground, hammering down blow after blow in a grotesque silent symphony of violence. Volkov raised its arms in a pathetic gesture of mercy to no avail. The creature on top continued to pound, smacking and tearing until Aldrin saw Volkov's neck snap. It continued to pound away until Volkov turned to pulp, a fine spray of blood and guts and flesh misting and crystallizing in the lunar atmosphere.

Aldrin had moved closer to Armstrong, until they were shoulder-to-shoulder. Armstrong pointed at Aldrin, then gestured to the side of his helmet. He repeated the gesture.

Armstrong was trying to tell him his comms were out. He grabbed Aldrin and turned him, reconnecting a stray cable on his suit antenna.

"—hear me? Dammit, Buzz, gimme—"

"Gotcha Neil, gotcha. We're on, we're on . . . "

"What in the hell is—"

Armstrong stopped, then turned Aldrin to face the creature that may have saved his life. It stood tall above the remains of the thing that had attacked Aldrin. It was easily seven feet, its arms and legs grotesquely elongated, the skin hard and swollen over sinew and muscle and mutated bone. The tattered remains of a spacesuit clung to its legs and lower torso, and one of its hands was still encased in a spacesuit glove. The other was bare, the fingers almost a foot long, pointing at the tattered piece of spacesuit in the soil that read SOKOLOV. Patchy hair covered the thing's front torso, growing thicker higher up its arms and shoulders. The creature was a wall of muscle, no neck, veins inky black beneath purple-blue skin. A mane of fur ringed its head, eyes flicking like black diamonds.

It arched its back, muscles flexing, jaw distending to an impossibly wide degree.

"You feel that buzzing?" Armstrong asked.

"It's howling," Aldrin replied.

"Of course it is. You want the shot, or should I—OOF!"

Armstrong was cut off as yet another creature bounded over the rim of the crater and barreled into his midsection. He felt strangely light after the initial collision, tumbling with the creature across the lunar landscape. The thing had latched its jaws onto his ankle, and although the pressure was great and painful his suit was still intact.

He twisted, bracing one hand against the lunar surface and jamming the barrel of his wrist rocket against the thing's shoulder, pulling the trigger twice. He felt the gun buck, his visor covered in thick black gore. The pressure on his ankle released immediately and he struggled to his feet. He swiped a hand across his visor, smearing away a clear streak that allowed him to see the creature leap to an impossible height, over the crater and out of his field of vision. He looked down at the huge splatter of blood on the lunar surface, chunks of flesh and fur mixing with the dirt, slowly freezing. He checked his oxygen levels. Everything was fine. As fine as someone being stalked on the moon by a werewolf could be.

"Aldrin? Aldrin, you copy?"

"I'm . . . here . . . " Aldrin puffed. "Could use . . . some help . . . "

"Where are you?"

Armstrong paced backwards, not taking his eyes of the stationary creature before him. Taking advantage of the low gravity, he jumped back twice, a flash of light catching his eye in the sky above. Collins wasn't scheduled to come around at this point, and he wouldn't be burning fuel unless there was a disaster. Could it be the Soviets?

"Neil! You're a lousy shot. This thing is still—ah shit—trying to lead it away from the lander. Can't go too much further. Could use some . . . "

"I'm coming," Armstrong replied, turning his back on the Sokolov creature and bounding back to the lander as quickly as he could.

"Dammit," Aldrin came back on the comms. "Looks like these wrist rockets aren't great from a distance. I winged him. He's running."

"You in pursuit?"

"We shouldn't. Protocol says we need to stay in line of sight of the cameras on Eagle."

"Did you set those up?" Armstrong asked.

"Thought you did," Aldrin said.

Armstrong arrived at the Lunar Exploration Module. Aldrin was there, cautiously unpacking a small crate from the base of the lander. He proceeded to set up the cameras.

"Aren't we supposed to wait until the first job is done to set those up?"

"If I'm going to get murdered on the moon by a twisted commie werebeast, I want it captured for eternity," Aldrin grumbled.

"You just want footage of you kicking that thing's ass," Armstrong said.

"Probably. Keep an eye on the hills there, huh?"

Aldrin moved away from the LEM and began setting up the camera. Armstrong watched the horizon, spinning constantly, arm at the ready with his wrist rocket. "How you doing on Oxygen, Buzz?"

"Burned through a lot. We've been moving faster than we budgeted for. Probably need to get inside to switch out within the hour, but we can't do that until we deal with our friends."

Armstrong surveyed the horizon. Everywhere he turned, the blackness of the void overwhelmed him. It felt like he was standing on a soundstage, a poorly crafted rocky landscape surrounded by an impossibly black sky. What could be stranger than this, more helpless than this? Survival had always been the primary mission, and the mission hadn't changed.

Armstrong turned again and saw one of the creatures crouched low to the ground on the horizon. It regarded him warily. He saw the tension in its arms and back, the way its eyes locked on to him, daring him to move.

Lions want their prey to run, Armstrong thought.

"We have company, Buzz."

"I see it. Where's the other one?"

"Sokolov?"

"You named it?"

"He didn't move. When I left to come find you, it was still standing there staring at me."

"One down, two to go. What's the plan? Do we flank that one and then go hunting?" Aldrin asked, turning slowly to stare at Sokolov the towering beast, which remained standing over the remains of their first attacker.

"We can't go too far. Oxygen. Supplies. Can't risk leaving the LEM alone in case one of them wants to make it into Swiss cheese."

"Where do you think the other one is?" Aldrin asked, swinging his gaze back to Armstrong.

An odd shadow crept up slowly from the top of the Eagle lander, drifting higher and higher, moving across Armstrong's back. Aldrin strained to turn his gaze upward. The final creature, wounded and bloodied from Armstrong's initial hits, slowly drifted down from the lander behind Armstrong.

"Neil, look out!"

Armstrong turned as the creature neared the ground, raising his wrist rocket. Aldrin dove at him.

"Hold your fire!"

Aldrin tackled his colleague down into the dirt, feeling the shot buck through his arm, cringing at the sound of his visor cracking against Armstrong's as they hit the dirt.

"Buzz, what are you—"

"Don't fire at the lander!"

"I wasn't firing at the lander, I was firing at the—whoa!"

The thing crouched low again and seized Armstrong's ankle, moving unnaturally quickly in the low grav. It had the advantage of being able to sink hooked claws into the lunar surface for traction. It hoisted him up, dangling the astronaut before its face and raising a clawed finger to pick at his spacesuit. Upside down, Armstrong made out the name GOLOVKIN on what was left of the thing's suit.

Aldrin rolled, struggling to get back to his feet, or any position close enough to upright to give him a good shot. He settled for flopping onto his side and raising up his arm. From this position, Armstrong's dangling body blocked most of his target. A miss on any of the remaining available tiny targets would mean a hole in the Eagle lander, which could mean no trip home.

"Buzz, shoot this god damned thing!"

"I'm trying. If I miss—"

"Then don't miss, damn it!"

Aldrin locked on to the creature's twisted foot, steadying his wrist. His whole body rocked before he could pull the trigger. Something had seized him from behind, lifting him form the lunar soil. He was brought upright with sickening quickness, set roughly on his feet. Sokolov had returned to the fray. It ignored Aldrin and charged at Armstrong's dangling form, seizing his arms and lifting him higher, so that he was suspended between the two creatures like a tug of war.

Sokolov stared at him, while Golovkin continued to pick at Armstrong's suit. Aldrin saw frayed fabric and thin metal filaments poking up from Armstrong's waist. He'd be done for soon.

Aldrin raised his wrist rocket, unsure of which creature to shoot, certain that killing one would only give the other enough time to finish them both.

Sokolov nodded at Aldrin, then jerked its chin at the other monster. It repeated the gesture. Aldrin hesitated. Had the thing's eyes been less beady, if it still had functioning eyelids, he would have sworn it rolled its eyes at him. Sokolov dug its feet into the soil and gave a sharp jerk on Armstrong, pulling Golovkin off balance and moving it away from the lander. As Golovkin stumbled forward, Sokolov pointed his free hand at Aldrin, then at the other monster's stomach. It repeated the gesture.

Aldrin got the message. It was helping, telling him where to shoot. Time for questions later, as Collins had said. Now was the time for violence.

Aldrin charged forward, diving, his arm extended straight at the monster's midsection. As soon as his fist made contact with Golovkin, he jerked his trigger, once, twice, three times, a strangely silent explosion bucking through his body as a spray of blood and organs exited the creature's other side. It spasmed, looking at him with an anger that would long haunt his dreams. It made one final attempt to scratch at Armstrong's spacesuit, but Sokolov grabbed its wrist, bending it back, then wrenching it side to side until it broke free from Golovkin's body.

Armstrong toppled to the ground as Sokolov went to work on its dying colleague, turning the severed forearm into a stabbing implement, riddling its remains with holes, stamping on its head until it flattened into silvery mud on the lunar surface. Sokolov pounded its chest, jaws extending into a soundless howl aimed at the blue sphere in the Lunar sky.

"Neil, get to cover! I'll draw this thing away from the Eagle. You just get ready to get out of here."

Before Aldrin could fire, Sokolov dropped what was left of Golovkin's arm and crouched low, bounding away in a single graceful leap, disappearing over the edge of the Western Crater.

Armstrong and Aldrin shared an uncomfortable silence.

"What the hell do we do now?" Armstrong asked.

"We need to get back inside, change out our oxygen tanks, and stop the soviets from bringing that thing back. Go hunt that thing down. We can't . . . imagine the Soviets bringing that thing to earth. Imagine your family having to—"

Aldrin looked up as the creature's shadowy form erupted again over the horizon, racing toward them, landing a few feet away from the Eagle.

"Arms down, Buzz," Armstrong said.

Aldrin hadn't even realized he had his wrist rocket armed and ready. The creature had smartly chosen to land between them and the Eagle. An errant shot would destroy their ride home.

"What's he holding?" Armstrong asked.

In one hand, it held the remains of a cosmonaut's space helmet, the visor intact. It carefully set the helmet down, dipping a finger into the remains of its enemy. It ripped a chunk of spacesuit from the thing's corpse, working slowly and carefully, bringing the debris close to its eyes for better focus. It stood, extending an arm toward them, holding the small piece of white metal with a symbol painted on it in fresh, shiny black blood.

"Is that a peace sign?" Armstrong asked.

"I don't give a shit if that thing went to Woodstock. We have a job to do."

"It doesn't want to hurt us, Buzz. You'd be in pieces if it did."

"Whatever gets us home faster."

The creature stood before them, looking between them, waiting. If there was such a thing as werewolf puppydog eyes, Sokolov had them trained on Aldrin, watching the barrel of his gun.

Aldrin lowered his wrist rocket. "Aw, hell. It's not what I came here for."

"Me neither," Armstrong said, lowering his arm. "Can it hear us? Can you hear us?" He shouted the question the second time, but Sokolov didn't move.

"I can hear you loud and clear enough to blow my eardrums out," Aldrin said. "Vacuum of space, remember?"

"Sorry." Armstrong moved so that his back was to the sun. He flicked open the gold sunvisor on his helmet, revealing his face to the creature. He spoke using exaggerated movement of his lips.

"Do you speak English?"

Sokolov didn't move.

Armstrong moved a bit closer, trying to assume the most peaceful stance he could think of. "I came here to . . . come to the moon. To here. Dammit, you know what I mean. This wasn't supposed to be a hunting trip. It's a peaceful mission to—"

As Armstrong spoke, the creature's face brightened. It bent slowly to retrieve the cosmonaut helmet from the ground, connecting a cable to the remains of the life support pack that clung to its massive frame. It lifted the helmet, poking its nose inside, looking as if it was drinking deeply. Sokolov moved its head out to look at them, paused, adjusted some dials on its pack, then put its head back in, repeating the sequence two or three times.

"I have wanted nothing more in my life than to stand where I am now," Armstrong said, "and I'd give anything right now to put this place behind me and never think of it again. But it's a mission of peace. This place, untouched by man, and the first thing we do, the god-damned first thing we do is spill blood on it. I can't—"

"Dobriy vyecher." The phrase broke into both of their headsets simultaneously. Weak, hollow. Unmistakably Russian.

They looked at the creature, who was half-bent over, the cosmonaut helmet pressed tightly over its cranium.

"Hello Americans," it said. "I find your frequency."

"How did he—"

"I make microphone work to you. I thank you. You will not kill me."

"Is that a request or an order?" Buzz asked, half laughing.

"You came in peace. Your government had other plans, much like mine. They are landing soon. They come for me."

Aldrin looked at the creature. "And your name is . . . you're . . . "

"Sokolov, Fedor. You know the name?"

"Sort of," Armstrong said.

"Your government sends you to kill and tells you nothing of your prey. Typical American."

"I came up here to get some rocks and take a few pictures. Plans change," Aldrin said. "We're supposed to stop them from taking you back to Earth."

"I will stop them. I could not kill the other Volk alone. The wolfs."

Armstrong raised a finger to correct his English, then thought better of it.

"I never wanted this. What they do to me. The others wolfs ready and want kill you. I am not so sure. I saw you land and you look so small and helpless. You are in shining white uniform, hope of mankind."

"Since we land here, I think only of how awful war would be, that my government will make more like me and send them to kill. They want put others through the pain of what we are to make this change. They send us all the way to moon for formula to work in correct manner. So much effort to increase human suffering. I was doctor before. I had wife and children. All gone now, in the name of progress. Such as me should not exist. I try many times to fight my colleagues, but they are too strong together. You provide great distraction."

"You will finish your mission. This is an age of wonder and fantaziya, no? So much we can do together. Show grace of humanity. Instead we use what we learn to fight. To kill. Your government made to come to the moon because they knew my government could not afford to follow. My government started a plan for . . . make the Volk so that you could never live in peace. They see us on a great hunt in America, feasting on your bones until whole continent is food. This medicine they give me could cure the sick, heal the weak. This technology America gives you could unite the planet. And instead we fight. Always fight. I am a man of peace. Nuclear weapons, nobody will use. Too risky. But things like me? What's to stop them from unleashing, yes?"

"We can . . . we can try to get you help," Armstrong said.

"No. I am nothing but horror. But I will find honor. You will finish your mission, your true mission. You could have killed me before, but you didn't. You search for peace. You go home, show the world the possibility of that peace, of working together. I will stop them. Soviets cannot afford to continue if this mission fails. So they will fail. I will see to it."

Sokolov raised his arm, pointing into the inky blackness at a tiny speck of light.

"Is that Collins? He's ahead of schedule . . . " Aldrin said.

"I think that was supposed to be his ride," Armstrong answered.

"Arrange your cameras. Clean your suits. They will not land."

Sokolov took two steps back and waited as the speck slowly grew into a larger point of light, then resolved into the unmistakable form of a lunar lander.

"They steal that from us or did we steal it from them?" Armstrong asked.

"It was wonderful to meet you, first men on moon."

Sokolov pulled his head from the helmet and tossed it aside, bouncing lightly on his toes. As the craft drew closer, he curled down, muscles flexing and hardening into a tight ball. The Soviet lander came within range, the flickering lights of its landing thrusters popping like camera flashes across Armstrong's visor.

Sokolov exploded upward into the lunar sky, sailing toward the Soviet lander. For a moment, it looked as if he'd misjudged his mark, sailing high, but as his path crossed the lander's, he snagged one of the metal feet with his long, curved claw. Momentum took over, the spacecraft spinning so quickly that it looked like a child's top rocketing over their heads.

The Soviet lander made impact fifty feet away from the Eagle, landing hard on its side, exploding into a shower of twisted metal until it was swallowed by an eerie orb of white and orange flame that snuffed out almost as soon as it started.

"Fuel tanks," Armstrong muttered.

"You think they survived?"

Their eyes followed the deep black scar made by the Soviet Lander over the horizon.

"Let's get to work," Aldrin said, heading back to the Eagle.

Armstrong stayed focused on the horizon as Aldrin climbed back into the Eagle. Now came the stillness that he'd sought, the majesty of the lunar soil, marked by a battle of political ideologies that would leave a permanent stain on the celestial body.

Over the horizon, Armstrong saw movement. Sokolov's head, slowly bobbing back and forth until the rest of him came into view. In his hands, he clutched the remains of the doomed cosmonauts. He came no closer to the Eagle, instead bounding away over the grey hills.

Armstrong got to work setting up the external cameras, preparing to go back into the Eagle so that he could properly become the first man on the moon. History was written by the winners, and he planned to give the people of earth an amazing story. He framed the landscape as Aldrin peered out of the hatch.

"Let's go, Neil. And uhh . . . make sure you frame it so you don't have all of that . . . that . . . in the shot." Aldrin dusted a hand toward the piles of gore and streaks of blood in the lunar soil.

Armstrong sheepishly turned the camera for a cleaner view. He climbed back into the lander and spent the next thirty minutes helping Aldrin clean off their gear, restock their oxygen, and get their equipment ready. When it was time for the grand entrance, he looked at Aldrin, holding the small box containing the American flag. There were no words. They stared at each other, shaking their heads.

"You're still gonna be the first man," Aldrin said.

Armstrong laughed, catching Aldrin by surprise. It was contagious. Soon both men were shaking, heads bent forward. Aldrin nodded to Armstrong and he got into position. The door opened, Aldrin in position behind the door.

"I just want to go home, Buzz."

Armstrong turned and exited the hatch. "Houston, do you copy?"

"Roger, we copy."

"Clear channel?"

A pause.

"Copy. This is private."

"First part of the mission is done, Houston."

"Roger that. You've done an invaluable service for your country." When Armstrong didn't answer, Houston broke in again. "Is everything okay, commander?"

"It could be. If we try."

"It's done, Houston," Aldrin broke in. "It's a mess up here. I don't think we can clean it or cover it."

"Roger that. We'll be back. Apollo program's not done yet. You just get ready to make history and come on home. And if you can get some samples of biological—"

"Hell no," Aldrin growled. "Not on my watch. This mess stays here. We spoiled it. Not even here a day and we spoiled it. It's a mess down there, Houston. We brought the same mess with us. It's gotta stop."

"Is the mission compromised?"

"Negative, Houston," Armstrong let out a sigh. "Look, we're done. We'll get your soil samples and do some readings, and that'll be it. Let's get it back on public channels and finish this."

"Copy that." A pause. "Proceed."

"I'm at the foot of the ladder. The LM footpads are only depressed in the surface about 1 or 2 inches, although the surface appears to be very, very fine grained, as you get close to it. It's almost like a powder. Down there, it's very fine."

Armstrong looked to his left one last time at the bloodied remains of the lunar monsters.

"I'm going to step off the LM now." As he drifted down to the moon, he cast a glance over his shoulder at the ever-shrinking speck of Sokolov, bounding into the inky blackness.

"That's one small step for a man, one giant leap for mankind."

THE PRINCE OF DARKNESS AND THE SHOWGIRL

JOHN PALISANO

EVEN FROM UP high, the green smell of the jungle overpowered them. The helicopter blades cut the air and thumped—Chop! Chop! Chop!—mirroring her nervous pulse. She held on tighter to the leather loop suspended from the roof of the cab, exchanging a glance with one of her steely-faced escorts.

You know how to do this. You can perform. You can be Marilyn. The country needs you.

She thought about her husband, back home, stewing because she answered the call to sing for the troops, cutting their honeymoon brutally short.

I just wish I could tell him it's bigger than anyone knows. It's a secret. They need my special electricity, they say. My magic stream. He's here, in the jungle, and they can't find him. And he's making all this bad stuff happen. Like he did before. But I can call him out.

She pictured a shiny, glistening worm at the end of a hook, a microphone dangling not far away, the worm's lips painted red like hers, a cheap blonde Marilyn wig on its head, bought from the Woolworths.

She laughed to herself at the absurdity. *Who'd have ever thought little old Norma Jean Baker could sing in front of so many troops one day? Someone out there believes in me.*

The fight at home had escalated just as she was leaving. Of course it had. It always happened the same way. He didn't want her to leave. She didn't want to leave. She had to. Things were bigger than both of them. The situation had left her feeling caught between two masters, protected by none, and immeasurably lonesome. Her insides felt lighter than air, and her stomach seemed as though it wouldn't be able to hold onto anything. Such was her destiny. She left an angry husband to help fight an angrier war.

It was more, of course. So much more.

Dressed in impeccable military uniform, his haircut tight and high, the chaperone sized her up. She could feel his judgment. *He thinks I'm ditzy. They all think I'm the airhead blonde just because I'm thinking. They don't know. They really have no idea what's behind all of me, do they?*

She knew, too, that they didn't suspect her real purpose. *How could they? My only existence to them is as a plaything. A Showgirl. A confection. Something to look at, a picture pinned to the wall. A sex symbol, of all silly things!*

Her image had been curated perfectly by the agents and producers back in Hollywood. That she had so much more was lost on most everyone. She carried a book with her everywhere. As much as she enjoyed the attention, she loved being a student of the world more.

They've got no idea how smart you have to be to play it so dumb and make it seem real. Can't be too dumb as to be ridiculous, but you can't come off too smart as to be no fun at all. You've got to be able to know when to bring that intelligence out, at just the right moment, stab the moment, and then pull it back in nice and neat like a knife slipped into a hidden sheath inside your vest.

Her acting teacher's words imprinted on her.

We're all acting, every single one of us, every day, whether we like to admit it or not. We're all portraying ourselves the way we wish to be seen, aren't we? People put on their costume and makeup, and they rehearse their lines in their heads. Everyone's an actor. We're always on stage. Even and especially to ourselves.

The helicopter descended, fast and abrupt. She imagined it was a safety precaution to avoid detection. The troops didn't know she was coming. Not yet, at least. She had business to take care of before then.

The base sprouted up in the midst of the jungle, reminding her of a child's set of blocks come to life. The camouflaged rectangular tents were hard to spot until they were close.

She'd fixated on the mechanics of it all as they landed on the helipad. Their voices and commands blurred into the background. She thought instead about how they'd managed to breach a foreign country and set up shop, and have food and water and bathrooms. She made a note to herself to ask questions once they were settled. How did the whole thing work? How did they do it? How were they not just run out?

As soon as she deplaned, she heard Sergeant Richards. "Miss Monroe? Thank you for coming."

Always 'Miss' and never 'Missis.' She'd been

married almost a year, yet, no one seemed to take her seriously.

She put on The Smile. "Wonderful to be here, darling. Where are we headed?"

"We've got a room for you all set up," he said. "Are you hungry?"

"I try not to eat before I perform," she said. "You understand."

"Of course. Whatever you're comfortable with."

She didn't feel comfortable in the jungle. Not one bit. Grasping the diamond on her ring finger, she felt a sense of control and ease she hadn't earlier. For the first time since leaving the States, she felt aligned and all right; she had a purpose again.

The show went off without any issues. The pickup four-piece band knew her material backward and forward. The acoustics were great, strangely, and she was glad to see film cameras recording.

Speaking to the men serving after the small set of songs, she was struck by how normal they were. Even though she was the only woman they'd seen in God knew how long, they all remained respectful and engaged, and warm.

I wish they were all home with their families. Maybe they will be soon. If I do things right.

As everyone drifted to sleep, she kept awake. By small lamp, she read several pages of Kerouac. She enjoyed the cadence of his writing, imagining his voice.

I wish you were here with me now.

Carry me into the jungle.

She looked over to the handsome sergeants guarding the doorway, their hair perfectly combed and black as coal, their faces chiseled and strong, and thought any one of them could have been Kerouac himself. Any one.

Take me.

They would.

She wouldn't have her privacy until she made it back to the ship. That was part of the deal.

One of the Sergeants came, hours later, in the deepest night. Her heart raced as she was led from the tent and into the adjacent thick jungle.

You're going to be okay. You were born for this. Your real job.

No. I'm an actor. A singer. A performer.

What did Stella always say?

We are being our best selves when we are not ourselves, darling. When we are being what we think we should be in our mind's eye.

So who am I?

Clear yourself.

Clear your head.

Channel. Focus.

Be.

She turned to find herself alone. The tough soldiers were gone, hiding behind tanks and guns and helmets and helicopters and camouflage.

She had no camouflage

The war would not be ended by hiding.

So she stood, waiting in the clearing just outside the camp. *There are poisonous snakes out here. Bugs. Monkeys that will rip your face off. Maybe a spy* patrol. *They'll catch me and torture me, more if they recognise me from the pictures.*

Shutting her eyes, she touched her ring. *Be strong. You can win this.*

"Good evening."

The voice startled her, even though she expected it.

She looked around and saw nothing.

"Hello," she said, using her best high speech.

"I know who you are," said the voice, "and I know why you're here."

"Well, it's good we understand each other," she said, again using her very practiced tone. *I know who you are.*

The voice roared. "Then you understand I'm going to peel off your pretty pink flesh and eat you from the inside out."

Her heart raced. Of course it did. But she steeled herself, taking in a breath and imagining a string holding her upright as though she were a marionette—it was a method she'd learned through her acting classes. *Step into it. Be Marilyn. Be larger than life. Be sure of yourself.* The jungle no longer smelled of banana leaves and dirt, but had become foul and fetid, as if the earth had opened and released the stench of a thousand rotting, liquified corpses.

"What I understand is that you and I have unfinished business," she said. Her mouth went dry.

"It's all your fault, you realize," said the entity. "You called me forth."

"We both know that's not true, Vanek. Not true one penny."

The ground shook. *He knows I recognize him.*

She had trouble keeping her balance.

Do the soldiers hear this? Do they know? They probably think it's a bomb.

Vanek stood before her, only he was no longer the form of the old man she'd met before. He'd taken David Lee Roberts. One of the great loves of her lives.

He still looked a lot like the David she'd known; he still had his charm and refined looks. *He's not David anymore. Not really human. Something has taken him over.* David's face looked the same, only filled with dark lines, as though they were tattooed. His jet black hair swept up in a wave, his skin was tanned and reddish, his eyes yellowed with fire. His arms stretched out just a little too long, his fingers uncoiled to twice the length they should have been. Their tips sharp and blackened.

His top lip curled back. A small group of albino flies escaped from his mouth, buzzed toward her, then disappeared into the jungle.

He's one of the Conflicted Ones. Don't forget it.

"Your circus tricks don't scare me, Vanek," she said. "And neither do you."

"You see what I can manifest," he said, swooping his arms around to showcase the area around them. In the sky, a munition flashed. Another example of his showboating, she was sure. "This is from me."

"This is from men who listened to you," she said. "I am not a man."

At that, Vanek's tongue prodded out, its tip as dark as his fingertips. He rolled it around his lips. "Oh, you are every bit the woman. You are the woman of all women. So many men . . . " he put his bony fingers down toward his middle, down toward his— " . . . have touched themselves hoping they were being touched by you."

He inched closer to her, his eyes steady, his rotten stench gaining. She wanted to put up a hand, but kept strong. She didn't want him to see her flinch.

"They could have made me out of anyone," she said. "That has nothing to do with why I'm here."

His face lit up. "You came for me. You couldn't resist." Vanek swayed. His face felt inches away; she smelled his breath. "I just want one hour with you to do with you what I want. Then all of this will go away. I'll make it happen," he continued, " . . . for . . . just . . . a . . . little . . . taste . . . of the one they're calling Marilyn. What I've always wanted. Since I was a man of flesh."

Her heart raced. *Find your strength.* She thought back to the helicopter. *Don't call him David, even though he's in his body. Don't think of him as anything other than Vanek.*

Chop!

Chop!

Went the blades.

Beat!

Beat!

Went her heart.

"How do I know you're good on your word? You haven't always been," she said.

He recoiled, just a bit. "That's not. The terms . . . changed . . . because the . . . situation . . . changed. Not my fault."

"One has to honor their word, or it becomes meaningless," she said.

He hollered. His arms fanned out. "My word is as

good as any. How dare you?" He pointed up. His long, black-tipped fingers twitched. "Would you rather believe them? They'll have you old and haggard in a blink, your body bones and dust before you can enjoy it. Your beauty won't be able to summon demagogues for long, my love. Your power will soon wane. Soon enough. Soon enough."

Calming himself, Vanek asked, "Wouldn't you want to look like this forever?"

She laughed, then. "I will."

"You won't!"

"I have my own . . . methods," she said.

"Is that so?" Vanek smirked. "Do tell."

"You took someone from me," she said. "Someone I loved. You're in David's body. So you owe me."

Vanek roared and the jungle shook. "How can I owe you anything?"

"You promised you wouldn't touch him, Vanek," she said.

"I did not," he said.

"You broke David's back and climbed inside," she said. "You took over him."

"I was desperate," Vanek said. "My other home was gone and I needed another right away."

"You broke him in a half," she said. "He was my love. Sent away to the war you stirred, and you knew exactly what you were doing when you killed him."

Vanek lowered his head. Then he raised his face, his expression sullen and remorseful. "Am I not still the face you love?" For a moment, she glimpsed David within the entity. Remembered the nights they'd shared on Malibu Beach. How he'd made her laugh. Then how he'd been stolen from her and whisked away as soon as the Conflicted Ones found out.

Don't believe a word he says. These dark entities are all at their best when they're lying. It's what they're made for. Spinning these traps to catch us off guard.

"So what do you come to the jungles for today, Norma? Normal. Norma. Doesn't have the same ring to it as Marilyn. That's just as phony as anything, isn't it?" He didn't look like David anymore. Just a shell being animated.

She shook her head. "Not phony, idealized. She is me. I am her."

"Yes. The sex symbol that brings a million little deaths a day. All that wasted energy," he said. "What . . . do . . . you . . . want?"

"I want you to leave this world, and stop this war. Stop the needless dying. Clarify the minds of the men fighting this war," she said. "Do it for me. You took David. You had your war . . . the blood and pain you have fed on for years to keep you all at bay . . . that was our deal . . . you made me a promise in return . . . to keep my David untouchable. You went back on your word. Now it's time to make it up to me."

Vanek sized her up. "The world doesn't know what's in your head. I do. I know you're not the ditz you play, and yet the world won't take you seriously. So why should I? Why shouldn't I just bend you over, belly over back, like I did to him? I can do it in a blink. I can snuff you out, right here. Why won't I?" He hovered over her again, his fingers threateningly close to her face.

"You're not the only one," she said. "There are others. I've spoken to all of them. The Conflicted are everywhere. And they all love me. And if anything were to happen to me, they'd know. They'd know so fast, and they'd take action so fast, and you know you'd suffer the hell of a thousand hells for it." She straightened her back. "So, Vanek? You owe me. You've fed off this war long enough. You've taken what you've asked for. So go away quietly. And I want your word on it, this time."

"I'm supposed to have another five years," he said.

"You took David," she said. "I think it's a fair deal."

He stood back, thought for a moment.

"If I don't?"

"The Conflicted have asked me to offer you this deal," she said. "They are tired of this war as anyone. It's time. They will come and ask for themselves if you don't agree, and we know that won't end well for you."

"You won't end well, either," he said. "Your time is limited. They'll be coming for you, too. One day, you may be sleeping, or walking along, and something that looks like something else will take you out. You can't last forever, either."

"Only in the hearts and minds of men," she said. "My legacy is sealed, no matter how I end. Now, will you concede?"

He looked at her and she went cold. *He's going to strike me down. Yup. This is it.*

But his eyes softened. "Can I have one more year?"

She thought for a moment. "I will ask them," she said. "It seems . . . reasonable."

"We wouldn't want the war to end too suddenly," he said. "Doing so might reveal the puppet's strings."

"Yes," she said. "That makes sense."

"Then we have a deal?" he asked.

"Not yet," she said. "I wanted something more than your word, as that seems to be questionable."

He smiled at this. "Oh? A romp in the jungle? A kiss? You cannot stop thinking about it, can you? Me instead of that dried up old husk of a husband."

She felt nothing for him. Maybe others did, but she was immune in ways most others weren't when confronted with one of the Conflicted.

"No," she said. "Nothing of the sort. I just want us to shake hands."

Vanek laughed. It rattled the leaves. "Oh, that's good. That's very good. Shake hands? Is that all? Do you really think . . . ?" He laughed. "Fine," he said, charging in. "You want to shake my hand." He put out his long left hand, the common gesture easy and strong. "We have a deal. We end the war in a year. Put 'er there, girlie?" He laughed again, his voice raspy and unnatural.

Marilyn put out her hand.

Hers close to his.

Before they touched, when they were mere inches apart, Vanek's face drooped.

"What . . . ?" he said, surprised.

The diamond on her ring glowed white, lighting the jungle around them brighter than daylight.

A sound like a million trumpets and violins sounded.

She wanted to clamp her hands over her ears, but couldn't.

She couldn't help but shut her eyes, it was so bright.

The music subsided, and in a moment, she sensed the light gone. She opened her eyes to find Vanek gone.

She looked at her ring. It glistened and sparkled like no other diamond. There seemed to be a light from within. So bright was it that it lit her way.

With each step back toward the camp, the diamond's light lessened, although it kept its sparkle.

Got you, you sonofabitch.

Soldiers surrounded her. They'd found her. "Are you alright, Miss Monroe?"

"Missis," she said, going right back into her Marilyn voice. "And I am, but that was close."

"Glad to hear it," the young man said.

Behind him, Sergeant Richards hurried toward her. He grabbed her by the crux of her arm. "So glad you're okay," he said.

He knows. Of course he knows. He led me here.

They crossed over into the camp again, and she was led back toward her quarters. "So glad everything worked out for this trip," Sergeant Richards said. "So glad you're not out there all alone in the jungle."

"I wasn't alone," she said, sitting on the cot. "I had this." She lifted her hand. "Haven't you heard the song, baby?"

She blinked twice and smiled.

"Diamonds are a girl's best friend."

<hr/>

Chop!

Chop!

Went the helicopter blades. She rode back from the camp, she rode out to the air strip, and then they flew her all the way back to the States.

She kept the ring until she was tragically lost.

And in her bungalow, near her bed, her last belongings catalogued, the diamond ring she'd worn

185

was gone, slipped from her finger––vanished, hidden, and lost––until it was thought to be glimpsed again in a desert plain, on a foreign land, with bombs exploding from underneath, and, it was whispered, a man lingered in doorways–– a man whose arms seemed just a bit too long, whose fingers stretched and curled, their tips blackened––a man who knelt and drank the blood of the fallen, a man who laughed at the sky and the sun, a man, who for a short time again, had won.

THE SECRET ENGRAVINGS

LISA MORTON

HANS TURNED THE corner and smelled death.

The odor, sudden and overwhelming, cascaded his memory back to four years ago, to 1519, when his brother Ambrosius had succumbed to plague. He'd gone against the advice of physicians and friends to attend to Ambrosius, and the scent in his brother's final hours had been this same nauseating mix of rotten meat and metallic blood and sour fear sweat.

Hans was yanked back to the present as he saw a body being taken from a house down the alley. Two men, common laborers with thick rags wrapped around their faces, lugged a shrouded corpse into a waiting cart. As they heaved it onto the creaking boards, a foot fell loose, and Hans saw:

The toes were almost completely black.

Plague. Again, here in Basel.

One of the laborers glanced up and saw Hans staring. He stepped a few feet away from the dead man, glanced back once, adjusted the improvised cloth mask. He was burly, with a long, unwashed beard and filthy peasant's garb, but his face and voice were surprisingly kind. "Best not come this way," he said.

"How far . . . ?" Hans couldn't finish the question.

The man understood. "Only this house. He was a merchant, been traveling, just came back last week. I doubt it'll spread."

'Doubt'? Precious little to put my mind at ease. But Hans nodded and turned away.

He clutched his satchel tighter—it held the drawings for the prayer book, his latest commission, and as such was precious—and walked down another lane, unseeing.

The Great Mortality . . . here, again.

He'd been on his way to visit Hermann, the engraver who would complete the woodcuts that would allow the drawings to be printed; but now he found himself walking aimlessly, too stunned to remember an alternate way.

After Ambrosius, Hans had lived in dread of encountering the plague again. Ambrosius, his beloved older brother, the one their father had believed would be a great artist. Ambrosius, who had his own studio while Hans was yet an apprentice to another artist; even if Hans was now accorded greater recognition than Ambrosius had ever been given, Hans knew the hole his brother's gruesome death had left in his soul would never fill. He couldn't forget watching the buboes form under his brother's arms, the black spots that spread up his face and limbs as he vomited blood. Four years later, not a day passed when he didn't see Ambrosius's dying face or—earlier—that sought-after smile of approval. He saw his brother in statues, in paintings, in other men, in children.

And he saw his own death by plague in everything else. The thought terrified him; he'd seen what his brother had endured, and he couldn't imagine doing the same. The fevers, the bursting skin, the blood . . .

Hans finally looked up, realizing he'd wandered far away now from the engraver's neighborhood, and was near the house of his friend Erasmus. Hans had recently painted the great man, and they'd become friends as a result. Erasmus had read parts of his essay *The Praise of Folly* to Hans during the sittings, and Hans had come to admire Erasmus for his wit and insight. He could use a precious dose of that today.

A few minutes later, the scholar was welcoming Hans into his study. Once seated before a warming hearth with a brandy ("good for all Four Humours," Erasmus assured him), surrounded by books and scrolls and writing desks and quills, only then did Hans finally begin to relax.

"Your fame is growing, young Hans," Erasmus told him, as he stood before the fire, his rugged face creased in pleasure. "I had reason to visit the Great Council Chamber in town hall today, and a traveler from Germany saw your mural and asked if it was the work of the Italian, Da Vinci. I was delighted to tell him that Basel had its own Da Vinci in the young Hans Holbein. He told me he would mark that name well."

Hans tried to smile, but wasn't entirely successful. Erasmus saw the attempt. "I fear you're not here for mere praise alone."

"No. I saw . . . plague. Plague has returned to Basel."

If Hans had expected some measure of panic or at least discomfort from his friend, he was surprised to see only a mild shrug. "Plague is always with us in some form or other. It's a constant companion. You of all people should know that, Hans—who was it but the artists who captured the 'Dance of Death' when the Great Mortality first struck a century ago?"

Erasmus rummaged briefly through a shelf, then pulled down a large vellum-bound volume, placed it in Hans's lap, and flipped through the parchment leaves until he came to an engraving that showed four skeletons, tufts of hair flying from their sere skulls, capering in a graveyard. Hans examined it briefly and then muttered, "I could do better."

His friend laughed and clapped his shoulder. "Indeed you could, young genius."

Hans spent another hour with Erasmus, discussing art and politics and the gossip surrounding a local aristocrat, and by the time he left the sun was setting and his spirits had lifted. As he lingered in Erasmus's doorway, pulling his fur-trimmed cloak tighter against the cooling air, Erasmus told him, "Paint, Hans. It's what God meant you for, and it will ease your mind."

Hans nodded and left.

He'd still been contemplative when he'd returned home. He ate dinner with his wife Elsbeth and their sons Franz and Philipp, then excused himself to the studio.

At first he wondered if he'd made a mistake; the studio had once belonged to his brother, whose spirit now seemed to infest every scrap of paper and brush and easel and ink bottle. Hans stoked the fire, shrugged out of his heavy outer garment, and tried to focus on his latest commission—an altarpiece design for the local church—but neither mind nor hand would bend to the task. Finally he lowered his head to the worktable and closed his eyes, seeking simple oblivion.

Someone was with him, in the studio.

He didn't know how much time had passed, and he hadn't yet opened his eyes to confirm what his other senses screamed at him; a quickening terror clutched his heart. His eyes popped open, involuntarily.

A tall shadow stood on the far side of the room, apparently draped in a black robe and cowl. "Good evening, Hans," it said, in a deep, somehow hollow voice.

Hans lifted his head, but he possessed no more strength. He opened his mouth, but couldn't form words.

"All will be made clear, my friend. Know for now that I mean you no harm." The visitor's rumbling tones sent shivers up Hans's back.

"How . . . " Hans managed to look back at the studio's door, and saw that it was as he'd left it—bolted from within.

His guest stepped forward, and Hans saw the gleam of something white from within the folds of the cowl.

Is that . . .

"Yes, bone. What else would Death be made of?" Two skeleton-hands emerged from the sleeves, pushed back the cowl, and let Hans see his visitor's face . . . or rather, see the skull where a face should have been. There was nothing but ancient, polished bone, no shred of skin or hair or muscle. Hans pushed back off his bench, and barely noticed when he fell to the floor.

His guest—Death—made a placating gesture. "You've nothing to fear from me, Hans Holbein."

"You're not here with . . . the plague?"

The skull moved back and forth. "Far from it. In

fact, I'm here to offer you a way to *save* yourself from plague. I come to claim your services, not your life."

Panic started to abate, replaced by curiosity. "My . . . services . . . "

"Yes. A commission."

Hans blinked in surprise and drew himself up. "You want me to . . . work for you?"

"I do. What you told your friend Erasmus earlier . . . "

Hans went back in his memory, and he knew immediately—he knew how he'd damned himself.

I could do better.

"The old depictions of me, those ridiculous images of dancing and cavorting like some mad witch in the moonlight . . . they no longer please me. I consider you to be the finest artist of this age, and I want you to render me, as I am, every day. I want you to record me the way I am—not as some prancing fool, but as one who practices his trade with care and respect for the craft."

"'Respect'?" Hans gasped out, before he could stop himself. "You kill innocents—"

"No. I merely perform the tasks assigned me. There are greater authorities above me, Hans. If you have complaints with choices, you'll need to address those elsewhere. I only control the day-to-day practice, and I am not cruel, callous, or uncaring. I take pride in my work, as you do in yours."

Hans wanted to sneer. He wanted to stand and hurl epithets at this monster, call him a liar, a hypocrite, deluded, but . . .

What if he's right?

"So how would you . . . ?"

"You will accompany me on some of my rounds.

Neither of us will be visible to those I must take. You will observe, and record exactly what you see."

"And in return, you'll keep me safe from plague? My family as well?"

"Yes. And also . . ."

Death ran his skeletal fingers into Hans's leather satchel, and removed the small bundle of prayer book drawings. The sheets flew across the table, and Death leaned down to examine them closely. "These are lovely. They're too good for Hermann, you know."

Hans *did* know. Hermann's work was often slipshod, erasing the lovely details that made a work live and breathe. "He's the best in Basel . . ."

"He's not. Seek out Hans Lützelburger."

"I know the name, but he's not in Basel . . ."

Death turned to face him, and somehow he knew the smile was intentional this time. "He has only recently come here. He will be my other gift to you. Shall we begin tomorrow?"

Holbein swallowed . . . and nodded.

―⁂―

They began at a convent.

Holbein felt like a voyeur, trespassing into the intimate inner realm of the brides of Christ, but when one initiate walked through him, he wondered which of them was really the ghost.

Death led him to a courtyard, where the elderly abbess knelt in a small garden. Even from a distance, Holbein could hear her rattling breath, see her faltering limbs. She was halfway dead, but her will kept her clinging stubbornly to life.

Death waited a few moments, then stepped forward and gently touched the old woman's shoulder.

She felt the tap, turned—and her mouth fell open in a silent shriek of protest. She tried to pull away, but Death clung to her habit's white scapulary and pulled her to her feet. Holbein watched, fascinated, as her body fell to the earth of the courtyard while her spirit was led off by determined Death. In one of the arched doorways leading out to the courtyard, a young nun saw the fallen body of her superior and she began to shout.

Holbein was too busy making preliminary sketches on a sheet of parchment to notice the grief that unfolded around him. He was surprised when he abruptly awoke, finding himself in his studio, alone, a half-finished sketch near his hands.

Death proved to be courteous, allowing Holbein enough time to completely finish one drawing before he reappeared. Holbein began to look forward to the visits, fascinated by his client's methods. He watched, invisible, as Death claimed a judge in the act of being bribed, a wealthy woman who felt the approach and dressed for the occasion, a peddler who tried in vain to flee to the next town, and a blind man who gratefully allowed himself to be led. He laughed when Death arrayed himself in the costume of a ragged peasant to claim a count; he allowed himself a measure of petty satisfaction when Death took a miser, and made the dead soul watch as he also took money from a counting table. Each of these excursions ended with Holbein awakening in his studio, and intuiting that he was not yet permitted to see what came next for each of those called by Death.

Hans continued working on his other commissions, but he found himself always returning to his Dance of Death. He added his own touches to the drawings: He included an hourglass in many of them; he did complete new drawings, depicting his new friend leading Adam and Eve out of Paradise, since they'd become part of his dominion. He drew a coat-of-arms for Death, and even an alphabet. He gave Death a sense of humor, although with subtler satire than earlier artists had provided.

He watched other citizens of his town die of plague. Not many—the sickness wasn't rampaging again, as it had in the past—and although the recognition left him uneasy, he had come to trust Death and knew he was safe. He took each new drawing to Hans Lützelburger, whose skill as an engraver surpassed his reputation. Holbein suspected that, if his Dances of Death were admired by future generations, it might be partly because of the brilliance of the engraver.

Then one day Death made him watch the taking of a child.

The boy was barely more than an infant, about the age and size of Hans's stepson Franz, his wife's son from her first marriage, which had ended when she was widowed. It was a poor family, living in a ramshackle cottage with no windows, a badly-thatched roof, and no fire but a cooking pit in the middle of the floor. Death showed no compassion nor consideration as he took the little one by a tiny wrist, leading it away from the body slumped on the floor, while the gaunt mother and older sister sobbed in a grief that Holbein had never seen, a grief born of a lifetime of desperation and loss. Holbein followed Death out of the cottage, and his face was still wet when his eyes snapped open to the familiar surroundings of his studio.

The beginnings of the drawing by his outstretched right hand repulsed him. But he didn't crumple it up or fling it into the fire. Instead he completed it.

He took it to Lützelburger, only to discover that the engraver had died in the week since Hans had last seen him. A terrible accident, involving a horse cart driven by a sot. The driver was in jail, and the engraver was dead.

Death came to Holbein that night. He was pacing in his studio, anticipating the visit. Still, his patron's first words surprised him: "I release you from our agreement, Hans. You have upheld your side of the bargain, and I'm very pleased with the work, which has re-inspired me."

"How could you take the child?"

The skull-head was unreadable, incapable of expressing emotion. "I've told you, I'm not the final authority—"

Hans cut him off, waving a hand in irritation. "Yes, yes, I know, I've heard all that. It's God's fault, isn't that it?"

Death hesitated, and Hans wondered if he'd finally provoked something that wasn't cold and rational. "Yes. Even I don't pretend to understand His wisdom."

"But doesn't it hurt you when it's a child, a babe, and the parents—"

"No, Hans, it doesn't."

Finally, Hans understood: He was dealing with a demi-god, a thing that was impossibly old and inhuman and with motives that nothing of flesh and blood could ever comprehend. And once again, he was frightened of Death.

"I leave you now, Hans . . . at least until we must

meet again. I am grateful for your skill, although I suspect it may make us both famous, and you must admit—you will owe part of that to me."

Hans stood, forcing himself into stone, as Death vanished again. Then he collapsed into a chair and poured himself a glass of ale that he hoped was big enough to make him as insensible as the drunkard who had killed Lützelburger.

<hr>

After that, Basel lost its charms, and in the autumn of 1526, Hans fled to England, where he'd heard artists were often highly paid. He left Elsbeth and the children in Basel, and over the next decade found fame in the court of Henry VIII, where he became the King's Painter. He prospered to the point where he acquired a mistress and two new children. He still visited Elsbeth when he could, and made sure she and their children were well provided for.

The plague returned to London in 1543. Hans heard the news from friends in the Royal Court. It was only a small outbreak, but Hans's anxiety rose like a black sun.

He was no longer protected.

On a cold night when fog covered London like grave dirt, Hans was returning from an audience with the King, who was inquiring again about the painting he'd commissioned from Hans in 1541, the one to commemorate the unification of the barbers' and surgeons' guilds. The painting was large, but size wasn't the issue; Holbein was, rather, simply bored by the subject. Of course he'd assured his royal patron that the work was progressing well, and would be completed soon.

Hans tried to negotiate his way through the fog, lighted windows providing little illumination until he'd nearly walked into them. He knew he was lost, and in fact he'd been walking for several minutes without even finding a shop or street sign. An overhead lamp revealed an intersection, he turned—

And smelled plague.

He froze, panic starting to rise up from his chest. The stench was nearly gagging him, and he staggered back as if physically assaulted by it. Then, from somewhere in the shrouded center of the lane, he heard:

"Hello, old friend."

No—

The black shape took form before him, hard white surfaces glinting within ebony folds, and Hans could only stare, immobile, sure that his time had arrived at last.

"You've come for me."

"Not yet, not that way. But I do come once again seeking your services. A new commission."

Hans felt exhausted at the mere idea. "We already showed you claiming your victims from nearly forty different walks of life—what can be left?"

"Exactly, Hans. I, too, have again grown weary of the limitations imposed on me. And that is why I want something different from you this: I want you to create entirely new works. This time, you will not accompany me on my rounds, but will work from your own imagination, placing me in fresh situations."

"You want me . . . " Hans struggled to find the words. "You want me to show you . . . "

"The station of the victims won't be important this time, but the method of passing will."

"New ways to die—is that what you're saying?"

Death's jaws made a slight clacking sound as he nodded. "Precisely."

Hans shook his head. "No. It's ghastly."

"Why? I'm asking you to entertain me, to renew and reinvigorate me. Surely that's a more worthwhile goal for art than memorializing some pompous blowhard and a bunch of barbers?"

"I . . . " Hans had no answer, because Death was right, and Hans knew that was why "King Henry VIII Granting the Charter to the Barber-Surgeon's Company" had already gone on for two years. Over the last few years here in England, he'd become little more than a gifted technician—a highly paid and praised one, but not a true artist. And wasn't Death the ultimate critic? If he could win the praise of this patron for original works, it would surely (ironically) be his life's greatest achievement.

"Yes." The word escaped his mouth almost of its own volition.

The reeking scent vanished instantly. "I'm delighted, my friend. I'll visit with you next week to view your progress."

Hans wasn't surprised to find the fog lifting by the time he'd reached the end of the lane.

Death became Hans Holbein's constant companion.

Hans began to notice new things about people, and about the world around them. He saw the potential for fatality in everything. A ship on the Thames could lose its rigging and hurl a sailor into the river's grimy depths. An urchin begging coins on a corner might be trod upon by a nobleman's horse, or perhaps fall victim to a far more outlandish accident—a bottle dropped from high overhead, an errant fist thrown by a bar brawler, a rare venomous spider inadvertently imported from a tropical region.

After his strolls, Hans returned to his studio and drew. For the first time in years, his work excited him. At the end of his first week, Death appeared by his side, and Hans wordlessly offered the first piece: A man convulsing at a dinner table while a woman sat at the head, raising a glass in toast, having just successfully poisoned her husband; Death stood nearby bearing a tray, the attentive waiter.

"Superb, Hans, superb," Death muttered, stroking a bone-tip over the art, "but you can go *further*."

Hans could barely sleep that night, his mind aflame with lethal possibilities.

When Death appeared next, Hans handed him two more works, and Death stood speechless for several seconds, before whispering one word: "Astonishing." The first of the drawings so praised showed a field of peasants in tattered rags torn apart by a wave of bullets from a giant gun mounted on a hill; Death held out strings of bullets to the gunner. The second new piece showed a man in a street being struck down by some sort of huge, horseless cart, a grotesque engine of destruction bellowing flame from its back.

Over the following weeks, Hans thought of little else but stranger and more horrible scenes of death. He drew on larger sheets, with bolder strokes. He drew scenes of soldiers enveloped in strange vapors on a battlefield, their mouths agape in their final dying breath, while Death stood above them, dangling long scarves that might have kept them safe. He drew a line of rail-thin, bent patients, all plainly dying as a wealthy doctor turned his back to them and accepted money from Death instead. He showed a priest gesticulating wildly from a pulpit, causing his flock to turn on each other in violence while Death stood behind him wearing a white mitre. He drew a man of science holding an open box from which emanated a blinding whiteness that caused all those below it to fling up arms in useless attempts to shield themselves, while Death stood behind the scientist making notes in a book.

Death was ecstatic. He stared with empty sockets at each new drawing, lingering for minutes, stroking them lovingly. "Exquisite," he might murmur, or, "brilliant."

Hans knew it was his finest work. After Death had rendered approval, each new piece went into a large wooden box that Hans had designed and specially made; the top was ornately carved and gilt with Death's coat-of-arms from the first set of drawings. Hans had already completed the engravings on the first two drawings of this new set, having decided that no other could be entrusted to accurately cut the wood for his masterworks. Someday, when the engravings were completed and the books printed, the world would recognize his achievement as well.

One afternoon, as Hans returned from another visit to Henry's court that had left him bored and annoyed and aching to get back to what he considered his real work, he passed an inn and saw a ring of onlookers standing around outside, peering in anxiously. He spotted a man he knew in the crowd, an apprentice to a printer he sometimes dined with, and he asked the man what the commotion was about.

"Lady murdered her husband," the young apprentice said, nodding his head toward the building's front windows.

Hans found a gap in the crowd, bent down to peer in through a square of glass—and his breath caught at what he saw:

Two armed men were questioning a woman who sat at the head of a table, a glass resting before her. A few feet away was a dead man slumped across his plate, still clutching an empty goblet in one hand.

It was an exact rendition of the first new drawing Hans had given Death; the only element missing was Death himself, in the position of the waiter.

Hans stumbled back in shock, carelessly bumping into others who cursed or cautioned him. He barely noticed when the apprentice laid a guiding hand on his arm. "Take care, there, sir—you don't want to hurt anyone . . . "

"Too late for that," Hans said, before turning to flee.

He staggered back to his studio, his thoughts racing past possibilities and deceptions: *It's a coincidence/Death put the image in my head and I didn't even realize it/perhaps I've gained some fortune-teller's ability . . .*

But only one explanation made sense: *Death copied my drawing.*

When he reached his studio, he bolted the door and raced to the box of drawings. He tore open the decorated lid, and reached to the bottom of the stack of drawings to pluck out the first.

THE SECRET ENGRAVINGS

A woman—no, *that* woman, who he'd just seen—poisoning a man. In that room. Even the glasses matched perfectly.

He slammed the drawing down, his motion causing some of the others to flutter aside. There was a woman being raped while Death kept her hands tied; there, a field of soldiers blown apart by some explosive, while Death stood apart, one arm still upraised from the deadly missile he'd just hurled.

Hans leafed frantically through the drawings, realization growing like a cancer within him:

He hadn't created entertainment for Death; Death had never intended to accept these works as art to restore his own flagging spirit.

No, this was an instructional guide.

These were signposts pointing to the future. Hans Holbein the Younger had assembled a manual of coming murders. Death had lied to him when he'd told him he had no control over who he took and how; He *was* the final authority. He *was* God.

Hans collapsed onto a work bench, his hands tearing at his beard, at his expensive collar. *What have I done? Is it too late to undo it?*

The drawings hadn't gone to the engraver yet, and these were the only copies. He could simply burn them now, destroy them. Death had already seen them, true, had committed them to memory; but perhaps a memory as well-used as His was faulty, wouldn't retain details.

Hans stayed up throughout the night, turning over options and possibilities, and by morning he knew there was only one course of action. But first . . .

There was one final drawing to be made.

Death returned a few nights later. Hans was waiting for Him.

"What have you got for me this week, friend?"

Hans passed him the last drawing he'd made. Death looked at it, perplexed. "What is this?"

"You lied to me. You've lied to me from the start. There is no authority over You, and I was a fool to ever believe there was. There is only You."

Death stood silently before Hans. After a few seconds he glanced aside—and noticed the wooden box full of drawings was missing. "Where are the others?"

"Gone. I burned the entire box."

The skull head twisted back and Death trembled, the first real display of emotion Hans had ever seen from Him. "You them all?!"

Hans held his ground. "Yes."

"You know what this will mean for you?"

"I do."

"Look under your arm."

Hans could already feel the skin there swelling, as heat began to course through him. "There's no need."

"You're a fool."

Smiling, Hans answered, "Not anymore."

With that, Death vanished.

Hans died two days later.

It was several more days before they found him; by then the blood had dried, but the smell hadn't abated. The messenger from the royal court and the neighbors who had battered down the door pulled back, nauseated. The young printer's apprentice had stopped by to visit Hans, and was there as the others were turning away.

"What's that he's got in his hands?"

The apprentice took a deep breath and stepped forward; he wanted to know what could have been so important to the great Hans Holbein that it was what he'd clung to as life had left him.

"Be mindful of the plague, lad," the messenger said. But the apprentice thought art was more important than death, and so he reached down and wrested the drawing from Hans's stiff fingers.

The sheet of parchment had been splattered heavily by Hans's blood, as he'd coughed up his life, but the apprentice could just make out the image: It showed a man who looked very much like Hans Holbein in a room that was undoubtedly this studio, dying of plague, his face blackened, (real) blood staining his bedclothes . . . but the man was smiling, at peace. Above the man's head was an hourglass, the upper compartment empty; from the side, a bony hand reached for the glass, but no more of Death was visible, a strange exclusion. At the bottom of the drawing was a Latin inscription; the apprentice had some familiarity with the language, and thought the words read, "Now I join Ambrosius."

He wondered who Ambrosius was.

"That's plague blood on that sheet, boy," muttered the neighbor. "Throw it on the fire."

The apprentice considered, and realized they were probably right. Who knew exactly how death passed from one man to another? Better not to take that chance.

He placed the drawing gently on the cold logs in the hearth, whispered goodbye to Hans Holbein, and left that chamber of death behind forever.

MUTTER ·

JESS LANDRY

S HE LIKED IT best in the dark. When the lights went out, when the sun went down, when she could walk freely without leering eyes following her every move. In the light they all looked at her funny, as though they could tell there was something different about her, something they couldn't put their fingers on. Whispers and giggles and averting gazes were the normal she'd known for the past few years, but all that was about to change. She needed one more thing and she knew exactly where to find it.

Under the blanket of night, she clicked open the cabin door and stepped inside.

———

Somewhere over the Atlantic, Edith startled awake. She jerked up in her cot, hand over her heart. That falling sensation, the one she'd been plagued by moreso over the past three days than before, never failed to rattle her. She peeled the thin cotton sheets off of her damp body and brought her feet over the side of the bottom bunk, catching her breath. Her other hand fumbled against the wall, searching for the light switch.

With a flick the yellow-lit bulb illuminated the tiny

room, washing over the same taupe windowless walls and prickly burgundy carpet that she'd seen for the past seventy-two hours. *I can't wait to wake up to sunshine*, she thought, her heart rate steadying itself. *And not in a room the size of a jail cell.*

Edith stood up, cracking her back and rubbing her hands over her skin to warm herself. The sheets of the top bunk were all over the place, the only hint that Hurricane Margot had blown through. Her room at home was always in a state—books strewn about, clothes tossed in places other than her closet—yet her sewing station was kept proper; it was the only thing Edith was truly strict on.

A teal flower-patterned dress hung off the sole chair in the room, a reminder Edith had left herself the night before. She'd made the dress for Margot in hopes that she'd wear it as they disembarked the ship, though clearly the girl had thought otherwise. *No matter*, Edith thought as she picked up the garment, noticing a slight tear at the hem. She sat back down on her bed, reached under, and pulled out her suitcase. Propping it onto the springy mattress, she tugged at her necklace which held two small keys to open the equally small locks she'd placed through the brown leather straps, and popped open the case, pulling out her sewing kit. Scissors, a needle, and thread—that's all Edith needed.

An important skill, Edith had told her daughter many times in their small home on the edge of Frankfurt. *Important for people like you and me.* Edith's own skills as a seamstress had kept her and Margot sheltered and fed, but tensions in Germany were reaching their boiling point—it was impossible to walk down the street without being bombarded by some kind of Nazi propaganda. Rumours were circling that German citizens were disappearing without a trace simply because of their religion, and that camps had been built far beyond the walls of the city where these people were being detained. All of this under the authority of one man, the Führer.

She'd known men and women like that in her lifetime, ones that hid in their fortresses while they commanded others to do their dirty work. That was not the life she wanted for her daughter. So when the opportunity arose for Edith to travel to New York City for work, she jumped at the chance, using the life savings she kept stored in a secret flap she'd sewn under her mattress to purchase a second ticket for Margot. She promised to take her daughter to see the Empire State building and to eat a hot dog and ride the subway, all things the little girl had read about in books. And after all the sights had been seen, they would disappear into the countryside under the cloud of the looming war.

If everything went according to plan, Germany would forget the faces of Edith and Margot Brandt.

A slight lurch caused Edith to reach out to the walls, her hands easily able to touch both sides of the narrow hallway, the rigid wallpaper rough under her fingertips.

"Guten Morgen," Peter Vogel, the ship's steward, squeezed by with a wink and a smile, beginning his last shift of this flight. He'd told Edith and Margot as he helped them to their cabin before departure that sudden movements of the airship were perfectly normal. Margot had taken to him right away, something she often did not do. Since they'd left Frankfurt, Vogel had been by their room a few times a day with a sweet for Margot who, he said, reminded him of his daughter back in Munich.

The same burgundy carpet from the cabin lined the entirety of the passenger deck, muffling the sound of Edith's Oxfords as she stepped into the lounge. The morning's breakfast crept in through the vents: bread fresh out of the oven, eggs cracked and scrambled, smoked meats grilled through and through, Edith could almost hear their sizzle. Margot had particularly taken to this part of the ship the first day, immediately pulling a chair to the wall of windows in the promenade. Maybe she felt like a giant or a bird watching the ground beneath her dwindle away, people and trees and cities reduced to nothing more than little dots. Edith often wondered what went through her daughter's mind; the 10-year-old with curly chestnut hair whose deep green eyes always said more than her mouth.

Margot sat in the far corner of the lounge, hands pressed against the windowpane, the only soul in a sea of brown tables and orange upholstered chairs. The wall behind her adorned with a mural painted by Professor Otto Arpke—apparently known for his work on a picture called *Das Cabinet des Dr. Caligari*, though Edith had never seen it. The mural depicted the world, showing the most notable transatlantic voyages in history: from Columbus to Magellan, from Cook to trips taken by the airship's predecessors, the muted browns and blues of the mural attempted to add a sense of adventure to the room, but to Edith it all seemed particularly sad for some reason. These voyages had been monumental, yes, but they'd all come to an end. Only a few names and faces remembered when there'd been more involved.

Margot pressed her hands and the tip of her nose against the closed windows, her breath lightly fogging the same spot over and over. She'd dressed herself in a pair of brown slacks and a blue striped shirt that they'd made together. Her tight brown curls sat lightly on her shoulder, and when she turned to acknowledge her mother, her green eyes gleamed.

Edith considered disciplining her daughter for leaving her side—something she had told her not to do under any circumstances—but the young girl had an adventurous side, a spirit that loved to learn and take in her surroundings. How could she deny a curious child the chance to explore? As it was, they were on an airship—what kind of trouble could she get into on a tin can a thousand metres above the ocean?

Edith walked over to her daughter, wrapping her arms around her. Margot was warm; her body loosened at her mother's touch. She stared off out the window, to the rising sun, to the waking world. Her right hand tapped against the pane. Edith kissed the top of her head, catching her daughter's reflection in the glass: those green eyes that if you looked hard enough, you'd notice they were about a centimetre too far apart, her full cheeks that were always a little rosy, and her smile—when she did—was thin-lipped but meaningful.

She followed Margot's gaze out the window, taking a moment to admire the new day. During their time on the airship, they'd seen nothing but blue skies and bluer oceans, and today was no different. The ocean rippled below them, and far off in the distance, faint beaches and deep forests were starting to take shape.

"It's going to be a beautiful day, isn't it?" Edith smiled and crouched beside the girl, sweeping a loose curl off her cheek. Margot paid her no mind.

Edith smiled at her in the window's reflection. Margot's green eyes remained locked on something just out of view. Her hand tapping in bouts of three with short pauses between, her breath fogging up the same spot.

The zeppelin swayed to the right, causing Edith to reach out a hand to steady herself. *Just a few more hours of this, then we'll be back on solid ground. Then we can disappear and leave it all behind.*

Margot's head shifted upwards, and Edith's followed. A dark shadow appeared over the edge of the ship's rounded frame. As Edith craned her head forward to get a better look, the door to the dining room opened and in poured the other passengers, some still in their nightgowns, some rubbing the sleep from their eyes. Children slept in the arms of their parents, parents muttered amongst themselves.

A rising din followed as what appeared to be about half the passengers on board the ship piled into the lounge. Vogel closed the door behind them, voices growing as he turned to face the crowd.

"If you'd please quiet down," he said. Faces Edith recognized from passing turned angry, the men shouting, their children crying. Edith stood up and Margot gripped onto her mother's belt. She placed her hand on her child's shoulder and gave it a tiny squeeze.

"Please!" Vogel pleaded. "If you'll quiet down I can explain the situation."

Women hushed their husbands and soothed their crying babies. Vogel cleared his throat.

"Thank you. Now, my apologies for the manner of which we've had to proceed, but a situation such as this has yet to occur on an airship."

The other passengers turned to each other, murmuring, exchanging worried glances.

"Please, please, quiet down." Vogel attempted once more. "There is no danger to you or your families."

"Then why have you herded us into the lounge?" a woman shouted, a crying toddler in her arms.

"Why can't we go back to our rooms?" asked another. Others joined in with a flurry of shouted questions.

"At this time," Vogel shouted over the clamor. "Please, everyone! At this time, it is in everyone's best interest to be here. Due to these circumstances, we will be conducting a search of your cabins—" the crowd roared "—please—with you present. Once we have concluded our search, you will be allowed to remain in your rooms until otherwise indicated."

"What exactly are you looking for?"

"Did you not search our luggage when we boarded?"

"Aren't we landing soon?"

Vogel cleared his throat, his hand moving to the door handle. "We have delayed landing at the Lakehurst Naval Base until further notice."

The crowd erupted as Vogel attempted his escape.

"Herr Vogel!" Edith shouted through the crowd, grabbing Margot's hand as they pushed through.

She grabbed him just as he was closing the lounge door, the other passengers livid amongst themselves.

"Herr Vogel," she said, holding onto Margot. "Please, will you at least tell me why we're not landing? What's happened?"

"I'm sorry," he said, attempting to shut the door, his attention leaning to something in the hallway.

"Please," she said, stuffing her fingers in between the door and its jamb. "What's going on?"

He frowned, his steel-blue eyes looking into hers. Though they'd only met three days prior, she'd taken to him, much like Margot had. There was a kindness about him. Though it was all a part of his job, he seemed to enjoy every minute he was on board the Hindenburg. He looked over his shoulder at the other crew members running by before turning back to Edith.

"A passenger was found dead this morning," he said as he closed the door.

<hr />

The hours dragged on as the crowd grew smaller and smaller. Whispers made their rounds, eyes shifted from one end of the room to the other. One by one families and single passengers were called out from the room until only Edith, Margot, and another woman and her child remained. The four of them sat in silence, the only sound the faint humming of the airship's motors, the smell of breakfast faded along with the ardor for the day. None of it affected Margot who tapped on the window repeatedly as the New York City skyline floated below—the statue of Liberty, the Empire State building, everything she wanted to see appeared before her eyes in the late afternoon sun. Edith was about to point her towards the Chrysler Building when Vogel and the ship's captain, Werner Richter, entered the room.

"Fräulein Brandt," he said. The two women exchanged glances, the worry clear in both their eyes. Edith then stood up and grabbed Margot by the hand. Richter said nothing, keeping a watchful eye on Edith and Margot from under his cap. His eyes burrowed, his thick white moustache covering his top lip, his stocky frame squeezed into his double-breasted uniform.

Vogel and Richter accompanied them to the cabin, Edith clutching onto Margot's shoulders. The cabin door sat open, everything as Edith had left it so many hours ago: Margot's flowered dress on the stool, patched and ready to be worn; Margot's sheets on the top bunk, tossed aside without a care. Their luggage however, which Edith had stuffed back under her bunk and locked after fixing Margot's dress, now sat on the floor in the middle of the room.

"Do you have the keys, Fräulein Brandt?" Richter asked. His voice echoed off every corner of the cabin.

"The keys?" She repeated, giving Margot's shoulders a pinch. Margot's hands found hers and squeezed back.

"To open your luggage."

She smiled thinly, thinking of how the scenario could go. Best case, Richter would open the suitcase, rummage through her personal belongings, perhaps embarrass himself a bit while he searched through her nightgown and underwear, but that would be it. They'd move onto the other woman and her child in the lounge.

Worst case, he'd find whatever he was looking for.

"The keys," Edith said, removing the necklace and handing it to Richter. "Of course. Though I have to ask, what is the meaning of all this?"

"It's simply a formality," Vogel piped up from behind them, shrugging himself into the room while two other crew members gathered at the door. Vogel slyly passed a sweet to Margot, who smiled then hid behind her mother.

Richter kneeled down. He used the two tiny keys on Edith's necklace and removed the locks, undoing the worn brown straps. She saw him hesitate for the briefest of moments, cocking his head slightly as though to see if she noticed, then he proceeded to open her luggage. Edith held her breath.

Every garment was neatly folded and placed, with Edith's sewing kit taking up a small section of one side.

Funny, Edith thought as Richter dug into the clothes. *Everything we own fits perfectly into this suitcase, this box with a handle.*

There had been much Margot wanted to bring with them: toys, gramophone records, photographs, all of which Edith had to deny. Edith herself had to leave behind her mother's ring—one passed down through the generations—a ruby stone set upon a silver band. She had planned on giving it to Margot one day, but taking sentimental items was too risky. They would have to rely on their memories instead.

Richter tossed their garments aside, carelessly and without shame, until the suitcase was empty, the plaid lining the only thing looking back at him, save for a few frayed strands of string where the seams met. Margot had sewed the lining herself; she'd beamed when she'd finished and rightly so. The girl would make a fine seamstress one day. Richter sighed and stood up. Edith exhaled.

"Apologies for the intrusion, Fräulein," he said, brushing by them without so much as a glance.

"It must be the other woman," Edith overheard one of the crewmen say from the hallway. She knelt down, re-folding her discarded clothing, Margot crunching on her lollipop behind her.

"I'm so very sorry, Edith," Vogel said, crouching beside her to help clean up.

"Please, it's fine," she replied, attempting to brush him away. "I've got it under control."

"It's no worry, here let me help." He folded one of her shirts. As he was about to place it in the suitcase, he noticed the stray threads dangling from the seam. Without a word, and before Edith could stop him, he tugged at them. As he pulled, the lining came loose exposing two tightly-wrapped flesh-coloured items roughly the size of a rolled up blanket.

Vogel looked up, his steel eyes meeting Edith's.

There was a moment of silence, of confusion; Vogel's gaze faltering between the two items and Edith. No time to save herself or grab Margot and run. No time to stop Vogel, to silence him before he opened his mouth. So as Vogel cried out for Captain Richter, the only thing she could do was turn her head to Margot and tell her to run.

"We've searched the whole ship, Captain," an exasperated crewman said, wiping his brow with his sleeve. "We can't find the girl anywhere."

"Keep searching," Richter muttered from under his moustache. "For God's sake, she's just a child."

Edith shifted uncomfortably, the handcuffs tight around her wrists, her hands behind her back. Confined to the officer's mess on the lower deck of the ship, she sat in a burgundy vinyl booth with the items in front of her, both rolled tightly and held together by strings of burlap. Photos of the Fuhrer and General Paul von Hindenburg hung in gold-lined frames on the wood-paneled wall, their eyes on her. Her brown blouse stuck to her shoulder where the blood dripped from the side of her face thanks to one of Richter's overzealous crewmen who tackled her in her cabin as she tried to pursue Margot.

Richter, Vogel, and two other burly crewmen huddled in the hallway whispering among themselves, their backs turned to her. The hum of the motors was more prevalent down in the officer's mess, a buzz that sounded like a swarm of bees just outside the walls waiting for the command to attack. The room stank of wasted alcohol and sweat.

"Do not disturb us," Richter told Vogel as he walked in, closing the door behind him. The zeppelin lurched slightly as the Captain took a seat across from Edith, checking his watch. She could see the hands ticking by, 3:28 pm. Richter cleared his throat.

"I'm not sure what to make of all this," he said, removing his cap and running a liver-spotted hand over his face and through his stark white hair. "In all my years, never have I come across this type of situation. I've been on battlefields. I've seen men cut in half. Women left bloodied and disfigured. Children . . . " he trailed off, his brown eyes lost in a memory. He exhaled and continued, "What I saw today, I do not understand. And I suppose I never will. How does someone so . . . delicate—my God, how could you do such a thing to another woman?"

He looked at her, genuinely puzzled by what he assumed she'd done.

He began to speak once more but closed his mouth before the words came. Instead, he fished in his pockets and pulled out a pair of gloves. He paused after he put them on, but proceeded to unfurl the thinner of the rolled objects in front of him, untying the burlap string with a shaky hand. It stretched over the length of the table as he flattened it out, and not an inch more, some bits stuck together as though they'd been glued. It had started to lose some of its rose colouring, except near the top. He smoothed it out with his hands, pure disgust across his face, until it finally became a tangible object, one that made him turn away in a gagging fit.

Edith gazed upon the piece before her: a well-preserved pelt with a perfect seam and near perfect stitching. Her daughter's finest work.

"What *is* this?" his voice shook as he asked the question, immediately correcting his posture, no doubt praying Edith wouldn't notice his falter. But she did. She had seen it in men like him before—the ones who cowered in their fortresses and demanded others do their dirty work. The ones who would—and had—come for her and her daughter time and time again. Unrelenting. Unwavering. But these men hadn't the slightest clue what they were up against. And now that they'd found her out, she had nothing to lose.

Behind him, a vent cover silently shook loose, a little hand reaching out to stop it from crashing to the ground.

"It's Margot," Edith smiled.

Vogel paced outside the door trying to listen to the conversation happening on the other side. The two mechanics waiting with him, Hans and Martin, watched him, smirking.

"They've been in there for quite some time," Vogel said, debating whether or not to interrupt.

"I doubt there's much going on," Hans said, scratching his jaw. "What's she going to do, beat him with her shoe?"

Martin chuckled. Vogel shook his head, "You didn't see what she did to that woman."

He'd passed Edith in the hallway that morning, smiling and unaware. She'd smiled back, her lips a deep red, her green eyes heavy. If only he'd known what she'd done. If only he'd checked on Ingrid Schmidt sooner. Maybe he could have done something. Maybe he could have helped.

"No one's afraid of a lady," Martin spat.

Vogel shook his head again, making his choice. He knocked on the door. When no answer came, he knocked again, calling out for Richter. When that proved useless, he threw the door open, the handle rattling as it hit the wall.

Upon first glance the room was empty. No Richter, no Edith. But as Vogel approached the booth where he had brought Edith, Hans and Martin staying precautiously behind, the captain's body came into view, a stream of blood spilling from multiple tiny wounds in his neck and onto the burgundy carpet.

"Perhaps we should be," Vogel said.

<hr />

Edith followed Margot through the vents, squeezing her way through the tight spaces with the two rolled up garments tucked under her arms. They eventually crawled up and out through a mesh of tangled wires and into the ship's interior hull, stepping onto a catwalk that led deeper into the ship's core one way and the other to a door marked ENGINE ROOM. The smell of rotted eggs slightly more prominent in the hydrogen-filled balloon.

The buzz was the loudest here, though it wasn't deafening—the ship's motors flanking them on either side. Around them were the Hindenburg's bones, the duralumin frames circled above and below like a thousand black Ferris wheels that stretched on as far as Edith could see; the reinforced cotton tarp covering every inch of its skeleton. It flapped and hummed as the winds pushed against it from the outside. Just beyond the tarp, the sun had begun its final descent.

Edith dropped the garments and grabbed hold of Margot as tight as she could, wishing she could squeeze her child into her to spare her from the world around them. She'd gone through so much at such a young age. It wasn't fair. This wasn't the plan. They were never supposed to have been found out. But Margot was young and inexperienced; she'd seen a pretty face and wanted her mother to have it. She hadn't thought about the consequences, how her actions wouldn't go unnoticed. And now, at the edge of their journey, the outcome was looking grim.

"Mama," Margot managed to say, her lips not quite glued down to the inside of her mouth, so Edith had told her to talk as sparingly as possible during their voyage. "Your face."

Edith crouched near a terminal with a reflective surface. A large chunk of flesh dangled off her cheek, the spot where she'd been struck earlier and where Richter had managed to strike her once more before she stuck him over and over with the curved needle she kept hidden in the skin of her wrist. He'd done some damage, exposing her true self underneath.

"Edith."

She turned to see Vogel standing on the catwalk ten feet away from them, an SS-designated dagger clutched in his fist, the words *Meine Ehre heisst Treue* carved on its blade. Margot cowered behind her mother, tiny fingers clutching at her belt.

"Herr Vogel," Edith said, raising her hands to chest-height in an attempt to show him she was disarmed and meant him no harm. "Please, you've been so kind to us on this journey, I feel selfish asking one more favour of you."

His chest heaved, he shifted his weight from one foot to the other, he said nothing.

"Look the other way. Go back to the other passengers and forget we were even here."

"You've killed the Captain. What you did to Ingrid Schmidt . . . I heard her cries from the hallway. When I entered her room . . . my God, Edith, you skinned her alive."

"I never meant for any of this to happen, please believe me," she paused, gently pushing Margot towards the engine room door, her eyes swelling. "I want a good life for my daughter. Surely you understand that much."

He lowered his dagger, his shoulders dropping. The kind eyes that once looked upon them returning to his face. He held back tears. "What are you?" he asked.

She smiled thinly. Edith started to answer him but before she could utter a word, Margot came blaring past, a flurry of brown curls and blue stripes. She charged at Vogel, knocking him off of his feet, the dagger tumbling onto the catwalk with a clang.

"Margot! No!" Edith cried, rushing for her daughter as she prepared to charge him again. Vogel scrambled, finding the blade just as Edith grabbed Margot and held her in her arms, her back to him.

At first she felt a tiny sting. Then the sting grew until it felt as though her whole back were aflame. She faltered, dropping Margot onto the metal catwalk. Blindly, she turned in place using her arms to shove Vogel away. She felt heat against her hands and she pushed, a crash sounding out as pain shot through her torso. She turned back to Margot, ushering the girl towards the engine room door.

"Mama," the word shook from Margot's lips as Edith felt the warm rush of liquid dripping down her back, her legs, her feet.

"Go, Margot, I'll be right behind you."

The little girl hesitated, but grabbed their new skins and went towards the door. Edith made a full turn towards Vogel. He lay tangled in wires and cables, blood saturating his black uniform and dripping through the catwalk grates underneath him.

"Do you want to know what I am?" she asked looking down at his broken body. He seemed smaller on his back, paltry, child-like.

He said nothing, his eyes wide. There was no need to hide anymore, not in this world. What good was a mother who kept her child hidden because of her own fears? She was no better than the others who sent their followers off to die while they sat in their castles.

Edith reached an arm behind her and dug the

blade out from where Vogel had made contact, shrieking as she did. The dagger hit the catwalk with a clang. She removed her clothing one excruciating item at a time until she stood nude. From the wound that Vogel forged in her shoulder, she bore her fingers in, pulling at the skin as though she were removing an adhesive. It ripped quickly, easily, and for the first time in a long while, Edith felt the night's air against her true self. Grabbing onto her brown curls, she tugged from the neck, pulling up and over. The fillers dropped from her face—a trick she'd picked up years ago, using strands of burlap to round out the parts under the skin that made her facial features more human. She'd gotten pretty good at it, though she often noticed Margot's eyes were slightly far apart. The girl was still growing so there would be imperfections. Edith yanked her claws out from her fingerholes, the blood sticking to her fur stringy like strawberry jam. And with a heave, she tore the rest of the skin away, tossing it into a pile between herself and Vogel. She stretched her arms out as far as they could go, bringing her hands to her back to her rear. Her fingers both found a thick strand of thread, and through a grimace, she pulled the thread, the fabric unspooling the wings she'd kept sewed down for years. She flexed her newly freed appendages, and though she'd clipped them long ago so they'd be better hidden—much like her horns— they were now free. Everything was unfettered.

Her body hummed as it released itself from the confines of her suit, one that she and Margot had become accustomed to to fit into a world that would not accept them in their natural form.

Vogel couldn't move. He glared at Edith, observing

every inch of her body; quick, uneven breaths escaping his chest.

"Is this not what you wanted to see?" Edith said as Margot opened the door to the engine room. "This is what I really am. This is why I have to hide. The way you're looking at me at this moment, that's how I've been looked upon my entire life."

A tear spilled from his eye, rolling softly down his cheek. "I'm sorry," he muttered, and pulled at the loosened wires.

Sparks from the disconnecting wires met the hydrogen-filled air. Before Edith could understand what was happening, a giant fireball sprang to life consuming all in its path. The off-white tarp lacing the Ferris wheel frame erupted in flames as though the sun had reached out from the sky and set it ablaze.

Edith was knocked down, hitting the metal grates hard. Through the blinding light and gaining heat, she turned onto her stomach, pain scorching her every move. But move she did.

Edith crawled to the engine room, passing by Vogel's screams, his body consumed by the inferno.

The zeppelin suddenly jerked downwards, Edith winding her claws through the catwalk, her hands desperately pulling her forward, feeling for a touch of fabric or her daughter's warm skin.

She crawled into the engine room and immediately noticed the little girl cocooned into a corner, the flames licking at her feet, her skin already beginning to melt away.

Through fire and smoke, she grabbed a hold of Margot, who dropped both their new, tightly-wrapped skins as she did, and squinted through the flames looking for an escape.

Margot shrieked in her arms. The fire kissed her fur, burning the skin of her wings. All seemed lost. But then, through the smog, she noticed a hatch on the underside of the catwalk.

"Hang onto me!" Edith shouted as her daughter wrapped her arms around her. She closed what remained of her wings around Margot, maneuvering her body through the climbing flames. The hatch lever seared her palms as she pulled, the door itself falling away into a black abyss. Exhaling, Edith tightened her grip on Margot and leapt into the night.

The wind rushed by them, caressing Edith's body in its gentle touch. With her back towards the earth, Edith expanded her charred wings as far as they could spread, hoping to catch a downdraft to ease the fall. Edith held onto her daughter with everything left in her. Around them, the Hindenburg burned, its massive frame melting away as though it were shedding its own skin.

There were screams, of that Edith was sure, and they were the last things she heard before they hit the ground.

Margot awoke in her mother's arms. She sat up, her body aching.

All that remained of the airship was its collapsed frame some 50 yards ahead of her, like old dinosaur bones sticking out from the earth. People closer to the wreckage were screaming at one another, men rushed the site attempting to put out what was left of the flames.

"Mama?" Margot turned to her mother, unsure of what to do next. She shook her mother but Edith didn't move.

They were here to start over, her mother and her.

226

MUTTER

She'd chosen a new face: the little girl who lived down the block with the straight red hair and pretty freckles. She'd chosen a new face for Mama: the lady in the cabin across from them, though Mama had gotten mad at her for getting it. They'd even chosen a new name, too. Mama would be Alice, and Margot, she picked a pretty one: Mary. No more Edith and Margot Brandt. They were Alice and Mary Leeds.

"Hello!" Someone called out from ahead, a silhouette making its way over to her. She shook her mother again but the woman didn't stir.

"Mama!" She cried, pulling at her fur, slamming her hands onto her chest, anything to get her to move.

"Are you all right?" Another voice said, the silhouette becoming that of two men.

Margot looked back to her mother, her face red and shiny, the fur burned away. Her head was turned to the forest, her green eyes staring blankly off to the distance.

The tears came as Margot stood up, all that remained of her burned skin falling from her body as she did. For the first time in her life, she felt the wind passing through her sprouting fur, over her growing horns, against her maturing wings. The men came closer. She hesitated for a moment, looking at her mother one last time. Margot then ran off, leaving behind the only one who'd ever meant anything to her.

"What's that?" One voice said as she ran, the trees growing closer and closer.

"It looks like the devil." Said the other.

The flames of the wreckage were nearly extinguished as Margot ran into the night; into the forests of New Jersey.

LA LLORONA

CULLEN BUNN

IT WILL BE SAID, I suppose, I disappeared without a trace. That I have cultivated fertile ground for wild speculation, I cannot deny. In my time, I have penned many tales of strangeness and spectral happenings. And, as to my personal affairs, I have crafted an air of secrecy, furtiveness, and—yes—even morbidity to fascinate idle minds. Therefore, a bit of mystery surrounding "The Demise of Ambrose Bierce" suits me well enough. Though it would please me just as well if no man, woman, or child considered my passing at all.

Yet, I write these words—scrawl them really on what few scraps of parchment I have managed to find in this place—in hopes that someone will one day read them and understand with some clarity what became of me.

Although my death—if it is truly death that awaits me—might be of such abnormal quality that it is beyond rational comprehension.

"As to me, I leave here tomorrow for an unknown destination."

I wrote this final line to my longtime friend, Blanche Partington, only a few days hence, not realizing the dark foreknowledge of the words. Certainly, I hinted at death and what lies beyond. (What man can grasp the concept of nothingness?) Even as I put pen to paper, I anticipated that it would not be long before I stood before a firing squad. After all, I was a "Gringo in Mexico," a respected position deserving of the thunderous fanfare of a five-gun salute. Pancho Villa, who humored me in the early days of my journey, had grown weary of my tequila-laced humors, and I surmised my time in his company was coming to a bloody end.

And so I fled.

From the city of Chihuahua, I stole away in the night, before Villa's men could drag me before a bullet-riddled wall and sent me to my final reward—a hole in the dirt! With me, I carried little more than the clothes on my back, a meager supply of tequila, and the sombrero given to me by the revolutionaries as a reward for marksmanship. I kept to the muddy banks the Rio Conchos as well as I could, with the intent of following the Rio Grande to Ciudad Juarez and back into the United States. The assassins who pursued me—if there were, indeed, assassins—surely anticipated my route. They, too, would stick to the river, and they would be traveling on horseback. I had also stolen a Colt Bisley pistol, and I kept it tucked in my belt and close at hand. Should my pursuers catch up with me, they would learn that an old man could be dangerous prey. Still, the journey was slow. I stayed hidden during the day and traveled the war-torn countryside at night when I could.

On the first night, I ran out of Mezcal. Dreadful business, that. In the wake of such a tragedy, my head throbbed painfully with every step of my flight, reminding me that perhaps the life I saved was not worth living.

On the second, my accursed asthma asserted itself and I made little progress on my journey. I huddled in a crumbling, abandoned cabin, wheezing and shivering in the hot and stagnant air, crouching in the purest darkness, jumping at every sound like a child frightened by sheet phantoms.

On the third night, I found the woman.

Before I saw her, I heard her, a desperate cry that seemed to be carried across the river's surface. The sound chilled me marrow-deep. The sound was unlike any I had heard before—hollow and mournful and lost. In my time, I had heard mortally-injured soldiers on the blood-soaked field of battle, crying for their mothers as they grasped fitfully at their wounds or crawled blindly in search of limbs severed by cannonball. Their cries were less haunting than the gut-wrenching sobbing I heard as I followed the river's bend through a forest of scattered, spindly, skeletal trees.

It was an otherworldly sound.

It was much worse than the sound of someone who was dying on the battlefield. It was the cry of one who had already died but had not moved on. It was—I could not shake the feeling—the wail of a ghost.

Perhaps, I should have turned away from the river and fled from the mournful wailing. To follow such a dirge could only invite misfortune. Still, my burgeoning fear did little to temper my incessant curiosity. I had penned many ghost stories, but I had never been a believer in such manifestations. If this was indeed a spirit, I wanted to see it with my own eyes, to disprove my years of skepticism. If it was not a wayward spirit, then I wanted to cast my speculation aside and continue, unencumbered by flights of fancy, accompanied only by my nagging headache, with my efforts to save my life from Pancho Villa's assassins.

Can you believe it? A man of my age, hunting for ghosts in the dead of night! Truly, the humor of youth resurfaces at the most unusual of times to remind you of what you once had and what you have lost!

Crouching behind a tree, I espied the woman.

My mind reeled. A ghost! She must have been! No living creature would have presented such a figure!

Dressed in a white gown and shawl, a flowing scarf covering her hair, she stood knee-deep in the sluggish river. The skin of her thin arms and giant face was perhaps more pale than the clothing—so stark as to be almost luminescent. She was weeping—yes—but the tears that ran down her cheeks and dripped into the water looked like black oil. Her eyes, too, were pitch black, and it was a simple matter to conceive that her skin was but a covering for naught but darkness, that her body was filled with those sorrowful black tears.

And the wailing—no creature of flesh and blood would have cried out in such a strange, sorrowful, chilling way.

With emaciated fingers, the woman grasped a wrapped bundle. At first, I could not identify what she held. Then, I saw two similarly swaddled shapes on the bank. The shapes squirmed on the ground, and as the wrapping pulled away from one, I saw an infant's face.

A baby—no more than a few days old!

A cry caught in my throat. I took half a step and then stopped myself.

The woman plunged the baby beneath the surface of the river.

Now, I moved. Now, I called out, damning the phantom and commanding her to release the infant in the same breath. In years past, I had faced mortality. On the battlefield, I had marched into the cold embrace of death. Here, though, I strode toward a being that transcended death, a creature that had peered beyond the veil of flesh and blood and seen the world beyond. With an angry yell, I stomped across the muddy bank, hoping my own voice might frighten this thing that seemed spawned unto the Earth for the sole purpose of terrorizing others.

The ghost looked at me. Her face—the features lost in a weird, shifting haze—betrayed no emotion.

She did as I asked.

She released the infant.

She pulled her hands out from beneath the water, and now she held no babe. She had cast the child into the depths. Surely, the current had already pulled the infant's small form away from us, sent it tumbling across the rocky river bed to unknown locales somewhere along the river's course.

In a rage, I screamed at the ghostly woman. I knew only too well the pain of losing a child. My sons, Day and Leigh, had both been stricken from the world before their times. The pain of their passing had almost been too much to bear. A new mother . . . a new father . . . should never face such torment. I knew not from where these newborns had been abducted. Perhaps there was some village nearby. I would not, however, allow this apparition to throw another baby into the unknown darkness. I had fled for my life from Pancho Villa's killers, but from this horror—for this purpose—I had found my courage once more.

And yet, as I splashed through the water toward the woman, I stopped. Cold water soaked my britches and filled my boots. The woman stared at me, curious. Had no one ever approached her in such a way? What would I do, I pondered, when I reached the woman? Would I strike her down? Would I tackle her and drive her beneath the surface? What would I do if she had no corporeal shape? If she were a ghost, she might have no form to speak of. She had held the baby, though, so surely—

The babies!

I wheeled away from the woman and splashed once more toward the bank. The two remaining children lay before me. Perhaps I had no means to brawl with a ghost, but I could steal away with her prey. I raced to the two small, bawling bundles. If I could grab them up, I would flee from the river until I found the nearest community, finding shelter for the babies and perhaps for myself.

The woman did not pursue me. Instead, she merely reached out with her long, pale fingers, an almost uncaring gesture. I felt myself hefted from the ground. As if I weighed nothing at all, I was hurled through the air. Although I felt light as a feather when I rose from the ground, I felt no such sensation when I landed. I crashed to the bank, my every bone jarred, my tongue nearly bitten in half by my teeth, several yards from the infants.

My head spun. The taste of blood filled my mouth.

Blood ran down my chin as I spat and picked myself up. I snatched the Coly Bisley from my belt and took aim. On any other day, I was an excellent marksman—my prize sombrero, now cast aside in the mud, was testament to that—but pain and disorientation threatened to spoil my aim.

I fired.

Again and again, the muzzle flash illuminated the night. I fired until all bullets were expended, and still I pulled the trigger a few more times for good measure. Spoiled aim or not, I hit her at least twice, but she seemed unaffected.

The ghostly woman glided to the bank and—gently—picked up the other children. She cuddled both of the infants to her breast. She was weeping still, as if she could not abide the very actions she took.

I cast the useless pistol aside. My legs trembled. With my first step, I almost collapsed. But I kept my legs beneath me. I took a second step. A third. I splashed into the water once more.

"Don't!" I cried through a mouthful of blood.

The woman dropped both infants into the water. For a second, they seemed to float. Then, they sank beneath the dark surface. In less than another second, they had vanished.

I stood before the woman now—closer than I liked—and looked into her black, oily eyes.

She spoke.

Her words sounded as if they were uttered from beneath the surface of the river, from beneath the deluge of those dark and inhuman tears. There was desperation in those words, as if she needed me to understand. But I did not. Even if she had spoken clearly, I would not have comprehended. I was the fool who had come to Mexico without a talent for their native tongue.

Behind me, I heard the calls of men. I heard footsteps along the bank. I heard a thunderous concussion.

For the second time that night, I felt myself thrown by an outside force. I staggered forward, my knees giving out underneath me, and collapsed against the woman. She wrapped her arms around me. Her embrace was cold—oh so frigid!—but had she not held onto me, I would have surely fallen. Trembling, I glanced down at myself, and I saw blood soaking through my shirt. There was no pain. There was only numbness and iciness, but I knew I had been shot.

I had been shot in the back, but the bullet had torn through my flesh, torn through my chest. My blood spattered the ghostly woman's white shawl. Shakily, I raised my head to look into her dark eyes. She gazed back at me, piteously, and whispered in her strange, otherworldly tongue. Although I did not recognize the words, I understood her meaning.

I was dying.

The woman looked past me as my killers cried out again.

"La Llorona!"

I turned my head to look upon the men. There were two of them, and they were staggering away in fright. One of them held a smoking rifle. The other aimed his rifle into the air and fired it wildly, as if trying to scare the woman—La Llorona—off. They hooted and hollered as they fled into the darkness.

La Llorona spoke softly to me.

Her cold arms pulled away from me.

"No!" I whimpered. "Please, no!"

This apparition had terrified me. Now, though, I did not want her to release me. I had written death . . . courted death . . . many times, but now I did not want to feel the final shroud of death pulled over my face. I clutched at her, but my trembling fingers could not find purchase.

I sank to my knees in the rushing water.

La Llorona looked down at me and spoke softly.

Slowly, I fell backwards. My blood uncoiled into the rushing water all around me. The river was not deep here, but it would cover my face once I was on my back. I thrashed about, trying to stand, but whatever strength I had left rushed out with my blood.

I gasped for breath. Even that was denied to me. My asthma playing one last, cruel trick on me as I sank beneath the water.

Through a rippling curtain of water, La Llorona stared at me.

The river was far deeper than I imagined—impossibly deep—and I found myself tumbling through cold darkness. Water filled my mouth, rushed in my ears, blinded me as I rolled through the void. As I spun head over feet, I glimpsed one of the infants the woman had tossed into the water. The child—it was a boy—floated only a few feet from me. The swaddling cloth had fallen away from the child. Blisters and sores covered his body, red and swollen and angry, and diseased, black, necrotic "veins" of discoloration seemed to crawl from one open sore to the next, connecting them. I reached out, but the darkness swallowed the child up.

Or perhaps it was I who was enveloped by emptiness.

This, I knew, is how it felt to drown, not in the waters of the river, but in the depths of the black tears of La Llorona.

Had I died already?

Was this some endless Purgatory?

And then—nothing.

No pain. No fear. No confusion. I saw nothing, heard nothing. I felt myself sinking—into the depths but also into nothingness. I was weightless for a time, and then even the sensation of weightlessness vanished. There was no movement. The passing of time ceased to exist. I had been wrong before. This—this!—was death.

But only for a short while.

It was not agony that awakened me. My wound caused me no more pain. It was the wailing of infants.

I opened my eyes and winced against the brightness. I was indoors now. I could see as much even though my eyes burned. But after the impenetrable darkness that had consumed me, even the meager glow of a dying candle might be blinding. I squeezed my eyes shut, then slowly opened them, letting only a little light in at a time. I ran my hands over my stomach. I was shirtless now, but I found no bandaged wound. After a moment, I opened my eyes. I am not ashamed to admit, I looked to myself first rather than tending to the crying infants around me. I sat up, gasping, finding no sign of injury at all. I was stretched out on a small bed, covered in a thin blanket.

I felt as though I had awakened from a dream. That

must be it! I had dreamed of the ghostly woman and of the infants. The cries of the infants around me must have somehow invaded my dreams!

I was in an infirmary tent not too dissimilar from those that might have been set up near the battlefield in the war. Now, though, instead of mortally injured men crying out in pain, the tent was filled with bassinets, many of which contained a mewling, kicking baby. I saw no other adult.

I swung my legs over the side of the bed. The ground beneath my bare feet was hard-packed earth, but at least it was dry. Sitting on a chair next to the bed was my clothing, also dry, and I quickly grabbed them up and started to dress. My mind reeled as I saw my shirt, tears in the cloth stitched together, but the telltale reddish brown stains of blood set into the cloth. Once more I checked my stomach for a wound that was not there.

I moved toward one of the bassinets and looked at the crying child within. I could not tell if this was one of the children I had seen at the river or not. One baby looks the same as the next to my eyes. This child, though, displayed none of the blisters or sores I had seen upon the baby's flesh as I sank beneath the water. Once more I ran a hand across my stomach. My shirt was stained by blood, but no bullet hole could be found beneath.

Light flooded into the tent as a flap was drawn back and a woman entered. Like the woman I had seen at the river, she was dressed all in white. She carried an infant in her arms. The infant, I saw, was dripping wet.

The woman paused for a second, looking at me curiously. Then she said something in Spanish and hurried across the room. Using a cloth, she dried the baby and placed it into one of the empty bassinets. She stood over the bassinet for a moment or two, regarding the child.

"La Llorona?" I asked.

The woman turned toward me, shook her head, and touched her cheek, using her finger to trace a line of a tear that was not there.

She spoke again, for all the good it did, and she motioned toward the entrance to the tent. She wanted me to see what I would find beyond. Or maybe she only wanted to be rid of me. Either way, I obliged her.

I stepped out of the tent and found myself in a small village. There were no permanent structures here, only more tents clustered together upon the grassy banks of a winding river. The air here smelled good, and the sun shone upon my face and warmed me. A lush forest rose up around the village.

As I took note of my surroundings, a group of children ran past, laughing and squealing. The youngest might have been four. The oldest, twelve. They were happy and carefree.

Elsewhere in the village, women in white hurried past. Some of them carried baskets of bread or buckets of water. Others carried swaddled infants. None of them were crying, and none of them paid me any mind. I wondered if I had been taken in by some sort of convent.

I walked toward the river, where I saw another woman in white standing ankle-deep in the rushing, crystal clear waters. She was not crying. Instead, she smiled happily as she scanned the water flowing past her feet. Still, she reminded me of La Llorona, and I called out to her. She paid me no mind as she stared into the river. She stood almost statue-like for a very long time.

When she finally moved, it was with a sudden quickness. She reached into the water with a splash. And when she pulled her hands back up, she held a crying baby in her hands. She shushed the baby, held it close, bouncing it gently, trying to console it. Carrying the child, she hurried to the bank and walked past me, barely acknowledging my presence. I watched as she took the child to the infirmary tent. Another white-clad woman passed me. She waded out into the river and assumed a statue-like stance, watching the water.

I laughed—laughed to assure myself that I was not going mad.

I turned in place, looking across the river and the tents and the women in white and the playing children.

"As to me, I leave here tomorrow for an unknown destination."

Though the people around me spoke Spanish, I realized that I was no longer in Mexico. I was no longer in the world I knew. I was in some . . . other place. Perhaps this was the world that lies beyond death, though I felt very much alive. Perhaps this was some hidden realm La Llorona and her sisters in white had discovered. Here, they took sickly children—and the occasional injured gringo—to heal them. Perhaps I had been brought here for a great purpose. The tents, I knew, could be replaced by permanent structures. There were trees and stones aplenty to raise homes and schoolhouses. The children might need a man of letters to share his knowledge. I stood upon the foundation of a new society in—

A new world.

How long had people been coming here?

There were no buildings, it was true, suggesting that this place was only newly discovered. Or perhaps the women in white moved from place to place, following the path of La Llorona in the real world. Could there be other people beyond the expanse of the forest? Other societies? Other cities? How long had La Llorona been casting babies into the waters of the river? Was she the only agent of this world at work in our own? Could it be that some of those infants had grown to adulthood here, in a place that might very well be free of sickness and pain, and might they have set out to explore and build on their own?

The laughing children ran by once more, happy in this world.

And if I—in my arrogance—thought I might help them build something better, might teach them of the "civilized" world, then I was entertaining cruelty.

Between cruelty and curiosity, I would much rather indulge one than the other.

Might I get myself into even more trouble in this world? Well, of course. After all, at first glance it looked very much like the world I had known up until now.

"A gringo," I mused, "in . . . wherever the Hell I am."

THE LONDON ENCOUNTER

VINCE A. LIAGUNO

SHE WAS WELL into her fourth glass of vodka and third Seconal when she heard the knock at the door. It was just past midnight, the overcast London sky as black as her mood. She paused, cigarette halfway to slightly parted lips, and considered answering it.

Probably just a fan wanting to see the goddamn ruby slippers.

She laughed aloud to no one in particular in the empty parlor of the mews flat she and Mickey were renting in the Chelsea suburb and took a long drag of the cigarette. She and Mickey—her husband of only three months—had fought earlier. They had been watching television—some laborious documentary on the royal family—when he had started in on her about the drinking. At that point, she was barely halfway through the second vodka and had exploded.

She liked to think anger was a sign of passion in a marriage, and she should know; Mickey was her fifth. She knew from experience with the others that the control started shortly after the honeymoon. The nagging would start disguised as innocuous concern over the amount of sleeping pills she took or—in tonight's case—her preference for an evening cocktail or two. Nagging turned to hounding, the hounding to open contempt. How she despised that arrogant male dominance, yet always seemed to find herself craving its stabilizing force in her life.

Tonight—*last* night, she corrected herself, glancing at the mantle clock—she had run from their flat in a tirade of profanity, screaming all the way down Cadogan Lane. She had no doubt the neighbors thought her a vulgar American of the worst sort. By the time she had walked off the rage and returned—popping the first Seconal—Mickey was gone. Likely off at the particular kind of gentlemen's clubs he had such fondness for and the patrons with whom he seemed to share such affinity.

A second knock at the door.

She heard the sound as if muffled through layers of gauze, the Seconal's anesthetic effect kicking in with its comforting numbness. Mickey wouldn't be knocking—unless he'd forgotten his keys. She rose from the settee on wobbly legs, expertly balancing vodka glass in one hand, lit cigarette in the other. She was nothing if not a pro.

"Who is it?" she asked through the door, the annoyance in her slurred voice impatient and unmistakable.

The response that came back was barely audible through the wood of the door, as if the light drizzle outside had dampened the caller's words, drowning them out. Or, more likely, the voice broke apart en route from ears and mind having been diluted and then fragmented as it traveled through the filter of the red devils in her system. Although muted and garbled to her conscious mind, subconsciously, she heard an accent, clipped and enunciated. Decidedly British.

Inhibitions lowered by the combination of booze and barbiturates, she threw the door open. Somewhere, deep in the recesses of the rational part of her mind the drugs and alcohol were suppressing, she knew this to be a reckless act bolstered by artificial nerve. She knew this on an instinctual level, just like she knew a man's—often a husband's—secret predilections or sexual proclivities.

"Yes?" she demanded impatiently. "What do you want? An autograph? You have some *goddamn* nerve coming to my home at this hour." In her mind, the words came out with precision and a hint of conceit. (She was, after all, a goddamn *celebrity* despite the appearance of her modest lodgings.) In reality, the words blended into each other with careless incoherence.

"Well?" she said when her caller didn't immediately answer. She stood in the open doorway, cigarette hand gripping the door but doing a poor job of keeping her from swaying. The air—despite being the end of June—had a slight chill, the light rain cooling her. She shuddered involuntarily as she considered her nocturnal visitor.

He was tall. Toweringly so, actually—or so it seemed through the sieve of her drug-addled perception. She was an unreliable narrator to the unfolding events, which she would readily admit to herself had she been of mind to do so. The man's face was shrouded in shadow beneath a tall top hat, his long torso cloaked in a lengthy, voluminous cape-like garment. There was something out of place about the man's appearance, but she was in no condition to identify what exactly it was.

"Good evening, Miss Garland." The words were soft-spoken, genteel, and incongruous to his imposing frame. "My sincerest apologies for calling on you at such a late hour but I've . . . just gotten in, as it were."

"Jesus," she said with no pretense of hiding her disgust, "even when you're being downright rude, you Brits are so *goddamn* polite about it." She took a swig of vodka before adding, "So? What do you want?"

"I'm a huge admirer, Miss Garland. And although my visit must appear to be quite unorthodox to you at this ungodly hour, I can assure you that I've traveled very far to meet you. Farther than you could ever imagine." The man's voice had an odd quality, like an echo in a cavernous chamber. She squinted to see his face, which seemed obscured by black grains of sand, shifting and ever-moving. She blinked to try and clear the optical illusion. The red dillies were working overtime on her sensory perception tonight.

"Listen, Mack," she said, unassuaged, "I don't give a good rat's ass where you're from or how far you came, but the show's over. Miss Garland has left the building. Got it, pal?"

"I've upset you," the man said, that oddly hollow voice suffused with an unmistakable note of regret. The effect was disarming. "I've thoughtlessly inconvenienced you, Miss Garland, and irrevocably cast myself in the poorest of lights. Please, accept my humblest of apologies. I bid you goodnight." Tipping the brim of his hat, he turned to leave.

She guzzled the rest of her vodka, looking down at the empty glass. She thought about her five-week supper club run at the Talk of the Town last December, a sudden flash of the crowd growing ugly, catcalling and throwing things—empty cigarette packs, crackers, rolls—onto the stage. She had been a few minutes late, yes—but that was no excuse for the abject rudeness of the crowd. It wasn't she who had changed, nor had her talent diminished—it was the crowds who grew vulgar and crass. Long gone were the MGM days and the throngs of adoring fans who lined up with their darling little autograph books, politely gushing praise and citations of favorite pictures. On days when she was in a rush, fans were happy just to get a glimpse of her, waving as she was ushered away from the studio or into a theater at a movie premiere. Now they heckled and hollered their impoliteness on whim.

"So . . . what's your name, anyway? I mean, if a gentleman is going to come calling after midnight, I think it's only fair that he have a name, no?"

The man stopped and turned back. "Please, call me Jack, Miss Garland. I'd be honored if you would do so." He extended his hand toward her. She looked down first at the hand holding the empty vodka glass, then at the one holding the cigarette. She flicked the latter to the ground just past the man's right leg, and extended her free hand. He took it gently in his hand—his very cold hand—and brought it up to meet his bending form. The brush of his equally cold lips against the top of her hand made her shiver, and she pulled away quickly.

"Now don't think I'm condoning this kind of thing," she said, regaining her baseline booze-and-barbiturates composure, "but since you *are* a fan and since you *did* travel all this way to meet me, who am I to disappoint? I could at least offer you a drink before I send you on your way."

"That would be delightful beyond words, Miss Garland," the man named Jack said.

She turned toward the parlor, too quickly, and teetered slightly before recovering her balance. Jack made no move to assist her, entering the flat at a dutiful distance behind.

"Please, Mr . . . *Jack*," she said motioning with exaggerated stateliness toward a garishly-upholstered armchair near the empty fireplace, "Won't you please sit down?" She was clearly in command of the room, the star of tonight's production, aided by the heightened effect of secobarbital and cheap vodka. She uncapped a half-empty bottle of Gilbey's and refilled her glass.

"So what's your poison, Jack?" she asked of her guest.

Jack motioned polite declination with his hand.

"You sure? A lady hates to drink alone." The question was met with continued silence. "Suit yourself."

"I don't suppose your housemaid could prepare a cup of hot tea?"

"My housemaid?"

"Surely, a star of your caliber and pedigree has at least one domestic . . . "

She threw her head back and laughed. She took a healthy swig from her refilled glass and then, as of considering the implications of not keeping up appearances, she said, "I've given the staff the evening off. They all wanted to see that dreadful documentary on the royal family on their televisions. *Tellies*, as you people say, isn't it?"

"Quite right, Miss Garland," Jack said with a slight nod.

She couldn't help sneaking looks at his face—trying both not to stare but to zero in on his features which seemed just out of focus, shifting. There was something simultaneously fascinating and unsettling about this lack of facial detail, and she wasn't entirely ruling out the effects of the pills as the cause. She remembered once—after a slight overindulgence on her part at dinner before a show—watching an entire audience whose heads seemed to ripple and swell, elongating right before her eyes in the middle of "The Man That Got Away."

"How terribly rude of me," she said snapping from her daydream, as if decorum suddenly pushed its way through the shroud of fog in her mind. "Can I at least take your coat, Jack?"

Again, he simply raised a gloved hand in courteous refusal. "No, please don't trouble yourself, Miss Garland. The truth is that I'm rather chilled from my travels through the London drizzle. I would just as well prefer to keep my topcoat on. Please don't think me rude for doing so."

She waved him off dismissively, the foggy tendrils once again dragging her remembered manners back into the recesses of her psyche. "So, let's get down to brass tacks, shall we, Jack? Why exactly are you here? You've got to be my biggest fan to trudge all the way out here in the middle of a rainy night for a *bloody* autograph!" She had taken to—and secretly enjoyed—incorporating some of the more colorful British colloquialisms into her own discernibly distinct speech pattern. *Bollocks* and *rubbish* being close runners-up to *bloody*.

THE LONDON ENCOUNTER

Jack laughed, his expression of lively amusement sounding impossibly echoey in the tiny drawing room. The sound seemed to oscillate all around her—eerie, disembodied. *Disconnected.*

Then, the merriment severed, abruptly and without transition: "I'm not here for an autograph." The declaration carried the gravity of a tolling bell, its severity of intonation driving a shiver through her body. Even through the miasma of narcotics and alcohol, she recognized her mistake—letting a stranger in the house in the middle of the night. How she wished Mickey was here at that moment; he'd know what to do.

"No?" she said with forced confidence, moving—staggering, really—away from the liquor cabinet, casually sidling between the back of the sofa where her guest sat—his back now to her—and the front door, eager to keep a clear channel of egress.

Jack sat motionless, (quivering) face forward. "No, Miss Garland. I assure you, although I am a great fan of your work, I have not traveled all this way for something so . . . *boorish* as an autograph."

Prone to shifting moods when under the influence, and accompanied by another swig from her glass, her demeanor swung from nervous to annoyed. "Well, then, just why in the *goddamn* hell are you here, Mr. . . . *Jack*?" To her ears, there was challenge and defiance in her voice; to anyone else's, just slurred inarticulacy.

There was the slightest of sighs—imperceptible to most, but certainly to the inebriated—before Jack replied. "I'm here to take your soul, Miss Garland."

Under normal circumstances, such an utterance

249

might have been met with a sense of surprise or even fear, but her artificially enhanced version of reality that evening processed her visitor's words through a distorted filter. Traveling through the warped kaleidoscope between her ears and brain, the words took on farcical meaning. The implied, if improbable, threat blossomed into garish absurdity—like juggling clowns riding unicycles at the circus. She erupted into laughter.

"Well, isn't *that* a relief?" she said. "And here I was beginning to worry about you, Jack. I had you pegged as an autograph hound, or one of those weirdos who think I travel with the ruby slippers. But, no, you're just a run-of-the-mill soul collector." More laughter, dissolving into coughing that rumbled up from somewhere deeper in her chest than the laughs.

Jack continued to sit staring forward, unmoving, as she stumbled around to the front of the sofa, slamming the empty vodka glass down and snatching a pack of cigarettes off the end table as she did so. With shaky hands, she fished a Player's No. 6 from the pack, plucked a match from a matchbook sporting an image of the Tower of London and the name of some charmless pub on its cover, and swiped its red charcoaled tip across the coarse strip on the matchbook's exterior.

She lit the cigarette and puffed a cloud of smoke into the room. "I've got some bad news for you, Jackie—mind if I call you that? See, you can't take something I don't have. I lost my *goddamned* soul a long time ago in this business."

"Yes, that is rather unfortunate."

"Unfortunate? My dear fellow," she began in full

affectation, "that's not *unfortunate* . . . it's a *goddamn* crime! I gave those studios the best years of my life . . . my career. I made those overfed pork bellies buckets of cold, hard cash with this talent. And what'd I get in return?"

"An unceremonious dismissal," Jack said, his hollow voice conciliatory, almost apologetic.

"Thrown out with the trash," she said, then added for emphasis, "Yesterday's *rubbish*."

"You're hardly yesterday's rubbish, Miss Garland. I daresay, you're being much too hard on yourself. Why, your motion pictures and recordings have brought immeasurable joy to countless men, women, and children over the years."

She considered his words for a moment, taking them in with another deep drag of the cigarette. "Well, that's very kind of you to say, Jack." His words, coursing through her on waves of Seconal and vodka, assuaged her, softening her alternating anger and apprehension.

"And it's been very kind of you to receive me, Miss Garland," Jack said, starting to rise from the couch, "but I'm afraid it's very late and I don't want to overstay my welcome. I'll just collect what I've come for and be . . . "

"Tea!" she exclaimed, snapping to attention and clapping her hands together, sending ash from the end of her cigarette airborne. "You asked for a cup of tea— *spot of tea*, isn't that what you people call it?—and that's the very least I can do before you head back out into this ghastly night."

Jack, mid-rise from the sofa, sat back quietly. "If you're certain it's no trouble . . . "

251

"None at all," she said, stubbing her cigarette out in the ashtray beside him. "I'll just boil some water." She tottered toward the kitchen, zigzagging as she exited the room. From the kitchen, the sound of a kettle banging against the stove and water pouring from the tap.

"I'm afraid I'm at a disadvantage, Jack," she called out to him as she set about the business of preparing her version of an English teatime. "You know everything about me, but I know nothing about you. Tell me, where in England are you from, anyway?"

His voice wafted in from the drawing room, the distance doing little to dispel its resonance. "I'm originally from London, but because I travel so much, my life has taken on a rather transitory quality, I'm afraid."

"And is there a special someone out there? A *Mrs.* Jack perhaps?"

"No, I'm afraid the nature of my . . . *work* makes any kind of romantic attachments quite impossible these days."

She appeared in the doorway, leaning against the frame, and regarded him sitting on the sofa, stock-still. "Come now, there's never been a special lady in your life? *Ever?*"

"I suppose there was the occasional young lady who caught my passing interest back in the Whitechapel days," Jack acquiesced. "But none of them quite worked out," he added, head bowed.

She smiled sadly, somehow understanding her visitor's loneliness which now stretched across the room and closed the distance between them. Even at the center of adoring crowds, she knew that kind of soul-crushing loneliness. She turned back toward the kitchen where the water began to boil on the stove.

Even under the influence, she knew how to function—and wooziness was no match for her ability to do so. She made quick work of transferring hot water to the delicate teapot, which sat in the middle of a sterling silver serving tray flanked by two equally delicate teacups and saucers. With an efficiency that belied her present state, she searched out the sugar bowl and retrieved milk from the icebox. With shaky hands that rattled the teacups against their saucers on the tray, she lifted the hastily thrown-together service and turned.

Jack was standing there. She let out a startled yelp as the tray slipped from her hands and crashed to the floor, sugar cubes quickly dissolving in the hot tea and milk all around their feet.

"Jesus Christ!" she shouted.

"I've startled you." Jack was mere inches from her now, somehow appearing even taller and more imposing than he had in the doorway earlier.

She struggled to regain her composure, her heart beating wildly in her chest, the adrenaline coursing through her veins momentarily eclipsing the sedative effects of the Seconal. "You're good *goddamned* right you startled me," she cried, her voice rising in volume and hysteria. She looked down at the remnants of her English teatime, now spreading across the floor in tandem with the terror spreading through her body.

"I think it's time for you to be on your way now," she said with forced sternness. She moved to sidestep around the widening coagulation of sweet tea and cream—and by extension, her visitor—but Jack moved with her, his cloak-like outer garment swinging with the movement like a displaced curtain over feet she couldn't see. It was as if he were floating across the tiled floor.

"You invited me in, Miss Garland," he said, "of your own free will and volition. You wanted something from me, and now I wish to take something from you." His voice was even, calm—almost preternaturally so.

"Please," she said, choking back the sob that was threatening to spill out from the back of her throat, "just leave. I don't want any trouble, hear?"

"Ah, but you've made a habit of inviting trouble into your life, haven't you, Miss Garland?"

She blinked through watering eyes, looking up into his featureless, molten face. "I don't . . . "

"The barbiturates, your fondness for the spirits and men. Your life has become one indulgence after another, and you've squandered your many talents on those immoderations."

"I . . . I don't understand. Who *are* you? Why are you doing this to me?"

"I wish to relieve you of your burdens, Miss Garland. You're a weak woman . . . a fallen woman."

"I demand that you leave. *Now!*" she said trying to summon some modicum of courage so she could shake off the fear that had now all but consumed her. The idea that this faceless man was deriding her, implying threat in her own home . . . it was outrageous. And terrifying. She again sidestepped, this time to the right, but Jack was right there, gliding in front of her to block any escape.

"Five husbands. Courting the affections of homosexuals. Leaving your devoted audiences waiting and often disappointed because you're off numbing yourself with medications and drink. You've failed, Miss Garland. You've become a miserable wretch . . . a common whore. Just like the others . . . "

She caught the glint of steel as Jack unsheathed the large butcher knife that seemed to materialize—as if by some kind of sorcery or cheap parlor trick, she wasn't sure which in the unreality of the moment—from the heavy fabric folds of his topcoat. She screamed, her legs—suddenly heavy under the weight of her terror and the cumulative effects of an evening of pills and booze—sliding out from under her. She hit the kitchen floor in a splash of warm tea and milk.

Her fight or flight instinct struggled to overpower the strong sense of surrender that told her to stay there on the floor, the latter an almost pacifying, maternal inner voice that coaxed her to let go. Suddenly, she was moving—scrambling, really—first backwards on all fours in crab-like movements away from where Jack towered above her, then forward on knees and palms that slipped and slid in the liquid mess on the floor. She could hear the *whoosh* as the knife sliced the air above her with tremendous force. Jack was apparently as strong as he was tall, she thought with almost logical detachment.

Finding traction just beyond the spill, she was up and on her feet. When Jack appeared in her left peripheral vision, she knew exit from the house was blocked so instead she sprinted forward, across the hall and into the bathroom. She slammed the door shut and slid the latch into place. She pressed her back to the door anticipating her visitor's imminent contact with the flimsy wood, knowing that it wouldn't likely withstand the force of impact.

255

She closed her eyes, images of Judy and Lorna and Joey playing out in motion picture images in her mind's eye. She thought of Mickey coming home to find her bloodied body there, on the bathroom floor, unceremoniously splayed. She could see the tawdry tabloid headlines now: *Dorothy Dead in Loo Bloodbath*. At least the *Sunday Times* header would be more dignified: *American Star Brutally Murdered in London*.

Star.

She *was* a star, critics be damned, and the irony that she'd likely enjoy a comeback in death that could never be rivaled in life wasn't entirely lost on her in what she knew to be her last terrifying moments. She wondered if her death would hurt, wondered how the knife would feel piercing her skin. The inevitability of it now weighed her down, made her legs feel like lead. She was so tired. Tired of the demands this life—a charmed life by all outside accounts anyway—had placed on her. She'd given it her all, but she was just so tired. Tired of the betrayals, of the judgements, of the impossible standards she was expected to live up to. She had always been the ugly duckling—apropos she should die in such an ugly manner.

She jumped at the sound of Jack's voice from the other side of the door.

"Let the world remember you as you once were, Miss Garland. Not as you've become," Jack said through the wooden panels. His voice had taken on a softer tone, a soothing elixir of logic and absolution that was lulling her into surrender. She backed away from the door, the backs of her knees eventually making contact with the cold porcelain of the toilet.

She sat as Jack's voice—that horrible, ghostly voice—continued to float through the door.

"You've been wicked, Miss Garland. And it's time to atone for your sins. Through death, your acquittal is all but guaranteed." His words eerily reflected her own thoughts, as if this horrible, murderous stranger could somehow read her mind at that moment. But he was right: In death, she'd find relief—and unending celebrity to the ends of time. Just as he had, this traveler of great distance and time, whose own incomprehensible identity she now understood.

"Your fans will mourn you, coming from great distances to pay tribute to your life and career. Your death will bring about a great riot in an even greater city, Miss Garland, so deep will the despair over your untimely passing run."

"But . . . I'm afraid," she said, her voice childlike and fragile in the stillness. It was a simple declaration told with her entire truth.

When the latch on the bathroom door gently slid back and the door opened, she didn't jump or try to run. She was raised to believe in a heaven and hell, with an interim purgatory for those whose fates were undecided—a last stop before either redemption or condemnation. She understood in that moment, perched atop the toilet bowl in the modest mews flat she shared with the last in a long string of men who loved the little girl in the blue gingham dress and red ruby slippers, that this was *her* purgatory, her chance to choose between deliverance and damnation.

Jack was now standing directly in front of her; the eddying blur of his face reflected in the gleam the knife's blade poised at her throat.

She nodded. "I'm ready, Jack." She suddenly felt the effects of a lifetime of red devils and hooch. Her eyelids became heavy, her limbs weak; it was a struggle to remain upright. She wavered but sensed Jack steadying her with a hand that never touched her.

So cold, this man's hands. So cold and brutal his heart.

But she understood his role in this last part of her journey—how his enduring brutality had transcended time and place to liberate her. As the light around her seemed to be gradually dimming now in a circle that grew smaller from the outside in, she looked up at the faceless man.

"In the silence of night, I have often wished for just a few words of love from one man, rather than the applause of thousands of people."

"I know, Miss Garland," Jack said as the knife cut down to caress her throat. "Wish no more."

Somewhere in the distance—as she slipped peacefully from the present while being viciously slain in another darker point in time someplace in the distant past—she heard an old gramophone playing, scratchy with comforting familiarity . . .

The night is bitter,
The stars have lost their glitter;
The winds grow colder
And suddenly you're older—
And all because of the man that got away . . .

BUBBA HO-TEP

JOE R. LANSDALE

ELVIS DREAMED HE had his dick out, checking to see if the bump on the head of it had filled with pus again. If it had, he was going to name the bump Priscilla, after his ex-wife, and bust it by jacking off. Or he liked to think that's what he'd do. Dreams let you think like that. The truth was, he hadn't had a hard-on in years.

That bitch, Priscilla. Gets a new hairdo and she's gone, just because she caught him fucking a big tittied gospel singer. It wasn't like the singer had mattered. Priscilla ought to have understood that, so what was with her making a big deal out of it?

Was it because she couldn't hit a high note the same and as good as the singer when she came?

When had that happened anyway, Priscilla leaving?

Yesterday? Last year? Ten years ago?

Oh God, it came to him instantly as he slipped out of sleep like a soft turd squeezed free of a loose asshole, for he could hardly think of himself or life in any context other than sewage, since so often he was too tired to do anything other than let it all fly in his sleep, wake up in an ocean of piss or shit, waiting for the nurses or the aides to come in and wipe his ass. But now it came to him. Suddenly he realized it had been years ago that he had supposedly died, and longer years than that since Priscilla left, and how old was she anyway? Sixty-five? Seventy?

And how old was he?

Christ! He was almost convinced he was too old to be alive, and had to be dead, but he wasn't convinced enough, unfortunately. He knew where he was now, and in that moment of realization, he sincerely wished he was dead. This was worse than death.

From across the room, his roommate, Bull Thomas, bellowed and coughed and moaned and fell back into painful sleep, the cancer gnawing at his insides like a rat plugged up inside a watermelon.

Bull's bellow of pain and anger and indignation at growing old and diseased was the only thing bullish about him now, though Elvis had seen photographs of him when he was younger, and Bull had been very bullish indeed. Thick-chested, slab-faced and tall. Probably thought he'd live forever, and happily. A boozing, pill-popping, swinging dick until the end of time.

Now Bull was shrunk down, was little more than a wrinkled sheet-white husk that throbbed with occasional pulses of blood while the carcinoma fed.

Elvis took hold of the bed's lift button, eased himself upright. He glanced at Bull. Bull was breathing heavily and his bony knees rose up and down like he was peddling a bicycle; his kneecaps punched feebly at the sheet, making pup tents that rose up and collapsed, rose up and collapsed.

Elvis looked down at the sheet stretched over his

own bony knees. He thought: My God, how long have I been here? Am I really awake now, or am I dreaming I'm awake? How could my plans have gone so wrong? When are they going to serve lunch, and considering what they serve, why do I care? And if Priscilla discovered I was alive, would she come see me, would she want to see me, and would we still want to fuck, or would we have to merely talk about it? Is there finally, and really, anything to life other than food and shit and sex?

Elvis pushed the sheet down to do what he had done in the dream. He pulled up his gown, leaned forward, and examined his dick. It was wrinkled and small. It didn't look like something that had dive-bombed movie starlet pussies or filled their mouths like a big zucchini or pumped forth a load of sperm frothy as cake icing. The healthiest thing about his pecker was the big red bump with the black ring around it and the pus-filled white center. Fact was, that bump kept growing, he was going to have to pull a chair up beside his bed and put a pillow in it so the bump would have some place to sleep at night. There was more pus in that damn bump than there was cum in his loins. The old diddlebopper was no longer a flesh cannon loaded for bare ass. It was a peanut too small to harvest; wasting away on the vine. His nuts were a couple of darkening, about-to-rot grapes, too limp to produce juice for life's wine. His legs were stick-and-paper things with over-large, vein-swollen feet on the ends. His belly was such a bloat, it was a pain for him to lean forward and scrutinize his dick and balls.

Pulling his gown down and the sheet back over himself, Elvis leaned back and wished he had a peanut butter and banana sandwich fried in butter. There had been a time when he and his crew would board his private jet and fly clean across country just to have a special made fried peanut butter and 'nanner sandwich. He could still taste the damn things.

Elvis closed his eyes and thought he would awake from a bad dream, but didn't. He opened his eyes again, slowly, and saw that he was still where he had been, and things were no better. He reached over and opened his dresser drawer and got out a little round mirror and looked at himself.

He was horrified. His hair was white as salt and had receded dramatically. He had wrinkles deep enough to conceal outstretched earthworms, the big ones, the night crawlers. His pouty mouth no longer appeared pouty. It looked like the drooping waddles of a bulldog, seeming more that way because he was slobbering a mite. He dragged his tired tongue across his lips to daub the slobber, revealed to himself in the mirror that he was missing a lot of teeth.

Goddamn it! How had he gone from King of Rock and Roll to this? Old guy in a rest home in East Texas with a growth on his dick?

And what was that growth? Cancer? No one was talking. No one seemed to know. Perhaps the bump was a manifestation of the mistakes of his life, so many of them made with his dick.

He considered on that. Did he ask himself this question every day, or just now and then? Time sort of ran together when the last moment and the immediate moment and the moment forthcoming were all alike.

Shit, when was lunch time? Had he slept through it?

Was it about time for his main nurse again? The good looking one with the smooth chocolate skin and tits like grapefruits? The one who came in and sponge bathed him and held his pitiful little pecker in her gloved hands and put salve on his canker with all the enthusiasm of a mechanic oiling a defective part?

He hoped not. That was the worst of it. A doll like that handling him without warmth or emotion. Twenty years ago, just twenty, he could have made with the curled lip smile and had her eating out of his asshole. Where had his youth gone? Why hadn't fame denied old age and death, and why had he left his fame in the first place, and did he want it back, and could he have it back, and if he could, would it make any difference?

And finally, when he was evacuated from the bowels of life into the toilet bowl of the beyond and was flushed, would the great sewer pipe flow him to the other side where God would—in the guise of a great all-seeing turd with corn kernel eyes—be waiting with open turd arms, and would there be amongst the sewage his mother (bless her fat little heart) and father and friends, waiting with fried peanut butter and 'nanner sandwiches and ice cream cones, predigested, or course?

He was reflecting on this, pondering the afterlife, when Bull gave out with a hell of a scream, pooched his eyes damn near out of his head, arched his back, grease-farted like a blast from Gabriel's trumpet, and checked his tired old soul out of the Mud Creek Shady Grove Convalescence Home; flushed it on out and across the great shitty beyond.

———

Later that day, Elvis lay sleeping, his lips fluttering the

bad taste of lunch—steamed zucchini and boiled peas—out of his belly. He awoke to a noise, rolled over to see a young attractive woman cleaning out Bull's dresser drawer. The curtains over the window next to Bull's bed were pulled wide open, and the sunlight was cutting through it and showing her to great advantage. She was blonde and Nordic-featured and her long hair was tied back with a big red bow and she wore big, gold, hoop earrings that shimmered in the sunlight. She was dressed in a white blouse and a short black skirt and dark hose and high heels. The heels made her ass ride up beneath her skirt like soft bald baby heads under a thin blanket.

She had a big, yellow plastic trashcan and she had one of Bull's dresser drawers pulled out, and she was picking through it, like a magpie looking for bright things. She found a few coins, a pocket knife, a cheap watch. These were plucked free and laid on the dresser top, then the remaining contents of the drawer—Bull's photographs of himself when young, a rotten pack of rubbers (wishful thinking never deserted Bull), a bronze star and a Purple Heart from his performance in the Vietnam War—were dumped into the trashcan with a bang and a flutter.

Elvis got hold of his bed lift button and raised himself for a better look. The woman had her back to him now, and didn't notice. She was replacing the dresser drawer and pulling out another. It was full of clothes. She took out the few shirts and pants and socks and underwear, and laid them on Bull's bed remade now, and minus Bull, who had been toted off to be taxidermied, embalmed, burned up, whatever.

"You're gonna toss that stuff," Elvis said. "Could I

have one of them pictures of Bull? Maybe that Purple Heart? He was proud of it."

The young woman turned and looked at him, "I suppose," she said. She went to the trashcan and bent over it and showed her black panties to Elvis as she rummaged. He knew the revealing of her panties was neither intentional or unintentional. She just didn't give a damn. She saw him as so physically and sexually non-threatening, she didn't mind if he got a bird's-eye view of her; it was the same to her as a house cat sneaking a peek.

Elvis observed the thin panties straining and slipping into the caverns of her ass cheeks and felt his pecker flutter once, like a bird having a heart attack, then it laid down and remained limp and still.

Well, these days, even a flutter was kind of reassuring.

The woman surfaced from the trashcan with a photo and the Purple Heart, went over to Elvis's bed and handed them to him.

Elvis dangled the ribbon that held the Purple Heart between his fingers, said, "Bull your kin?"

"My daddy," she said.

"I haven't seen you here before."

"Only been here once before," she said. "When I checked him in."

"Oh," Elvis said. "That was three years ago, wasn't it?"

"Yeah. Were you and him friends?"

Elvis considered the question. He didn't know the real answer. All he knew was Bull listened to him when he said he was Elvis Presley and seemed to believe him. If he didn't believe him, he at least had the courtesy not to patronize. Bull always called him Elvis, and before Bull grew too ill, he always played cards and checkers with him.

"Just roommates," Elvis said. "He didn't feel good enough to say much. I just sort of hated to see what was left of him go away so easy. He was an all right guy. He mentioned you a lot. You're Callie, right?"

"Yeah," she said. "Well, he was all right."

"Not enough you came and saw him though."

"Don't try to put some guilt trip on me, Mister. I did what I could. Hadn't been for Medicaid, Medicare, whatever that stuff was, he'd have been in a ditch somewhere. I didn't have the money to take care of him."

Elvis thought of his own daughter, lost long ago to him. If she knew he lived, would she come to see him? Would she care? He feared knowing the answer.

"You could have come and seen him," Elvis said.

"I was busy. Mind your own business. Hear?"

The chocolate-skin nurse with the grapefruit tits came in. Her white uniform crackled like cards being shuffled. Her little white nurse hat was tilted on her head in a way that said she loved mankind and made good money and was getting regular dick. She smiled at Callie and then at Elvis. "How are you this morning, Mr. Haff?"

"All right," Elvis said. "But I prefer Mr. Presley. Or Elvis. I keep telling you that. I don't go by Sebastian Haff anymore. I don't try to hide anymore."

"Why, of course," said the pretty nurse. "I knew that. I forgot. Good morning, Elvis."

Her voice dripped with sorghum syrup. Elvis wanted to hit her with his bed pan.

JOE R. LANSDALE

The nurse said to Callie: "Did you know we have a celebrity here, Miss Jones? Elvis Presley. You know, the rock and roll singer?"

"I've heard of him," Callie said. "I thought he was dead."

Callie went back to the dresser and squatted and set to work on the bottom drawer. The nurse looked at Elvis and smiled again, only she spoke to Callie.

"Well, actually, Elvis is dead, and Mr. Haff knows that, don't you, Mr. Haff?"

"Hell no," said Elvis. "I'm right here. I ain't dead, yet."

"Now, Mr. Haff, I don't mind calling you Elvis, but you're a little confused, or like to play sometimes. You were an Elvis impersonator. Remember? You fell off a stage and broke your hip. What was it . . . Twenty years ago? It got infected and you went into a coma for a few years. You came out with a few problems."

"I was impersonating myself," Elvis said. "I couldn't do nothing else. I haven't got any problems. You're trying to say my brain is messed up, aren't you?"

Callie quit cleaning out the bottom drawer of the dresser. She was interested now, and though it was no use, Elvis couldn't help but try and explain who he was, just one more time. The explaining had become a habit, like wanting to smoke a cigar long after the enjoyment of it was gone.

"I got tired of it all," he said. "I got on drugs, you know. I wanted out. Fella named Sebastian Haff, an Elvis imitator, the best of them. He took my place. He had a bad heart and he liked drugs, too. It was him died, not me. I took his place."

"Why would you want to leave all that fame," Callie said, "all that money?" and she looked at the nurse, like *Let's humor the old fart for a lark.*

"'Cause it got old. Woman I loved, Priscilla, she was gone. Rest of the women . . . were just women. The music wasn't mine anymore. I wasn't even me anymore. I was this thing they made up. Friends were sucking me dry. I got away and liked it, left all the money with Sebastian, except for enough to sustain me if things got bad. We had a deal, me and Sebastian. When I wanted to come back, he'd let me. It was all written up in a contract in case he wanted to give me a hard time, got to liking my life too good. Thing was, copy of the contract I had got lost in a trailer fire. I was living simple. Way Haff had been. Going from town to town doing the Elvis act. Only I felt like I was really me again. Can you dig that?"

"We're digging it, Mr. Haff . . . Mr. Presley," said the pretty nurse.

"I was singing the old way. Doing some new songs. Stuff I wrote. I was getting attention on a small but good scale. Women throwing themselves at me, 'cause they could imagine I was Elvis—only I was Elvis, playing Sebastian

Haff playing Elvis . . . It was all pretty good. I didn't mind the contract being burned up. I didn't even try to go back and convince anybody. Then I had the accident. Like I was saying, I'd laid up a little money in case of illness, stuff like that. That's what's paying for here. These nice facilities. Ha!"

"Now, Elvis," the nurse said. "Don't carry it too far. You may just get way out there and not come back."

"Oh fuck you," Elvis said.

The nurse giggled.

Shit, Elvis thought. *Get old, you can't even cuss somebody and have it bother them. Everything you do is either worthless or sadly amusing.*

"You know, Elvis," said the pretty nurse, "we have a Mr. Dillinger here too."

And a President Kennedy. He says the bullet only wounded him and his brain is in a fruit jar at the White House, hooked up to some wires and a battery, and as long as the battery works, he can walk around without it. His brain, that is. You know, he says everyone was in on trying to assassinate him. Even Elvis Presley."

"You're an asshole," Elvis said.

"I'm not trying to hurt your feelings, Mr. Haff," the nurse said. "I'm merely trying to give you a reality check."

"You can shove that reality check right up your pretty black ass," Elvis said.

The nurse made a sad little snicking sound. "Mr. Haff, Mr. Haff. Such language."

"What happened to get you here?" said Callie. "Say you fell off a stage?"

"I was gyrating," Elvis said. "Doing 'Blue Moon,' but my hip went out. I'd been having trouble with it." Which was quite true. He'd sprained it making love to a blue-haired old lady with Elvis tattooed on her fat ass. He couldn't help himself from wanting to fuck her. She looked like his mother, Gladys.

"You swiveled right off the stage?" Callie said. "Now that's sexy."

Elvis looked at her. She was smiling. This was great fun for her, listening to some nut tell a tale. She hadn't had this much fun since she put her old man in the rest home.

270

"Oh, leave me the hell alone," Elvis said.

The women smiled at one another, passing a private joke. Callie said to the nurse: "I've got what I want." She scraped the bright things off the top of Bull's dresser into her purse. "The clothes can go to Goodwill or the Salvation Army."

The pretty nurse nodded to Callie. "Very well. And I'm very sorry about your father. He was a nice man."

"Yeah," said Callie, and she started out of there. She paused at the foot of Elvis's bed. "Nice to meet you, Mr. Presley."

"Get the hell out," Elvis said.

"Now, now," said the pretty nurse, patting his foot through the covers, as if it were a little cantankerous dog. "I'll be back later to do that . . . little thing that has to be done. You know?"

"I know," Elvis said, not liking the words "little thing."

Callie and the nurse started away then, punishing him with the clean lines of their faces and the sheen of their hair, the jiggle of their asses and tits. When they were out of sight, Elvis heard them laugh about something in the hall, then they were gone, and Elvis felt as if he were on the far side of Pluto without a jacket. He picked up the ribbon with the Purple Heart and looked at it.

Poor Bull. In the end, did anything really matter?

Meanwhile . . .

The Earth swirled around the sun like a spinning turd in the toilet bowl (to keep up with Elvis's metaphors) and the good old abused Earth clicked about on its axis and the hole in the ozone spread slightly wider, like a shy lady fingering open her vagina, and the South American trees that had stood for centuries, were visited by the dozer, the chainsaw and the match, and they rose up in burned black puffs that expanded and dissipated into minuscule wisps, and while the puffs of smoke dissolved, there were IRA bombings in London, and there was more war in the Mideast. Blacks died in Africa of famine, the HIV virus infected a million more, the Dallas Cowboys lost again, and that Ole Blue Moon that Elvis and Patsy Cline sang so well about, swung around the Earth and came in close and rose over the Shady Grove Convalescent Home, shone its bittersweet, silver-blue rays down on the joint like a flashlight beam shining through a blue-haired lady's 'do, and inside the rest home, evil waddled about like a duck looking for a spot to squat, and Elvis rolled over in his sleep and awoke with the intense desire to pee.

All right, thought Elvis. *This time I make it.* No more piss or crap in the bed. (Famous last words.)

Elvis sat up and hung his feet over the side of the bed and the bed swung far to the left and around the ceiling and back, and then it wasn't moving at all. The dizziness passed.

Elvis looked at his walker and sighed, leaned forward, took hold of the grips and eased himself off the bed and clumped the rubber padded tips forward, and made for the toilet.

He was in the process of milking his bump-swollen weasel, when he heard something in the hallway—a kind of scrambling, like a big spider scuttling about in a box of gravel.

There was always some sound in the hallway, people coming and going, yelling in pain or confusion, but this time of night, three a.m., was normally quite dead.

It shouldn't have concerned him, but the truth of the matter was, now that he was up and had successfully pissed in the pot, he was no longer sleepy; he was still thinking about that bimbo, Callie, and the nurse (what the hell was her name?) with the tits like grapefruits, and all they had said.

Elvis stumped his walker backwards out of the bathroom, turned it, made his way forward into the hall. The hall was semi-dark, with every other light out, and the lights that were on were dimmed to a watery egg yolk yellow. The black and white tile floor looked like a great chessboard, waxed and buffed for the next game of life, and here he was, a semi-crippled pawn, ready to go.

Off in the far wing of the home, Old Lady McGee, better known in the home as The Blue Yodeler, broke into one of her famous yodels (she claimed to have sung with a country and western band in her youth), then ceased abruptly. Elvis swung the walker forward and moved on. He hadn't been out of his room in ages, and he hadn't been out of his bed much either. Tonight, he felt invigorated because he hadn't pissed his bed, and he'd heard the sound again, the spider in the box of gravel. (Big spider. Big box. Lots of gravel.) And following the sound gave him something to do.

Elvis rounded the corner, beads of sweat popping out on his forehead like heat blisters. Jesus. He wasn't invigorated now. Thinking about how invigorated he was had bushed him. Still, going back to his room to lie on his bed and wait for morning so he could wait for noon, then afternoon and night, didn't appeal to him.

He went by Jack McLaughlin's room, the fellow who was convinced he was John F. Kennedy, and that his brain was in the White House running on batteries. The door to Jack's room was open. Elvis peeked in as he moved by, knowing full well that Jack might not want to see him. Sometimes he accepted Elvis as the real Elvis, and when he did, he got scared, saying it was Elvis who had been behind the assassination.

Actually, Elvis hoped he felt that way tonight. It would at least be some acknowledgment that he was who he was, even if the acknowledgment was a fearful shriek from a nut.

'Course, Elvis thought, *maybe I'm nuts too. Maybe I am Sebastian Haff and I fell off the stage and broke more than my hip, cracked some part of my brain that lost my old self and made me think I'm Elvis.*

No. He couldn't believe that. That's the way they wanted him to think. They wanted him to believe he was nuts and he wasn't Elvis, just some sad old fart who had once lived out part of another man's life because he had none of his own. He wouldn't accept that. He wasn't Sebastian Haff. He was Elvis Goddamn Aaron Fucking Presley with a boil on his dick. 'Course, he believed that, maybe he ought to believe Jack was John F. Kennedy, and Mums Delay, another patient here at Shady Grove, was Dillinger. Then again, maybe not. They were kind of scanty on evidence. He at least looked like Elvis gone old and sick. Jack was black—he claimed The Powers That Be had dyed him that color to keep him hidden—and Mums was a woman who claimed she'd had a sex change operation.

Jesus, was this a rest home or a nut house?

Jack's room was one of the special kind. He didn't have to share. He had money from somewhere. The room was packed with books and little luxuries. And though Jack could walk well, he even had a fancy electric wheelchair that he rode about in sometimes. Once, Elvis had seen him riding it around the outside circular drive, popping wheelies and spinning doughnuts.

When Elvis looked into Jack's room, he saw him lying on the floor. Jack's gown was pulled up around his neck, and his bony black ass appeared to be made of licorice in the dim light. Elvis figured Jack had been on his way to the shitter, or was coming back from it, and had collapsed. His heart, maybe.

"Jack," Elvis said.

Elvis clumped into the room, positioned his walker next to Jack, took a deep breath and stepped out of it, supporting himself with one side of it. He got down on his knees beside Jack, hoping he'd be able to get up again. God, but his knees and back hurt.

Jack was breathing hard. Elvis noted the scar at Jack's hairline, a long scar that made Jack's skin lighter there, almost grey. ("That's where they took the brain out," Jack always explained, "put it in that fucking jar. I got a little bag of sand up there now.")

Elvis touched the old man's shoulder. "Jack. Man, you okay?"

No response.

Elvis tried again. "Mr. Kennedy."

"Uh," said Jack (Mr. Kennedy).

"Hey, man. You're on the floor," Elvis said.

"No shit? Who are you?"

Elvis hesitated. This wasn't the time to get Jack worked up.

"Sebastian," he said. "Sebastian Haff."

Elvis took hold of Jack's shoulder and rolled him over. It was about as difficult as rolling a jelly roll. Jack lay on his back now. He strayed an eyeball at Elvis. He started to speak, hesitated. Elvis took hold of Jack's nightgown and managed to work it down around Jack's knees, trying to give the old fart some dignity.

Jack finally got his breath. "Did you see him go by in the hall? He scuttled like."

"Who?"

"Someone they sent."

"Who's they?"

"You know. Lyndon Johnson. Castro. They've sent someone to finish me. I think maybe it was Johnson himself. Real ugly. Real goddamn ugly."

"Johnson's dead," Elvis said.

"That won't stop him," Jack said.

Later that morning, sunlight shooting into Elvis's room through Venetian blinds, Elvis put his hands behind his head and considered the night before while the pretty black nurse with the grapefruit tits salved his dick. He had reported Jack's fall and the aides had come to help Jack back in bed, and him back on his walker. He had clumped back to his room (after being scolded for being out there that time of night) feeling that an air of strangeness had blown into the rest home, an air that wasn't there the day before. It was at low ebb now, but certainly still present, humming in the background like some kind of generator ready to buzz up to a higher notch at a moment's notice.

And he was certain it wasn't just his imagination. The scuttling sound he'd heard last night, Jack had heard it, too. What was that all about? It wasn't the sound of a walker, or a crip dragging their foot, or a wheelchair creeping along, it was something else, and now that he thought about it, it wasn't exactly spider legs in gravel, more like a roll of barbed wire tumbling across tile.

Elvis was so wrapped up in these considerations, he lost awareness of the nurse until she said, "Mr. Haff!"

"What . . . ?" He saw that she was smiling and looking down at her hands.

He looked too. There, nestled in one of her gloved palms was a massive, blue-veined hooter with a pus-filled bump on it the size of a pecan. It was *his* hooter and *his* pus-filled bump.

"You ole rascal," she said, and gently lowered his dick between his legs. "I think you better take a cold shower, Mr. Haff."

Elvis was amazed. That was the first time in years he'd had a boner like that. What gave here?

Then he realized what gave. He wasn't thinking about not being able to do it. He was thinking about something that interested him, and now, with something clicking around inside his head besides old memories and confusions, concerns about his next meal and going to the crapper, he had been given a dose of life again. He grinned his gums and what teeth were in them at the nurse. "You get in there with me," he said, "and I'll take that shower."

"You silly thing," she said, and pulled his nightgown down and stood and removed her plastic gloves and dropped them in the trash can beside his bed.

"Why don't you pull on it a little," Elvis said.

"You ought to be ashamed," the nurse said, but she smiled when she said it.

She left the room door open after she left. This concerned Elvis a little, but he felt his bed was at such an angle no one could look in, and if they did, tough luck. He wasn't going to look a gift hard-on in the pee-hole. He pulled the sheet over him and pushed his hands beneath the sheets and got his gown pulled up over his belly. He took hold of his snake and began to choke it with one hand, running his thumb over the pus-filled bump. With his other hand, he fondled his balls. He thought of Priscilla and the pretty black nurse and Bull's daughter and even the blue-haired fat lady with Elvis tattooed on her butt, and he stroked harder and faster, and goddamn but he got stiffer and stiffer, and the bump on his cock gave up its load first, exploded hot pus down his thighs, and then his balls, which he thought forever empty, filled up with juice and electricity, and finally he threw the switch. The dam broke and the juice flew. He heard himself scream happily and felt hot wetness jetting down his legs, splattering as far as his big toes.

"Oh God," he said softly. "I like that. I like that."

He closed his eyes and slept. And for the first time in a long time, not fitfully.

Lunchtime. The Shady Grove lunch room.

Elvis sat with a plate of steamed carrots and broccoli and flaky roast beef in front of him. A dry roll, a pat of butter and a short glass of milk soldiered on the side. It was not inspiring.

278

Next to him, The Blue Yodeler was stuffing a carrot up her nose while she expounded on the sins of God, the Heavenly Father, for knocking up that nice Mary in her sleep, slipping up her ungreased poontang while she snored, and—bless her little heart—not even knowing it, or getting a clit throb from it, but waking up with a belly full of baby and no memory of action.

Elvis had heard it all before. It used to offend him, this talk of God as rapist, but he'd heard it so much now he didn't care. She rattled on.

Across the way, an old man who wore a black mask and sometimes a white Stetson, known to residents and staff alike as Kemosabe, snapped one of his two capless cap pistols at the floor and called for an invisible Tonto to bend over so he could drive him home.

At the far end of the table, Dillinger was talking about how much whisky he used to drink, and how many cigars he used to smoke before he got his dick cut off at the stump and split so he could become a she and hide out as a woman. Now she said she no longer thought of banks and machine guns, women and fine cigars. She now thought about spots on dishes, the colors of curtains and drapes as coordinated with carpets and walls.

Even as the depression of his surroundings settled over him again, Elvis deliberated last night, and glanced down the length of the table at Jack (Mr. Kennedy) who headed its far end. He saw the old man was looking at him, as if they shared a secret. Elvis's ill mood dropped a notch; a real mystery was at work here, and come nightfall, he was going to investigate.

Swing the Shady Grove Convalescent Home's side of the Earth away from the sun again, and swing the moon in close and blue again. Blow some gauzy clouds across the nasty, black sky. Now ease on into three a.m.

Elvis awoke with a start and turned his head toward the intrusion. Jack stood next to the bed looking down at him. Jack was wearing a suit coat over his nightgown and he had on thick glasses. He said, "Sebastian. It's loose."

Elvis collected his thoughts, pasted them together into a not-too-scattered collage. "What's loose?"

"It," said Jack. "Listen."

Elvis listened. Out in the hall he heard the scuttling sound of the night before. Tonight, it reminded him of great locust wings beating frantically inside a small cardboard box, the tips of them scratching at the cardboard, cutting it, ripping it apart.

"Jesus Christ, what is it?" Elvis said.

"I thought it was Lyndon Johnson, but it isn't. I've come across new evidence that suggests another assassin."

"Assassin?"

Jack cocked an ear. The sound had gone away, moved distant, then ceased. "It's got another target tonight," said Jack. "Come on. I want to show you something. I don't think it's safe if you go back to sleep."

"For Christ's sake," Elvis said. "Tell the administrators."

"The suits and the white starches," Jack said. "No

thanks. I trusted them back when I was in Dallas, and look where that got my brain and me. I'm thinking with sand here, maybe picking up a few waves from my brain. Someday, who's to say they won't just disconnect the battery at the White House?"

"That's something to worry about, all right," Elvis said.

"Listen here," Jack said. "I know you're Elvis, and there were rumors, you know . . . about how you hated me, but I've thought it over. You hated me, you could have finished me the other night. All I want from you is to look me in the eye and assure me you had nothing to do with that day in Dallas, and that you never knew Lee Harvey Oswald or Jack Ruby."

Elvis stared at him as sincerely as possible. "I had nothing to do with Dallas, and I knew neither Lee Harvey Oswald or Jack Ruby."

"Good," said Jack. "May I call you Elvis instead of Sebastian?"

"You may."

"Excellent. You wear glasses to read?"

"I wear glasses when I really want to see," Elvis said.

"Get 'em and come on."

Elvis swung his walker along easily, not feeling as if he needed it too much tonight. He was excited. Jack was a nut, and maybe he himself was nuts, but there was an adventure going on.

They came to the hall restroom. The one reserved for male visitors. "In here," Jack said.

"Now wait a minute," Elvis said. "You're not going to get me in there and try and play with my pecker, are you?"

Jack stared at him. "Man, I made love to Jackie and Marilyn and a ton of others, and you think I want to play with your nasty ole dick?"

"Good point," said Elvis.

They went into the restroom. It was large, with several stalls and urinals.

"Over here," said Jack. He went over to one of the stalls and pushed open the door and stood back by the commode to make room for Elvis's walker.

Elvis eased inside and looked at what Jack was now pointing to.

Graffiti.

"That's it?" Elvis said. "We're investigating a scuttling in the hall, trying to discover who attacked you last night, and you bring me in here to show me stick pictures on the shit house wall?"

"Look close," Jack said.

Elvis leaned forward. His eyes weren't what they used to be, and his glasses probably needed to be upgraded, but he could see that instead of writing, the graffiti was a series of simple pictorials.

A thrill, like a shot of good booze, ran through Elvis. He had once been a fanatic reader of ancient and esoteric lore, like *The Egyptian Book of the Dead* and *The Complete Works of H. P. Lovecraft,* and straight away he recognized what he was staring at. "Egyptian hieroglyphics," he said.

"Right-a-reen-O," Jack said. "Hey, you're not as stupid as some folks made you out."

"Thanks," Elvis said.

Jack reached into his suit coat pocket and took out a folded piece of paper and unfolded it. He pressed it to the wall. Elvis saw that it was covered with the same sort of figures that were on the wall of the stall.

"I copied this down yesterday. I came in here to shit because they hadn't cleaned up my bathroom. I saw this on the wall, went back to my room and looked it up in my books and wrote it all down. The top line translates something like: *Pharaoh gobbles donkey goober*. And the bottom line is: *Cleopatra does the dirty*."

"What?"

"Well, pretty much," Jack said.

Elvis was mystified. "All right," he said. "One of the nuts here, present company excluded, thinks he's Tutankhamun or something, and he writes on the wall in hieroglyphics. So what? I mean, what's the connection? Why are we hanging out in a toilet?"

"I don't know how they connect exactly," Jack said. "Not yet. But this . . . thing, it caught me asleep last night, and I came awake just in time to . . . well, he had me on the floor and had his mouth over my asshole."

"A shit eater?" Elvis said.

"I don't think so," Jack said. "He was after my soul. You can get that out of any of the major orifices in a person's body. I've read about it."

"Where?" Elvis asked. *Hustler?*

"The Everyday Man or Woman's Book of the Soul

by David Webb. It has some pretty good movie reviews about stolen soul movies in the back, too."

"Oh, that sounds trustworthy," Elvis said.

They went back to Jack's room and sat on his bed and looked through his many books on astrology, the Kennedy assassination, and a number of esoteric tomes, including the philosophy book, *The Everyday Man or Woman's Book of the Soul.*

Elvis found that book fascinating in particular; it indicated that not only did humans have a soul, but that the soul could be stolen, and there was a section concerning vampires and ghouls and incubi and succubi, as well as related soul suckers. Bottom line was, one of those dudes was around, you had to watch your holes. Mouth hole. Nose hole. Asshole. If you were a woman, you needed to watch a different hole. Dick pee-holes and ear holes—male or female—didn't matter. The soul didn't hang out there. They weren't considered major orifices for some reason.

In the back of the book was a list of items, related and not related to the book, that you could buy. Little plastic pyramids. Hats you could wear while channeling. Subliminal tapes that would help you learn Arabic. Postage was paid.

"Every kind of soul eater is in that book except politicians and science fiction fans," Jack said. "And I think that's what we got here in Shady Grove. A soul eater. Turn to the Egyptian section."

Elvis did. The chapter was prefaced by a movie still from *The Ten Commandments* with Yul Brynner playing Pharaoh. He was standing up in his chariot looking serious, which seemed a fair enough expression, considering the Red Sea, which had been parted by Moses, was about to come back together and drown him and his army.

Elvis read the article slowly while Jack heated water with his plug-in heater and made cups of instant coffee. "I get my niece to smuggle this stuff in," said Jack. "Or she claims to be my niece. She's a black woman. I never saw her before I was shot that day in Dallas and they took my brain out. She's part of the new identity they've given me. She's got a great ass."

"Damn," said Elvis. "What it says here, is that you can bury some dude, and if he gets the right tanna leaves and spells said over him and such bullshit, he can come back to life some thousands of years later, and to stay alive, he has to suck on the souls of the living, and that if the souls are small, his life force doesn't last long. Small. What's that mean?"

"Read on . . . No, never mind, I'll tell you." Jack handed Elvis his cup of coffee and sat down on the bed next to him. "Before I do, want a Ding Dong? Not mine. The chocolate kind. Well, I guess mine is chocolate, now that I've been dyed."

"You got Ding Dongs?" Elvis asked.

"Couple of PayDays and Baby Ruth too," Jack said. "Which will it be? Let's get decadent."

Elvis licked his lips. "I'll have a Ding Dong."

While Elvis savored the Ding Dong, gumming it sloppily, sipping his coffee between bites, Jack, coffee cup balanced on his knee, a Baby Ruth in one mitt, expounded.

"Small souls means those without much fire for life," Jack said. "You know a place like that?"

"If souls were fires," Elvis said, "they couldn't burn

much lower without being out than here. Only thing we got going in this joint is the pilot light."

"Exactamundo," Jack said. "What we got here in Shady Grove is an Egyptian soul sucker of some sort. A mummy hiding out, coming in here to feed on the sleeping. It's perfect, you see. The souls are little, and don't provide him with much. If this thing comes back two or three times in a row to wrap his lips around some elder's asshole, that elder is going to die pretty soon, and who's the wiser? Our mummy may not be getting much energy out of this, way he would with big souls, but the prey is easy. A mummy couldn't be too strong, really. Mostly just husk. But we're pretty much that way ourselves. We're not too far off being mummies."

"And with new people coming in all the time," Elvis said, "he can keep this up forever, this soul robbing."

"That's right. Because that's what we're brought here for. To get us out of the way until we die. And the ones don't die first of disease, or just plain old age, he gets."

Elvis considered all that. "That's why he doesn't bother the nurses and aides and administrators? He can go unsuspected."

"That, and they're not asleep. He has to get you when you're sleeping or unconscious."

"All right, but the thing throws me, Jack, is how does an ancient Egyptian end up in an East Texas rest home, and why is he writing on shit house walls?"

"He went to take a crap, got bored, and wrote on the wall. He probably wrote on pyramid walls, centuries ago."

"What would he crap?" Elvis said. "It's not like he'd eat, is it?"

"He eats souls," Jack said, "so I assume, he craps soul residue. And what that means to me is, you die by his mouth, you don't go to the other side, or wherever souls go. He digests the souls 'til they don't exist anymore—"

"And you're just so much toilet-water decoration," Elvis said.

"That's the way I've got it worked out," Jack said. "He's just like anyone else when he wants to take a dump. He likes a nice clean place with a flush. They didn't have that in his time, and I'm sure he finds it handy. The writing on the walls is just habit. Maybe, to him, Pharaoh and Cleopatra were just yesterday."

Elvis finished off the Ding Dong and sipped his coffee. He felt a rush from the sugar and he loved it. He wanted to ask Jack for the PayDay he had mentioned, but restrained himself. Sweets, fried foods, late nights and drugs had been the beginning of his original downhill spiral. He had to keep himself collected this time. He had to be ready to battle the Egyptian soul-sucking menace.

Soul-sucking menace?

God. He was really bored. It was time for him to go back to his room and to bed so he could shit on himself, get back to normal.

But Jesus and Ra, this was different from what had been going on up until now! It might all be bullshit, but considering what was going on in his life right now, it was absorbing bullshit. It might be worth playing the game to the hilt, even if he was playing it with a black guy who thought he was John F. Kennedy and believed an Egyptian mummy was stalking the corridors of Shady Grove Convalescent Home, writing graffiti on toilet stalls, sucking people's souls out through their assholes, digesting them, and crapping them down the visitors' toilet.

Suddenly, Elvis was pulled out of his considerations. There came from the hall the noise again. The sound that each time he heard it reminded him of something different. This time it was dried corn husks being rattled in a high wind. He felt goose bumps travel up his spine and the hairs on the back of his neck and arms stood up. He leaned forward and put his hands on his walker and pulled himself upright.

"Don't go in the hall," Jack said.

"I'm not asleep."

"That doesn't mean it won't hurt you."

"'It' my ass, there isn't any mummy from Egypt."

"Nice knowing you, Elvis."

Elvis inched the walker forward. He was halfway to the open door when he spied the figure in the hallway.

As the thing came even with the doorway, the hall lights went dim and sputtered. Twisting about the apparition, like pet crows, were flutters of shadows. The thing walked and stumbled, shuffled and flowed. Its legs moved like Elvis' own, meaning not too good, and yet, there was something about its locomotion that was impossible to identify. Stiff, but ghostly smooth. It was dressed in nasty looking jeans, a black shirt and a black cowboy hat that came down so low it covered where the thing's eyebrows should be. It wore large cowboy boots with the toes curled up, and there came from the thing a kind of mixed-stench: a compost pile of mud, rotting leaves, resin, spoiled fruit, dry dust and gassy sewage.

Elvis found that he couldn't scoot ahead another inch. He froze. The thing stopped and cautiously turned its head on its apple stem neck and looked at Elvis with empty eye sockets, revealing that it was, in fact, uglier than Lyndon Johnson.

Surprisingly, Elvis found he was surging forward as if on a zooming camera dolly, and that he was plunging into the thing's right eye socket, which swelled speedily to the dimensions of a vast canyon bottomed by blackness.

Down Elvis went, spinning and spinning, and out of the emptiness rushed resin-scented memories of pyramids and boats on a river, hot, blue skies, and a great silver bus lashed hard by black rain, a crumbling bridge and a charge of dusky water and a gleam of silver. Then there was a darkness so caliginous it was beyond being called dark, and Elvis could feel and taste mud in his mouth and a sensation of claustrophobia beyond expression. And he could perceive the thing's hunger, a hunger that prodded him like hot pins, and then—

—there came a *popping* sound in rapid succession, and Elvis felt himself whirling even faster, spinning backwards out of that deep memory canyon of the dusty head, and now he stood once again within the framework of his walker, and the mummy—for Elvis no longer denied to himself that it was such—turned its head away and began to move again, to shuffle, to flow, to stumble, to glide, down the hall, its pet shadows screeching with rusty throats around its head. *Pop! Pop! Pop!*

As the thing moved on, Elvis compelled himself to

lift his walker and advance into the hall. Jack slipped up beside him, and they saw the mummy in cowboy clothes traveling toward the exit door at the back of the home. When it came to the locked door, it leaned against where the door met the jamb and twisted and writhed, squeezed through the invisible crack where the two connected. Its shadows pursued it, as if sucked through by a vacuum cleaner.

The popping sound went on, and Elvis turned his head in that direction, and there, in his mask, his double concho-studded holster belted around his waist, was Kemosabe, a silver Fanner Fifty in either hand. He was popping caps rapidly at where the mummy had departed, the black spotted red rolls flowing out from behind the hammers of his revolvers in smoky relay.

"Asshole!" Kemosabe said. "Asshole!"

And then Kemosabe quivered, dropped both hands, popped a cap from each gun toward the ground, stiffened, collapsed.

Elvis knew he was dead of a ruptured heart before he hit the black and white tile; gone down and out with both guns blazing, soul intact.

The hall lights trembled back to normal.

The administrators, the nurses and the aides came then. They rolled Kemosabe over and drove their palms against his chest, but he didn't breathe again. No more Hi-Yo-Silver. They sighed over him and clucked their tongues, and finally an aide reached over and lifted Kemosabe's mask, pulled it off his head and dropped it on the floor, nonchalantly, and without respect, revealed his identity.

It was no one anyone really knew.

Once again, Elvis got scolded, and this time he got quizzed about what had happened to Kemosabe, and so did Jack, but neither told the truth. Who was going to believe a couple of nuts? Elvis and Jack Kennedy explaining that Kemosabe was gunning for a mummy in cowboy duds, a Bubba Ho-Tep with a flock of shadows roiling about his cowboy-hatted head?

So, what they did was lie.

"He came snapping caps and then he fell," Elvis said, and Jack corroborated his story and when Kemosabe had been carried off, Elvis, with some difficulty, using his walker for support, got down on his knee and picked up the discarded mask and carried it away with him. He had wanted the guns, but an aide had taken those for her four-year-old son.

Later, he and Jack learned through the grapevine that Kemosabe's roommate, an eighty-year-old man who had been in a semi-comatose condition for several years, had been found dead on the floor of his room. It was assumed Kemosabe had lost it and dragged him off his bed and onto the floor and the eighty-year-old man had kicked the bucket during the fall. As for Kemosabe, they figured he had then gone nuts when he realized what he had done, and had wandered out in the hall firing, and had a heart attack.

Elvis knew different. The mummy had come and Kemosabe had tried to protect his roommate in the only way he knew how. But instead of silver bullets, his gun smoked sulphur. Elvis felt a rush of pride in the old fart.

He and Jack got together later, talked about what they had seen, and then there was nothing left to say.

Night went away and the sun came up, and Elvis, who had slept not a wink, came up with it and put on khaki pants and a khaki shirt and used his walker to go outside. It had been ages since he had been out, and it seemed strange out there, all that sunlight and the smells of flowers and the Texas sky so high and the clouds so white.

It was hard to believe he had spent so much time in his bed. Just the use of his legs with the walker these last few days had tightened the muscles, and he found he could get around better.

The pretty nurse with the grapefruit tits came outside and said: "Mr. Presley, you look so much stronger. But you shouldn't stay out too long. It's almost time for a nap and for us, too, you know . . ."

"Fuck off, you patronizing bitch," said Elvis. "I'm tired of your shit. I'll lube my own transmission. You treat me like a baby again, I'll wrap this goddamn walker around your head."

The pretty nurse stood stunned, then went away quietly.

Elvis inched his way with the walker around the great circular drive that surrounded the home. It was a half hour later when he reached the back of the home and the door through which the mummy had departed. It was still locked, and he stood and looked at it amazed. How in hell had the mummy done that, slipping through an indiscernible chink between door and frame?

Elvis looked down at the concrete that lay at the back of the door. No clues there. He used the walker to travel toward the growth of trees out back, a growth of pin-oaks and sweet gums and hickory nut trees that shouldered on either side of the large creek that flowed behind the home.

The ground tipped sharply there, and for a moment he hesitated, then reconsidered. *Well, what the fuck?* he thought.

He planted the walker and started going forward, the ground sloping ever more dramatically. By the time he reached the bank of the creek and came to a gap in the trees, he was exhausted. He had the urge to start yelling for help, but didn't want to belittle himself, not after his performance with the nurse.

He knew that he had regained some of his former confidence. His cursing and abuse had not seemed cute to her that time. The words had bitten her, if only slightly. Truth was, he was going to miss her greasing his pecker.

He looked over the bank of the creek. It was quite a drop there. The creek itself was narrow, and on either side of it was a gravel-littered six feet of shore. To his left, where the creek ran beneath a bridge, he could see where a mass of weeds and mud had gathered over time, and he could see something shiny in their midst.

Elvis eased to the ground inside his walker and sat there and looked at the water churning along. A huge woodpecker laughed in a tree nearby and a jay yelled at a smaller bird to leave his territory.

Where had ole Bubba Ho-Tep gone? Where did he come from? How in hell did he get here?

He recalled what he had seen inside the mummy's mind. The silver bus, the rain, the shattered bridge, the wash of water and mud.

Well, now wait a minute, he thought. Here we have water and mud and a bridge, though it's not broken, and there's something shiny in the midst of all those leaves and limbs and collected debris. All these items were elements of what he had seen in Bubba Ho-Tep's head. Obviously there was a connection.

But what was it?

When he got his strength back, Elvis pulled himself up and got the walker turned, and worked his way back to the home. He was covered in sweat and stiff as wire by the time he reached his room and tugged himself into bed. The blister on his dick throbbed and he unfastened his pants and eased down his underwear. The blister had refilled with pus, and it looked nastier than usual.

It's a cancer, he determined. He made the conclusion in a certain final rush.

They're keeping it from me because I'm old and to them it doesn't matter. They think age will kill me first, and they are probably right.

Well, fuck them. I know what it is, and if it isn't, it might as well be.

He got the salve and doctored the pus-filled lesion, and put the salve away, and pulled up his underwear and pants, and fastened his belt.

Elvis got his tv remote off the dresser and clicked it on while he waited for lunch. As he ran the channels, he hit upon an advertisement for Elvis Presley week. It startled him. It wasn't the first time it had happened, but at the moment it struck him hard. It showed clips from his movies, *Clambake, Roustabout,* several others. All shit movies. Here he was complaining about loss of pride and how life had treated him, and now he realized he'd never had any pride and much of how life had treated him had been quite good, and the bulk of the bad had been his own fault. He wished now he'd fired his manager, Colonel Parker, about the time he got into films. The old fart had been a fool, and he had been a bigger fool for following him. He wished too he had treated Priscilla right. He wished he could tell his daughter he loved her.

Always the questions. Never the answers. Always the hopes. Never the fulfillments.

Elvis clicked off the set and dropped the remote on the dresser just as Jack came into the room. He had a folder under his arm. He looked like he was ready for a briefing at the White House.

"I had the woman who calls herself my niece come get me," he said. "She took me downtown to the newspaper morgue. She's been helping me do some research."

"On what?" Elvis said.

"On our mummy."

"You know something about him?" Elvis asked.

"I know plenty."

Jack pulled a chair up next to the bed, and Elvis used the bed's lift button to raise his back and head so he could see what was in Jack's folder.

Jack opened the folder, took out some clippings, and laid them on the bed.

Elvis looked at them as Jack talked.

"One of the lesser mummies, on loan from the Egyptian government, was being circulated across the United States. You know, museums, that kind of stuff. It wasn't a major exhibit, like the King Tut exhibit some years back, but it was of interest. The mummy was flown or carried by train from state to state.

When it got to Texas, it was stolen.

"Evidence points to the fact that it was stolen at night by a couple of guys in a silver bus. There was a witness. Some guy walking his dog or something. Anyway, the thieves broke into the museum and stole it, hoping to get a ransom probably. But in came the worst storm in East Texas history. Tornadoes. Rain. Hail. You name it. Creeks and rivers overflowed. Mobile homes were washed away. Livestock drowned. Maybe you remember it . . . No matter. It was one hell of a flood.

"These guys got away, and nothing was ever heard from them. After you told me what you saw inside the mummy's head—the silver bus, the storm, the bridge, all that—I came up with a more interesting, and I believe, considerably more accurate scenario."

"Let me guess. The bus got washed away. I think I saw it today. Right out back in the creek. It must have washed up there years ago."

"That confirms it. The bridge you saw breaking, that's how the bus got in the water, which would have been as deep then as a raging river. The bus was carried downstream. It lodged somewhere nearby, and the mummy was imprisoned by debris, and recently it worked its way loose."

"But how did it come alive?" Elvis asked. "And how did I end up inside its memories?"

"The speculation is broader here, but from what I've read, sometimes mummies were buried without their names, a curse put on their sarcophagus, or coffin, if you will. My guess is our guy was one of those. While he was in the coffin, he was a drying corpse. But when the bus was washed off the road, the coffin was overturned, or broken open, and our boy was freed of coffin and curse. Or more likely, it rotted open in time, and the holding spell was broken. And think about him down there all that time, waiting for freedom, alive, but not alive. Hungry, and no way to feed. I said he was free of his curse, but that's not entirely true. He's free of his imprisonment, but he still needs souls.

"And now, he's free to have them, and he'll keep feeding unless he's finally destroyed . . . You know, I think there's a part of him, oddly enough, that wants to fit in. To be human again. He doesn't entirely know what he's become. He responds to some old desires and the new desires of his condition. That's why he's taken on the illusion of clothes, probably copying the dress of one of his victims.

"The souls give him strength. Increase his spectral powers. One of which was to hypnotize you, kinda, draw you inside his head. He couldn't steal your soul that way, you have to be unconscious to have that done to you, but he could weaken you, distract you."

"And those shadows around him?"

"His guardians. They warn him. They have some limited powers of their own. I've read about them in *The Everyday Man or Woman's Book of the Soul*."

"What do we do?" Elvis asked.

"I think changing rest homes would be a good idea," Jack said. "I can't think of much else. I will say this. Our mummy is a nighttime kind of guy. Three a.m. actually. So, I'm going to sleep now, and again after lunch. Set my alarm for before dark so I can fix myself a couple cups of coffee. He comes tonight, I don't want him slapping his lips over my asshole again. I think he heard you coming down the hall about the time he got started on me the other night, and he ran. Not because he was scared, but because he didn't want anyone to find out he's around. Consider it. He has the proverbial bird's nest on the ground here."

After Jack left, Elvis decided he should follow Jack's lead and nap. Of course, at his age, he napped a lot anyway, and could fall asleep at any time, or toss restlessly for hours. There was no rhyme or reason to it.

He nestled his head into his pillow and tried to sleep, but sleep wouldn't come. Instead, he thought about things. Like, what did he really have left in life but this place? It wasn't much of a home, but it was all he had, and he'd be damned if he'd let a foreign, graffiti-writing, soul-sucking sonofabitch in an oversized hat and cowboy boots (with elf toes) take away his family members' souls and shit them down the visitors' toilet.

In the movies he had always played heroic types. But when the stage lights went out, it was time for drugs and stupidity and the coveting of women. Now it was time to be a little of what he had always fantasized being.

A hero.

Elvis leaned over and got hold of his telephone and dialed Jack's room. "Mr. Kennedy," Elvis said when Jack answered. "Ask not what your rest home can do for you. Ask what you can do for your rest home."

"Hey, you're copping my best lines," Jack said.

"Well then, to paraphrase one of my own, 'Let's take care of business.'"

"What are you getting at?"

"You know what I'm getting at. We're gonna kill a mummy."

The sun, like a boil on the bright blue ass of day, rolled gradually forward and spread its legs wide to reveal the pubic thatch of night, a hairy darkness in which stars crawled like lice, and the moon crabbed slowly upward like an albino dog tick striving for the anal gulch.

During this slow rolling transition, Elvis and Jack discussed their plans, then they slept a little, ate their lunch of boiled cabbage and meatloaf, slept some more, ate a supper of white bread and asparagus and a helping of shit on a shingle without the shingle, slept again, awoke about the time the pubic thatch appeared and those starry lice began to crawl.

And even then, with night about them, they had to wait until midnight to do what they had to do.

Jack squinted through his glasses and examined his list. "Two bottles of rubbing alcohol?" Jack said.

"Check," said Elvis. "And we won't have to toss it. Look here." Elvis held up a paint sprayer. "I found this in the storage room."

"I thought they kept it locked," Jack said.

"They do. But I stole a hair pin from Dillinger and picked the lock."

"Great!" Jack said. "Matches?"

"Check. I also scrounged a cigarette lighter."

"Good. Uniforms?"

Elvis held up his white suit, slightly greyed in spots with a chili stain on the front. A white silk scarf and the big gold and silver and ruby-studded belt that went with the outfit lay on the bed. There were zippered boots from K-Mart.

"Check."

Jack held up a grey business suit on a hanger. "I've got some nice shoes and a tie to go with it in my room."

"Check," Elvis said.

"Scissors?"

"Check."

"I've got my motorized wheelchair oiled and ready to roll," Jack said, "and I've looked up a few words of power in one of my magic books. I don't know if they'll stop a mummy, but they're supposed to ward off evil. I wrote them down on a piece of paper."

"We use what we got," Elvis said. "Well then. 2:45 out back of the place."

"Considering our rate of travel, better start moving about 2:30," Jack said.

"Jack," Elvis asked. "Do we know what we're doing?"

"No, but they say fire cleanses evil. Let's hope they, whoever they are, are right."

"Check on that, too," said Elvis. "Synchronize watches."

They did, and Elvis added: "Remember. The key words for tonight are *Caution* and *Flammable*. And *Watch Your Ass*."

The front door had an alarm system, but it was easily manipulated from the inside. Once Elvis had the wires cut with the scissors, they pushed the compression lever on the door, and Jack shoved his wheelchair outside, and held the door while Elvis worked his walker through. Elvis tossed the scissors into the shrubbery, and Jack jammed a paperback book between the doors to allow them re-entry, should re-entry be an option at a later date.

Elvis was wearing a large pair of glasses with multi-colored gem-studded chocolate frames and his stained white jumpsuit with scarf and belt and zippered boots. The suit was open at the front and hung loose on him, except at the belly. To make it even tighter there, Elvis had made up an Indian medicine bag of sorts, and stuffed it inside his jumpsuit. The bag contained Kemosabe's mask, Bull's Purple Heart, and the newspaper clipping where he had first read of his alleged death.

Jack had on his grey business suit with a black-and-red-striped tie knotted carefully at the throat, sensible black shoes, and black nylon socks. The suit fit him well. He looked like a former president.

In the seat of the wheelchair was the paint sprayer, filled with rubbing alcohol, and beside it, a cigarette lighter and a paper folder of matches. Jack handed Elvis the paint sprayer. A strap made of a strip of torn sheet had been added to the device. Elvis hung the sprayer over his shoulder, reached inside his belt and got out a flattened, half-smoked stogie he had been saving for a special occasion. An occasion he had begun to think would never arrive. He clenched the cigar between his teeth, picked the matches from the seat of the wheelchair, and lit his cigar. It tasted like a dog turd, but he puffed it anyway. He tossed the folder of matches back on the chair and looked at Jack, said, "Let's do it, amigo."

Jack put the matches and the lighter in his suit pocket. He sat down in the wheelchair, kicked the foot stanchions into place and rested his feet on them.

He leaned back slightly and flicked a switch on the arm rest. The electric motor hummed, the chair eased forward.

"Meet you there," said Jack. He rolled down the concrete ramp, on out to the circular drive, and disappeared around the edge of the building.

Elvis looked at his watch. It was nearly 2:45. He had to hump it. He clenched both hands on the walker and started truckin'.

Fifteen exhaustive minutes later, out back, Elvis settled in against the door, the place where Bubba Ho-Tep had been entering and exiting. The shadows fell over him like an umbrella. He propped the paint gun across the walker and used his scarf to wipe the sweat off his forehead.

In the old days, after a performance, he'd wipe his face with it and toss it to some woman in the crowd, watch as she creamed on herself. Panties and hotel keys would fly onto the stage at that point, bouquets of roses.

Tonight, he hoped Bubba Ho-Tep didn't use the scarf to wipe his ass after shitting him down the crapper.

Elvis looked where the circular concrete drive rose up slightly to the right, and there, seated in the wheelchair, very patient and still, was Jack. The moonlight spread over Jack and made him look like a concrete yard gnome.

Apprehension spread over Elvis like a dose of the measles. He thought: *Bubba Ho-Tep comes out of that creek bed, he's going to come out hungry and pissed, and when I try to stop him, he's going to jam this paint gun up my ass, then jam me and that wheelchair up Jack's ass.*

He puffed his cigar so fast it made him dizzy. He looked out at the creek bank, and where the trees gaped wide, a figure rose up like a cloud of termites, scrabbled like a crab, flowed like water, chunked and chinked like a mass of oil-field tools tumbling downhill.

Its eyeless sockets trapped the moonlight and held it momentarily before permitting it to pass through and out the back of its head in irregular gold beams. The figure that simultaneously gave the impression of shambling and gliding, appeared one moment as nothing more than a shadow surrounded by more active shadows, then it was a heap of twisted brown sticks and dried mud molded into the shape of a human being, and in another moment, it was a cowboy-hatted, booted thing taking each step as if it were its last.

Halfway to the rest home it spotted Elvis, standing in the dark framework of the door. Elvis felt his bowels go loose, but he was determined not to shit his only good stage suit. His knees clacked together like stalks of ribbon cane rattling in a high wind. The dog-turd cigar fell from his lips.

He picked up the paint gun and made sure it was ready to spray. He pushed the butt of it into his hip and waited.

Bubba Ho-Tep didn't move. He had ceased to come forward. Elvis began to sweat more than before. His face and chest and balls were soaked. If Bubba Ho-Tep didn't come forward, their plan was fucked. They had to get him in range of the paint sprayer. The idea was he'd soak him with the alcohol, and Jack would come wheeling down from behind, flipping matches or the lighter at Bubba, catching him on fire.

Elvis said softly, "Come and get it, you dead piece of shit."

Jack had nodded off for a moment, but now he came awake. His flesh was tingling. It felt as if tiny ball bearings were being rolled beneath his skin. He looked up and saw Bubba Ho-Tep paused between the creek bank, himself, and Elvis at the door.

Jack took a deep breath. This was not the way they had planned it. The mummy was supposed to go for Elvis because he was blocking the door. But, no soap.

Jack got the matches and the cigarette lighter out of his coat pocket and put them between his legs on the seat of the chair. He put his hand on the gear box of the wheelchair, gunned it forward. He had to make things happen; had to get Bubba Ho-Tep to follow him, come within range of Elvis' spray gun.

Bubba Ho-Tep stuck out his arm and clotheslined Jack Kennedy. There was a sound like a rifle crack (no question Warren Commission, this blow was from the front), and over went the chair, and out went Jack, flipping and sliding across the driveway, the cement tearing his suit knees open, gnawing into his hide. The chair, minus its rider, tumbled over and came upright, and still rolling, veered downhill toward Elvis in the doorway, leaning on his walker, spray gun in hand.

The wheelchair hit Elvis' walker. Elvis bounced against the door, popped forward, grabbed the walker just in time, but dropped his spray gun.

He glanced up to see Bubba Ho-Tep leaning over the unconscious Jack. Bubba Ho-Tep's mouth went wide, and wider yet, and became a black toothless vacuum that throbbed pink as a raw wound in the moonlight; then Bubba Ho-Tep turned his head and the pink was not visible. Bubba Ho-Tep's mouth went down over Jack's face, and as Bubba Ho-Tep sucked, the shadows about it thrashed and gobbled like turkeys.

Elvis used the walker to allow him to bend down and get hold of the paint gun. When he came up with it, he tossed the walker aside, eased himself around and into the wheelchair. He found the matches and the lighter there. Jack had done what he had done to distract Bubba Ho-Tep, to try and bring him down closer to the door. But he had failed. Yet by accident, he had provided Elvis with the instruments of mummy destruction, and now it was up to him to do what he and Jack had hoped to do together. Elvis put the matches inside his open-chested outfit, pushed the lighter tight under his ass.

Elvis let his hand play over the wheelchair switches, as nimbly as he had once played with studio keyboards. He roared the wheelchair up the incline toward Bubba Ho-Tep, terrified, but determined, and as he rolled, in a voice cracking, but certainly reminiscent of him at his best, he began to sing "Don't Be Cruel," and within instants, he was on Bubba Ho-Tep and his busy shadows.

Bubba Ho-Tep looked up as Elvis roared into range, singing. Bubba Ho-Tep's open mouth irised to normal size, and teeth, formerly non-existent, rose up in his gums like little, black stumps. Electric locusts crackled and hopped in his empty sockets. He yelled something in Egyptian. Elvis saw the words jump out of Bubba Ho-Tep's mouth in visible hieroglyphics like dark beetles and sticks:

Elvis bore down on Bubba Ho-Tep. When he was in range, he ceased sing-ing, and gave the paint sprayer trigger a squeeze. Rubbing alcohol squirted from the sprayer and struck Bubba Ho-Tep in the face.

Elvis swerved, screeched around Bubba Ho-Tep in a sweeping circle, came back, the lighter in his hand. As he neared Bubba, the shadows swarming around the mummy's head separated and flew high up above him like startled bats.

The black hat Bubba wore wobbled and sprouted wings and flapped away from his head, becoming what it had always been, a living shadow. The shadows came down in a rush, screeching like harpies. They swarmed over Elvis' face, giving him the sensation of skinned animal pelts—blood-side in—being dragged over his flesh.

Bubba bent forward at the waist like a collapsed puppet, and bopped his head against the cement drive. His black bat hat came down out of the dark in a swoop, expanding rapidly and falling over Bubba's body, splattering it like spilled ink. Bubba blob-flowed rapidly under the wheels of Elvis' mount and rose up in a dark swell beneath the chair and through the spokes of the wheels and billowed over the front of the chair and loomed upwards, jabbing his ravaged, ever-changing face through the flittering shadows, poking it right at Elvis.

Elvis, through gaps in the shadows, saw a face like

---

[1] *By the unwinking red eye of Ra!"*

an old jack-o'-lantern gone black and to rot, with jagged eyes, nose and mouth. And that mouth spread tunnel wide, and down that tunnel-mouth Elvis could see the dark and awful forever that was Bubba's lot, and Elvis clicked the lighter to flame, and the flame jumped, and the alcohol lit Bubba's face, and Bubba's head turned baby-eye blue, flowed jet-quick away, splashed upward like a black wave carrying a blazing oil slick. Then Bubba came down in a shuffle of blazing sticks and dark mud, a tar baby on fire, fleeing across the concrete drive toward the creek. The guardian shadows flapped after it, fearful of being abandoned.

Elvis wheeled over to Jack, leaned forward and whispered: "Mr. Kennedy."

Jack's eyelids fluttered. He could barely move his head, and something grated in his neck when he did. "The President is soon dead," he said, and his clenched fist throbbed and opened, and out fell a wad of paper. "You got to get him."

Jack's body went loose and his head rolled back on his damaged neck and the moon showed double in his eyes. Elvis swallowed and saluted Jack. "Mr. President," he said.

Well, at least he had kept Bubba Ho-Tep from taking Jack's soul. Elvis leaned forward, picked up the paper Jack had dropped. He read it aloud to himself in the moonlight: "You nasty thing from beyond the dead. No matter what you think and do, good things will never come to you. If evil is your black design, you can bet the goodness of the Light Ones will kick your bad behind."

That's it? thought Elvis. That's the chant against evil from the *Book of the Soul*? Yeah, right, boss. And what kind of decoder ring does that come with? Shit, it doesn't even rhyme well.

Elvis looked up. Bubba Ho-Tep had fallen down in a blue blaze, but he was rising up again, preparing to go over the lip of the creek, down to wherever his sanctuary was.

Elvis pulled around Jack and gave the wheelchair full throttle. He gave out with a rebel cry. His white scarf fluttered in the wind as he thundered forward.

Bubba Ho-Tep's flames had gone out. He was on his feet. His head was hissing grey smoke into the crisp night air. He turned completely to face Elvis, stood defiant, raised an arm and shook a fist. He yelled, and once again Elvis saw the hieroglyphics leap out of his mouth. The characters danced in a row, briefly—

2

—and vanished.

Elvis let go of the protective paper. It was dog shit. What was needed here was action.

When Bubba Ho-Tep saw Elvis was coming, chair geared to high, holding the paint sprayer in one hand, he turned to bolt, but Elvis was on him.

Elvis stuck out a foot and hit Bubba Ho-Tep in the back, and his foot went right through Bubba. The mummy squirmed, spitted on Elvis' leg. Elvis fired the paint sprayer, as Bubba Ho-Tep, himself, and chair,

---

2 *"Eat the dog dick of Anubis, you ass wipe!"*

went over the creek bank in a flash of moonlight and a tumble of shadows.

Elvis screamed as the hard ground and sharp stones snapped his body like a piñata. He made the trip with Bubba Ho-Tep still on his leg, and when he quit sliding, he ended up close to the creek.

Bubba Ho-Tep, as if made of rubber, twisted around on Elvis' leg, and looked at him.

Elvis still had the paint sprayer. He had clung to it as if it were a life preserver. He gave Bubba another dose. Bubba's right arm flopped way out and ran along the ground and found a hunk of wood that had washed up on the edge of the creek, gripped it, and swung the long arm back. The arm came around and hit Elvis on the side of the head with the wood.

Elvis fell backwards. The paint sprayer flew from his hands. Bubba Ho-Tep was leaning over him. He hit Elvis again with the wood. Elvis felt himself going out. He knew if he did, not only was he a dead sonofabitch, but so was his soul. He would be just so much crap; no afterlife for him; no reincarnation; no angels with harps. Whatever lay beyond would not be known to him. It would all end right here for Elvis Presley. Nothing left but a quick flush. Bubba Ho-Tep's mouth loomed over Elvis' face. It looked like an open manhole. Sewage fumes came out of it.

Elvis reached inside his open jumpsuit and got hold of the folder of matches.

Laying back, pretending to nod out so as to bring Bubba Ho-Tep's ripe mouth closer, he thumbed back the flap on the matches, thumbed down one of the paper sticks, and pushed the sulphurous head of the match across the black strip.

Just as Elvis felt the cloying mouth of Bubba Ho-Tep falling down on his kisser like a Venus flytrap, the entire folder of matches ignited in Elvis' hand, burned him and made him yell.

The alcohol on Bubba's body called the flames to it, and Bubba burst into a stalk of blue flame, singeing the hair off Elvis' head, scorching his eyebrows down to nubs, blinding him until he could see nothing more than a scalding white light.

Elvis realized that Bubba Ho-Tep was no longer on or over him, and the white light became a stained white light, then a grey light, and eventually, the world, like a Polaroid negative developing, came into view, greenish at first, then full of the night's colors.

Elvis rolled on his side and saw the moon floating in the water. He saw too a scarecrow floating in the water, the straw separating from it, the current carrying it away.

No, not a scarecrow. Bubba Ho-Tep. For all his dark magic and ability to shift, or to appear to shift, fire had done him in, or had it been the stupid words from Jack's book on souls? Or both?

It didn't matter. Elvis got up on one elbow and looked at the corpse. The water was dissolving it more rapidly and the current was carrying it away.

Elvis fell over on his back. He felt something inside him grate against something soft. He felt like a water balloon with a hole poked in it.

He was going down for the last count, and he knew it.

But I've still got my soul, he thought. Still mine. All mine. And the folks in Shady Grove, Dillinger, the Blue Yodeler, all of them, they have theirs, and they'll keep 'em.

Elvis stared up at the stars between the forked and twisted boughs of an oak. He could see a lot of those beautiful stars, and he realized now that the constellations looked a little like the outlines of great hieroglyphics. He turned away from where he was looking, and to his right, seeming to sit on the edge of the bank, were more stars, more hieroglyphics.

He rolled his head back to the figures above him, rolled to the right and looked at those. Put them together in his mind.

He smiled. Suddenly, he thought he could read hieroglyphics after all, and what they spelled out against the dark beautiful night was simple, and yet profound.

ALL IS WELL.

Elvis closed his eyes and did not open them again.

THE END

JOE R. LANSDALE

Thanks to

(Mark Nelson) for translating East Texas "Egyptian" Hieroglyphics.

 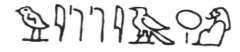

312

GORILLA MY DREAMS

JONATHAN MABERRY

"LET ME GET this straight, Mr. Karlson," said Abraham Schuster, "you want me to get you a major Broadway theater booking for a . . . gorilla?"

"Did I say 'gorilla'?" cried Jack Karlson. He began waving his hands, because that usually worked with people. They thought something important was happening. "No, did I say that it was 'just a gorilla?' I did not."

"You did say gorilla," Shuster assured him. "Those exact words. You hear that? It's inflection. Did I say this was only a gorilla? Did I, in fact, say it was only a regular gorilla? No, sir, that is not how I said it. Mr. Schuster, hold onto your toupee because I'm talking about the biggest damn ape you ever saw!"

Schuster leaned back in his chair. He wore a nice suit, but not a new one. Everything in the office was nice, but not new. It had been new before the Depression mugged the entire entertainment industry, picked everyone's pockets, and engendered within Schuster and all of his colleagues a talent for squeezing all the life out of every single penny.

"I've seen a lot of apes in my time," he said dryly. "One of them is dating my daughter."

"Yeah, well this one is different?"

Schuster steepled his fingers. "And, pray, *how* is he different? And please note that I, myself, have inflected, just to show you that I understand the concept. Now, tell me how your gorilla is different from every other gorilla in every monkey act that has come through vaudeville and the grander stages since . . . oh, let me see . . . Nero's Rome?"

"Well," said Karlson, "mine is big."

"As opposed to all of the midget gorillas walking around Manhattan?"

"No, no—I mean *really* big."

Schuster sighed. This was giving him a pain in one of his internal organs. His spleen perhaps. "How big is big?"

"Big is, well . . . really pretty big."

"Oh, thanks," said the booking agent, "that makes it so much clearer."

"No, I mean really, really, really big."

"That's a lot of reallys. Gadzooks, he must be a corker."

"Oh, he is!"

"Pardon me while I yawn."

"Yeah, yeah, crack jokes, Schuster, but I'm telling you, this is no ordinary ape."

"Oh, I believe you, Mr. Karlson, truly I do. You see it's just a matter of my not caring one little—"

"There's a girl."

Schuster paused. He leaned forward and placed his elbows on the desk, made fists, put them together like a ledge and leaned his chin on them. "Oh?" he said, drawing it out.

Karlson's eyes twinkled and he gave Schuster a

small wink of the kind that would make the father of any female children reach for something with which to hit him. However, Abraham Schuster had no daughters. He had sons. Four of them, and they were looking for wives. With the economy continuing its slide down a very smelly pipe and business as bad as it was, Schuster was hoping for one of them to marry money. Right now they all worked for Abraham's brother's meat packing plant, which was teetering on the edge of financial ruin because meat was expensive and without which there was nothing to pack. If something didn't turn things around, then the whole Shuster family was going to fold up and they would all be living in a car parked somewhere in New Jersey, most probably an unpaved road in the Pine Barrens. The booking agency right now was paying some of the bills, but the two bottom drawers of his desk were filled with the real truth about how things were going. The left-hand drawer was filled with unpaid bills, and the right was filled with bottles of very illegal gin.

The gin had been a gift from Uncle Morty, who was now doing six to twelve for running booze down from Canada. There was some talk in the papers about Prohibition being repealed, maybe as soon as December, but it hadn't happened yet.

"A girl, you say?"

"A pretty blonde," said Karlson.

"For future reference," said Schuster dryly, "your pitch would have been better if you'd led with the blonde."

"Instead of a really big gorilla?"

"In almost every instance, yes."

"It's a pretty special gorilla," Karlson assured him.

"Let's stick with the blond. What does she do?"

"Do?"

"Yes. What's her talent? What's the act?"

"She works with the ape."

"'Works with' . . . ?"

"I mean she has a special relationship with the ape."

"Ah," said Schuster, sitting back. "I see. Mr. Karlson, although times are tough here in New York, and although some members of my profession have taken to showcasing more, shall we say, outré, acts . . . I have just enough self respect left to abstain. I'm sure there are those other agents who would be eager for that kind of show, but surely Times Square is not the place for—"

"No, you don't get what I'm saying," growled Karlson, throwing up his hands. "The girl and the ape aren't like that. Don't be disgusting. They have a link, a bond. She's the queen to his king."

"A link? Yes. Yes, I'm sure they do; and there are doctors who can help the poor girl. But it just doesn't belong in front of a family audience."

"I'm telling you, this is a great act. The Eighth Wonder of the World!"

"Why are there always exclamations points implied in many of the things you say?"

Karlson ignored him because he was clearly in gear. "This is a classic, Schuster. It's a real 'Beauty and the Beast' story."

"Yes, I have read French magazines, but I—"

"No, no, this is on the level. Garganto is head over heels for the broad."

"Garganto?"

316

GORILLA MY DREAMS

"The ape."

"The ape's name is Garganto?"

"Yes."

"He's Chinese then, is that it?"

"No, he isn't Chinese. I don't think there are gorillas in China anyway. Not like this."

"What is he then?"

"Well, I dunno . . . I guess he's kind of South Pacifican. Comes from a place called Kaiju Shima."

"What's that mean?"

"Island of Very Big Monster Things. Or something like that."

"Mm. Sounds like a garden spot. Nicely lurid, though. Is this a real place?"

"Real? Why, it's a savage tropical jungle filled with monsters the likes of which man has never seen! Creatures from the very dawn of time."

"How would you know?"

"I've been there, I've seen them, I tell you!"

"Which means man *has* seen them, then . . . "

"Well, yes . . . but—"

"Well, I'm sure Garganto of Kaiju Shima is very interesting, Mr. Karlson, but this Broadway."

"We could call him *Prince Garganto*!"

"'Prince Garganto'?"

"Sure, he was the prince of that island."

Schuster smiled thinly. "Was he an actual prince? I mean with a crown and all? Was there a king? Or a queen? Or is this more of an honorary title, him being an actual simian, I mean?"

Karlson looked momentarily flustered. "More of a stage name, but he makes it work. When you see him you'll understand."

"Oh, I'm positively breathless with anticipation." Schuster opened his desk drawer and removed a packet of sourballs. He shook one into his palm and put it in his mouth. He did not offer one to his guest. "Mr. Karlson," he said as he sucked, "if this ape of yours is so big and impressive, how could you assure me he wouldn't terrorize the audience. How do you control him?"

"Gas. He has a problem with it, you see."

"Gas? Your Mr. Garganto has problems with gas? Wouldn't that present a rather distasteful problem onstage?"

"Huh? What? Oh. God . . . no! That's not what I meant. I mean we *control* him with gas. We caught him by using gas grenades. Now he's chained up."

"I . . . see. Exactly what do you plan to do with a large, gassed-out ape onstage? Does he do tricks?"

"No."

"Is he funny?"

"Not really."

"Do you dress him up in a clown suit and have him ride a bicycle? I saw a bear do that once in a circus and it was quite clever."

"No. He doesn't do anything like that."

"Well, then, what does he do?"

"Well, he'd just be standing there. In chains."

Schuster sat there. He did not say anything. He tapped his fingers slowly on his desk top. Waiting for more. Not getting anything.

"Stands there," he said after a very long time.

"Well . . . yes."

"In chains."

"Kind of has to," said Karlson. "He's really big."

318

GORILLA MY DREAMS

"Uh huh."

"And strong."

"Right."

"And dangerous."

"Sure," said Schuster. "But . . . to make sure I grasp the central conceit of your act . . . a pretty blond girl is on stage with a big gorilla who doesn't do anything except stand there in chains?"

"Sure. She'll tell her story. It's a corker."

"It would have to be," said Schuster. "I can see how that could guarantee at least a dozen curtain calls."

Karlson cleared his throat. "And we'd talk about how we captured him."

"Sure. Let me see if I have this clear in my mind, Mr. Karlson. You want me to book you and your ape into the biggest theater on Times Square so the audience can see an overgrown monkey stand there in chains while you explain how he was captured with knock-out gas while mooning over some blonde? Is that about it?"

"Well . . . yes. In a nutshell."

"If we're going to talk about 'nuts', Mr. Karlson, let's start with you."

-2-

Residence of New York Mayor John P. O'Brien
December 2, 1933—12:01 a.m.

"Your honor? Sir?"

"It's after midnight," grumbled Mayor O'Brien in a vaguely threatening tone. "If this isn't a fabulously gorgeous redhead I'm hanging up the phone."

"Sorry to wake you, sir."

319

"If you're not sorry, you will be. Who in the flaming hell is this?"

"Commissioner Murphy, sir," said the caller. "We have a situation happening near Times Square."

"I'm not sure I like the word 'situation', Murphy."

"No sir."

"What kind of a 'situation' are we talking about? Is it the Meat Packers union again? I spent all day trying to explain to them that the meat that was shipped in from the Midwest was unfit and we just can't have them package it for sale. I told them today that we—"

"Well . . . sir . . . not to interrupt, but apparently a giant gorilla is rampaging through Manhattan."

" . . . ."

"Sir?"

"I'm sorry, I must not be awake yet. It almost sounded like you said a giant . . . "

"Ape, sir. Yes."

"Rampaging."

"Yes, sir."

"Who did you say this was?"

"Murphy, sir. Police commissioner."

"Did I appoint you?"

"Yes, sir."

"Should I regret that, Murphy?"

"Well, sir . . . there really is a giant ape. And he is on a rampage, mostly through the theater district."

The mayor sat up and rubbed his eyes. Despite the ban on all alcohol sales across the United States, he was a bit hung over. Drinking from his private stock. Drinking, in fact, quite a lot from that stock. Very good whiskey. The kind that went down easy but later dragged you outside and roughed you up. His head hurt. "When you say 'giant', Murphy . . . what are we talking here?"

"Well," said the commissioner, "let's see. I guess thirty, thirty-five feet. Give or take."

The mayor nearly slid off the edge of the bed. "Thirty-five-*feet*?"

"Give or take, sir."

"Murphy, are you aware of something called prohibition?"

"I'm sober as a judge, sir," said Commissioner Murphy.

"Frankly, Murphy, that's a pretty poor example to hide behind."

"I haven't touched a drop, your honor. Not in years."

"We both know that's not entirely true."

"Your honor, I—"

"And yet you insist there is a thirty-five-foot ape tearing up the theater district?"

"Yes, sir. There has been considerable damage already to several buildings, a theater, and the elevated train."

"By a *gorilla*?"

"It is a very large one, sir."

"I see. A giant gorilla tearing up Times Square. Thank you for calling me. I sit up late every night hoping for calls like this."

"I . . ."

"It's why I ran for office, just waiting for the day when giant monkeys attack the city. Now I know my hour has come."

"Sir," said Murphy, "this is a genuine crisis. There is a giant ape and something needs to be done."

"And . . . just what exactly do you expect *me* to do about it, Murphy? I'm a politician, not a zookeeper."

"I really don't know, sir. But you are the Mayor—"

"My job description didn't say anything about giant rampaging apes."

"Mine neither, sir."

"You'd better call the governor, Murphy. He's trying to get re-elected. I'm not."

-3-
Observation Deck of the RCA Building
30 Rockefeller Plaza
December 2, 1933—12:41 a.m.

"You can see him from here, your honor," said the commissioner of police.

The mayor gaped. "You mean he's way up *there!*"

"Yessir."

"Would you like to tell me, Commissioner Murphy, how in the flaming hell he got *up* there?"

"He, um . . . *climbed*, sir."

"Climbed?"

"Yes, sir."

"To the top of the Empire State Building?"

"Yes, sir."

"Oh, come *on* . . . "

"Well, sir," said Murphy, "there he is. I doubt he took the elevator . . . "

"Watch yourself now, Murphy."

"Sorry, sir."

They stood looking up at the large, dark, hairy figure clinging to the top of the world's tallest building. Spotlights painted it with pale silver light.

GORILLA MY DREAMS

"And, um," said Mayor O'Brien, "*why* would a giant ape go up there anyway?"

"I . . . actually don't know the answer to that, sir."

There were a lot of people on the street. The windows of every building around the skyscraper were lit and tiny figures were silhouetted against the glow. Thousands upon thousands of New Yorkers were watching this. And on the ground the flash of camera bulbs was as constant as fireworks on the Fourth of July.

"Well, Murphy, what are you going to do now?"

The police commissioner flinched as if dreading that question. "Well, sir, per your suggestion I called the governor."

"And . . . ?" There was no great love between the mayor and the governor.

"And, he authorized the use of airplanes from Roosevelt Field."

"Airplanes?"

"Yes, sir. There they are. Can you hear them?"

"What, let's stay on topic. The governor ordered airplanes to do *what*, exactly?"

"To shoot the ape off a skyscraper, sir."

"Shoot?"

"Yes, sir."

The mayor closed his eyes and bent forward to quietly bang his head on the guard rail. He said something in Gaelic that Murphy, whose Irish language skills were rusty, was pretty sure involved the governor and livestock, and was not something one would say in church.

"Is there a problem with that plan, sir?" asked Murphy.

"I should have stayed in bed, Murphy."

323

"Don't fret, Mr. Mayor, those pilots are aces. They'll get him for sure."

Above them the sky was torn apart by the roar of engines and the rattle of machine gun fire.

-4-
Observation Deck of the RCA Building
30 Rockefeller Plaza
December 2, 1933—12:49 a.m.

"He looks about done-in, sir," said Murphy.

"Wouldn't you be?" said the mayor. He wondered if he looked as green and sick as he felt. "They must have put ten thousand rounds into him."

Murphy was grinning. "Oh, at least, sir."

"Though . . . tell me something, Murphy," said the mayor slowly.

"Yes, sir?"

"Surely a fair amount of those rounds had to have missed. I mean, with the planes circling, high winds, and that big ape swinging at them. Some of the shots *had* to have missed, am I right?"

"I expect so, sir."

"Maybe quite a lot of them?"

"Maybe, but I'm sure they hit him enough times—"

"Don't get ahead of me, son. If they fired all those shots, and some of them missed . . . tell me, Murphy—where'd the other bullets go?"

"Sir?"

"The ones that missed. Where'd they go?"

"Ummm . . . ."

"That's not the reassuring answer I was looking for, Murphy."

"Well, I . . ."

"Nor was that."

"I . . . guess . . . they hit something, sir."

"That would be my guess, too. Big city, isn't it, Murphy?"

"Yes . . ."

"Lots of people."

"Sure"

"I'll bet everyone in this city is either at a window watching this thing happening, or standing down there in the street looking up."

"Yes."

"Makes you think, doesn't it?"

"Sir?"

"All those people standing at the windows in all those buildings surrounding that one. With all those bullets—the ones that missed—having to go somewhere."

"Oh dear," said the commissioner.

"Oh dear is right."

The planes gunned their engines and circled back for another round. The night sky seemed to pop with fire as if strings of firecrackers were exploding up there. The dying roar of the mortally wounded gorilla bounced like thunder from the walls of the surrounding buildings.

"And, Murphy?"

"Sir?" croaked the commissioner, who now looked ever more green and sickly than the mayor felt.

"Have you thought about what's going to happen when that ape falls?"

"Falls, sir?"

"I believe that the planes are attempting to shoot

him *down*. Note the emphasis on 'down', Murphy. I use the word with precision."

"I . . . uh . . . ."

"Well, maybe I'll get lucky and he'll fall on the lawyer from the meat-packers union."

-5-

Headline of the New York Times (morning edition):

GIANT APE RAMPAGES!

Headline of the New York Times (afternoon edition):

APE KILLS THIRTY!
ARMY PLANES KILL NINETY-SEVEN
FALLING APE KILLS FORTY-THREE

Headline of the New York Times (evening edition):

MAYOR FIRES POLICE COMMISSIONER OVER APE ANTICS

-6-

Office of New York Mayor John P. O'Brien
December 3, 9:38 a.m.

"Gentlemen. *Gentlemen*! Please, one at a time!" roared the mayor. He had to repeat it and then finally slam his fist down on the table before they all jumped and fell silent. "Okay," he said into the uneasy quiet, "that's better. This meeting will proceed with some decorum, and I want to get this settled sooner rather than later. I have the lawyers from the meatpacking union outside for another round of mudslinging. They think I can produce fresh supplies of sirloin and hamburger out of thin air and I need time to figure out exactly how to tell them where to go and what they can do when they get there. So, I'd like to clear this matter off my slate by noon, or they'll be in here yelling louder than you lot. And they're union boys, so you know they can yell." He cleared his throat. "Now, Mr. Delpino, we'll hear from you first."

A thin, lugubrious fellow who smelled faintly of rotten eggs stood. "It's simply this way, your honor," he said in a nasal Bronx voice, "I don't think it's the problem of the Department of Sanitation to remove a giant ape carcass."

"Someone has to do it, Mr. Delpino."

"I respect that, sir, but that someone is not my department. Let someone *else* do it. My people are flat out not going to do it, that's for sure. We have enough problems with the nine-hundred pounds of 'droppings' our late friend left in Times Square. I mean, have you ever *smelled* giant ape droppings, Mr. Mayor?"

"No, can't say I have."

"I have. I'm what you might call an expert in all of the varieties of excremental leavings, and I have smelled everything up to, and including, rat poop, fifty breeds of dog poop, cat poop and even alligator poop."

"Alligator poop, Mr. Delpino? In New York?"

"Have you been down in the sewers, Mr. Mayor?"

"I have not, I'm happy to say."

"We have alligators in the sewers," said Delpino. "Well-known fact. My point is that I have smelled poop in all of its varieties but I have never before smelled giant gorilla poop. And it isn't good, Mr. Mayor. No sir, it is not good at all. It is causing distress to some of my most hardened and experienced poop management engineers."

"And you say that with a straight face," murmured the mayor, but Delpino ignored the comment.

"Our job is to haul those nine hundred pounds of gorilla droppings away, Mr. Mayor. That's what we're here for, and that's how we will serve this city. But . . . we won't haul away the body."

The mayor cocked an eyebrow. It was a trademark move. "May I remind you, sir, that you are an appointed official?"

"May I remind *you*, sir, that we're also a union, and the union reps are jerking my strings over this? Go ahead and fire me. It would be a relief, I can tell you, but you still wouldn't have a sanitation department working to scrape gorilla *tartare* off the streets. Just not going to happen." With that he sat back and laced his fingers together over his stomach and affected a look of immoveable stoicism.

"Very well, Mr. Delpino," sighed the mayor, "we'll come back to you. Mr. Sanders?"

"Sir?" replied a short, fat man with Ben Franklin glasses and a complexion like an old, sweaty tomato.

"What about your organization?" asked the mayor.

Mr. Sanders had one of those smiles that looked like a wince. As if every action he took, every word he spoke troubled him and made his hemorrhoids throb. "Sir," he said in a reedy voice, "the American Association for the Prevention of Cruelty to Animals is outraged by this whole affair. The treatment of this poor animal is reprehensible to say the least, and displays the poorest regard for life in general."

"Does it, Mr. Sanders?"

"It certainly does, Mr. Mayor."

The mayor sighed. "While I applaud your viewpoints, Mr. Sanders, we are not discussing a living animal, are we? Surely your society had some provision for disposing of animal remains?"

"Yes, we do," said Sanders carefully, "but for standard animal carcass disposal we use a furnace that could accommodate anything up to a very large dog, say a Saint Bernard. We once cremated a mountain lion that, regrettably, died at the Central Park Zoo. But . . . Mr. Mayor, we are in no way equipped to handle the cremation of an animal roughly the size of the Hindenburg."

"Are you saying you won't?"

"I'm saying that we *can't*. He won't fit in the vans and he won't fit in the crematory."

"Well . . . couldn't you, uh, cut him up some."

Mr. Sanders looked truly appalled. "*'Cut him up some'*? Surely, you're joking, sir."

"Am I smiling?" asked the mayor.

"Do you understand how difficult that would be?"

"Perhaps you could use buzz-saws?"

"You're missing the point, Mr. Mayor. Our people aren't hardened as much as you'd think. I have drivers who nearly throw up when they have to scrape a dead poodle up on West 57th—how do I get them to chainsaw twenty-five tons of gorilla?"

"You could ask them."

"With respect, your honor, but that's just as absurd as asking the meatpacker's union to do it. If we're going to be ridiculous why don't you have them slice him up and sell him as top round? Didn't you say you were meeting with them anyway?" Sanders paused. "Sir? Your Honor . . . ?"

"Hmmm . . . ?" murmured the mayor distractedly.

"Sir," said Sanders, "are you unwell?"

"As a matter of fact, I feel better than I have all day."

"Oh?"

"Oh yes." A laugh bubbled from the mayor's chest and everyone glanced queerly him.

Mr. Sanders licked his lips. "Did I say something amusing, sir?"

"Amusing? No . . . not exactly."

"Then may I ask why you are smiling like that, sir? This is a rather serious matter, sir."

"Yes, it is," said the mayor. And he chuckled again.

"Mr. Mayor . . . ?" asked his deputy, but his words trailed off.

The mayor sat up straight and glanced at the closed door. Through the frosted glass he could see men pacing up and down, their bodies hunched with agitation. His next meeting. It made him chuckle again.

"These are hard times," he said, addressing his comment to no one in particular. Everyone in the room studied him. They were all confused. "Hard times. Can't buy a drink when we really need one. Can't even buy a hot dog because no one has meat to see. Keeps going the way it's going and more people are going to be put out of work."

"I agree, sir," said the deputy mayor, "which is why the meatpackers union are waiting. But we have to deal with one matter at a time."

"Do we?" asked the mayor, smiling.

The deputy mayor frowned. "What do you mean, sir?"

"Weren't you listening? Mr. Sanders came right out and said it."

"Did I?" asked Sanders, confused. "What did I say?"

But from the look on the deputy mayor's face, it was clear he got it. All the color drained from his cheeks and he stared at his books with a look of complete and utter horror.

"Desperate times," said the mayor, as if in response to an actual question from his aide. "Desperate times, desperate measures."

"Sir . . . you can't actually . . . I mean, you wouldn't ever really consider . . ."

The mayor reached over and patted his hand. "Look at it as killing two birds with one stone."

"But . . . but . . . but . . ."

"I think we should let the gentlemen from the meatpackers union come in," said the mayor happily. He looked around. "Don't you?"

ARTICLES OF TELEFORCE

MICHAEL BAILEY

FROM A CLASSIFIED transcription of a conversation held in the Situation Room beneath the West Wing of the White House [also known as the John F. Kennedy Conference Room], retrieved from the hacker group Anonymous, dated September 11th, 2011:

> [name redacted]—"We need to bring down a commercial plane."
> [name redacted]—"How many civilian lives?"
> [name redacted]—"Does it matter? With what's happened—"
> [name redacted]—"All lives matter, [salutation & name redacted]. How many civilian lives?"
> [name redacted]—"The events that transpired early this morning in New York with the towers have—"
> [name redacted]—"How many civilian lives?"
> A long pause . . .

In a letter addressed to Milutin Tesla from the head of Gymnasium Karlovac in Croatia, postmarked April

ARTICLES OF TELEFORCE

13th, 1870 [translated to English by E. Glenn Tharpe of the Nikola Tesla Museum archive in Belgrade]:

To the parents of Nikola:

Following a recent lecture and demonstration of 'mysterious phenomena' by a certain professor of physics at our institution, your son has taken an interest in what our faculty has reported as 'unhealthy interests and unsafe personal studies.'

I am sure you are also aware of your son's progress with his treatment of malaria, to which he [unable to translate] shortly upon his arrival in Karlovac, and for which we have granted permission to bring home school books to self-study when he is unable to attend because of his bedriddenness. Despite this malady, Nikola is an apt pupil and has excelled to the top of his class in a matter of months. However . . .

In our efforts to continue providing safety to our students, we have interviewed your son in private regarding these matters of unsafe personal studies and 'experiments,' to which he has stated nothing more than his interest "to know more of this wonderful force." It should also be stated that his workspace is constantly littered with 'tools' and 'components' used for these unknown and unsafe experiments, and we are currently investigating the danger of having such items in his possession and around other students—as well as their proper ownership.

Furthermore . . .

Found written on a torn strip of notepaper underneath a loose stone during a remodel of Gymnasium Karlovac sometime in early 2010 [German translator unknown]:

> The world is full of many wonderful marvels, some of which mankind may never fully understand, but death will not have me until I have at least pried opened Pandora's Box.

From a medical diagnosis in Smijan sometime in 1873, after which Milutin Tesla is noted as promising to send his son—near death and requiring nine months of bedside care—to "the best engineering school available" upon his full recovery:

> Cholera.

In a letter addressed to Milutin Tesla from the head of Gymnasium Karlovac, postmarked March 30th, 1873 [translated to English by E. Glenn Tharpe of the Nikola Tesla Museum archive in Belgrade]:

> To the parents of Nikola Tesla:
> Notwithstanding our constant efforts to put an end to your son's interest with what can only be described as 'unknown forces of the universe,' Nikola has far-surpassed our expectations as a student—and twice there have been reports of extinguished small fires resulting from his 'experimentations,' but this is not the purpose of this letter, although the issue should soon be addressed.

ARTICLES OF TELEFORCE

The reason is to inform you that Nikola is on a path to graduate early, with honours, in as little as three years.

In a letter to his father [date illegible because of deterioration; although determined to have been written sometime prior to 1874]:

[top of page missing]
—of the Smijan Austro-Hungarian Army, so I must evade such conscription and flee to Tomingaj, which is near Gračac. I must make amends with nature, clear my head, and prepare mentally for what is to come. War is a pointless act of cruelty mankind parades upon itself. To enter a war without consent of soldiers is utterly . . . [illegible]. Have you per-chance read anything by a man by the name of Mark Twain? I have recently— [remainder missing]

Transcribed from a telegram sent from Graz University of Technology in Styria, Austria, dated December 24th, 1875:

Father,
I am saddened to hear of your diminishing health, so I would like to attempt to elevate your spirits by letting you know I am excelling at TU Graz this last year under the Military Frontier Scholarship, and have to-date not missed a single class nor assignment. I must admit I've seen the Dean's letter he plans to send your way—he felt the need to share his

words with me as well—in which he states, "Your son is a star of first rank!" That said, you may find yourself reading some rather harsh words from a certain Professor Poeschi, as we have had mixed words—near fisticuffs, if I may be honest—about the necessity of commutators in use with the Gramme dynamo, which is a type of electronic generator capable of producing direct current. The contraption involves a series of armature coils wound about a revolving ring of iron. The coils are thus connected in series and there is a great deal of magnetism involved. Poeschi is insistent upon connecting the junction between pairs to these commutators, which is rubbish!

In a letter to Samuel Langhorne Clemens, postmarked June 19th, 1878:

Mr. Clemens:

I wanted to send you this note of thanks for helping me through a period of self-enlightenment. I had the pleasure of familiarizing myself with your short fiction over these last few years, and your recent novel, *The Adventures of Tom Sawyer*. Although your fictitious world is set in the town of St. Petersburg—which I assume is also fiction because it is not to be found on a map that makes any logical sense, I can't help but feel this town you created is inspired by your very own Hannibal, Missouri, and that this is an autobiographical novel of sorts.

I have taken a liking to your work, and have to ask the question: Do you also write under Thomas Jefferson Snodgrass? I have read a few humorous articles by a writer of that name—the name is also humorous: Snodgrass, ha!—and he shares something similar with his prose.

We should make an appointment to meet, sooner rather than later, as I would like to share with you some interesting ideas I have for a particular word we mutually admire: "peace."

Sincerely,
N.T.

In a letter from Milutin Tesla to Graz University of Technology in Styria, Austria, dated March 3rd, 1879:

To whom it may concern:

I am writing to inquire about the location of my son, Nikola Tesla, who I have heard recently dropped out of your institution, despite his continued education relying on my finances. I have not heard from him in some time, nor from the school, and am highly concerned of his whereabouts. He has cut all ties with family and seems to have vanished from this very earth. There are rumors he has moved to Maribor, Slovenia, where I will travel next if his location is still uncertain following your reply. Any information you can provide would be greatly appreciated . . .

There are numerous letters and transcriptions concerning the whereabouts of Nikola Tesla over the thirty-five years that follow, following Milutin's sudden and unexpected death on April 17th, 1879, but none are relevant for the purpose of this collection of articles. The relationship between Thomas Edison and Nikola Tesla is well-known, as well as their quarrels with patents and ownership of original ideas for both direct and indirect electrical circuits. And there are other non-relevant matters, so the timeline of these articles quickly shifts through the years covering Tesla's stint in Hungary, Budapest, and Paris—where he worked for the Continental Edison Company—and through his emigration into the United States in 1884 when he was brought to New York—Manhattan's Lower East Side—to manage Edison Machine Works. And the timeline quickly shifts through 1885 to the start of Tesla Electric Light & Manufacturing, through the inventions of the polythermal induction motor, and various transformer designs. His work helped journey him to places like Niagara, to assist in generating power from the falls. And over the years, and through many inventions, Nikola became independently wealthy from licensing patents, giving him both the time and funds to pursue his own interests, both brilliant and peculiar, resulting in inventions still in use today, such as the Tesla coil. He alternated, like some of his machines, between wealthy and broke.

Yet his ideas always reached farther than his funds would allow, often beyond the scope of imagination; his ideas becoming what most considered *fantastic*, but in the way that word can also mean *lunacy*, *crazy*, something composed of '*fantasy*;' ideas one might read in *fiction*.

ARTICLES OF TELEFORCE

Thus, in a letter written by Samuel Langhorne Clemens, addressed to Nikola Tesla at his South Fifth Avenue laboratory, postmarked June 19th, 1894:

Greetings, Mr. Tesla:
  After so many letters back and forth, it is finally time we meet in person, don't you think? Your name is all over the papers, like a brand, so your whereabouts were not difficult to track. There is even a picture of your laboratory in New York in the latest Times, and I must say, the building looks garish and, well, clayey! You gave me strife with that word in your last letter: clayey, saying I had made up a word that was not yet a word. This makes us more similar than differing, don't you think? You invent new things out of nothings, much like I do with words. I happen to be making my way north and will be passing through New York in my travels. I'll stop by if you'll allow, and we can talk about your "ideas" for a better world that you touched on in your last correspondence, and I would love for the opportunity to "hold the lightning," or to walk through it, at least, as you have been noted as doing in some of your recent public experiments. You were right about Hannibal, by the way. I love the damn Mississippi! It's liquid chocolate, 'tis true! [the 2nd page of the letter is water-damaged and unreadable]

In a letter to Samuel Langhorne Clemens, postmarked July 31st, 1894:

Sam / Mark (you are one in the same, so what does it matter?):

My most recent experiments in finding a means to bring light to our so very dark world has taken much of my time, in fact nearly all of it. I write these words under the light provided by wireless electricity, if you can imagine such a thing. Apologies for the delay since your last meeting, but I have found a way inside Pandora's Box and have flung it wide open, thus breaking its hinges; I'm not sure it will be capable of closing ever again.

What we discussed when we last met, I won't write about here, but wanted you to know that I've found a way! There can be an end to all war—not by offense, but by defense . . . I only need to find the means to fund such exhaustive research.

Your friend,
N. Tesla

From a classified transcription of a conversation held in the Situation Room, retrieved from the hacker group Anonymous, dated September 11th, 2011:

[name redacted]—"Where is Flight [number redacted] headed?"
[name redacted]—"Origination was J.F.K. with a destination of Chicago/O'Hare, sir."
[name redacted]—"Chicago? [Emphasized]"
[name redacted]—"We have reason to believe the hijackers will attempt to fly the aircraft into either the Willis Tower, or the John

Hancock building. Both building names
have been mentioned—"
[name redacted]—"How do we know this?"
[name redacted]—"Text messages obtained
from passengers onboard the flight, sir."
A long silence . . .

From a letter to John Pierpont "Jack" Morgan Jr. (also
known as J.P. Morgan, Jr., philanthropist, banker, and
finance executive), dated November 29th, 1934:

I have made recent discoveries of inestimable
value . . . The fly machine [war plane] has
completely demoralized the world, so much
that in some cities, as London and Paris, people
are in mortal fear from aerial bombing. The
new means I have perfected afford absolute
protection against this and other forms of
attack. . . . These new discoveries, which I have
carried out experimentally on a limited scale,
have created a profound impression.

Published in the *New York Times*, in an article
headlined "Beam to Kill Army at 200 Miles, Tesla's
Claim on 78th Birthday," dated July 11th, 1934:

My apparatus projects particles which may be
relatively large or of microscopic dimensions,
enabling us to convey to a small area at a great
distance trillions of times more energy than is
possible with rays of any kind. Many thousands of
horsepower can thus be transmitted by a stream
thinner than a hair, so that nothing can resist . . .

341

Also claimed on Nikola Tesla's 78th birthday, as published in the *New York Times* in an article headlined "'Death Ray' for Planes," published September 22nd, 1940:

> ... The nozzle would send concentrated beams of particles through the free air, of such tremendous energy that they will bring down a fleet of 10,000 enemy airplanes at a distance of 200 miles from a defending nation's border and will cause armies to drop dead in their tracks.

Snippets from the treatise "The New Art of Projecting Concentrated Non-Dispersive Energy through Natural Media: System of Particle Acceleration for Use in National Defense" concerning charged particle beam weapons in an attempt to explicate technical descriptions of an alleged 'superweapon' that could potentially put an end to all war, dated sometime between 1935 and 1937 [currently located in the Nikola Tesla Museum archive in Belgrade]:

> The advances described are the result of my research carried on for many years with the chief object of transmitting electrical energy to great distances. The first important practical realization of these efforts was the alternating current power system now in universal use. I then turned my attention to wireless transmission and was fortunate enough to achieve similar success ...

ARTICLES OF TELEFORCE

I mastered the technique of high potentials sufficiently for enabling me to construct and operate, in 1899, a wireless transmitter developing up to twenty million volts . . .

After preliminary laboratory experiments, I made tests on a large scale with the transmitter referred to and a beam of ultra-violet rays of great energy in an attempt to conduct the current to the high rarefied strata of the air and thus create an auroral such as might be utilized for illumination, especially of oceans at night . . .

Much time was devoted by me to the transmission of radiant energy, in various forms, by reflectors and I perfected means for increasing enormously the intensity of the effects, but was baffled in all my efforts to materially reduce dispersion and became fully convinced that this handicap could only be overcome by conveying the power through the medium of small particles projected, at prodigious velocity, from the transmitter. Electrostatic repulsion was the only means to this end and an apparatus of stupendous force would have to be developed . . .

When I undertook to carry out this plan in practice, the difficulties seemed insurmountable. In the first place, a closed vacuum tube could not be employed as no window could withstand the force of the impact. This made it absolutely necessary to project the particles in free air which meant that each could hold only an insignificant charge. Thus, no matter how high the potential of the terminal, the force of repulsion would be necessarily too small for the purpose contemplated . . .

The successful carrying out of the plan involves a number of more or less important improvements but the principal among these includes the following:

1. A new form of high vacuum tube open to the atmosphere.
2. Provisions for imparting to a minute particle an extremely high charge.
3. A new terminal of relatively small dimensions and enormous potential.
4. An electrostatic generator on a new principle and of very great power.

From a classified transcription of a conversation held in the Situation Room, retrieved from the hacker group Anonymous, dated September 11th, 2011:

[name redacted]—"Where is the plane currently?"
[name redacted]—"Just entering airspace over Ohio."

A letter from Samuel Langhorne Clemens, addressed to Nikola Tesla at [address illegible], postmarked January 27th, 1933:
Nikola,

Does the newsprint speak the truth? Have you perfected the [illegible] vacuum and completed your "ray?" The Times reads as though your purpose is to find a means not only to end all war, but to create a device capable of annihilating innumerous lives in the blink of an eye, without a trace . . . yet those are your words they are printing, are they not? My heart is telling me you have higher plans, that your "death ray" is in fact a "peace ray," in the same manner a country capable of manufacturing a bomb of atomic proportions would rely on its possession more so than its use.

Your friend,
S. Clemens

A postcard from Nikola Tesla to Samuel Langhorne Clemens, postmarked February 28th, 1933, the back of which contains a photograph of an unknown street in New York:

S.C.—My plans for "peace" have expanded beyond the vision of plain-folk minds. Papers enjoy the term "death ray," and so do I, but only because it brings financiers to the table.—N.T.

In a letter mailed from Hotel New Yorker, addressed to S.W. Kintner, Esq. of Westinghouse Electric & Manufacturing Company in Pittsburgh, PA, dated April 7th, 1934:

My dear Mr. Kintner;

I was glad that you did not put the matter before Mr. Merrick for I found after careful thought and figuring that it would take much more money to carry out my proposal which I made to you on the spur of the moment stimulated by the pleasure of our meeting and your warm response. The Westinghouse people made a friendly gesture and I wanted to meet them in the same spirit by giving them the first opportunity on discoveries which I honestly believe to be more important than any of recorded in the history of invention.

[page missing]

I note your suggestion but am at a loss to see how to carry it out. Rest assured though, that I shall always hold your people in high regard and if I ever find it in my power to advance their interest I shall spare no effort.

The skepticism of your expert was expected. He is probably under the sway of the modern illusionary ideas and the abler he is the more apt he is to be in error. But I have demonstrated all the principals involved and am going ahead with perfect confidence which all the experts in the world could not shake.

Yours very truly,
Nikola Tesla

Published in the *New York Sun* in an article titled "Tesla Invents Peace Ray: Tesla Describes His Beam of Destructive Energy," dated July 10th, 1934:

Invention of a "beam of matter moving at high velocity" which would act as a "beam of destructive energy" was announced today by Dr. Nikola Tesla, the inventor, in his annual birthday interview. Dr. Tesla is 78, and for the past several years has made his anniversary the occasion for announcement of scientific discoveries.

The beam, as described by the inventor to rather bewildered reporters, would be projected on land from power houses set 200 miles or so apart and would provide an impenetrable wall for a country in time of war. Anything with which the ray came in contact would be destroyed, the inventor indicated. Planes would fall, armies would be wiped out and even the smallest country might so ensure "security" against which nothing could avail.

Dr. Tesla announced that he plans to suggest his method at Geneva as an assurance of peace.

From the *New York Sun*, in an article titled "Death-Ray Machine Described: Dr. Tesla Says Two of Four Necessary Pieces of Apparatus Have Been Built," published July 11th, 1934:

Amplifying his birthday anniversary announcement of the prospective invention of an electrical death-ray, or force beam, that would make any country impregnable in time of war, Dr. Nikola Tesla says that two of the four pieces of necessary apparatus already have been constructed and tested.

Four machines combine in the production and use of this destructive beam, which, according to Dr. Tesla would wipe out armies, destroy airplanes and level fortresses at a range limited only by the curvature of the earth. These four are:

First, apparatus for producing manifestations of energy in free air instead of in a high vacuum as in the past. This, it is said, has been accomplished.

Second, the development of a mechanism for generating tremendous electrical force. This, too, Dr. Tesla says, has been solved. The power necessary to achieve the predicted results has been estimated at 50,000,000 volts.

Third, a method of intensifying and amplifying the force developed by the second mechanism.

Fourth, a new method for producing a tremendous electrical repelling force. This would be the projector, or gun of the invention.

While the latter two elements in the plan have not yet been constructed, Dr. Tesla speaks of them as practically assured. Owing to the elaborate nature of the machinery involved, he admits it is merely a defense engine, though battleships could be equipped with smaller units and thus armed could sweep the seas.

In addition to the value of this engine for destruction in time of war, Dr. Tesla said it could be utilized in peace for the transmission of power . . .

ARTICLES OF TELEFORCE

From a classified transcription of a conversation held in the Situation Room, retrieved from the hacker group Anonymous, dated September 11th, 2011:

> [name redacted]—"This 'device' [emphatically], we can pinpoint its focus to a single location in the sky, to a moving plane, even, with minimal civilian casualties?"
> [name redacted]—"The beam can be directed to Flight [number redacted]'s exact location in the sky. Everyone onboard will be lost, sir, instantaneously. Ground control will simply see its blip vanish from radar. Those on the flight . . . there is no avoiding—"
> [name redacted]—"Besides those on the plane, [salutation & name redacted], can we avoid further loss of life?"
> [name redacted]—"Flight [number redacted] will become debris, a minimal amount, with trajectories uncertain."
> [name redacted]—"Debris over Ohio."
> [name redacted]—"Farmland, sir."

In a letter from Samuel Langhorne Clemens to Nikola Tesla, August 1st, 1934:

> I understand now, my friend. Much success in carrying out this burden! To imagine . . . a world without war!

From the *New York Herald Tribune*, pp. 1, 15, in an article by Joseph W. Alsop, Jr., titled "Beam to Kill Army at 200 Miles, Tesla's Claim on 78th Birthday:

Death Ray Also Available as Power of Agent in Peace Times, Inventor Declares," also published July 11th, 1934:

> He came to the idea of a beam of force, he said, because of his belief that no weapon has ever been found that is not as successful offensively as defensively. The perfect weapon of defense, he felt, would be a frontier wall, impenetrable and extending up to the limits of the atmosphere of the earth . . .
>
> The beam of force itself, as Dr. Tesla described it, is a concentrated current—it need be no thicker than a pencil—of microscopic particles moving at several hundred times the speed of artillery projectiles. The machine into which Dr. Tesla combines his four devices is, in reality, a sort of electrical gun.
>
> He illustrated the sort of thing that the particles will be by recalling an incident that occurred often enough when he was experimenting with a cathode tube. Then, sometimes, a particle larger than an electron, but still very tiny, would break off from the cathode, pass out of the tube and hit him. He said he could feel a sharp, stinging pain where it entered his body, and again at the place where it passed out. The particles in the beam of force, ammunition which the operators of the generating machine will have to supply, will travel far faster than such particles as broke off from the cathode, and will travel in concentrations, he said.

As Dr. Tesla explained it, the tremendous speed of the particles will give them their destruction-dealing qualities. All but the thickest armored surfaces confronting them would be melted through in an instant by the heat generated in the concussion . . .

In a New York World Telegram from Nikola Tesla, dated July 24th, 1934, in response to an article written by William Engle re: hydro-electric development in an issue published June 24th, in which the author announces Tesla's inexhaustible source of power as "nebulous":

We are all fallible, but as I examine the subject in the light of my present theoretical and experimental knowledge I am filled with deep conviction that [I] am giving to the world something far beyond the wildest dreams of inventors of all time.

From *Every Week Magazine*, published October 21st, 1934, p. 3 in an article titled "Dr. Tesla Visions the End of Aircraft in War" by Helen Welshimer:

Now, 15 years after the War has ended, Tesla, one of the greatest inventors of all time, has announced that his invention to end all wars, by a perfect means of defense which any nation can employ, is ready . . .

Dr. Tesla wishes it to be understood that the means he has perfected has nothing in common with the so-called "death ray."

"It is impossible to develop such a ray. I worked on that idea for many years," he says, "before my ignorance was dispelled and I became convinced that it could not be realized. This new beam of mine consists of minute bullets moving at a terrific speed, and any amount of power desired can be transmitted by them. The whole plant is just a gun, but one which is incomparably superior to the present."

From a Western Union Telegram from [name redacted], a past and sometimes frequent financier of Nikola Tesla, dated October 13th, 1934:

We regret to inform you that your persistent requests for additional funds will continue to be denied. Please cease and desist further requests for support from [business name redacted]. Consider all ties cut.

In a letter mailed from Hotel New Yorker, New York, NY, addressed to J.P. Morgan Esq. at 23 Wall Street, New York, NY, dated November 29th, 1934:

Dear Mr. Morgan:
I have made recent discoveries of inestimable value which are referred in the marked passage of the clipping enclosed. Their practical application should yield an immense fortune.
The flying machine has completely demoralized the world, so much that in some cities, as London and Paris, people are in

mortal fear from aerial bombing. The new means I have perfected afford absolute protection against this and other forms of attack . . .

Yours most faithfully,
N. Tesla

Following the ellipses in the letter above, Nikola details Mr. Morgan in the urgency and importance of continuing the development of his recent discoveries, requesting substantial funds:

Words cannot express how much I am aching for the same facilities which I then had at my disposal and for the opportunity of squaring my account with your father's estate and yourself. I am no longer a dreamer but a practical man of great experience gained in long and bitter trials. If I had now twenty five thousand dollars to secure my property and make convincing demonstrations I could acquire in a short time colossal wealth.

Mr. Morgan, you are still able to help an undying cause but how long will you be in this privileged position? We are in the clutches of a political party which caters openly and brazenly to the mob and believes that by pouring out billions of public money, still unequalled, it can remain in power indefinitely. The democratic principles are forsaken and individual liberty and incentives are made a joke. The "New Deal" is a perpetual motion scheme which can never work but is given a semblance of operativeness by an unceasing supply of the peoples' capital. Most of the measures adopted are a bid for votes and some are destructive to established industries and decidedly socialistic . . .

From a classified transcription of a conversation held in the Situation Room, retrieved from the hacker group Anonymous, dated September 11th, 2011:

[name redacted]—"How does this device work, this system?"

From a Western Union Telegram from Nikola Tesla to his nephew, Sava Kosanović, in New York, NY, dated March 1st, 1941:

In the system there are no electrons. Energy goes into the same direction without any distribution [dissipation] and the same on all sides of distance. It contains neutrons. [In] the air [its size] is equal to a diameter of hydrogen. It can destroy the largest ships afloat. There is unlimited distance of travel. The same is for airplanes.

From a classified transcription of a conversation held in the Situation Room, retrieved from the hacker group Anonymous, dated September 11th, 2011:

[name redacted]—"We have used teleforce for years, sir, in Afghanistan, in Kuwait, in Syria, home abroad—"
[name redacted]—"So tell me again why the

towers are gone. So many lives lost, so
many lives."
[name redacted]—"We cannot defend against
the unexpected, and the use of such a
weapon requires an executive order."
[name redacted]—"Weapon? [emphasized]"
[name redacted]—"Yes, a defensive weapon . . .
of sorts."

Snippets from the article "A Machine to End War,"
dated February 1935, in which Nikola Tesla discusses
humanity in his future, subtitled "A Famous Inventor,
Picturing Life 100 Years from Now, Reveals an
Astounding Scientific Venture which Believes Will
Change the Course of History":

No man can look very far into the future.
Progress and invention evolve in directions
other than those anticipated . . .

Life is and will ever remain an equation
incapable of solution, but it contains certain
known factors. We may definitely say that it is
a movement even if we do not fully understand
its nature. Movement implies a body which is
being moved and a force which propels it
against resistance . . .

There is no conflict between the ideal of
religion and the ideal of science, but science is
opposed to theological dogmas because science
is founded on fact. To me, the universe is
simply a great machine which never came into

being and never will end. The human being is no exception to the natural order. Man, like the universe, is a machine . . .

In the course of ages, mechanisms of infinite complexity are developed, but what we call "soul" or "spirit," is nothing more than the sum of the functionings of the body. When this functioning ceases, the "soul" or the "spirit" ceases likewise . . .

Today the most civilized countries of the world spend a maximum of their income on war and a minimum on education. The twenty-first century will reverse this order. It will be more glorious to fight against ignorance than to die on the field of battle. The discovery of a new scientific truth will be more important than the squabbles of diplomats . . .

Progress [illegible] will be impossible while nations persist in the savage practice of killing each other off . . .

I believed at one time that war could be stopped by making it more destructive. But I found that I was mistaken. I underestimated man's combative instinct, which it will take more than a century to breed out. We cannot abolish war by outlawing it. We cannot end it by disarming the strong. War can be stopped, not by making the strong weak but by making every nation, weak or strong, able to defend itself.

ARTICLES OF TELEFORCE

From the *Baltimore Sun* in an article titled "Aerial Defense 'Death Beam' Offered to U.S. by Tesla," dated July 12th, 1940:

> "All my inventions," he [Nikola Tesla] said, "are at the service of the United States Government."
>
> The death beam, he said, is "based on an entirely new principle of physics that no one has ever dreamed about." The principle, he added, was different from those relating to the transmission of electrical power by wireless . . .
>
> The beam, he said, would be only one hundred-millionth of a square centimeter in diameter and could be generated from a special plant that would cost no more than $[redacted] and would take only about three months to construct. A dozen such plants, located at strategic positions along the coast, he said, would be enough to defend the country against all possible aerial attack.

From an article titled "'Death Ray' for Planes," published in the *New York Times*, September 22nd, 1940, Sec. 2, p.7:

> Nikola Tesla, one of the truly great inventors who celebrated his eighty-fourth birthday on July 10, tells the writer [name redacted] that he stands ready to divulge to the United States Government the secret of his "teleforce" . . .
>
> In the opinion of the writer [name redacted], who has known Mr. Tesla for many

357

years and can testify that he still retains full intellectual vigor, the authorities in charge of building the national defense should at once look into the matter. The sum is insignificant compared with the magnitude of the stake.

From the *Philadelphia Inquirer* in an article titled "Proposing the 'Death Ray' for Defense," published October 20th, 1940:

> "If only they will let me try out my new teleforce." exclaimed Nikola Tesla, who has been called one of the greatest electrical inventors since Benjamin Franklin flew his kite. "If only they will let me show how this Nation can be made invulnerable to air attack . . ."

Nikola Tesla continued to work on plans for the directed-energy weapon until his death on January 7th, 1943. At a luncheon in his honor, concerning this "death ray" turned "peace beam," he is noted as declaring, "But it is not an experiment! I have built, demonstrated and used it. Only little time will pass before I can give it to the world."

Thus, from the *New York Times* in an article titled "'Death Ray' for Defense an Unobtainable Mad-Man's Fantasy," published April 23rd, 1943:

> . . . the death of famed inventor, Nikola Tesla, brought upon a great deal of investigation into his work from disgruntled investors. His highly-sought-after "death ray," sometimes

referred to as a "peace ray" because of its proposed use/non-use to bring an "end to all wars," as Tesla was often noted to claim, has been debunked as a farce, with much of his notes and experimentations in building such a device lost in the fire that burned down his most recent laboratory. What remains of Tesla's estate is a mystery . . .

In a letter from Nikola's nephew, Sava Kosanović to [name redacted], [address redacted], Belgrade, Serbia, postmarked November 5th, 1952:

> Dearest [name redacted],
> I am shipping Nikola Tesla's entire estate to you in 80 crates, simply marked with the initials N.T. Please take care of my deceased uncle's notebooks and remaining possessions, and make sure they do not fall into the wrong hands. The contents of which are not to be sold, not to be used in any means oth— . . . [the rest of the letter is water-damaged and indecipherable].

From a classified transcription of a conversation held in the Situation Room, retrieved from the hacker group Anonymous, dated September 11th, 2011:

> [name redacted]—"Flight [number redacted] is gone, sir. Other than those on the aircraft, zero civilian casualties are being reported in northern Ohio, although a water tower—"
> [name redacted]—"Sir?"
> A long silence . . .

SIC OLIM TYRANNIS

DAVID WELLINGTON

THERE WAS NO banner of fire trailing across the sky. It happened too fast for that.

No roar as the atmosphere was torn open, no sound at all, from so far away. There was a flash of light, there and gone so fast it barely irritated the dull eyes of the watchers. Then darkness swallowed the sun.

And the dust began to fall.

Thick fat flakes descended to cover a world that had forgotten what snow looked like. The dust piled up in great drifts, filling valleys, staining the sea. The giant fern trees, the tall, swaying grasses were buried, suffocated, already well on their way to fossilization. The dust clogged the burrows of the smaller animals, asphyxiating them in their sleep. It made the air so thick the leather-winged hunters couldn't fly, but only perch in high places, in hollows up on rocky cliffs, their long pickaxe-shaped heads pressed together, their wings wrapping each other up for protection.

The dust fell, and fell, and fell, and it seemed it would never end. As the first day passed it only got hotter, the air volcano-mouth hot. Hot dust kept falling, hot enough to scorch feathers and burn exposed, scaly skin. The smart ones, the ones with brains bigger than a walnut, dug deep, dug down into the ash pits, and tried not to breathe.

For days the dust fell and accumulated, soft avalanches of it slipping down the sides of young, ragged mountains. For days it covered the whole world, and filled the air.

But there came a day when it stopped, when the massive dark clouds that choked the sun began to part, and the light came back.

On the third day, the tyrant began to stir. To move. He lifted his massive square head from the ground, and dust fell away from his ridged snout in great cascades. His foreclaws twitched and scratched at the dusty ground. His long tail swayed behind him, stirring up a great cloud.

He opened one long suspicious eye—and squeezed it shut again almost instantly, as fine dust slipped in under his nictitating membrane, irritating, caustic dust. He coughed and spat and sneezed and gray freshets of snot burst from his nostrils.

One limb at a time, one cautious, scrabbling foot after another found purchase. The tyrant had never laid down on his side before—even in sleep he had simply crouched on his hind legs. It took some tricky maneuvering just to get back on his feet.

But he managed. He rose, his head up out of the dust, his eyes clearing, his stomach rumbling.

He lived.

Nor was he alone.

There had been a valley, a long, sloping descent toward a broad and silver lake. There had been forests clothing the mountainsides, and marshy ground where the big meat animals wallowed, and herds of the little runners, the little fleet-of-foot that the tyrant loved to chase and snatch up in his great jaws. There had been cries and shrieks in the branches of the trees, and dark little eyes glinting there. The thing from another world, the world-killer, had tried to take all of that away. It had hidden the sun and turned the air to poison and it had flooded the world with its dry rain. And it had wreaked a terrible change, it was true—the valley was a dustheap now, a stir of fine powder that flew up into the air in a choking haze every time the tyrant moved or turned around. Yet life had not drained out of the world, not entirely. Those lizards, those terrible runners and hunters and armored herbivores were survivors, gifted by a hundred million years of evolution, engineered to live. As the tyrant turned his square head from side to side, he saw movement everywhere he looked. He heard a lowing sound, a long, low bellow and saw an armored behemoth shake itself clear of the dust, its great war club of a tail slapping at the armored plates on its back as if it were clearing away parasites. From across the valley he heard the gruff snorting of his three-horned nemesis, king of the plant-eaters, and saw it rear back its vicious head and cry at the sun. All around him the dust boiled and furrowed as the little ones, his meat, stirred beneath the dust and dug their way toward clear air.

And overhead a flier took wing, leaping from the rocks and gliding from one mountain peak to another, its shadow flickering across the broken sky.

The tyrant could not laugh, but it could smile. A great, wide beaming grin that showed its long, swordlike teeth. It was a grin that drove the little ones to panic, a grin of pure rapacious malice. The tyrant grinned now at the sky that had tried to kill him, had tried to destroy his empire of blood and life. The world-killer had failed—the world yet lived—and life alone felt so good. It felt like victory.

The tyrant was no fool. His brain was larger than one might have expected, big and convoluted. He needed all that brainpower to see past the tricks and feints of his prey, to catch them as they tried to escape. He knew that while he had beaten back extinction for the moment there were no guarantees. His belly rumbled angrily, after so many days without a kill, and his lungs were still clotted with the dust. He needed to move, to find a way out of this powdered labyrinth. Perhaps he would scale the peaks, and pounce upon the fliers, and be whole again. Perhaps he would travel north, away from the place where the world-killer struck, into the cooler valleys of the uplands. He knew he needed to move, to migrate. Always in the past he had been the overlord of this valley, its sure and potent master, but now time had called for a change. He would need to find a new land to conquer, one perhaps still unknown to the rule of an apex predator. He lifted his legs high, and balanced with his massive tail as he plunged through the dust, headed up the gentle slope, away from the deepest drifts. He paused only once, barely slowing down as something stirred in the dust right in front of him. Pure instinct was enough to send his snout flying downward, into the powder, his jaws closing like a blast of lightning on the thing that was foolish enough to wriggle there. Slaver poured down his gums and made mud of the dust as he lifted his head again, snapping it upward on his thick neck, and his teeth crushed the bones and tore the flesh of his meal.

Something was wrong, though. The meat was foul and bitter. Perhaps he'd grabbed up too much of the dust along with the anonymous little snack, perhaps it was one of those tricky little animals that secreted poison from its skin. The tyrant spat out the mouthful of corruption, spat and hawked up mucus to clear his mouth of the terrible taste. He blinked his eyes rapidly as the smell of the toxic meal filled his sinuses and he barked out a coughing cry of disgust.

No matter. He was hungry, still—starving—but there would be other prey. Other animals he could chomp and rend, in the higher altitudes.

The thing he'd tried and failed to eat he left behind him, still twitching though its bones were shattered, its flesh in ribbons. He paid it no attention as he passed on by, having no interest in sticking around to watch it die. He was not at all aware of the way it dragged itself through the dust, crippled limbs convulsing in slow motion, pulling itself along the ground with the dulled claws.

In a minute's time, he was far enough away he couldn't even smell its sour reek anymore.

The armored behemoth trumpeted a call of defiance as the tyrant came near, but it had nothing to worry about. The bony plates that covered its skin were proof against his jaws, and he was not so stupid as to risk getting close enough to face its weaponized tail. He sought softer, smaller prey as he always had. Like the tyrant, the behemoth was headed north, up the slope, out of the deep, restless cauldron of the dust. They followed parallel tracks as they sought out their chosen food, one looking for meat, one for anything green. Behind them, but moving fast, the horned nemesis joined their quest. There was only the one way out of the valley, one route to higher ground, and the survivors of the world-killer were racing to get there first.

The stakes might be survival. Predators lived always on the raw knife edge of hunger; herbivores needed to stuff themselves constantly, gorge all day long on plants that offered only a bare trickle of nutrition. If they didn't get out of the dust-choked land in a hurry, they were all likely to starve.

It was hard going. The tyrant was a speed demon on the flatlands below, on the long stretches of slickrock and grass that ringed the vanished lake, but on these slopes he had to pick his way a step at a time, bracing himself with his tail as he constantly tottered, facing a long backward slide through the dust if he once lost his grip. It took focus, and concentration—and the behemoth just wouldn't shut up. Its bellows, its mooing, filled the air, a constant distraction.

Hungry as he was the tyrant wondered if maybe, just once, he ought to take his chances with that club of a tail. Until he came over a rise and saw the behemoth beset, and knew its meat was beyond his reach.

Someone had beaten him to it. No—a lot of someones.

The behemoth must be near death, he thought. Its ribs were exposed to the air, long bloody arches over a heap of viscera that had been ripped apart like wet cloth. Its armor plates had been cracked open as if by implacable machines. Blood stained the dust all around it, turning the dust a nasty orange.

And yet—it kept screaming. Its eyes searched the horizon, eyes growing dull and glassy but still, still they moved.

What monster could have done this? The tyrant knew of no predator greater than himself. No virtuoso of violence with the power, the will, to break apart that armor to snack upon the wet calories within. Whoever they were, they were long gone. He worried, briefly, that he might have to face them farther up the trail. He was capable of imagining the future, though only in the most abstract terms.

It was when he saw the dying behemoth that he first felt fear.

He was no stranger to scavenging. No meal too old or ripe that it could be passed up. He stomped over toward the soon-to-be corpse, his jaw flexing in the air, spilling saliva. He darted in for a quick bite of its liver, knowing its tail wouldn't strike as fast or as quick as it used to. Yet even as he claimed his prize he caught a whiff of that same strange corruption he'd tasted before, the awful inedible stink of the dying lizard. He reared back, red meat spilling unchewed from his mouth.

He reared back—just in time. The behemoth was already in mid-retaliatory strike. Not with its dangerous tail but with its beak-like mouth, which snapped at the air right where the tyrant's throat had been, a moment before.

Utter nonsense, of course. The behemoth was a plant eater. Its teeth couldn't tear and rend meat. Yet even as the tyrant stepped slowly backwards, away from the giant herbivore, it snapped again and again at his skin. At his life.

It raised itself up on broken legs, pushed upright by sheer will. Its guts trailed behind it, its ravaged tail dragging.

Its eyes glowed, positively glowed not with reflected sunlight but with an inner, evil illumination. The color of the dust all around them.

Its liver fell to the ground behind it. Its lungs slithered out, dangling on stringy blood vessels that ripped and tore. Its heart plopped onto the dusty soil.

And still it came, lurching for his blood.

The tyrant, utterly incapable of understanding what he saw, ran.

He ran as fast as he could.

He came along a bend in the trail, a place where a lip of rock jutted out over the valley. Short of breath and weak with hunger, he slowed and came to a panting stop, and simply let his chest heave for a moment, sucking in oxygen that was tainted with the blowing drifts of dust, even this high up. He breathed, and let his pulse slow, and tried to regain his composure. And then he looked down on the valley, on what had been his empire. And he saw.

He saw what had brought the behemoth low. He saw what had come of the little meat animals that burrowed through the dust. He saw they had gone to war.

Final, apocalyptic war. A war of all against all.

The dust boiled with impossible combat. Animals that once had known their place in the web of life now driven mad by insatiable hunger. Plant-eaters ganging up on predators, tearing them to gobbets of meat, then turning on each other. Long, loping herd beasts turned killers, their blunt teeth chewing and chewing on tough skin. He saw legs torn off, he saw skulls cracked, little ones feasting on the brains of giants, giants that had never tasted flesh now lifting maws caked with gore. And their eyes—

Their eyes all burned. That same dull fire blazed in their eyes, in every eye.

The tyrant could not imagine hell, or the end of all things. Yet in the heart of every emperor and king lurks the same nightmare, the possibility of revolution. That moment when the rightful rulers are tossed from their thrones by the ravening mob. The tyrant could understand that wrongness, that irruption of propriety, and he knew that impossible day had come.

The little ones, the meek, the helpless. They were devouring their former masters, eating forbidden meat with reckless abandon. They were torn apart themselves, ripped to pieces. And yet the pieces kept moving. Kept returning to the melee, as long as they had jaws to snap, claws to tear.

This was a revolution not just against the proper order, but against the greatest monarch of them all, the satrap that would one day come even for the tyrant himself. This was a revolt against death itself.

And the little ones were already climbing the slope. Coming for the tyrant. Coming for anything that still lived. It looked like the world-killer, which had surely brought this madness, was going to live up to its name.

The tyrant turned his face upward again, running now not even for survival but simply for fear, for the fear of being torn apart by tiny blunt teeth. He ran, slipping and sliding and losing ground, he ran on pure instinct.

A grumbling roar met him as he ran. A warning shout. He lifted his square head and looked, and saw the nemesis above him on the trail. Standing between him and safety.

They had met in combat before, though never with this ferocity, this level of panic. The struggle of jaws versus horns was an old one and it followed certain rules. There were moves, gambits to be attempted, feints and ripostes hardwired into the tyrant's brain. He came in quickly from the left, and as the nemesis swung its massive frilled skull that way, the tyrant darted right, trying to get behind the giant's armored head. Its flanks and belly, those were the weak spots, and if he could just—

The nemesis shrieked in fury and the tyrant did too, as he felt one of those three horns dig a deep trench through his own soft-fleshed chest. Blood ran and the tyrant's breath came hot and fast. He scrabbled at the enemy with his short forelimbs, his tiny claws that could never gain purchase on the smooth bony frill. He snatched with his teeth at the nemesis's eyes, trying to make it flinch. The nemesis stood its ground. It stamped its elephantine feet and snorted, defying the tyrant to try again.

The tyrant heard something, a pattering of feet from behind. He risked a glance backwards and saw they had an audience. A thousand, a million burning eyes coming up on their heels, ready to interrupt this duel of the ages, ready to devour them both.

SIC OLIM TYRANNIS

It was now or never.

The nemesis had backed up, a little, readying itself for a charge. Its head was down, horns pointed forward like three lances. It was a lumbering beast, but once it got up to speed it would run at him like a fiery comet, a fast blur of motion and then it would gore him, pin him on its horns and push him back, push him as his little arms beat at its plow-shaped face. It would disembowel him—

If he let it.

The nemesis charged with all the strength in its massive legs, hurtling toward him in a perfectly straight line. The tyrant waited, standing there as if he'd given up, as if he'd accepted this final pass—until the last possible moment. Then he broke left, his feet slapping at the ground. He didn't quite get out of the way, but instead of goring him those horns knocked him ass-over-head rolling up the path. The tyrant scrabbled to recover his footing. The nemesis started to wheel around, loosing horrible cries. It knew the game, just as the tyrant did. The tyrant was behind it now, ready to strike at its unprotected sides, and it turned as quickly as it could.

But for once—just this once—the tyrant didn't take the opportunity. Instead he turned tail and ran. Because he knew what was about to happen.

Behind him, even as the nemesis prepared for another charge, the wave of dead-eyed plant-eaters rolled up the trail. It broke over the nemesis, all those dead mouths clamoring for living flesh.

The nemesis' screams chased the tyrant all the way to the top of the world.

The air was better up there. Cleaner. As the tyrant's lungs surged, they no longer sucked in great snootfuls of dust. He could see what lay ahead of him, and it was good. A long, easy slope leading down into a new world, a hidden world of canyons that wound between the mountain peaks. He saw nothing moving down there, neither living nor dead.

He could hide in those canyons. He could nurse his wounds down there and consider his options.

He was going to make it.

He wanted to rest. He needed to eat. Those things didn't matter. He was going to head down into those shadowy canyons and he was going to live. He would survive. A hundred million years of evolution had made him the master of this world. One rock from space couldn't end that winning streak. He, perhaps alone, would remain, would outlast the end times.

And it was good. So very, very good to be alive.

His lips peeled back in his trademark evil grin as he headed down the slope. So much easier to climb down than up. He settled into a relaxed, energy-conserving lope, and the fear began to subside. The things behind him could have the valley, the dead things. The not-dead things, they could consume one another all day if they wanted. He had made it out, passed beyond the vale of death. He would find something to eat, and then he would think about how to reconsolidate. How to regain his crown, as the undisputed master of the food chain. He would—

There was no sound, but something moved. He froze and looked around. And saw it had been a shadow. A dark spot flashing across the rocky ground, there and then gone.

It came again. He twitched his head back and forth, looking for what made that shadow. What was up there with him, up in the heights.

Then he heard a piercing cry, a warbling ululation. And he looked up.

He'd forgotten about the fliers.

One wheeled above him, now, its streamlined head cutting through the wind. Its wings were ragged, torn. Its chest had been torn open and its ribs exposed. It was missing one of its feet.

Its eyes burned with unearthly fire.

It cried again, a shrieking that cut through the tyrant's brain like a drill.

And then it dove to attack.

Tiny claws scrabbled at a bit of loose soil, sending grains of dirt rolling back, down the long ramp of the burrow. A little face, ringed with fur, pressed out into the light, and a pink nose twitched at the air. Bright eyes looked out on a world still clogged with dust from the stars, but there was less of it then there had been before. It was blowing away, blowing down toward the sea.

The furry creature climbed a little further out of its burrow, one foot still underground, ready to dart back into the safety of darkness at the slightest provocation. The mammals of this time were timid things. They needed to be.

The shrew-like animal saw nothing moving. It crept a little further into the world. It saw a wall of fallen flesh before it. A heap of meat as big as a hill. The mammal was an omnivore, and not picky about eating dead things. It took a few tentative steps toward that massive windfall of calories. It twitched its nose at the smell.

The tyrant's eye opened like a portal into a burning abyss. Its head started to lift from the ground. Much of its face had been chewed away, but that only revealed more of its massive, toothy grin.

The mammal bolted back into its tunnel, scrabbling down the slope of loose dirt, and it didn't stop until it was curled in a ball with its mate and its children. Some of them looked up with curious eyes. They saw what had happened in their father's aspect, his quick, spasmodic breaths.

It wasn't safe out there.

Not yet.

Shh, their mother whispered, in that language every mother shares with her children. Calm yourselves. It'll be a while longer, yes. But just a little while longer.

Soon, she told them,

Soon.

THE WASHINGTONIANS

BENTLEY LITTLE

I WILL SKIN your Children and Eat Them.
Upon Finishing, I will Fashion Utensils of Their Bones.

"It's authentic," Davis admitted. "It was written by George Washington." He flipped off the light and, with gloved fingers, removed the parchment manuscript from underneath the magnifier. He shook his head. "Where did you get this? I've never come across anything like it in all my years in the business."

Mike shook his head. "I told you. It was in a trunk of my great- grandmother's stuff that we found hidden in her barn."

"May I ask what you intend to do with it?"

"Well, if it was authentic, we were thinking we'd donate it to the Smithsonian or something. Or sell it to the Smithsonian, if we could. What's the appraisal value of something like this?"

Davis spread his hands in an expansive gesture. "It's invaluable."

"A ballpark figure."

He leaned forward, across the counter. "I'm not sure you realize what you have here, Mr. Franks. With this one sheet of paper, you can entirely rewrite the history of our country." He paused, letting his words sink in. "History is myth, Mr. Franks. It's not just a collection of names and dates and facts. It's a belief system that ultimately tells more about the people buying into it than it does about the historical participants. What do we retain from our school lessons about George Washington? About Abraham Lincoln? Impressions. Washington was the father of our country. Lincoln freed the slaves. We are who we are as a nation because of what we believe they were. This letter will shatter that belief system and will forever change the image we have of Washington and perhaps all our Founding Fathers. That's a huge responsibility, and I think you should think about it."

"Think about it?"

"Decide if you want to make this knowledge known."

Mike stared at him. "Cover it up? Why? If it's true, then people should know."

"People don't want truth. They want image."

"Yeah, right. How much do I owe you?"

"The appraisal fee is fifty dollars." Davis started to write out a receipt, then paused, looked up. "I know a collector," he said. "He's had feelers out for something of this nature for a very long time. Would you mind if I gave him a ring? He's very discreet, very powerful, and, I have reason to believe, very generous."

"No thanks."

"I'd call him for you, set up all the—"

"Not interested," Mike said.

"Very well." Davis returned to the receipt. He finished writing, tore the perforated edge of the paper, and handed Mike a copy. "But if I may, Mr. Franks, I'd like to suggest you do something."

"What's that?" Mike asked as he took the receipt.

"Sleep on it."

He thought about Washington's letter all the way home. It was lying on the passenger seat beside him, in a protective plastic sleeve that Davis had given him, and he could see it in his peripheral vision, dully reflecting the sun each time he turned north. It felt strange owning something so valuable. He had never had anything this rare in his car before, and it carried with it a lot of responsibility. It made him nervous. He probably should've had it insured before taking it anywhere. What if the car crashed? What if the parchment burned? His hands on the wheel were sweaty.

But that wasn't why his hands were sweaty. That wasn't really why he was nervous. No. That was part of it, but the real reason was the note itself.

I will Skin your Children and Eat Them.

The fact that the words had been written by a real person and not a character in a novel would have automatically made him uneasy. But the fact that they had been written by George Washington . . . Well, that was just too hard to take. There was something creepy about that, something that made a ripple of gooseflesh crawl up the back of his neck each time he looked at the plastic-wrapped brown parchment. He should have felt excited, proud, but instead he felt dirty, oily. He suddenly wished he'd never seen the note.

Ahead of him on a billboard above a liquor store, a caricature of George Washington-green, the way he appeared on the dollar bill-was winking at him, promoting the high T-bill rate at the Bank of New York.

He looked away from the sign, turned down Lincoln Avenue toward home.

Mike paced up and down the length of the kitchen. "He implied that rather than give it to the Smithsonian or something, I should sell it to a private collector who would keep it a secret."

Pam looked up from the dishes, shook her head. "That's crazy."

"That's what I said."

"Well, don't get too stressed out over it—"

"I'm not getting stressed out."

"Will you let me finish my sentence? I was just going to say, there are a lot of other document appraisers, a lot of museum curators, a lot of university professors. There are a lot of people you can take this to who will know what to do with it."

He nodded, touched her arm. "You're right. I'm sorry. I'm just . . . I don't know. This whole thing has me a little freaked."

"Me too. This afternoon I was helping Amy with her homework. They're studying Johnny Appleseed and George Washington and the cherry tree."

"Two myths."

"There's a picture of Washington in her book . . . " She shivered, dipped her hands back into the soap suds. "You ought to look at it. It'll give you the willies."

He smiled at her. "I could give you my willy."

"Later."

"Really creepy, huh?"

"Check it out for yourself."

"I will. You need me in here?"

"No."

He patted the seat of her jeans, gave her a quick kiss on the cheek. "I'll be out front then."

"All right. I'll be through here in a minute. Go over Amy's math homework, too. Double-check."

"Okay." He walked into the living room. Amy was lying on the floor watching a rerun of Everybody Loves Raymond. Her schoolbook and homework were on the coffee table. He sat down on the couch and was about to pick up the book, when he saw the cover: mountains and clouds and a clipper ship and the Statue of Liberty and the Liberty Bell. The cover was drawn simply, in bright grade school colors, but there was something about the smile on the Statue of Liberty's face that made him realize he did not want to open up the book to see the picture of George Washington.

A commercial came on, and Amy turned around to look at him. "Are you going to check my homework?" she asked. He nodded. "Yes," he said. "Do it quick, then. I'm watching TV." He smiled at her. "Yes, boss."

The pounding woke them up.

It must have been going on for some time, because Amy was standing in the doorway of their bedroom clutching her teddy bear, though she'd supposedly given up the teddy bear two years ago.

Pam gave him a look that let him know how frightened she was, that told him to go out to the living room and find out who the hell was beating on their front door at this time of night, then she was no longer Wife but Mom, and she was out of bed and striding purposefully toward their daughter, telling her in a calm, reasonable, adult voice to go back to bed, that there was nothing the matter.

Mike quickly reached down for the jeans he'd abandoned on the floor next to the bed and put them on. The pounding continued unabated, and he felt more than a little frightened himself. But he was Husband and Dad and this was one of those things Husbands and Dads had to do, and he strode quickly out to the living room with a walk and an attitude that made him seem much braver than he actually felt.

He slowed down as he walked across the dark living room toward the entryway. Out here, the pounding seemed much louder and much . . . scarier. There was a strength and will behind the pounding that had not translated across the rooms to the rear of the house and he found himself thinking absurdly that whatever was knocking on the door was not human. It was a stupid thought, an irrational thought, but he stopped at the edge of the entryway nevertheless. The door was solid, there was no window in it, not even a peephole, and he did not want to just open it without knowing who-what-was on the other side.

He moved quickly over to the front window. He didn't want to pull the drapes open and draw attention to himself, but he wanted to get a peek at the pounder. There was a small slit where the two halves of the drapes met in the middle of the window, and he bent over to peer through the opening.

Outside on the porch, facing the door, were four

men wearing white powdered wigs and satin colonial garb.

He thought for a second that he was dreaming. The surrealistic irrationality of this seemed more nightmarish than real. But he saw one of the men pound loudly on the door with his bunched fist, and from the back of the house he heard the muffled sound of Pam's voice as she comforted Amy, and he knew that this was really happening.

He should open the door, he knew. He should confront these people. But something about that bunched fist and the look of angry determination on the pounder's face made him hesitate. He was frightened, he realized. More frightened than he had been before he'd peeked through the curtains, when he'd still half thought there might be a monster outside.

I will Skin your Children and Eat Them.

These weirdos were connected somehow to Washington's note. He knew that instinctively. And that was what scared him.

He heard Pam hurrying across the living room toward him, obviously alarmed by the fact that the pounding had not yet stopped. She moved quickly next to him. "Who is it?" she whispered.

He shook his head. "I don't know."

He peeked again through the split in the curtains, studying the strangers more carefully. She pressed her face next to his. He heard her gasp, felt her pull away. "Jesus," she whispered. There was fear in her voice. "Look at their teeth."

Their teeth? He focused his attention on the men's mouths. Pam was right. There was something strange about their teeth. He squinted, looked closer.

Their teeth were uniformly yellow.

Their teeth were false.

George Washington had false teeth.

He backed away from the window. "Call the police," he told Pam. "Now."

"We want the letter!" The voice was strong, filled with an anger and hatred he had not expected. The pounding stopped. "We know you have it, Franks! Give it to us and we will not harm you!"

Mike looked again through the parted curtains. All four of the men were facing the window, staring at him. In the porchlight their skin looked pale, almost corpselike, their eyes brightly fanatic. The man who had been pounding on the door pointed at him. Rage twisted the features of his face. "Give us the letter!"

He wanted to move away, to hide, but Mike forced himself to hold his ground. He was not sure if the men could actually see him through that small slit, but he assumed they could. "I called the police!" he bluffed. "They'll be here any minute!"

The pounder was about to say something but at that second, fate stepped in and there was the sound of a siren coming from somewhere to the east. The men looked confusedly at each other, spoke quietly and quickly between themselves, then began hurrying off the porch. On their arms, Mike saw round silk patches with stylized insignias.

A hatchet and a cherry tree.

"We will be back for you!" one of the men said. "You can't escape!"

"Mom!" Amy called from her bedroom.

"Go get her," Mike said.

"You call the police then."

382

He nodded as she moved off, but even as he headed toward the phone, he knew with a strange fatalistic certainty that the police would not be able to track down these people, that when these people came back-and they would come back-the police would not be able to protect him and his family.

He heard a car engine roar to life, heard tires squealing on the street.

He picked up the phone and dialed 911.

He left Pam and Amy home alone the next morning, told them not to answer the door or the telephone and to call the police if they saw any strangers hanging around the neighborhood. He had formulated a plan during the long sleepless hours between the cops' departure and dawn, and he drove to New York University, asking a fresh-faced clerk in administration where the history department was located. Following the kid's directions across campus, he read the posted signs until he found the correct building.

The secretary of the history department informed him that Dr. Hartkinson had his office hours from eight to ten-thirty and was available to speak with him, and he followed her down the hallway to the professor's office.

Hartkinson stood upon introduction and shook his hand. He was an elderly man in his mid- to late sixties, with the short stature, spectacles, and whiskers of a Disney movie college professor. "Have a seat," the old man said, clearing a stack of papers from an old straight-backed chair. He thanked the secretary, who retreated down the hall, then moved back behind his oversized desk and sat down himself. "What can I do for you?"

Mike cleared his throat nervously. "I don't really know how to bring this up. It may sound kind of stupid to you, but last night my wife and I were . . . well, we were sleeping, and we were woken up by this pounding on our front door. I went out to investigate, and there were these four men on my porch, calling out my name and threatening me. They were wearing powdered wigs and what looked like Revolutionary War clothes—"

The old man's eyes widened. "Washingtonians!"

"Washingtonians?"

"Shh!" The professor quickly stood and closed his office door. His relaxed, easygoing manner no longer seemed so relaxed and easygoing. There was a tenseness in his movements, an urgency in his walk. He immediately sat back down, took the phone off the hook, and pulled closed his lone window. He leaned conspiratorially across the desk, and when he spoke his voice was low and frightened. "You're lucky you came to me," he said. "They have spies everywhere."

"What?"

"Dr. Gluck and Dr. Cannon, in our history department here, are Washingtonians. Most of the other professors are sympathizers. It's pure luck you talked to me first. What do you have?"

"What?"

"Come on now. They wouldn't have come after you unless you had something they wanted. What is it? A letter?"

Mike nodded dumbly.

"I thought so. What did this letter say?"

Mike reached into his coat pocket and pulled out the piece of parchment.

The professor took the note out of the plastic. He nodded when he'd finished reading. "The truth. That's what's in this letter."

Mike nodded.

"George Washington was a cannibal. He was a fiend and a murderer and a child eater. But he was also chosen to be the father of our country, and that image is more important than the actuality."

"Someone else told me that."

"He was right." The professor shifted in his seat. "Let me tell you something about historians. Historians, for the most part, are not interested in truth. They are not interested in learning facts and teaching people what really happened. They want to perpetuate the lies they are sworn to defend. It's an exclusive club, the people who know why our wars were really fought, what really happened behind the closed doors of our world's leaders, and most of them want to keep it that way. There are a few of us altruists, people like myself who got into this business to learn and share our learning. But the majority of historians are PR people for the past." He thought for a moment. "Benjamin Franklin did not exist. Did you know that? He never lived. He was a composite character created for mass consumption. It was felt by the historians that a character was needed who would embody America's scientific curiosity, boldness of vision, and farsighted determination, who would inspire people to reach for greatness in intellectual endeavors. So they came up with Franklin, an avuncular American Renaissance man. Americans wanted to believe in Franklin, wanted to believe that his qualities were their qualities, and they bought into the concept lock, stock, and barrel, even falling for that absurd kite story.

"It was the same with Washington. Americans wanted him to be the father of our country, needed him to be the father of our country, and they were only too happy to believe what we historians told them."

Mike stared at Hartkinson, then looked away toward the rows of history books on the professor's shelves. These were the men who had really determined our country's course, he realized. The historians. They had altered the past and affected the future. It was not the great men who shaped the world, it was the men who told of the great men who shaped the world.

"You've stumbled upon something here," Hartkinson said. "And that's why they're after you. That note's like a leak from Nixon's White House, and the President's going to do everything in his power to make damn sure it goes no further than you. Like I said, the history biz isn't anything like it appears on the outside. It's a weird world in here, weird and secretive. And the Washingtonians . . . " He shook his head, "They're the fringe of the fringe. And they are a very dangerous group indeed."

"They all had wooden teeth, the ones who came to my house—"

"Ivory, not wood. That's one of those little pieces of trivia they're very adamant about getting out to the public. The original core group of Washingtonians screwed up on that one, and subsequent generations have felt that the impression that was created made Washington out to be a weak buffoon. They've had a hard time erasing that 'wooden teeth' image, though."

"Is that how you can spot them? Their teeth?"

"No. They wear modern dentures when they're not in uniform. They're like the Klan in that respect."

"Only in that respect?"

The professor met his eyes. "No."

"What . . . " He cleared his throat. "What will they try to do to me?"

"Kill you. And eat you."

Mike stood. "Jesus fucking Christ. I'm going to the police with this. I'm not going to let them terrorize my family—"

"Now just hold your horses there. That's what they'll try to do to you. If you listen to me, and if you do exactly what I say, they won't succeed." He looked at Mike, tried unsuccessfully to smile. "I'm going to help you. But you'll have to tell me a few things first. Do you have any children? Any daughters?"

"Yes. Amy."

"This is kind of awkward. Is she . . . a virgin?"

"She's ten years old!"

The professor frowned. "That's not good."

"Why isn't it good?"

"Have you see the insignia they wear on their arms?"

"The hatchet and the cherry tree?"

"Yes."

"What about it?"

"That was Professor Summerlin's contribution. The Washingtonians have always interpreted the cherry tree story as a cannibal allegory, a metaphoric retelling of Washington's discovery of the joys of killing people and eating their flesh. To take it a step further, Washington's fondness for the meat of virgins is well documented, and that's what made Professor Summerlin think of the patch. He simply updated the symbol to include the modern colloquial definition of 'cherry.'"

Mike understood what Hartkinson meant, and he felt sick to his stomach.

"They all like virgin meat," the professor said.

"I'm going to the police. Thanks for your help and all, but I don't think you can—"

The door to the office was suddenly thrown open, and there they stood: four men and one woman dressed in Revolutionary garb. Mike saw yellowish teeth in smiling mouths.

"You should have known better, Julius," the tallest man said, pushing his way into the room.

"Run!" Hartkinson yelled.

Mike tried to, making a full-bore, straight-ahead dash toward the door, but he was stopped by the line of unmoving Washingtonians. He'd thought he'd be able to break through, to knock a few of them over and take off down the hall, but evidently they had expected that and were prepared.

Two of the men grabbed Mike and held him.

"My wife'll call the police if I'm not back in time."

"Who cares?" the tall man said.

"They'll publish it!" Mike yelled in desperation. "I gave orders for them to publish the letter if anything happened to me! If I was even late."

The woman looked at him calmly. "No, you didn't."

"Yes, I did. My wife'll—"

"We have your wife," she said.

A stab of terror flashed through him.

She smiled at him, nodding. "And your daughter."

He was not sure where they were taking him, but wherever it was, it was far. Although he was struggling as they hustled him out of the building and into their van, no one tried to help him or tried to stop them. A few onlookers smiled indulgently, as though they were witnessing the rehearsal of a play or a staged publicity stunt, but that was the extent of the attention they received.

If only they hadn't been wearing those damn costumes, Mike thought. His abduction wouldn't have looked so comical if they'd been dressed in terrorist attire.

He was thrown into the rear of the van, the door was slammed shut, and a few seconds later the engine roared to life and they were off.

They drove for hours. There were no windows in the back of the van, and he could not tell in which direction they were traveling, but after a series of initial stops and starts and turns, the route straightened out, the speed became constant, and he assumed they were moving along a highway.

When the van finally stopped and the back door was opened and he was dragged out, it was in the country, in a wooded, meadow area that was unfamiliar to him. Through the trees he saw a building, a white, green-trimmed colonial structure that he almost but not quite recognized. The Washingtonians led him away from the building to a small shed. The shed door was opened, and he saw a dark tunnel and a series of steps leading down. Two

389

of the Washingtonians went before him, the other three remained behind him, and in a group they descended the stairway.

Mt. Vernon, Mike suddenly realized. The building was Mt. Vernon, George Washington's home.

The steps ended at a tunnel, which wound back in the direction of the building and ended in a large warehouse-sized basement that looked as if it had been converted into a museum of the Inquisition. They were underneath Mt. Vernon, he assumed, in what must have been Washington's secret lair.

"Where's Pam?" he demanded. "Where's Amy?"

"You'll see them," the woman said.

The tall man walked over to a cabinet, pointed at the dull ivory objects inside. "These are spoons carved entirely from the femurs of the First Continental Congress." He gestured toward an expensively framed painting hanging above the cabinet. The painting, obviously done by one of early America's finer artists, depicted a blood-spattered George Washington, flanked by two naked and equally blood-spattered women, devouring a screaming man. "Washington commissioned this while he was president."

The man seemed eager to show off the room's possessions, and Mike wondered if he could use that somehow to get an edge, to aid in an escape attempt. He was still being held tightly by two of the Washingtonians, and though he had not tried breaking out of their grip since entering the basement, he knew he would not be able to do so.

The tall man continued to stare reverently at the painting. "He acquired the taste during the winter when he and his men were starving and without supplies or reinforcements. The army began to eat its dead, and Washington found that he liked the taste. During the long days, he carved eating utensils and small good luck fetishes from the bones of the devoured men. Even after supplies began arriving, he continued to kill a man a day for his meals."

"He began to realize that with the army in his control, he was in a position to call the shots," the woman explained from behind him. "He could create a country of cannibals. A nation celebrating and dedicated to the eating of human flesh!"

Mike turned his head, looked at her. "He didn't do it, though, did he?" He shook his head. "You people are so full of crap."

"You won't think so when we eat your daughter's kidneys."

Anger coursed through him and Mike tried to jerk out of his captors' grasps. The men's grips tightened, and he soon gave up, slumping back in defeat. The tall man ran a hand lovingly over the top of a strange tablelike contraption in the middle of the room. "This is where John Hancock was flayed alive," he said. "His blood anointed this wood. His screams sang in these chambers."

"You're full of shit."

"Am I?" He looked dreamily around the room. "Jefferson gave his life for us, you know. Sacrificed himself right here, allowed Washingtonians to rip him apart with their teeth. Franklin donated his body to us after death—"

"There was no Benjamin Franklin."

The man smiled, showing overly white teeth. "So you know."

"Shouldn't you be wearing your wooden choppers?"

The man punched him in the stomach, and Mike doubled over, pain flaring in his abdomen, his lungs suddenly unable to draw in enough breath.

"You are not a guest," the man said. "You are a prisoner. Our prisoner. For now." He smiled. "Later you may be supper."

Mike closed his eyes, tried not to vomit. When he could again breathe normally, he looked up at the man. "Why this James Bond shit? You going to give me your whole fucking history before you kill me? You going to explain all of your toys to me and hope I admire them? Fuck you! Eat me, you sick assholes!"

The woman grinned. "Don't worry. We will."

A door opened at the opposite end of the room, and Pam and Amy were herded in by three new Washingtonians. His daughter and wife looked white and frightened. Amy was crying, and she cried even harder when she saw him. "Daddy!" she screamed.

"Lunch," the tall man said. "Start up the barbecue."

The Washingtonians laughed.

The woman turned to Mike. "Give us the letter," she said.

"And you'll let me go? Yeah. Right."

Where was the letter? he wondered. Hartkinson had had it last. Had he destroyed it or ditched it somewhere, like a junkie flushing drugs down the toilet after the arrival of the cops?

And where was Hartkinson? Why hadn't they kidnapped him, too?

He was about to ask just that very question when there was the sound of scuffling from the door through which Pam and Amy had entered. All of the Washingtonians turned to face that direction.

And there was Hartkinson.

He was dressed in a red British Revolutionary War uniform, and behind him stood a group of other redcoats clutching bayonets. A confused and frightened youth, who looked like a tour guide, peered into the room from behind them.

"Unhand those civilians!" Hartkinson demanded in an affected British accent.

He and his friends looked comical in their shabby mis-matched British uniforms, but they also looked heroic, and Mike's adrenaline started pumping as they burst through the doorway. There were a lot of them, he saw, fifteen or twenty, and they outnumbered the Washingtonians more than two to one.

Two of the Washingtonians drew knives and ran toward Pam and Amy.

"No!" Mike yelled.

Musket balls cut the men down in midstride.

Mike took a chance and tried his escape tactic again. Either the men holding him were distracted or their grip had simply weakened after all this time, but he successfully jerked out of their hands, broke away, and turned and kicked one of the men hard in the groin. The other man moved quickly out of his way, but Mike didn't care. He ran across the room, past arcane torture devices, to Pam and Amy.

"Attack!" someone yelled.

The fight began.

It was mercifully short. Mike heard gunfire, heard ricochets, heard screams, saw frenzied movement, but he kept his head low and knew nothing of the specifics of what was happening. All he knew was that by the time he reached Pam and Amy they were free. He stood up from his crouch, looked around the room, and saw instantly that most of the Washingtonians were dead or captured. The tall man was lying on the floor with a dark crimson stain spreading across his powder blue uniform, and that made Mike feel good. Served the bastard right.

Both Pam and Amy were hugging each other and crying, and he hugged them too and found that he was crying as well. He felt a light tap on his shoulder and instinctively whirled around, fists clenched, but it was only Hartkinson.

Mike stared at him for a moment, blinked. "Thank you," he said, and he began crying anew, tears of relief. "Thank you."

The professor nodded, smiled. There were flecks of blood in his white Disney beard. "Leave," he said. "You don't want to see what comes next."

"But—"

His voice was gentle. "The Washingtonians aren't the only ones with . . . different traditions."

"You're not cannibals, too?"

"No, but . . . " He shook his head. "You'd better go."

Mike looked at Pam and Amy, and nodded.

From inside his red coat, Hartkinson withdrew a piece of parchment wrapped in plastic.

The letter.

"Take it to the Smithsonian. Tell the world." His voice was low and filled with reverence. "It's history."

"Are you going to be okay here?"

"We've done this before." He gestured toward the tour guide, who was still standing in the corner. "He'll show you the way out." He shook his head, smiling ruefully. "The history biz is not like it appears from the outside."

"I guess not." Mike put his arm around Pam, who in turn pulled Amy toward the door. The tour guide, white-faced, started slowly up the steps.

"Don't look back," Hartkinson advised.

Mike waved his acquiescence and began walking up the stairs, clutching Washington's letter. Behind them, he heard screams-cries of terror, cries of pain-and though he didn't want to, though he knew he shouldn't, he smiled as he led his family out of the basement and into Washington's home above.

SCENT OF FLESH

JESSICA MARIE BAUMGARTNER

"**W**HERE ARE YOU, you damn varmint?" Annie clutched her father's busted up muzzle-loading rifle. Her ragged hair rustled in the wind. The chill didn't bite her though; she preferred hunting in winter.

Too easy. Her father had laughed when she expressed her fondness of it as a child. The game got no place to hide, "'specially if it snows," he had said.

The frayed ends of her skirt were pulled tight over her thick boots. She held steady, squatting in layered pairs of thick pantaloons. Fighting off her father's memory, she focused on the shadows, darted her gaze from side to side.

She had already laid down a deer, and caught a couple of rabbits. The meat would feed her family well. The money earned from the Willowdell butcher often nourished them more than a meal could. But the fleshy scent of the carcasses was what she relied on at this moment.

"I know you're out there." She growled through her teeth.

Her sharp eyes had glimpsed something unnatural. Its image followed her, haunted her waking hours, until the past dredged through her dreams. Dreams they were.

Annie refused to believe in nightmares. Anything she feared at night, she knew she could kill once awake.

"Phoebe," the unmistakable baritone of her father's voice called from her left.

She breathed slow and tilted her head toward it. Long lines of timber and fur jetted through the grey darkness that dimmed with each moment.

Night. Her mouth curved. Night hunts brought peace once the bullet was released. Her fingers itched for the trigger, but she held steady.

It's a wallop of a game, she thought.

The ground crunched on the hill some forty yards to her left. She narrowed her eyes and met the glowing yellow gaze that crested the hilltop for only a second.

Gotcha! She fired. But the lanky frame brushed aside, like a tree in a storm.

She slapped her knee and grabbed her rifle rushing forward, weaving through trees left and right, working to confuse the giant before her. Its grey flesh matched the moonlight on the tree trunks. She fought off the urge to hold her nose against the putrid smell of death that wafted around her. She knew the haggard breathing better than anything. The croaking rasp was often mistaken for dead branches swaying, but she had hunted enough to decipher the difference.

Nearing the icy cannibal, her pulse thumped from her ears to her toes. Her chest drummed with each drop of her quick feet, until she froze.

Her legs shook and she whimpered. "Daddy?"

"Phoebe?"

How dare it mimic her father's voice. Only he had ever called her by her first name. To everyone else she was Annie.

"Daddy?" She lowered the rifle, relaxed her grip.

"I've missed you, Phoebe."

She glanced around the darkened branches. Scanning the conifers with hope she sighed. "Me too, Daddy."

"Stop hunting and come with me."

"Okay." She let the rifle fall.

With one sharp jerk, the festering monster raced toward her with long sharp teeth ready.

Annie fell to her knees, caught the rifle with her left hand, and pulled up enough to get off a clear shot. Straight between the eyes. They're getting smarter. She cried out, howling like a wolf, into the night.

"I hate having to play the sad little girl." She stood and prodded the dead creature with the barrel of her gun. The beast's tongue protruded from its mouth. Ice clung to the mats in its wiry fur.

Annie scratched her nose. She pulled her collar over her face and inhaled through her mouth to dull the stench. "One deer, two rabbits, and one less monster to terrorize the town."

Daddy'd be proud. She closed her eyes for a moment and took in the silence. Soon the wolves would be back. Coyotes could howl in safety again. Foxes and owls would roam.

She walked back to her pack and untied her shovel. I've lost two fathers to these beasts. Ain't gonna lose another.

Despite her hatred of the ice creatures, she couldn't leave the slain. Even after being attacked, her father had made it home to die with dignity. Her step-father hadn't been so lucky, but it never settled her stomach to leave any kill behind.

"You cain't keep running off so late."

Annie eyed her mother's new husband with a straight face. Lord knows he wouldn't make it a day in the woods. She bit down on her tongue and held in the laughter.

His tailored jacket and perfect pants said it all.

"Mama." She turned in her seat.

Her mother set a plate of biscuits before her brothers and sisters.

"You scared me half to death."

"Ain't nothing to fear for me," Annie said.

"Phoebe."

The children stopped.

Annie glared at her new step-father. How dare he call her by that name.

Her mother rushed to him and patted his back. "Joe, let me handle her."

Annie stiffened. She sat up with perfect posture.

Her step-father raised his coffee to his lips and grunted.

"Annie, it's been hard enough to keep tabs on everyone what with me and your father working all day."

Her third father seemed less prepared than her second, who was nothing of note compared to the man who bore her.

"Nobody gets a shot past me. And if it weren't for my efforts, we'd all starve." Annie rose, anxious to escape back to the hunt.

Her step-father shot her a dark scowl. His beady eyes were as black as his coffee. His moustache twitched.

"You may be excused," her mother called after her.

Excused? She grabbed her father's Kentucky rifle this time and pulled her pack over her shoulder. Mama's always excusing something.

It seemed to be her mother's place to brush off what she couldn't understand. She had never accepted the truth of Annie's importance. Even after losing a second husband she refused to believe anything Annie had tried to tell her about the monsters.

I'll leave her to her fancies. Annie straightened her skirt and marched out. The clearing around their meager home ended in a tangled brush. She pushed beyond the burrs and stepped around a few vines.

She scanned the leaves coating the ground before her. Their thick bed made it easier to walk, but her heel toe movements were harder to stifle.

Slowing her steps, she gripped her father's gun. No shadows reached for her. No limbs quickened to grab for flesh. Disappointment nearly took over, but she had a job to do.

The exhilaration of destroying a monster had worn off. It left the dull duties of attempting to appease her mother more burdensome than ever. Annie grew angry at the denial.

She grabbed some sticks and propped them in the knobs of a sickly tree. How can she be so blind? Annie jogged away.

The freedom of the clean air cut her lungs with a burning chill. She glanced over her shoulder and slowed to a walk. "I will always look for what my eyes cain't see."

Turning to face her mark, she contemplated stepping further back. The twigs stuck out of the tree like mere match sticks from the distance, but she needed to shoot. The heat of her rifle would cool her senses.

Setting up, she blasted off her first mark. It struck the stick in half. Annie frowned. Nope. Too close.

She put more space between the range. Forty paces. Spinning around once more, she didn't even need a breath. The squeeze came off the trigger like a born reflex, and the tip of the next twig was shot off.

"Hooey!" She grinned. "How's that for keeping tabs?"

She backed up fifteen more paces and fired again, and again, and again; until the sticks and the knobs on the tree were shot off.

The smoke darkened the air with a musty curtain of powder. She breathed it in. "Nothing like gunpowder to get a girl going." She laughed to herself and moved deeper into the forest.

Distance from civilization always cleared her head. She softened her movements and carefully held her skirt with one hand. Focusing ahead, she sought her favorite tree. The sturdy Pin Oak that offered a crooked smile with its empty branches.

She slung her rifle on her back and spit onto her hands. Moving in, she gripped the nearest branch to her head and pulled up. She pushed off the tree with her boots, swinging herself onto the bough, and a few small twigs scratched her cheeks.

Again, she climbed. Her dress snagged. Strands of hair broke loose from her braid and tugged on some wayward branches. Annie tucked the folds of her skirt close. She tilted her head away and didn't stop ascending until her palms throbbed.

Perching above, she was like a hawk with new eyes. Every jack-rabbit and squirrel were found. The deer would be out later.

Annie waited. Each day, she hunted with exercised patience. During night hunts, her game multiplied. She provided enough food for her family that she took some extra meat to the grocer.

"Does your ma know you're here?"

Annie pursed her lips and held up the trio of rabbits by the ankles. "Mr. Kratzenberger, would I be here if she didn't?"

He furrowed his thick black eyebrows.

She held her breath as his deep chestnut eyes seemed intent on finding a lie, but she didn't squirm or fidget.

"How is it that you can bring in enough for all your little brothers and sisters, and still have meat to sell?" His features warmed.

Annie shuffled her feet side-to-side. "Just a good shot."

"Uh-huh." Mr. Kratzenberger rubbed his fingers over his long mustache. "In winter too?"

She smiled at his joking tone. "I love winter."

"Even after your father . . . " He coughed and blinked hard. "No matter. We can always take these off your hands." He grabbed the rabbits by their feet, swinging their lifeless bodies as if they were rag dolls. "Provided that you have plenty at home."

Annie nodded. She waited for her payout before strolling home like she'd won a county fair shoot-out.

"Where you been?" her step-father called after her when she pushed open the door.

"Here's where I been." She walked toward the supper table and handed her mom the money she'd been paid.

Her mother's mouth hung open in a perfect oval. "Lord, Annie. Where on Earth did you come by that?"

"Well," Annie shooed her youngest sister away and made a face at her brothers. "I sold some kill to Mr. Kratzenberger."

"Child, in the middle of winter?"

Annie scrunched up her face. "We have more than enough to get by."

"You don't know how the weather's gonna turn." Her step-father bit off a hunk of bread from his plate.

Her mother got up and grabbed a steel round for her, and put a cut of meat on it. "Here, you eat." She set it down on the table and gestured for Annie to sit. Her eyes shimmered with maternal pride. "Thank you, my dear."

It was like old times. Annie's resentment toward her mother all but vanished with the encouragement.

She took to the trees more often. Longer. Day and night, she hunted. The money helped, and the praise aided, but the longer Annie found safety surrounding her solitude, the more she began to doubt herself. "Ain't no way these woods are cleared."

She studied the trees, hoping to find some unnatural twisting limb. Her ears pricked, but nothing but slight murmurs sounded from the inhabitants of the forest. The dark stillness seemed empty. Too comfortable.

"The monsters have left, but they'll never be gone."

She hugged her gun to her. A shiver rippled through her body and the soft padding of a creature met her ears.

Annie crouched in a fir this time. She allowed the needles to prick her forehead. Sap stuck to her boots, slowing the slightest movements.

Ice beast. She squinted ahead, steadying her eyes. She slowly brought her rifle into position and licked her lips. Sick of the silence, she fired the second its shadow crested the moonlight paling the grass below.

The dead thump of an elk rang in her ears. Annie screamed. She clutched her rifle in her right arm and turned to punch the tree trunk with the other. Another shout of frustration escaped her before she could control the anger, the disappointment.

"I'm a hunter," she reminded herself.

Maybe the monsters ARE gone. A twinge of bitter emptiness filled her. She draped her gun over her shoulder and grasped the branch beneath her.

Steadying her feet, she stepped down to continue lowering herself until she could jump to the ground with ease. Then this is all that's left. She glared at the dead elk's glazed eyes.

Unable to fathom the amount, Annie gaped at Mr. Kratzenberger.

"It's all yours. Take it." He held the money out to her.

She grasped it with a sigh. It would be more than enough, but it still solidified her fate. I came back home for more than this. She imagined the last monster. There has to be more.

"Thank you." She turned to go. Her thoughts

switched to the possibility of keeping every pence-traveling, finding another icy beast, and preventing its terrors.

"Now wait now." Mr. Kratzenberger stopped her. He adjusted his vest and held up a paper. "Ever heard of Mr. Butler?"

She shook her head. Mr. Anyone never much amused her. No one could ever be like her father, and he'd died years before.

"Frank E. Butler is the best shot this side of the Mississippi. Or so says the papers."

Annie's neck itched. Her fingers twitched and she suddenly longed for her gun. "So they say."

Mr. Kratzenberger leaned forward and chuckled. "I know better." He winked at her. "What if I told you I was acquainted with Frank and could set up a contest between the both of you?"

Annie couldn't fight the grin that spread across her entire face. "I'd be inclined to call you a liar. Or a fool. Maybe both."

"Annie, you know your eye." He nodded at the money in her hand. "That there will take care of your ma, but you can do more for yourself."

She balled her fist tight around her earnings and stared at it. Looking back at his assuring gaze, she nodded. "If you can arrange this contest, there's not much I can do but oblige."

"Atta girl!" He almost jumped with excitement.

Annie rushed home, shaking her head. "Ain't no way this'll go off." She set her sight on the faded little shack at the edge of town and went in like she did every day.

Her brothers were running circles around her

sisters hooting and hollering. "Boys, get yourselves outside before I go deaf," her mother shouted from the stove.

Annie bopped them on their heads and hugged her sisters. "There now, you're saved. Come help us bake." She led them toward the worn wooden table beside their mom, and helped knead some dough.

Once it went into the oven, she rubbed her hands on her skirt and pulled the money out from her boot. "Annie, how many times do I hafta tell you not to store things in there?"

Annie pushed back a laugh. She glanced up and placed the money on the table.

Her mom froze.

"It's enough, ain't it?" Annie studied her mother's ashen face. The wrinkles around her eyes pulled straight.

"Enough?"

"To pay off the house, of course."

"Girls, go play." Her mom nudged her sisters away. Then she fell into the chair closest to her. Fanning herself, she gasped.

Annie knelt before her and clasped her mother's hands in her own. "It should be enough."

Her mom squeezed her grip. Tears dripped from her eyes. "I never wanted to send you away. Before. You know."

Annie refused to respond.

"You'd seen it. That thing. It took your father, but you were a child. No one listened. But after it took another, people talked. I know'd you'd seen it when it took my second husband. I'm not that blind. That thing took 'em both from me. Almost took you. I had to send you away for a while. People didn't wanna hear the truth. They were gonna hurt you if it didn't."

Annie's jaw quivered. She fought off tears, but her fingers shook. "I thought you didn't believe me either. That I'd been a burden."

"No!" Her mother gripped Annie's arms and pulled her into a tight hug. She stroked her hair. "But you're back now. And you've done more for me than I ever could for you." Annie gave in. She snuggled against her mom's breast and sobbed. "That asylum, it was . . . cold. They didn't care."

"And you're never going back there." Her mother kissed the top of her head.

Annie sighted her gun. The winds rushed in from the west and set her skirt flapping before the crowd.

Her mom struggled to keep her brothers and sisters back. She nodded at Annie. Her features beamed with approval.

Mr. Kratzenberger scratched his chest and tapped Annie on the shoulder.

She turned to face him. "The mark's too close."

She furrowed her brow and found a tall stranger beside him. Clenching her jaw, she tightened her grip on her gun.

"Let me introduce you two. Annie, this is Frank E. Butler. The best shot this side of the Mississippi." Mr. Kratzenberger's lip curled at one end of his face.

Mr. Butler tipped his hat at her.

"And this is—"

"Put her there." Annie became too aware of her breathing and extended her hand before Mr. Kratzenberger could finish. She meant to shake like any rifleman, but Mr. Butler grasped her hand with a gentility that baffled her teenage mind. He raised it to his lips like some storybook hero and her entire face went hot.

One of her brothers pointed and laughed.

Her mom smacked his hand. Annie couldn't escape the anger that flooded her throat. She grew rigid and repeated herself, "The mark's too close."

Mr. Butler rubbed the back of his neck and chuckled. "She's right, Mr. Kratzenberger. If this is to be a real contest, we need to shoot further and harder."

Mr. Kratzenberger sent Annie a look of puzzlement, but whistled to his brother at the end of the clearing. "Further back, and don't make it too easy!"

His brother, who was almost identical to the sturdy grocer, waved back and took the box of cans 20 paces out.

"Far enough?" Mr. Butler eyed Annie with a curiosity she did not know if she appreciated. Something lay deep in his hazel eyes, a question, or an interest she'd witnessed between men and women but always distanced herself from.

She looked ahead to avoid it. Tall grasses swayed over the flat land. Just outside of town, it was already speckled with a few patches of wildflowers. Winter was dying like the creatures Annie could no longer find.

The townsfolk held back, curving around them. Annie felt puny and beaten already. How can I win against a name like Frank E. Butler?

But he seemed more than a name. He smiled at her. "Ladies first."

"Thank you kindly." She could have spit in his eye.

She stepped aside and touched her rifle against her shoulder. Keeping a firm grip on it, she nodded at Mr. Kratzenberger who whistled for his brother to toss her first mark.

He threw the rusted can overhead.

Annie followed it up until it curved, and fired.

Ding!

Another can. Ding!

And another.

She pulled the trigger, forgetting everyone. The cheers were a dull hum. All she needed was the smoke and the echo of a hit.

More. Ding! More. Ding!

The cans went up faster, higher. Each time they fell, there was a new hole in the metal.

Annie gave herself over to the rhythm, loading and firing as fast as she could.

Twenty-five cans later and she had a perfect record. She looked at the clouds rolling across the sapphire sky, like boats sailing the ocean. The breeze reminded her of why she had come, and she turned to bow.

It seemed the thing to do. Her mother had snuck her into a traveling show to watch a performance once, and they all bowed to the delight of the audience. Now, she straightened to the welcome applause of her family and neighbors. An overwhelming warmth ignited within her.

She scanned the wide eyes and broad grins. Then Mr. Butler stepped up.

He flashed her a charming sideways smirk. "You sure know how to put on a show."

She stared at her boots and clutched her rifle. "It's my first."

He looked back to Mr. Kratzenberger and then moved closer. He lowered his tone, "You mean to tell me, you ain't never competed?"

"No, sir." She stretched her neck up high and dared to meet his eyes.

"Well I'll be. You're a natural."

She smiled at his praise, but the wind shifted, bringing with it a familiar scent. The stench of rotting flesh flooded her senses. A few people fanned their noses, others seemed oblivious.

Mr. Butler focused on Mr. Kratzenberger's brother. "Let 'er rip!"

Annie longed to watch. She found it difficult to avoid staring at Mr. Butler's broad shoulders, and the hits. Despite the excitement, she stared at the surrounding trees beyond.

Somewhere, it lurked.

"You missed one." Mr. Kratzenberger took off his hat and held it over his chest when the shots were done. "Annie, Annie you won!"

"What?" She blinked at Mr. Kratzenberger.

Mr. Butler kicked the ground. He ripped off his hat and stalked away.

"I give you our winner." Mr. Kratzenberger gestured to her and her mother ran forward bringing the flood of Annie's younger siblings with.

Annie lost sight of Mr. Butler getting swept away by the crowd that enclosed her. She accepted their kind words and thanked everyone. When the crowd finally dispersed, her mother insisted on serving supper in her honor.

It wasn't until hours later that Annie slipped out into the night, ready to hunt. A strange stillness settled around her as she grabbed her gun and stepped outside. The trees even seemed afraid to blow in the gales. Not one animal made a sound.

She tip-toed onward. Placing her feet like a trained dancer, Annie knew this symphony, the sound of approaching death. Death never scared her, not the prospect of it—but prolonged suffering, that she could not bear. Her father had survived the attack long enough to shiver, vomit, and cry out for days.

I will not let that happen again. She crept forth, relying on her olfactory prowess along with sharp hearing.

A twig snapped behind her and she refused to jump. Holding steady, she kept her back to the beast. It can't be this close already.

She closed her eyes, but the scent of balm and pine threw her off. She steadied her hands, sliding her finger near the trigger of her gun held safely in her arms.

Whirling about, she slammed the muzzle against Mr. Butler's hand.

"Oh!" She dropped her rifle.

He laid a finger over his lips, picked up her gun, and handed it to her. He nodded for her to follow and she put a hand on her hip, unable to comprehend what he was doing.

"I didn't mean to startle you," he whispered. "But I'm tracking something big."

Bigger than a tall tale. She realized the danger he was in and searched his face. "I know where it is."

"You?" He gaped at her.

"Come." She sprinted on light toes.

He kept up, hopping from tree to tree, mimicking

her movements as she grew more careful to hide herself along the way.

If I can just lead him back, she thought.

But he stopped. "We're heading toward the town?"

She hugged her rifle to her and looked over her shoulder to study Mr. Butler's face. His square jaw sat tight.

"Annie." He grasped her free hand. "You're in danger."

She swallowed her laughter, but her smile took over. "Not me." She shook her head and pushed her hair away from her shoulders.

"This ain't no game." Even through the shadows, his frown stood out beneath his piercing gaze.

"Don't tell me. This is my town." She became aware of the stars brightening the sky overhead. The clouds were dissipating. Light shone down to unveil them. A stench as thick as soup wrapped around the trees. Annie turned away from Mr. Butler and raced away breathing through her mouth. Pumping her legs beneath her thick skirt, she leapt over fallen logs and retraced old haunts.

The night air stung her eyes until they watered. Through blurry vision, she tracked every elongated shadow. The twitching darkness moved incessantly.

It's near. Her heart matched the light padding behind her. She spun around and pursed her lips at Mr. Butler. "We're being hunted."

"I know." He tapped his rifle. "Where'd ya think I went after ya outshot me?"

"The tavern?" She sniffed and grimaced, working hard not to cough. Meat and decay met her so strong she wished Mr. Butler would disappear so she didn't have to talk.

"Annie," He gripped her arm. "Is this why you're such a good shot? Them?" He extended his elbow at the trees ahead.

"Trees are not exactly game." She couldn't bring herself to say it.

After spending years in an asylum, admitting what she knew out loud seemed terrifying and dangerous. He can't know, can he?

He huffed at her. "Tight lipped, but quick." He let out a chuckle and the rumbling of something beyond cut the chatter.

"Move." He nudged her aside.

She jogged in front of him, looking above. No time to climb. She thought of the numerous animals she'd killed from position alone.

A grunt came and then her entire body was pushed down. She rolled forward, tucking her gun in the crook of her arm to spin around and fire. The shot grazed the beast, but nearly hit Mr. Butler who charged. Unable to get a clean shot without hitting him, Annie grabbed some rocks off the ground and pelted the monster's thick hide. Her arm was as true as her gun.

Mr. Butler wrestled well enough to avoid the snapping jaws. Long sharp teeth bit at him. All he had were a couple of sticks to beat it with.

"Where's your damn gun?" she yelled at him.

"Fire now!" he ordered as he jammed one of the sticks down the creature's throat.

Annie grit her teeth and pulled the trigger.

Mr. Butler fell off the beast and she shot again, just to be sure. The mass of matted fur didn't move.

"I didn't hurt you, did I?" She went to Mr. Butler and knelt before him, checking his arms and legs.

He bellowed hard laughter. "You didn't aim for me, did you?"

"No." She sat back.

"And you never miss. Mr. Kratzenberger was right about you."

She breathed in. "You too, I think."

He sat up. His shoulder brushed against hers. "Glad I'm not the only one chasing these things." He stood and kicked it.

Annie stared at the lifeless giant. "What are they?"

"Wendigo." He pulled a knife from his boot and set to carve out the monster's teeth.

"Don't." She hopped up and balled her fists.

"These are sharp. We can trade 'em with the tribes."

Annie's breath rushed in and out. "The t-t-tribes? You mean Injuns?"

"M-hmm." He cut a tooth out.

"What do they want with 'em?" She moved closer.

He struggled to cut the bleeding gum. "Good for tools."

She crouched beside Mr. Butler. "And you don't have any qualms?"

"Not a one." He ripped out the second tooth and blood splattered her face.

She spat on the ground and wiped her cheeks with her skirt. "And here I thought you was just a sore loser." She stood and twirled her hair around her finger. "No one's ever hunted with me. Well . . . not these."

"Now I have." He stopped to wink at her before extracting another tooth.

She turned to face the trees. "But you travel. A lot, I hear."

His feet scuffed the ground behind her and she found his hand on her shoulder a moment later. "This bastard followed me. You cleared these woods yourself, I reckon. Ever think of taking up other parts?"

"Me?" She looked over her shoulder.

"I get jobs on the traveling shows. Kill Wendigo wherever I go. They seem to follow me."

"I thought that too, for a while. It's like they come after certain people." She laughed with a bitter heaviness. "But I'm easy to track. Don't go far."

"You could."

Her mother's visage flashed across her mind. Her new step-father had seemed off-put by her presence, and she barely knew her baby brothers and sisters after having been locked up. With the house taken care of, Annie knew her family would be set. Still, she didn't know anything about traveling.

"I'll be in town for some time. Why don't you think on it?"

Annie's muscles relaxed. "Thank you, Mr. Butler." She turned to him.

He took her hands in his and rubbed them. "Call me Frank."

With one look back to the house she was born in, Annie waved at her mom. The only other time she'd left town was after her first step-father died and she'd been sent to the asylum.

Turning to Frank, she punched him on the shoulder. "Damn you, Mr. Butler, don't you dare think of trying to subdue me into a life of domestics."

He chuckled and pushed his hat back, holding the

reins of the buggy tight. "Ball and chain that you are, I doubt I could keep you caged, Mrs. Butler." The sun tinted his eyes with golden flecks as he winked at her.

"Gee up, then." She looked ahead to the wagons leading them west. She sat tall, working to stay balanced after every bump. The horses clip-clopped at a fine pace and Annie gripped her skirt.

Frank had loaded up all their worldly possessions. Her tiny bag had seemed puny in comparison to his travel tack, but Mr. Kratzenberger had been right. She was destined for a greater life.

The countryside opened up, spilling golds and pinks along the emerald spans of grass and shrubs that led them away. Frank patted her leg.

She jerked her head at him and he grinned. "Yer doing it again."

"Naw?" She wiggled her jaw.

"Yes, ma'am. You've been humming since we laid down that last Wendigo."

She glanced around half-hoping the mention of its name would bring another.

"Now tell me, my dear, you humming 'cause of me?" He furrowed his brow. "Or you thirstin' for a kill?"

She leaned over and hit the reins in his hands.

He nudged her back with his arm.

"You were getting behind." She waved ahead.

The wind tickled her cheeks and sent her hair flying from her face. Frank bent forward and eyed the horses, keeping a firm hand on the reins. "I asked you a question."

She blew out a breath that rivaled the next gust.

He chewed his lip.

"They cain't all be gone," she said.

"And here I thought you was getting musicality on my account."

She laughed at his tone. "I get plenty of something over you." She glanced at him from the corner of her eye and offered a coy smile. "Now, you jest focus on getting us to the show, and I'll hum or sing as much as you like."

She fanned herself in the late summer heat, wondering when the breeze tapered off. Her mind wandered and she longed for a break. She couldn't avoid hunting on the trail. Each stop left her sniffing-searching for tracks. Nothing but common forest animals were found for long spans.

By the time they reached Chicago, the only thing abating her disappointment was the show, and Frank. He knew the road, got her out and settled in their tent.

"I still cain't believe we didn't find head nor tail of a damn beast." She paced the tight space sheltering them.

Frank kissed her and handed her his rifle. "You shoot with this today."

She blinked at him. Her mouth hung open as she attempted to think of some appreciative words that expressed her deepest gratitude.

"That!" He held up his hands like a picture box. "If I could capture that face." He gripped her free hand and gave it a squeeze. "I vowed myself to you, woman. And once we kilt every damn Wendigo, I'll keep you so busy with exciting stunts, you won't miss tracking 'em."

She curled her hair around her finger. The thin beat of her pulse climbed through her fingers. With a nod, she pulled the gun up to sight it. The weight pressed into her shoulder with more power. The barrel was longer, but easy to stare down. "It's a little off—"

"To the left." He chuckled. "Now you know why I always lean right."

She lowered the barrel and he pulled her into his arms. "I married the right man." She kissed him until Bill announced them for the show.

Wild Bill had hired her as soon as Frank had shown him she could shoot. His outspoken honesty had won her over. Leaving home seemed natural when traveling with her husband and folks who respected her.

Stepping onto the fairgrounds, everything had transformed from when they first arrived. The empty space that she left when going into the tent was now filled with others like it. A world of performers: men, women, and children had filled the dusty clearing. It had spirit-lifted the lands. What was once empty now erupted with life and wonder.

"You ready?" Frank linked arms with Annie and they marched out to the center stage in front of a daring crowd.

"I fear if I blink I'll miss everything." She took in the faces staring at them—at her.

Bill announced them with an air of greatness. His charisma seemed to place a spell over everyone. Annie brought her gun up and fired off a few rounds for show.

"She never misses!" Frank warmed up the audience. He ran for the end of the fairway and pulled off his hat.

She snickered at the thinning hair sticking up off his head. He'd never looked better.

418

He pulled an apple from his pocket and she turned to speak up. "I'll be your William Tell for the day." She cocked her head, basking in the warmth of the gentle laughs she instigated.

Without warning, she lifted her gun and cleared a bullet right through the apple on her husband's head before anyone knew she'd pulled the trigger.

The audience cheered with a great roar.

Frank pulled out another apple and tossed it above him.

Annie sighted it and fired a hit.

He pulled out three more and began to juggle.

She laughed with the crowd and lowered the barrel of the gun to the ground, leaning on the shoulder rest. "Show off."

"You gonna show me up, or what?" He fired back.

Annie soaked up the smiles. The onlookers' awe filled her with pride. She took up the rifle once more. With a careful breath, she focused on his rhythm and shot.

One. Two. Three.

The smoke awakened her senses and she bowed when the crowd erupted even louder.

"What a shot!"

"Glad to meet you."

"What a show!"

Annie welcomed her audience as they descended upon her. She played her part and it was fulfilling for the time.

Once back on the road, the old longing crept back into her soul. Frank juggled faster, got smaller objects for her to hit. He went so far as to have her shoot a cigarette from his mouth until they reached St. Paul, Minnesota.

"I've never smelt air like this." She gazed at Frank as he pitched their tent.

"That's snow."

"Already?" She scanned the sunlight playing peek-a-boo through misty gray clouds.

Bill waltzed over and slapped her on the back. "There's always snow in the air up here. No matter what time a year it 'tis."

She spun around and shook out her skirt. "Sounds like my kinda place."

The colder the better. Wendigo always stalked in the cold. If there were any in these parts, Annie would find them.

"Jest don't get too bold."

"Whatcha mean?" She eyed Buffalo Bill's scowl.

The deep lines on his forehead matched the wrinkles around his mouth. They gave him a masterly air, and he stood as tall as his name. "They say people's gone missing around these parts lately. Not yer usual runaways neither."

Annie glanced at Frank and he nodded with a knowing glow on his features.

The thrill of the show had kept Annie going, but her hands ached to clasp her gun and once again meet the hunt of the Wendigo.

<hr>

"This show better go off without a hitch." Bill lowered his gaze on Annie and she stuck her chest out.

Frank stepped forward, mouth open, but she held her hand out. "What's got you so riled up, Bill?"

"Other 'n the fact that you nearly shot off your husband's face last show?"

She remained steady until he let out a laugh. Frank

followed and she joined in. "If I wanted to shoot someone's face, they'd know it."

"Yes, ma'am." Bill looked at the gun in her arms. "Just keep true."

Annie followed Bill in front of the largest stage she'd ever been on. The raised platform made her feel like a giant trampling over worshippers. The sea of eyes below her boots held a desperation she had not experienced in previous towns.

No matter how poor or drought-stricken a city was, most folks had some hope for fun shining in their eyes. Before her, Annie found lifeless stares surrounded by dark circles. Fear seemed to hang in the air.

She swallowed hard and flashed a smile at them. "Thank y'all for coming. I've often been called the best shot around—"

"Often?" Her husband interjected. "You mean always, my dear."

The crowd murmured with a few chuckles, but the banter only prolonged the awkward pretense.

Annie blushed and nodded at Frank. "We'll see. Maybe today'll be the day I miss."

He jogged a-ways off. Holding up a silver dollar for all to see, he tossed it above his head. The metal flickered in a beam of sunshine.

Too easy. Annie pulled up her gun and blasted a hole through the coin.

She reloaded, ready for a triple.

Frank took three silver dollars out at once and threw them up together.

One. Two. Three. And a fourth shot for good measure.

Frank rolled a cigarette and winked at her. Then

turning to the audience, he asked, "Anybody got a light?"

A short fat man obliged him, but Annie found it difficult to avoid the distrust seated in the man's posture.

"Filthy habit. Makes you smell like a skunk." She cackled—all part of the show.

"You ain't got to breathe it in, woman." He puffed long and hard for everyone to see. Then he blew smoke at Annie.

Her face twitched, but she could act. "I'll show you."

The moment he went to take another puff, she had the cigarette sighted, and blew off the smoking ember.

A shriek pierced her ears. Gasps and whispering grew louder until the crowd split open for a very excited audience member. The man hopped forward, dodging people to make his way to the stage.

When in sight, Annie wandered forward with Frank and knelt at the front of the stage. Before her stood a sun dyed man clad in a hide suit. His long hair laid in braids on each shoulder, as black as the ink of the last letter she had written to her ma.

Frank jumped down and held out his hand in greeting.

The man gestured to Annie and helped her get offstage before Frank could. "You are the one I've been waiting for."

"Annie Oakley." She grabbed his hand and gave it a firm shake.

"Sitting Bull." She found his grip equal in firmness. Something in his earthy eyes outmatched the townsfolk.

Annie grew certain he knew more than he was letting on. She released her grip and moved closer to Frank. Linking her arm with her husband's, she beamed on their new acquaintance, oddly aware of the spectacle they had become.

"And this is?"

"Frank E. Butler." He offered Sitting Bull his hand and they shook, but Sitting Bull kept his attention on Annie.

"We must speak," he said.

Annie sighed at her husband. Frank's puzzlement lay in each contemplative feature. She admired his attentive nature. "My husband is my partner in everything." She patted his hand.

Sitting Bull studied her.

"Everything," she assured him.

"Follow me." Sitting Bull gestured away.

Bill had already stepped onstage as if this had been part of the plan. "And there you have it, folks." His voice echoed behind them, but Annie's curiosity left her stunned, unable to react, until they passed her tent.

Frank spoke of the weather with Sitting Bull. He asked about hunting success. That's when Annie noticed the growl in Sitting Bull's tone.

She let the men talk while she studied the grasses that popped up around them as they moved farther out. Matted. Up yonder sat a small dwelling with smoke rising from the hole in the center.

Annie swished saliva over her teeth. "You live there?" She nodded to the teepee.

"I would rather die than live like the white man." Sitting Bull frowned.

423

She blinked hard, unsure of herself and this new acquaintance. "Are we all that bad?"

He stopped and gazed over the trees that ran up the hills leading beyond the valley. A glimmer of pain sat in his stare. "Not all." He cocked his head at her. "You do good in the land."

She held silent. Something in the air or his voice made her feel as if she knew him. A rush of uncertainty struck her and she pointed to his teepee. "I've never been in a real jig like that."

"It is no jig. It is life."

Her chest grew heavy. Whatever had put the low mournful tone in his voice made her wish to help. "Oh."

He led them closer, but stopped them at the entrance. "You stay."

Slipping in and out, he held a long sharp object in his hand. "You know this?"

Annie lost control of her breathing. She sniffed at the tooth, reached for it to hold the monstrous artifact with revelry. "Wendigo."

"Yes." A curve appeared, growing slightly on Sitting Bull's mouth. "I knew you were the one." He sat down on the ground and patted the grass beside him. "There is death again. A herd of them. Worse than ever."

Frank sat, but Annie gripped the tooth and paced the area in front of them. "A herd. Even with my eye, and his . . . " she glanced at Frank who was as still as a statue, "sticks, we'd be destroyed."

Sitting Bull leaned back. "Sit."

She rubbed her forehead and lowered herself beside them.

Frank twirled his mustache against pinched fingers. "Those sticks do more than you know."

Annie made a face at him.

"No teasing. Learned it from the Algonquin."

"He's right." Sitting Bull laughed. "Sumac."

"What?" Annie pulled a handful of grass from the dirt and left it fall.

"Sumac sticks send them away," Sitting Bull said.

Annie wrapped her legs before her like Sitting Bull and leaned her elbows on her knees. "Those beasts eat everything and everyone. A little stick cain't do much."

Frank rubbed her shoulder. "Not any stick, Mrs. Butler. Sumac."

"The oils burn it." Sitting Bull nodded.

Annie rested her chin in her hands. "So you want me—"

"Us," Frank reminded her.

"Us, to go kill a herd of Wendigo with some sumac sticks?"

Sitting Bull's dark gaze seemed to look into her soul. It may as well have reached into her heart and pulled a lever. A wave of calm wrapped about her and she began to imagine a different option.

"The oils!" She jumped up and started pacing again. "We could coat my bullets in sumac oil!"

Frank stood with a jolt. "You sure got a mind on ya." He pulled her into a hug.

Sitting Bull remained seated. He turned an approving eye on Annie. "I knew you'd come."

She dropped to her knees before him. "But why? What are the monsters? Where do they come from?"

"Frank, lend me a puff." Sitting Bull held out his hand.

Her husband rolled him a cigarette and handed it over with his matchbox.

425

Sitting Bull inhaled before speaking again. He let the smoke curl from his lips. "Last winter, the snow kept on. Many starved. My people have been forced away. I return hoping to stay. This is my place, but many white men came and built. A family lost their home. It fell under the cold. They wandered, froze. The father lived and bloodied with frost, ate the flesh of his dead children." Annie bit back the bile tickling her throat. She shivered and closed her eyes at the thought.

"Wendigo were men. They grow wild once they drink the blood of man. A dark spirit takes over, twists their soul, stretches their bodies, and the hunger takes over."

Unable to breathe, Annie held her head in her hands. Sitting Bull had told her everything she never realized she didn't wish to know.

Frank's voice revived her faculties, "But that would make one. How is there a herd?"

Annie dared to watch the contemplative expression on Sitting Bull's face change to disgust. "It was not the only time. News got back. Many were angered, but some used it to survive the rest of the winter. They sought murder for flesh. The power it gave them was a prize."

"They chose it?" Annie kicked the ground. Unable to control herself, she waved her hands as she talked, "My father, my second father, my life has been set by these creatures, and they chose it? I need my gun!"

"Wait. I have too many wounds from battle." Sitting Bull pushed himself up from the ground. He rubbed his back and straightened himself. "I had hoped for one of my people to do this. But maybe if you can, it will bond you to the land and you'll be able to rid the white man of his crimes." He ducked back into the small teepee and returned with a thick pair of hide shoes.

Frank nudged her.

Sitting Bull smiled at Annie. "These will grant your feet more speed."

Annie took them, marveling at the smooth edges with ripples of texture along the sides. "Thank you."

Her mind filled with more thoughts than she could decipher. She turned to her husband and found her focus. "You knew about the sumac and never told me?"

He shrugged. "Didn't have a mind to worry over it."

She bit her lip and lowered her eyelids with frustration.

"Ah, the difference between man and wo-man." Sitting Bull pointed at them and laughed.

The absurdity struck Annie. She giggled with him and Frank, but a deeper calling rumbled. Her desire to hunt overcame her.

"We best be tracking, if we're gonna get this herd." She looked to Frank with wide eyes.

"Best be," he said. "But we need to wait 'til nightfall."

The forest hummed with the moans of death and bloodlust. Annie strode ahead of Frank, her hands still itching from the fresh sumac oil. But my bullets are ready. Powder too.

Frank held so close to her, she could feel his breath on the back of her neck. His foot pressed on her heel and she stopped.

"What is it?" he whispered, bumping into her. The

end of his stick poked her through the wool of her dress.

She reached back and shooed him off. "Cain't hunt if you knock me down."

She squinted around. The trees swayed with the night breeze, moving shadows like a theatre show. Her throat went dry. The shifting winds held the pungent smell of death. Then the whining began.

"Pitiful." Frank growled.

Annie pursed her lips. The monsters would try and prey on their sympathies—draw them out with cries and shots, before lunging with the dastardly tones of decay and degradation. She wanted none of it.

"Blast em all!" she shouted.

Frank gripped her arm. "Annie?" "I thought I missed the hunt, but this is absurd." She unbuttoned her overcoat and tossed it on the ground.

"That ain't necessary." Frank tapped his stick at the fabric heaped on the leaves.

"I'm ready now. They can't resist good meat, so I'll give it to em." She ripped her dress laces open and pulled her arms free

"Now what in lan' sakes you doing?" He eyed her figure.

She stepped out of her dress and stripped off her undergarments, leaving her pantaloons where they fell. "Drawing them out with my scent, of course."

"Of course." He rubbed his hands together and sighed. "Baiting them won't keep pneumonia away."

"I've survived worse." She glared at him.

He tugged at his belt. "Best be joining you, then." He had his pants half pulled down when Annie dropped in a low crouch, digging the butt of her rifle in the ground. "They're coming."

She shivered in the night air, but tilted her ear forward and cupped her hand to it.

"There." Frank stepped out of his pants and leaned down. He placed his arms around her and she welcomed the warmth of his bare skin.

Something glowed in the shadows before them. Great hungry eyes glowed behind the tree roots nearby, lit under the gaze of a herd of monstrous cannibals in a dusty patch of moonlight. Their contorted and sunken features twitched.

Annie only had one breath before the tallest of them sped toward her. Its lanky arms flailed as it charged, jumping from tree to tree, shadow to shadow. Annie gripped her gun to her naked body, no longer feeling the cold.

Frank hollered and ran out to meet the giant beast. He held the stick up like a spear and Annie screamed, "Not yet. You'll drive the rest away."

Frank threw the stick aside and stood, arms out.

The smaller Wendigo snarled, gurgling as they licked their lips and moved in. Annie lost sight of the leader. She could feel its eyes up in the trees. But where?

She fired at the first to get close to her husband. It fell and the others scattered. They threw sticks at her, crying out in unnatural guttural moans.

"You need your damn gun." She nodded off the way they had come.

"This is your show." He chuckled. "I came to speculate."

"You mean spectate." She attempted a laugh, but lost all humor, desperately searching the shadows. "And you's a liar." She nodded back to the stick he tossed.

"Come on." She raced behind a tree and sniffed. The stench nearly knocked her over. It seemed to coat her skin. A searing pain tore into her shoulder and she was shoved to the ground. She struggled to roll over. The weight was too much. She kicked back to no avail. Closing her eyes, she held her breath and knocked her head back against the beast's mouth.

It whimpered and Annie rolled over and fired. She stared at the blood trickling down its fangs as it went limp. Rubbing the back of her head, she clenched her teeth and got up quick. "Frank!"

She aimed for the Wendigo stalking him, but it slipped into the shadow of a nearby tree. Frank jogged over to where the first had charged. "I need the sumac stick."

She followed. "No time."

Annie kicked their clothes and panted. Her ears rang with a low rumble that sounded from above. She shot into the trees. A Wendigo fell, dead.

Her triumph melted into disappointment when she found it was the smallest one. Barely four feet, she imagined it as a child.

Biting her lip, she weaved through the trees, trusting Frank to keep up.

"Annie!" he gasped. The giant Wendigo had seized her in its crushing claws.

She squirmed under the jolt of pain that surged down her shoulder. The creature drooled on her breasts and pressed its icy fur against her naked thighs. The cold seemed to consume her. Her teeth chattered and she shook.

This is it, she only had time for one thought.

She gnashed her teeth and tore into the cannibal's

face. The rotting meat made her vomit in her mouth, but she continued to bite, mixing bile and coagulated blood, until Frank worked his arm through and jammed the sumac stick between them.

The Wendigo stumbled back, relaxing its grip. Annie shoved the sumac stick down its throat. It dropped her and she felt about for her rifle, spitting out the horrid taste again and again.

Her fingers knocked against the familiar muzzle, and she drew it up enough to blow a hole through the creature's head.

She dropped her gun and tore through the leaves, digging up handfuls of dirt and rubbing them on her tongue to rid herself of the awful taste.

Frank patted her back and handed her her dress. Before she could get it over her head, two more Wendigo grumbled in sync, mixing their deadly tones with a nefarious harmony.

Frank dove for her rifle and got off three shots. Both remaining monsters fell.

"Three shots?" Annie stepped back into her dress and raised an eyebrow.

"We cain't all hit every time." He staggered forward and she caught him.

"You're hurt."

"So are you." He motioned to her shoulder.

"Ain't we a pretty picture." She brushed off her skirt and reached for his clothes.

He winked at her. "It'll be one hell of a tale to tell."

They collected themselves and went to their tent for a bit of rest before going to Sitting Bull the next day. He offered them a balm to help heal their wounds and vowed to look after Annie always.

A newfound love for him and his tribe consumed her and she promised to be watchful of him, as a daughter cares for a father.

After fighting for so long, Annie finally found contentment as a performer. Frank talked Wild Bill into taking the show to Europe so they could see new things and leave the past behind. But as always, desperate men turn to monsters, and Annie and Frank often found themselves on the hunt.

ROTOSCOPING TOODIES

MORT CASTLE

SNOW WHITE WAITS in darkness, if you can call it "waiting" if there is no expectation. Snow White is a Toody. Not being human, Toodies do not have anything tantamount to the full range of human emotion, though some Toodies can mimic certain aspects of human feelings without experiencing any degree of effect. Likewise, *most* Toodies also lack such human physical characteristics as pores, bladders, spleens, warts, etc.

Toodies never become ill, as we understand illness, though some, like the Dwarf Sneezy, might present a condition similar to chronic rhinitis, which has neither cause nor cure (the Dwarf Sneezy does little else but sneeze in explosively comic fashion). Other Toodies exhibit severe stuttering, OCD conditions, such as seeking and collecting dots, or addictions to such foods as spinach or carrots. Toodies do not die. If they are forgotten or totally ignored, they simply cease to exist, either fading away relatively slowly or departing with a quiet "pop."

The Toody Snow White does not long for anyone, nor care for anyone, nor miss anyone, nor hope for anyone.

But can we explain why, on some days, her face seems—might it be, *wistful*—and voice soft and trembly and musical, she sings, "Someday my prince will come?"

———

Rotoscoping: a frame by frame technique that animators use to produce realistic action. In the rotoscope process, live action film images are projected onto a glass panel and traced over and colored by pen and brush. The original equipment employed in the process was dubbed a "rotoscope," invented and employed by the Polish-American animator Max Fleischer. At one time, many animators and critics held rotoscoping in low regard, seeing it as a lazy way to cut corners and requiring only the most rudimentary art skills.

Animation: History and Future
by James Oliver Firkins, published
November, 2030 by Vintage, Hachette,
Random, Triangle Productions

———

ROTOSCOPING TOODIES

My Christmas Eve, 1966

Walt Disney died and was cremated and interred at Forest Lawn Memorial Park in Glendale, California last week.

A day before he passed, he called me to his bedside in Providence Saint Joseph Medical Center. He asked his brother Roy, the only other visitor at the time, to step out for a moment.

He said in a bubbly dying whisper, "Bish, you are my friend."

I said I was.

He said, "We share secrets."

We did.

"There is a promise you must make me."

He said it as a question: "Will you take care of her now?"

I made the promise.

Walt was my friend. He was a genius and a son of a bitch, and I got a maximum dose of one and sometimes the other, but had you been there when Walt was pitching *Snow White and the Seven Dwarfs*, acting out each scene, playing it broad full gesture, expressions and moves as smooth as anything Chaplin ever put on film, you would have known the power of the man. He became Snow White and the Wicked Queen and all seven of the dwarfs.

Walt Disney was a shaman, a wizard, and when he stepped into a room, the air charged with ozone, and you swore lightning jumped from his fingers and if he said, "Let us climb Mt. Sinai and kick God in the ass!" you would have cheered and followed him in your mountain climbing ass-kicking boots.

Along with the veterans, Art Babbitt, Hardie Gramatky, Johnny Cannon, and Bill Cottrell, I was present at that mesmerizing performance. I was still the new guy, Bish (Bishop) Leffords, 26 years old, but already a lead animator and not a backgrounder or in-betweener.

(It is significant who was not there: Ub Iwerks. With Iwerks we might not have been forced into the great deception. But Walt had offended his former partner and master animator by taking credit for everything from sound cartoons to the sinuous whip of Mickey Mouse's tail, and Iwerks said, "Fuck you and the fucking mouse, too," and opened his own New York studio in 1930.)

Snow White and the Seven Dwarfs would be the first feature length animated film—and the greatest. Cartoon short subjects? A frivolous novelty, produced with the artistry of a failing student in a high school mechanical drawing class, with cacophonous soundtracks comprised of xylophones, Jew's harps, musical (!?!) saws, and whoopee cushions.

We would transform the medium.

We would transcend the medium.

We believed.

We were determined.

We were destined.

We would create—*drum roll*—

ART!

Ours was a holy mission.

It would cost an unbelievable $250,000 but we would get it. That is, Roy Disney, the company's money man, would get it (the initial estimate was off. *Snow White* came in at just under a million and a half). It was only money. What did we care about money?

ROTOSCOPING TOODIES

WE WERE ARTISTS!

Development of *Snow White and the Seven Dwarfs* began in 1934.

I had been hired late in the previous year.

Flashback: My Welcome to Disney Studios

I was told, "We think he will hire you, but Walt makes all the final decisions."

I was shown into his office.

Smoke.

Walt Disney smoked all the time.

The pencils in the utilitarian holder on the desk all stood sharp points up. There was a pristine blotter. There was a framed 8 x 10 of a woman. She looked like a librarian who could tell you the Dewey Decimal number for any category of book you might desire. There was nothing of The Mouse.

Behind the desk sat Walt Disney, smoking.

He said, "You're Bish?"

I commanded myself to smile. I knew that is what you do when you are meeting someone you wish to please.

I said, "Yes. Ha, ha. Bish, short for Bishop. Ha, ha."

Walt Disney gestured to the chair alongside his desk.

"I've seen your samples. I've seen your pitch reel. You're good, Bish."

I said what I was supposed to say. "Thank you, Mr. Disney. Ha, ha." I did not say more. You can have problems if you say too much. You can have problems if you try too hard.

He said, "Call me Walt."

I said, "Okay. I can. Okay . . . Walt."

He smoked and raised an eyebrow.

He said, "You're not comfortable calling me 'Walt,' but I do insist on it. I am 'Walt' to everyone who works here. I want to hire you, Bish. You are a very talented animator."

He held out his hand.

It took a while for me to take it and pump it up and down a short ways, *one-two-three, ha, ha, ha*. Back then, it was not easy for me to touch or be touched.

Walt did not say anything for a little while, then he said, "You're not comfortable with people, are you, Bish?"

"Ha, ha," I said. "No, sir, I am not. Walt."

"You are not comfortable in this world, are you, Bish?"

"I do not know what you mean . . . "

"You are not comfortable because everything is all fucked up in this world and everyone is all fucked up, can't help it, all fucked up, that's just the fucking way it is. Fucked up. That's why you want to create something beautiful and pure and *just how it should be* instead of all of it being all fucked up."

"Ha, ha," I said.

Then he told me about himself. Later, I came to understand he wanted me to know him so I could be a friend.

This is what he said:

"So the other day, it was so nice and I finished lunch early and I thought I'd take a little walk and as soon as I was out the door, I stepped into a big pile of dogshit. With the sky so blue and a gentle breeze and the sun shining so bright, I step in FUCKING DOGSHIT!

"That is fucked up, Bish.

"So I'm at Bullock's Wilshire Department Store. I want to buy some pocket squares for the guys I play polo with. I'm going to the elevator and there's this nicely dressed lady with this cute little boy, maybe seven, maybe just six, and she's slapping him in the back of the head, steady like a metronome and hard: Whap, Whap, Whap! Kid is crying. Screaming. Whap, whap, whap!

"So I softly and calmly tell her, 'Ma'am, you must be upset, I know, but you don't have to do that to the child.'

"And she yells right in my face and there's spittle flying, 'Tomorrow they cut off my husband's leg! They started with his toe when it went black. Then they cut off his foot. And tomorrow they do his leg! How can you work on the railroad without a leg? You have to have legs to work on the railroad!'

"Bish," Walt puffed smoke and whispered, "I have decided to tell you something personal. I believe you will understand.

"Lillian, that's my wife, wants another child. So last night, we did sex. It's never been easy. But last night, well, it never seemed more disgusting. The noises she makes. You make your own sounds just so you won't have to listen to hers. There's that damp skin wriggling under your skin. There are . . . smells . . . It's, oh, God! It's horrible, as horrible as horrible can be."

He slapped his palm down hard on the desktop. "None of it! IT SHOULD NOT BE THAT WAY!"

I remember I nodded.

Walt said, "I knew you would understand me, Bish. And I understand. *I understand you, Bish.*"

Years later, I would learn about autism and conclude the term had once applied to me, but being with others who made hippopotamuses in tutus dance ballet and sailor suited ducks sputter like a tongue-tied King Lear and elephants fly by flapping their fucking ears, working in such a gloriously frantic freak show for such a long time, I learned to fake the protocols of necessary social interaction.

I learned to *pretend* to be all right.

It made my life considerably easier.

In fact, over the years, there were times pretending to be all right that I had to wonder if I actually was all right.

The day Walt hired me, I had a friend.

January 4, 1937

Walt led us into the screening room. It was hot and cramped. We were outgrowing the Hyperion Studio (in 1940 we moved to Burbank).

Today the screening room mood was tense because Walt was "getting desperate," is what he had said. He said he was "feeling pressured." He said he was getting "fucking pissed off."

Of course, all of us were desperate and feeling pressured. But if we were "pissed off," it was at ourselves: We were not getting the job done.

Walt, dead center, first row, cigarette screwed into his mouth.

On the screen, no soundtrack: Woodland scene.

Great depth, a sense of moving into and being enveloped by the setting. That was the multiplane camera. Better than the real world. It was what the real world should have been, not the usual view through a glass darkly. You intuited forest life that you did not see. Humming bees. Sassy chipmunks. Chattering squirrels.

Magic.

Enter fluffy little rabbit, so damned cute someone had named him "Diabetes Bunny."

Bunny wrinkles nose.

Aw . . .

Good. Damned good.

We had nailed it. Animals had to be as expressive as people.

Enter bluebird.

Gentle ripple of feathers. Flutter of the heart.

Cut to:

Medium close-up on crying Snow White.

Boo-hooing.

Oh, boo.

Oh, hoo.

Boo hoo fuck!

Bad. Very bad.

Film click-ticks on sprocketed black and lights come up.

An awful reverential moment.

Walt calmly rises and like a high school geography teacher instructing none-too-bright sophomores says, "Well, what do we—heh-heh-heh—think of that?" The *heh-heh-heh* was the clue.

Bill Cottrell says, "Backgrounds couldn't be better. Lush. The dolly to the tree trunk is amazing."

Art Babbitt says, "That bluebird . . . I worked on that and I don't believe it came out so well."

Johnny Cannon, "Love the bunny."

Walt claps his hands and laughs. "*Wunderbar!* We've got a background and a bluebird and a bunny."

Then he looked at Roy like he was taking aim. "Roy, do you have an opinion?"

Getting to his feet, you half expected Roy to lift his arms in a defensive posture. He said flatly, "It was pretty good."

Walt nodded. "Agreed. I totally agree . . . " Walt's voice trailed off. And then he started screaming. "It was pretty good, if you like total shit. If you like shit soufflé, shit on your shoes, shuffled shit, stirred shit, shit through a tin horn, and comin' round Kilkerry fucking Mountain, shit!

"Snow fucking White," Walt raged, "moves like she's made out of nothing but arthritic elbows. She's got the winsome charm of leprosy. She dances like Vitus is her patron saint. She klumps around with the subtle grace of a concrete mixer. She bows to her woodland chums like she's getting a barbed wire enema while being electrocuted. And that face"—Walt actually shuddered—"only a mother could love that, a mother barracuda."

It was all aimed at Roy, and there wasn't one of us who wasn't grateful then not to be Roy Oliver Disney.

" . . . of course you like shit. That's because you're an asshole! That is why you just stick to the financial side, Brother Asshole, because you can con and screw over the other assholes who do money and you won't fuck that up . . . "

Roy did not slink. He walked out.

Walt said quietly, "Guys, let's take a break."

We were getting up, thinking about earning a living designing corset ads for the *Los Angeles Times* or maybe using a three-inch brush dipped in orange paint for butcher signs, when Walt said, "Bish, come to my office, please."

When we were seated he took the Cutty Sark from the third desk drawer. We used paper cups.

We are friends, I said to myself.

"I really lambasted Roy," he said.

I said, "Yes."

Walt lit a cigarette.

I said, "I am surprised Roy did not punch your nose, Walt. People do that sometimes when they are insulted, don't they?"

"Roy and I, we're okay." Walt shook his head. "My father, he was the one did the hitting. Bastard always had plenty for both Roy and me. We promised we'd never hit one another. And my kid, Diane, I will never, never *ever* strike her." Walt looked at the cup in his left hand, the cigarette in his right. "My old man, tight assed sonofabitch, hated smoking and drinking."

"Oh," I said, "that is why you smoke and drink."

"Thank you, Dr. Freud," Walt said. "And I make art. That's something else Daddy said 'no' to. So, fuck him."

Then he looked at me in a way that I truly understood meant *help me.* "Bish, what can we do?"

"I do not know."

"We have to, Bish. We're in hock up to Roy's ass and my ears. *Snow White* premieres in December of this year and it takes off or I'm drawing puppies and rainbows for Hallmark Cards and Lillian's selling ribbons at Woolworth's.

"Iwerks could have done it," Walt said. "Ub Iwerks is the total animator. The cartoons he's doing nowadays, *Flip the Frog* . . . Ub could not tell a story if you gave him the beginning, the end, and filled in the parts between, but *Flip the Frog* . . . Fucking frog is more real than any pond frog, bullfrog, or Florida Everglades frog that ever zapped a fly."

Walt sighed. "Snow White has to be real like that. The dwarfs have to be real like that."

"What can we do?" I said.

Walt said, "Rotoscope."

I said, "As soon as you see rotoscope, you know. It does not look created, it looks *copied*. It's just tracing. It's fake. A copy can never be real."

Walt said. "That is why we will not use real people."

"What will we use?" I asked.

Walt said, "Toodies."

———————

December 1, 1996: A Reminiscence Filtered through Hindsight

What I tell you will be no noteworthy revelation for many. Perhaps you have seen the 1988 box office smash *Who Framed Roger Rabbit*, or, less likely, the 1992 box office floppola, *Cool World*. Though it was never bandied about all that much, both movies cast Toodies in leading and lesser roles. *Framed*'s Roger Rabbit, Jessica Rabbit, Baby Herman, Benny the Taxicab, and *World*'s Nails the Spider, Chico the Bouncer, and sexy Holli Would were Toodies, though called respectively *Toons* and *Noids*.

They all come from a domain known as *2D*, pronounced . . . That is correct. We here on Planet Earth, are referred to by Toodies as . . . Threedies!

How did 2D come into existence?

ROTOSCOPING TOODIES

Given the irrational ways of most of its inhabitants, Unintelligent Design is an answer not without merit. The more philosophical might speculate about the Collective Unconsciousness manifesting itself physically.

Whatever, 2D is real. That is that.

In 2D, you can find Popeye the Sailor, the Yellow Kid, Smoky Stover, Barney Google, Snuffy Smith, Little Orphan Annie, Blondie, Mutt and Jeff, Felix the Cat, Buck Rogers, Tarzan, Mary Worth, and Little Iodine, etc. They look pretty much as they have been presented to us in comic strips and books, single panel cartoons, and animated films. It would not be wrong to refer to Toodies as Archetypes. Like all types, thus, they are limited in function and intellect. Their behaviors are prescribed and repetitive: Popeye, seemingly vanquished, eats his spinach and knocks hell out of Bluto—again and again. Tubby pranks Little Lulu Moppet and she counter-pranks with greater and more comic success.

Final point of interest: You will not know it from their representations in the Sunday Funnies or Looney Tunes, but Toodies are approximately half the size of 3D *homo sapiens*. In the 2D realm, Superman stands a perfectly proportioned three feet and an inch tall. Similar in many respects, but small, that's 2D.

From the time of Rudolph Dirks's *Katzenjammer Kids*, 1897, Hearst's *New York Journal,* to Calvin and Hobbes, from the earliest animations of *Krazy Kat* to today's *Simpsons,* certain artists have seemed to know of 2D, perhaps psychically, and some discovered a way to journey there.

If you ask *Cool World*'s Ralph Bakshi or *Roger*

Rabbit's chronicler Gary K. Wolf about their crossing from 3D to 2D and back again, you might get a wink and a knowing smile or a dismissive "I imagine you believe in leprechauns, too."

In 1937, in Hollywood, if you wished to, let us say, *utilize* Toodies, you needed a mover, a shaker, all around grifter and connection man, and the one Walt Disney engaged was a certified sleaze merchant named Powell Benjamin. Powell Benjamin wore a sports coat with lapels wide enough to accommodate drippings of his last 12 meals, had a pencil thin mustache, and eyes that made a hyena's glare remind you of Lassie.

I never learned how Walt came to know Powell Benjamin.

I never asked.

Roy somehow secured another loan.

Three hundred thousand dollars was paid to Powell Benjamin for three months—*usage*—of eight Toodies.

Walt's carefully selected small crew—*our* crew, for I was Walt's Majordomo—sign an oath of secrecy in India ink.

We believe in our mission.

We believe in Art.

We believe in Walt Disney.

Late one night, Powell Benjamin drove to Hyperion Studio in a panel truck and unloaded them.

We had Seven Dwarfs.

We had Snow White.

With their size, we needed only a few props and limited, minimized sets.

Once they were dressed, we were in business.

We began rotoscoping.

What did they look like? Please, unless you are a Survivalist-Fundamentalist Mormon living with your ridiculously extended family in a desert cave, you have seen the movie. Bashful looked like Bashful, Doc looked like Doc, Sleepy looked like staggering narcolepsy and Grumpy looked like a crabby old bastard, etc.

And Snow White? She looked like a cool 31 inches of sweetness, goodness, and light, inadvertently inaugurating the line of what would become Disney Princesses.

Except for Sleepy, the dwarfs did not sleep; they did not need to. Once a day, for perhaps 15 minutes, there was a meal of soup served by a singing Snow White. They appeared to be eating, although one was never sure. They did not require exercise. They did not even need bathroom breaks, in that they lacked the requisite plumbing.

Powell Benjamin became our director in everything but screen credit. While the Toodies seemed to listen to Walt or me, we apparently confused them. When Powell Benjamin said, "Here's what you do," they did it, toot sweet. Pratfall? Plop-bop. March of the dwarfs, lips puckered in a whistle, and it's off to work we go. Do a triple back flip and land in a two finger handstand while wiggling your ears? No problem. Shed flowing tears big as Oldsmobile headlights, it's the Seven Sobbers Ensemble.

We rotoscoped hell out of them. No need to rotoscope Nasty Queen/Ugly Witch. Traditional free hand art proved more effective; cartoony exaggeration a perfect fit for a hag/bitch. The Prince? Use a Hollywood chorus boy as a model and he gets his 37 seconds on screen. Who's looking at him, anyhow?

Working only at night, everyone else gone, shooting in a shed that looked like it had been constructed by the Little Rascals, it took just under three months to get the necessary Toodies footage. Powell Benjamin loaded up the cast, or so I thought, and *adios*. Into the "rendering" stage, with splashes of hand painted primary color and fuzz focus to make Snow White and the dwarfs just a tad more cartoon-like—then, the voice actors, and . . .

Snow White and the Seven Dwarfs premiered at the Carthay Circle Theatre on December 21, 1937, followed by a nationwide release on February 4, 1938. It was a critical and commercial smash: $8 million earnings before distribution plans were drawn up for a return engagement.

By March of 1938, we had *Dumbo* underway, so I thought we'd be discussing that when, one night, Walt asked me to return to Hyperion after dinner. He had something to show me.

And what that was apparently required him to fortify himself before the unveiling; he reeked of alcohol as he led me to what had been a small storeroom for Bristol board pads, cellulose acetate cells, pens, brushes, and other art supplies but was now a dimly lit, sparsely furnished room. It was small: about half scale. There was a proportional table, chairs, and sofa. There was a painted half-sized window that showed a distant verdant hill beneath a sunny sky. And on a half-sized armchair by that phony window sat the Toody Snow White.

She looked at us. She smiled a perfunctory smile, reflecting neither thought nor emotion.

"I kept her," Walt said. "I paid Benjamin. I bought her."

"Oh," I said. "Oh."

Walt said, "She's mine."

Then he said to the Toody, "Snow White, please stand up and remove your clothes."

She did. Undressed, she stood before us, her head tipped slightly to the left. I cannot say she was naked. I cannot say she was nude.

She had no nipples. She had a navel or at least an indentation. She had nothing of those other physical characteristics we associate with the female gender— the *human* female.

Walt whispered, "Not a mole, a bleb, a pimple or a birthmark. She is just what she should be. There will never be a trace of wrinkle at the edges of her eyes. No root canal, no sinus infection, no pneumonia, no . . . "

Walt gripped my upper arm. "Bish, do you see? She is perfect."

I said, "Walt, she is not human. She is not alive."

Snow White waved to me. She smiled.

Walt said, "She is *perfect* and she is mine."

"Walt," I said, "it's not right."

"It's right for me," Walt said. "I love her."

<hr>

For many years, I did not see the Toody Snow White. Walt and I did not speak of her. She was the unspoken obstruction in our friendship and we dealt with it by not speaking of her.

But when Walt lay dying, all that mattered was he was my friend.

Yes, I would take care of her, the Toody Snow White.

I did.

I have.

But now, I am 86 years old. Next week, I will go to Providence Saint Joseph Medical Center for cardiovascular surgery which is expected to take seven to nine hours. It is possible I will survive but not expected.

I have taken care of most everything. I have no family, so charities and casual friends (I had only one close friend) will be the beneficiaries of the Bishop Leffords's estate.

There is one item which I have not seen to.

I have time before my scheduled surgery.

I trust I will think of something.

<hr/>

Snow White waits in darkness.
On some days she sings, "Someday my prince will come."

LONE WOLVES

PAUL MOORE

"The wolf is the arch type of ravin, the beast of waste and desolation. It is still found scattered thinly throughout all the wilder portions of the United States, but has everywhere retreated from the advance of civilization."
Theodore Roosevelt, 1902

December 13th, 1886
49 miles northwest of Medora, Dakota Territories
12:42 AM

ROOSEVELT WINCED AS he rolled onto his side. This close to Montana, the ground was always rough and the particularly harsh winter had frozen it hard. He peeled back the sheepskin sleeping bag as he glanced over at the remains of the campfire.

It was little more than ash and fading embers. A thin wisp of smoke spiraled upward as it disappeared into the clear night sky.

Beautiful night, he thought. *Been awhile since I've seen one of those.*

The sight of the cloudless sky lifted Roosevelt's

spirits. He and his companions had been scouring the plains for three miserable days. Heavy winter storms filled with snow, ice and all the frigid fury Mother Nature could muster had slowed their progress significantly. However, Roosevelt had insisted that they stay the course. They were closer to the pack than they had ever been, and he was not about to relinquish the hunt when they were so near.

Roosevelt sat upright and glanced over at the other men. Both Jake Cutler and Avonaco continued to slumber inside their tightly wrapped sheepskin cocoons. He could barely make out their misting breath across the waning coals. As if sensing his restlessness, one of the horses snorted in the dark recesses beyond the camp.

"Couldn't have said it better myself," Roosevelt muttered to himself as he stood and approached the remains of the fire. He reached into the ring of stones and pulled a tin kettle from the ashes. The handle was still warm, and Roosevelt silently thanked the Maker for small favors.

The coffee was, at best, tepid, but compared to the biting winds that rose and fell across the plains, the dark liquid felt almost volcanic. Roosevelt poured himself a cup and gulped a mouthful. It had little effect on him these days. His time in Cuba had altered his perception on many things.

Something about finding comfort in a hot cup of Jamoke while his wounded men wailed through the night had left a sour taste in his mouth. The heat had been oppressive, the jungle dense and unforgiving, and too much blood had been spilled on both sides. Roosevelt had a stomach for combat and the fortitude for victory, but he took no pleasure in taking another man's life.

Wolves, on the other hand, were a completely different story.

As far as Roosevelt was concerned, wolves were ravenous agents of unbridled destruction. They were little more than forces of pure *id* who continued to kill long after they had satiated their gluttonous appetites. Roosevelt could cite many instances where wolves had not killed for food, defense or survival. Instead, they had hunted and killed purely for pleasure. As far as he knew, there was only one other animal on Earth that behaved in a similar manner.

Human beings.

Much like wolves, humans were social creatures that sought the company of like-minded individuals. Also much like wolves, a man's pack could accomplish great things to help ensure survival. There was a problem with these shared traits, however. Whether a group of wolves or a group of men, the result was always the same.

Put enough of them together, for any reason, and the result was inevitably violence.

The difference, in Roosevelt's opinion, was that men possessed *ego* as well as *id*. It was this conflicted nature that often compelled men to curtail their baser instincts and appeal to their better angels. And even if a single man did succumb to his darker appetites, other men would challenge his transgressions. It was the rule of law. The cornerstone of civilized society.

A wolf knew no such conflict, neither within itself or its pack. They were driven only by a need to spill blood, whether for necessity or for sport. Either way, death did not follow them; they delivered it.

PAUL MOORE

After mealtime on the ranch he used to call home, Roosevelt had often enjoyed a cigar on the porch as he watched the sun surrender to the night. It was during that changing of the guard that he would muse on a variety of challenging thoughts, dabbling in conjecture and the darker brooding that had crept into his mind after his wife's death. Those shadowed thoughts often involved the wolves, their natures and their deeds.

He had come to the conclusion that he did not loathe the animals for their single-minded nature, nor for the wanton devastation they left in their wake. The real reason was that they represented the worst of humanity. Roosevelt had seen war. He had seen the worst that man had to offer. He had seen men who were no better than wolves.

Men with no use for family, or companionship, or society as a whole.

When the Rough Riders were formed, volunteers from all over the nation had applied. Most of them were good, decent men who wanted to serve their country, or had left the military and not yet found their place in the world. The brotherhood of soldiers provided a camaraderie seldom found elsewhere; the crucible of combat forged powerful bonds. For many men, the military was where they felt most comfortable. It was their home.

And then there was the other type of volunteer. The kind that Roosevelt abhorred, even if he had found uses for them on occasion.

These were the men who wanted to kill. They enjoyed murder. Savored it. The type of men who not only took pleasure in killing other men, but took even

454

greater pleasure in watching them die. Sadists. Degenerates. Cruel men who knew neither empathy nor honor.

Lone wolves.

While effective on the battlefield for their sheer blood lust, they disgusted Roosevelt. They had no code of ethics or sense of loyalty. They were opportunists of the worst sort: only happy once their hands were soaked in blood; hands that could have built homes, bridges and churches; hands that could have sown fields, reaped harvests or folded themselves into prayer. They were men who thrived on destruction and chaos and despised creation. Just like wolves.

Roosevelt drained the lukewarm coffee from his cup. He was not disposed to sleep, but knew it was a necessity. The day before them was long. The day after that would be longer. Hunting was not a game of pursuit, it was a game of patience. A tired man was not a patient man.

He returned to his sleeping bag and pulled it tight to ward against the crippling cold. He closed his eyes. The sound the wind carried was faint, but unmistakable.

The distant howling of wolves.

Jake Cutler cinched the cord around his bedding before loading it onto his horse. He looked around as Roosevelt and the Indian performed similar tasks. Jake knew the other men had more years of hunting experience between them than he himself had years of living. Roosevelt had brought him along for only two reasons.

The first was that he needed the extra hands. Jake

was not yet old enough to grow a proper beard, but he was a hard worker and stronger than his lean frame suggested. He was as good with a knife as with an axe, and he knew just about all there was to know about wilderness life.

He owed those skills to the miserable son-of-a-bitch that had been his father. The man had been an intolerable and abusive drunk, but a skilled trapper. Once Jake reached his manhood, his father had decided it was time for him to learn the family trade. For the next five years, Jake had spent most of his time traveling the Territories with his father as the old man trapped just enough to put food on the table and keep himself in liquor.

Jake learned everything there was to know about living under the stars. He could fashion snares, start a fire in a thunderstorm, pull water from the driest soil, and even scavenge for plants to be used as food or medicine. He learned these skills because he had his mother's wits, and because the price for failing a lesson or task was a savage beating at the hands of his soused father.

The second reason Roosevelt had hired him was that Jake was a crack shot with a rifle.

Jake had learned humility growing up and, for obvious reasons, seldom drank. However, on those rare occasions that he found himself in his cups, his humility disappeared and he spoke the truth. *Crack shot* was an understatement. If there was a better man with a rifle in the Territories, Jake had yet to meet him. He could take down a rabbit on the move at six hundred yards and most people on the western side of the Territories knew it.

Eventually, the word of Jake's prowess spread to Bill Sewall and Wilmot Dow, friends of Roosevelt that had benefited from his interest in politics and the diminishing returns on Elkhorn. Roosevelt's renewed presence in the Dakota Territories had become a sensational subject of conversation among the locals after his exploits in Cuba and his incumbent status as Governor of New York. However, it was still a surprise to Jake when a young Indian boy arrived at his homestead and handed him a letter written by the man himself.

Jake's ability to read was limited as he had never had a formal education. Jake's father had begrudgingly allowed his mother to teach her son rudimentary reading and writing in addition to basic arithmetic, but the letter had proved beyond him.

His mother had read it to him. He could still remember her scarred face transforming in the lamplight as she read aloud. Jake had listened halfheartedly as he watched her read. It was not for lack of interest; it was that his attention was arrested by the change in her disposition. The further she read, the more her spirits lifted.

Her son was being considered for employment by the great Theodore Roosevelt. A national hero. A man of station and respect, the exact opposite of the monster she had wed. An esteemed man who had taken interest in her only son. For the first time since his father had died, she looked genuinely happy.

In his mind, Jake had already accepted the job, whatever it may have been. He was eternally grateful to Roosevelt for giving his mother that single moment of joy. She had suffered too much in her life for Jake to deny her the pleasure of telling the other women in town that her son had been hand selected by none other than the legendary Roosevelt.

"Secure that tight, son," Roosevelt called from across the camp, "We've got some rough terrain ahead and we'll be picking up the pace. We need to make the valley by nightfall or we'll be wishing for the Devil himself to warm our beds tonight."

"Yessir," Jake responded, "I don't suppose we've got a resupply anywhere out there?"

"The Garnett ranch," Avonaco offered.

Though Jake was careful not to show it, the sound of Avonaco's voice startled him. It was not because the Indian's voice was loud, in fact, it was low and raspy due to a lifetime affinity for tobacco and alcohol. It was simply because the man rarely spoke; and if he did, it was never more than a handful of words. Jake originally assumed the Native's English was simply limited, but after a few nights of shared campfires, he realized that the man's taciturn demeanor was far more calculated.

Avonaco was what Jake's mother would have referred to as a *quick one*. He listened more than he spoke; and as Jake had learned, when he spoke, he spoke carefully. He chose his words for maximum efficiency and minimum scrutiny.

At first, Avonaco's reserved nature had roused Jake's suspicions. He had known many Indians in his time, and he felt that the majority of them fell into one of two categories: broken spirits or silently enraged. The broken spirits had simply accepted the new world order imposed upon them and were doing their best to carve a niche in a society that viewed them as less than human. The silently enraged held their tongues and averted their eyes, but their contempt and fury was palpable on the rare occasions they had dealings with anyone of European descent.

Avonaco fell into neither of those categories. He, like Roosevelt, was a unique beast. He was a survivor, not a victim. It was evident in his posture, demeanor and his speech. He was neither angry nor afraid. However, it was most evident in his interactions with Roosevelt.

The Native spoke to the American legend as an equal. They always met one another's gaze when they spoke, never equivocated their positions and, most importantly, always ended their conversations in agreement. Jake had never seen a relationship between two men built on such deep levels of respect. That had led the young man to one inescapable conclusion.

What he knew about the world beyond the Territories amounted to a little less than a cup of horse piss.

"That ranch is too far," Roosevelt countered. "If we wind up within shooting distance of Garnett's land, we'll have lost the pack."

"Not these wolves," Avonaco said in a tone that implied the statement should have been common knowledge.

Jake had never been very keen when it came to social dynamics, so he was usually reticent to join conversations in progress. However, there was something about Avonaco's statement that unsettled him. It was not the content, but the context. Jake was suddenly struck with the feeling that Roosevelt and

Avonaco were aware of information to which he himself was not privy.

"What makes these wolves so special?" Jake asked.

Avonaco turned to face the younger man. Despite the distance between them, Jake could clearly see the Indian's coal black eyes narrow. Even Roosevelt ceased packing. Jake sneaked a glance in the man's direction and saw what he expected: Roosevelt's expression was passive and relaxed. Jake had come to learn that meant their employer was observing and evaluating.

"The wolf hunts prey," Avonaco began, "It stalks. It separates the herd. It kills."

"And these wolves are different."

"These beasts are not hunting," Avonaco explained, "They are leading us."

Jake pondered his response.

"Maybe they're just running scared."

"Not this pack," Avonaco dismissed, "These animals do not know fear."

Jake opted to stand his ground.

"All animals know fear, Avonaco," Jake rebutted, "If you've ever come across one in a trap, you'd know that."

Avonaco nodded in agreement, turned and resumed readying his mount.

Jake looked over at Roosevelt.

"Did I miss something?"

Roosevelt eyed Jake for a long moment. The younger man felt an overwhelming urge to avert his eyes, but a voice inside him, a voice his drunken, tyrannical father had done his best to silence, urged him otherwise.

Jake held both his ground and Roosevelt's gaze.

460

The pregnant moment hung in the crisp, morning air. Whatever was happening, it was a crucial moment. An excruciating moment.

Just when Jake concluded he had made a critical miscalculation, Roosevelt produced a wry smile.

"You didn't miss a thing, young man."

Jake opened his mouth to respond, but the older man had already turned away. Jake considered pressing the point, but it was obvious the other two considered the matter settled. Whatever the matter had been.

Whatever it was, I guess I'll know the answer soon enough.

Another voice quietly chimed inside his head. A voice he had not heard since the night his father died. A voice Jake had hoped he would never hear again.

Are you sure that is what you want?

I can't answer that until I know the thing I don't know.

True, but by then it will be too late.

Jake shrugged the voice away and finished preparing his mount. His enthusiasm for the day ahead had waned considerably.

Though dark clouds hovered in the sky, the snowstorms had abated. The horses cut shallow furrows of mud and slush as the three men urged them onward.

Like many men, Roosevelt viewed horses as companions. And like many men, he had learned the consequences of that sentiment in the most brutal fashion imaginable. War was the ugliest of enterprises, and not all of its casualties were human.

As dark as those days had been for man and beast, Roosevelt had also learned that the friendship between men was no different than that between a man and his horse. Both required fundamental respect and communication. Over the years, his attitude toward the animals had elicited more than a few belly laughs from his contemporaries.

Their ribbing had not perturbed Roosevelt. Those men saw horses as beasts of burden; nothing more than tools used to accomplish goals. Roosevelt had a different perspective. He had never gone into battle with an untested rifle. Only a fool gambled his life with nothing more than blind faith. Preparation was the key to success in any endeavor. Thus, he maintained his firearms with meticulous care, and he felt his animals should be treated no differently.

The end result of Roosevelt's attitude was that his horses did not resist when pushed by their riders. They made good time, even under poor conditions. The animals tolerated the most unpleasant weather without complaint and if the need arose, they would run themselves into the ground if he deemed it necessary.

Roosevelt truly hoped their situation would not come to that. If he and the others were smart and fleet, they might resolve their hunt efficiently and decisively. Although he knew that was only if everything from the timing to the weather broke in their favor. Unfortunately, in Roosevelt's experience, those were long odds.

Very long odds.

Avonaco discovered the body.

The party had stopped for lunch. Avonaco had led them to a small stream where the horses could slake their thirst and Jake had provided venison jerky in addition to canned peaches, an unexpected treat. After the brief meal, Avonaco and Jake had excused themselves to tend to nature's call.

In the interim, Roosevelt had busied checking each of the mounts' shoes. He was carefully inspecting Jake's mount when a voice sounded behind him. Startled, Roosevelt dropped his hand to his pistol. It was an act of pure instinct, and he felt almost foolish as Avonaco finished speaking.

"Follow me," the Native instructed in a tone devoid of urgency.

I swear that man is part ghost, Roosevelt thought.

Not many men could get the jump on Theodore Roosevelt Jr. Avonaco was among that elite group. By all outward appearances, the Native was, at best, an aging man with less years to spend than years he had banked. At worst, he looked like a career drunk who split his time evenly between the bottom of a bottle and the ditch behind the saloon that served it to him.

In Roosevelt's experience, judging a man from his appearance was often a critical mistake, sometimes fatal. When he had been a much younger man, Roosevelt had taken up boxing, a noble sport that tested both the mind and body. During that time, he witnessed more than one cocksure lad laid out by a fat opponent that they had believed to be slow, or a small opponent that they believed to be weak. It was one of the most valuable lessons that his time in the ring had taught him.

Never assume the outside of a man is his is total measure. If you do, prepare yourself for disappointment.

"What is it?" Roosevelt asked as he stood.

Avonaco's face remained inscrutable.

"Best if you see."

The corpse lay prone at the edge of the icy creek. Three things immediately struck Roosevelt. The body was Native, naked and had been shredded by teeth and claws. The dead man's back and thighs had been sliced to ribbons in an unusually brutal and savage fashion.

He had not been eaten.

There were no signs of predation. The flesh had been mutilated, but not consumed. Both the tissue and muscle had been riven to the bone. Purple bruising had formed at the edges of the ragged wounds, although most of the blood had been swept away by the running water. The entire milieu led Roosevelt to a single conclusion.

It had not been an act of hunger. It had been an act of murder.

Roosevelt knelt beside the corpse as he spoke.

"No sign of clothing? Horse tracks?"

"None," Avonaco replied in his usual terse manner.

"Then . . . " Roosevelt began as he faced Avonaco, "Why? Why murder him?"

Avonaco scanned the opposite bank of the creek as he considered his response. After a moment, he spoke.

"A challenge," he replied, "Or an offense."

"What kind of offense?"

"Mating. Theft. Disrespect."

"I've known more than a few men who've been shot

for less," Roosevelt quipped as he continued to inspect the wounds. "We should—"

"What the hell is that?!"

Both Roosevelt and Avonaco reached for their sidearms as they pivoted. Jake was oblivious to their actions. His attention was tightly focused on the mutilated corpse laying at the water's edge. Roosevelt and Avonaco exchanged glances, then relaxed as the stunned youth continued to stare at the naked body.

"Christ on a cross!" Jake exclaimed to no one in particular, "What happened here?"

"That is what we are trying to discern," Roosevelt said as he returned his attention to the corpse, making a mental note about Jake's silent approach. Apparently the elite group, of which Avonaco was a member, was growing larger by the day.

Jake traversed the bank with ease as he spoke.

"No mystery there, sir."

"Why's that?" Roosevelt asked without turning away.

"That's the work of some mighty big wolves if you ask me."

Avonaco tipped the brim of his derby upwards as he eyed the younger man with a cold stare more commonly seen in reptiles and dead men. Regardless, Jake met the Native's gaze and decided not to demure.

Of the few lessons worth learning from his father, one was that you never broke eye contact with a wild animal. Jake did not consider Avonaco an animal in any way, but he knew a man with talents when he saw one. Avonaco was such a man, and Jake suspected his skills were both very particular and very dangerous. He was also certain that the Indian was still forming an opinion about the young man's worth.

"Am I right?"

Avonaco offered a slight nod in response.

"Except it can't be wolves," Jake stated.

"And why is that?" Roosevelt asked as he stood.

"That boy's chewed up, but ain't nothing missing," Jake observed. "Wolves would've taken the meaty parts down to his ass and pecker."

Roosevelt studied him for a few seconds before starting toward the embankment. Avonaco began following him as Jake continued to gawk at the body. As the two older men mounted the embankment, Jake called after them.

"HEY!"

Both men turned to face Jake, expectantly.

"Am I the only one who finds it peculiar that this boy ain't wearing a stitch of clothes?"

Avonaco remained impassive, but Roosevelt allowed himself a thin hint of a smile.

"I told you," Roosevelt said to Avonaco with a tinge of self-satisfaction.

The Indian gave the barest shrug, turned and walked away. Roosevelt chuckled softly. Jake watched as Roosevelt followed his friend over the embankment and disappeared from sight.

Jake resisted expressing his own satisfaction at Roosevelt's nod of approval, but internally he was beaming. He cast one last look at the naked corpse decaying on the wet rocks before starting after the two men.

As he climbed the embankment, Jake began to wonder about Roosevelt's agenda. It was obvious he was not a scheming man, but it was equally obvious that he was a methodical planner. Jake had no idea what his plan was, or why the two men were reticent to share it with him. He wished they would tell him soon, but he trusted Roosevelt and his judgment.

Jake did not know it then, but soon he would wish that he had never laid eyes on the dead brave. He would wish that he had never left his homestead. He would wish that he could sit by the fire with his mother one last time.

But most of all, he would wish that he had never met Theodore Roosevelt.

The sun had almost set when Avonaco discovered the tracks. There were no distinct paw prints, only divots and depressions leading toward the horizon. That was not unusual after such a heavy snowfall, but the erratic direction of the tracks unsettled Avonaco.

By his count, the pack now consisted of seven members. Another disconcerting revelation. When they began tracking the pack there had been nine. Seven males, two females, all very large.

Most male wolves in the Territories averaged one hundred pounds. The females were smaller by about twenty or thirty pounds. The largest Avonaco had seen outside of a traveling carnival or Wild West show was nearly one hundred and thirty pounds. It had taken half a dozen braves to run it to ground, and it still managed to maul and cripple two of his tribesmen. An anomaly. A rare example of nature unbridled.

This pack was different. By Avonaco's estimation, the smallest members of the pack weighed somewhere between one hundred ten and one hundred thirty pounds. And those were the females.

The males weighed significantly more. It was

possible that a few of them exceeded two hundred pounds. They were not animals. They were monsters.

Even as a child, Avonaco had been a gifted tracker. His father had been the first to recognize his potential and had encouraged his son with a quiet sense of pride. His talents had not escaped the attention of the tribal elders, either. Even before Avonaco had reached the age of manhood, he had been allowed to join the hunting parties, and he was soon after considered indispensable.

If it were not for the US Army Cavalry and the Dakota Wars, he would have been one of the youngest braves to sit on the tribal council. However, the United States government had different plans for his people. Bloody designs that, once the smoke had cleared, left Avonaco's people broken and scattered. The few that were left attempted to adhere to the old ways, but that behavior was often rewarded with persecution, imprisonment and death.

Avonaco had fought fiercely and bravely during those times. Like most of his tribe, he had conducted himself with valor and honored the memories of his forefathers. He had spilled more than his fair share of the white man's blood, but a noble defeat was still a defeat.

During those years, he had turned many wives into widows. Too many. Sometimes when the nights grew long and the darkness too deep, the spirits of those slain soldiers cried out to him. He heard them as clearly as he heard the pleas of his own fallen brethren. At times the cacophony of voices had been almost overwhelming, but the world had moved on from those blood-soaked days. Like many of his people, Avonaco had learned that escaping the past was impossible. His only option was to bury it. And there was only one way he had found to do that.

Whiskey and rye.

He was under no illusions about what he had become. He was a drunk. A man out of place in a world that was unforgiving of his kind. Yet he was still one of the best trackers in the Territories, and that was a valuable skill. The kind of skill that kept a roof over a man's head and a bottle in his hand.

The night he and Roosevelt had crossed paths, Avonaco was in just such a state. After spending his last dollar, the Native had stumbled out of the saloon and into the presence of two equally intoxicated men. *White men.*

Even steeped in alcohol, Avonaco's brain registered alarm. They had a look and demeanor about them that Avonaco had seen far too many times in his life. They were stupid, angry and looking for someone to blame for whatever perceived misery had befallen them.

Perhaps their wives had abandoned them. Perhaps they had lost their livestock or their claims. Perhaps a beloved family member had passed away. Perhaps someone had shot their trusted and faithful hound. Avonaco did not know, nor did he care. All he saw was the hate burning behind their dull eyes and it made him angry.

If they had witnessed an enemy's people repeatedly raping their wives and slaughtering their children, he would have understood their rage. He was certain that those men had not experienced such horrors.

Avonaco had not been so fortunate.

He had no memory of who landed the first blow.

He did have a vague recollection of knocking one of the men flat, but he attributed the memory more to wounded pride and revisionist history. Regardless of how the altercation began, Avonaco had quickly found himself in the dirt doing his best to ward off a seemingly endless barrage of kicks and punches.

Bruises spread and blood had flowed as Avonaco's consciousness had begun slipping away. In his alcohol fueled fugue, he had decided he was ready. He had tried to carve a life in the White Man's world, but every day saw new obstacles and new setbacks. Not to mention that he was not welcome in his own lands. The ancestral lands of his people.

He did not remember the exact moment of surrender. Avonaco had only two clear memories after reaching that moment.

He recalled that though the beating grew more severe with each kick, he felt an overwhelming sense of peace at the thought of seeing his family again. In that moment, he had wished his attackers had been wearing their pistols. His misery could have ended, his journey to the sacred land could have begun with a single pull of a trigger. One shot would have freed him.

The second thing he remembered was the abruptness with which the assault had ended. His eyes had been screwed shut and his ears bleeding, so all Avonaco heard were raised, muffled voices. Seconds later, a few loud thumps sounded, followed by two heavy thuds. When Avonaco did open his eyes, he was staring into the face of a bespectacled, barrel-chested *Wašicu* who appeared to be more mustache than man.

"I don't know what you said to them fellas," the

man began as he bent and offered his hand, "But it sure got their dander up."

Avonaco reached forward and gripped the man's hand, however it was apparent to them both that the wounded man was going to require medical attention. The good Samaritan curled his arms beneath Avonaco's shoulders and hauled the Native to his feet.

"Looks like we're waking up Doc Myers tonight," the man said as he steadied Avonaco, "Do you think you can make it?"

Avonaco had been dazed and not fully comprehending. His words slurred as he spoke.

"No medicine."

"What? You don't believe in the white man's medicine?"

"No money," Avonaco had murmured.

"We'll discuss that when the sun comes up," the man had stated, "But you won't live to see it unless you come with me."

Between the alcohol and the thrashing, Avonaco was in no condition to refuse. He did manage to mutter a few words before the night dimmed into complete darkness.

"Many thanks," Avonaco offered.

"Don't thank me," the man advised as he prompted Avonaco to take a step, "You're not out of the woods yet."

"Still," Avonaco mumbled, "I am in your debt."

The man urged Avonaco forward.

"Do you have a name?" the man asked in a completely conversational tone.

Upon reflection, Avonaco had realized that the man's questions were designed more to keep him conscious than to gather information. However in that moment, Avonaco's thinking had been far from lucid and his mind had been operating on conditioning and instinct.

"Means Lean Bear," the man speculated, "Is that right?"

If Avonaco had not been impressed with the man before, he was definitely impressed with him then. He had never met a white man who had taken the time to learn even the most rudimentary elements of his language.

He offered a weak nod to the man and the man rewarded the effort with a smile.

"In that case, it is my pleasure to meet you, Avonaco," the man announced, "And allow me to introduce myself."

The man's words had sounded like distant echoes in a long tunnel.

"My name," the distant voice began, "is Theodore Roosevelt. It is good to make your acquaintance."

Avonaco liked to believe he responded, but all that was left in his memory was an expanding pool of blackness.

Where are they headed? And why?

The thought pulled the tracker from his reverie. This pack was subtler than others, but their tactics were still detectable by a trained eye. They were doing their best to conceal their ultimate destination while attempting to prolong the pursuit as much as possible.

They are trying to exhaust us.

Avonaco knew that tactic well. He and the other braves had employed it many times when warring with neighboring tribes. The idea was simple; tire your enemy with unnecessary travel in senseless directions. The end result was fatigued men on weary horses. Not only was your quarry physically drained, but their minds would begin to buckle.

Strong, intelligent men would begin to bicker over incidental behavior. Disagreements would balloon into arguments and those arguments would escalate into violence. The tactic was designed to sow the seeds of distrust and paranoia. When it worked, Avonaco and his men often found themselves facing a disorganized assembly of men too aggravated to function as a unit.

As a pack.

Avonaco had no such worries. His debt to Roosevelt was far from being repaid and thus his allegiance to the man was unwavering. As for the kid, Avonaco had begun to understand why Roosevelt chose him. He was different from most of the white men Avonaco had dealt with.

Jake was still young and not the most worldly of men. However, he was sharp and even more importantly, respectful. Not only to his employer, but to Avonaco as well. When Avonaco met the younger man's gaze, he saw no resentment or hatred in his eyes. This told Avonaco something very crucial about Jake's character. Whatever problems Jake had had in life, he did not blame others for his misfortunes. Avonaco had learned that was a trait that only true men possessed.

The Indian had been waiting and watching for Jake's prejudice to reveal itself. It had yet to emerge. Even in moments of exhaustion or frustration, Jake had remained calm and affable. He had kept his good humor and had never flagged in his obligations. All totaled, Avonaco was forced to arrive at one inexorable conclusion.

Jake Cutler was not a bigot, and a basically decent human being.

Avonaco was a little disappointed with that conclusion; not with the boy, but with himself. With as much respect and lifelong loyalty he had bestowed upon Roosevelt, he should never have doubted his friend's judgment. Avonaco had let his own prejudices cloud his perceptions and, in that way, he was no better than the men who had beaten him outside the saloon. It was a shameful admission, but facing unpleasant truths about one's self was yet another measure of being a man.

Avonaco came to two realizations as he stood alternating his gaze between the tracks and the horizon. The first was that he should be less guarded when dealing with Jake Cutler. The second was that their party needed to become less reactive and more proactive in their pursuit. Avonaco was convinced that the pack was leading them into a trap.

But where? Where would they have the advantage?

Wherever it was, it would have to be some place where their weapons were useless and the pack would have the—

The answer bloomed like a thunderclap in his mind. Avonaco had found yet another reason to chastise himself. It was an old tactic. A Native tactic. If he was correct, there were only two places the wolves could spring their trap. Unfortunately, those points on the map were separated by two days of hard riding. And that was at a full gallop.

Avonaco began the trek back to the others. If they were to get ahead of the pack, Roosevelt had to make a choice.

And Avonaco was certain that he was not going to care for his options.

"Are you certain?"

Avonaco nodded.

"Do you see any alternative?"

Avonaco responded with a faint shaking of his head.

Jake, who had been nurturing the beginnings of a campfire, ceased his efforts and stood. Whatever was being decided in that moment was obviously of great importance and though he had not been invited to participate in the discussion, Jake felt it deserved his full attention.

Roosevelt looked skyward and sighed.

"How is that fire coming along?" he asked while he continued to study the emerging stars.

"She'll be roaring soon enough, sir," Jake answered. "Do you want me to heat a few tins of beans?"

"You should tell him, Theodore."

Jake was not sure if he was more surprised by Avonaco's unsolicited remark or by Roosevelt's reaction to it. If it had been any other man, the reaction would have been negligible. Roosevelt was not just any man, and for him, his reaction was nothing short of an emotional outburst.

Abandoning his usual measured demeanor, Roosevelt swiveled his head toward the Native and furrowed his brow. His hands came together. Jake noticed his employer was worrying his palms with his thumbs. Avonaco appeared unfazed, but Jake had observed the man long enough to recognize that he was uncomfortable with Roosevelt's response. It was his face. His expression was almost always inscrutable, but when Avonaco was anxious, it became tight. Immobile.

The moment hung in the air as the last of the daylight surrendered to the oncoming night. To Jake, it felt like an eternity, when in actuality only seconds had passed. Roosevelt glanced between the two men before nodding to himself as he accepted Avonaco's suggestion.

Roosevelt sighed, again.

"I suppose we have reached that juncture," he admitted in a soft spoken tone.

The big man walked to Jake and looked at the young man and looked him straight in the eye.

"What do you say you get those tins and put on some coffee," Roosevelt suggested as he placed his hand on Jake's shoulder. "Because we've got a lot to talk about, son."

Firelight flickered and danced across Jake's face as Roosevelt finished speaking. The hour was growing late, but Jake was not the least bit tired. Truthfully, he doubted he would sleep at all if one tenth of what Roosevelt had said was anything other than pure fantasy.

The man had detailed every event leading up to the day of their departure. It was an incredible story. The kind of thing one might have read in a penny dreadful or heard in a campfire yarn. Even though it came straight from, arguably, the most respected man in the United States, Jake would have thought his leg was being yanked if Avonaco had not occasionally interjected to support Roosevelt's recounting of events.

Despite the fantastic nature of their tale, the two men were serious. Deadly serious.

The crackling of the fire was the only relief from the silence that had settled over the camp. Roosevelt and Avonaco exchanged curious glances as Jake studied the twirling flames.

"I know it sounds like a whopper, son," Roosevelt admitted, "But, I can swear to you, it's the God's honest truth. Every word."

"I'd never call you a liar, sir," Jake said as he watched the popping embers. "I know you to be an honest and plainspoken man."

"Most men would think I'm off my chump," Roosevelt chuckled, "Don't tell me you haven't even considered the possibility that I've gone batty."

"The thought crossed my mind, but . . . " Jake looked up from the campfire, "Both of you? No. Neither of you suffer fools, so I can't reckon you indulge in foolish pursuits."

Roosevelt leaned back and smiled as he spoke.

"I can't say I disagree with you, son, but I'm not above confessing I've played the fool for more than one lass with a pretty smile and a coy wink."

"I've met a few of those myself, sir," Jake replied, his tone devoid of mirth. "But I never met one that turned into a wolf."

"Are you certain?"

The question caught Jake off guard. It was not only

the fact that if they had been shining him, he doubted they would carry such a charade so far for so long. It was also because it was not Roosevelt who asked the question, but Avonaco. Jake still knew very little about Roosevelt's Indian friend, but he would bet a round of drinks that the man was not much of a practical joker.

Jake looked across the rising flames of the campfire as he answered the question.

"Can't say that I am," Jake acknowledged, "But to be honest, I'm mostly concerned about catching the drip. I really don't ask too much about being eaten alive."

"Then I'm sorry, Jake," Roosevelt's expression was as sincere as his voice. "Because you'll never see this world the same way once we're done. I wish I could have done this differently. I wish I could undo a lot of what's been done. But that ship sailed long ago," Roosevelt concluded. "What's done is done. Now we need to focus on the task at hand."

"And what is the task at hand, sir?"

Roosevelt nodded as he addressed Avonaco.

"Now's as good a time as any. Give 'em over."

Avonaco's only acknowledgment of Roosevelt's order was to stand and disappear into the darkness beyond the campfire. Jake watched as the night swallowed Avonaco. He turned his attention back to Roosevelt. The elder statesman clenched a cigar between his teeth as he plucked a sliver of wood from the fire. He touched the glowing splinter to the tip of the cigar and inhaled.

"How familiar are you with Native lore, Jake?" Roosevelt asked as he exhaled a plume of thick smoke. Jake watched as the smoke tumbled and expanded in the firelight. As the cloud dissipated, Jake answered.

"If I take your meaning, not much, sir. I've heard a few stories about medicine men and witch doctors, but nothing that didn't sound like superstitious nonsense."

Roosevelt took a keen interest in the smoldering tip of his cigar. He rolled it between his thumb and forefinger as he spoke.

"So you don't give much credence to tales of witches, ghosts and goblins?"

"No, sir," Jake confirmed, "I'm not going to say I haven't heard a few things in these parts that made my nape hairs stand up. Some of these night creatures can give you the willies when you're out late and alone. But it's never anything unnatural. Just an angry owl or a fox with his horn up."

Roosevelt chuckled. "What if I told you that some of those stories weren't for children, and some of those midnight calls were something other than a fox looking for company?"

"If it were anybody else, I'd tell them to lay off the hooch," Jake admitted, "But on account of your reputation and your plain-spoken mind, I'd be inclined to listen."

Avonaco appeared at the periphery of the campfire.

Christ Almighty, Jake thought. *That man is as silent as a shadow.*

The tracker was holding small boxes that Jake immediately recognized, boxes of ammunition. Avonaco held them for Roosevelt to inspect. Roosevelt nodded his approval and Avonaco stepped over to Jake as he presented the boxes.

Jake looked up at the Native with querulous eyes. Avonaco's expression remained impassive as he patiently waited for Jake to relieve him of the boxes.

"Thanks."

Avonaco offered the slightest of nods before returning to his seat by the fire. Jake looked over at Roosevelt who simply indicated the boxes with a casual wave of his cigar. Jake turned his attention to the boxes.

The print indicated he was holding a box of .56-56 Spencer rimfire cartridges. Jake's brow furrowed. It was not the caliber of the ammunition that perplexed him. They were the correct rounds for his rifle, a Spencer 1860. It was the fact that it was common knowledge among the group that he had five boxes totaling a hundred rounds in his saddle bags and about half that for his double-action Colt revolver.

"I don't understand," he said as he looked over at Roosevelt, "Just as you asked, I brought enough rounds to fight a whole tribe of Apaches." Jake glanced sideways at Avonaco, "No offense."

"None taken," Avonaco did not look away from the campfire as he spoke. "I'm not Apache."

"One of those boxes is for your rifle and one for your pistol," Roosevelt explained, "Why don't you open it up and take a gander?"

Jake obeyed. He leaned forward into the firelight as he pulled the top from the box. For a moment, he stared, uncomprehending. With a hint of amusement, Roosevelt watched as realization spread over Jake's features. Jake plucked a rifle round from the box and scrutinized it in the firelight.

"Is this what I think it is?"

"Can't read your mind, son," Roosevelt responded as he took a long drag from his cigar.

"Are these bullets silver?"

"Indeed they are."

"These must have cost a fortune," Jake quietly exclaimed.

"I wouldn't say a fortune; I will admit they were not cheap," Roosevelt clarified, "But they are essential."

"I'm man enough to admit that I'm a might bit confused, Mr. Roosevelt."

"I'd feel the same way if you weren't confused, Mr. Cutler. However now that we've arrived at this moment, I can indulge in some of that plain speech of which you are so fond."

Roosevelt stubbed his cigar into the damp earth and sipped a lukewarm cup of coffee before continuing. "I'm afraid I told you a half-truth at the beginning of our journey. The politicians in New York would refer to it as a lie of omission. I prefer to think of it in military terms."

For the first time since meeting Roosevelt, Jake experienced something truly unexpected. Doubt. Despite the older man's and Avonaco's occasional cryptic behavior, Jake had never questioned their intentions or integrity. Roosevelt was known for both his honesty and strength of character and Jake had long decided the Indian was a straight shooter.

"I never enlisted, sir," he began, "So, you understand I might need a little explaining."

"In the Cavalry, information is only offered on a need to know basis," Roosevelt said, "And the further you are down the chain of command, the less you need to know."

"If we're not out here to hunt wolves, Mr. Roosevelt, then I would sure appreciate you telling me why we've been churning earth for the last four days.

Not to mention," Jake added as he tapped the box of ammunition, "what I'm supposed to do with these."

"Well, son," Roosevelt said between sips of coffee, "We are here to hunt wolves and we aren't."

Jake stared at him with a blank expression.

"Maybe I should let Avonaco take it from here. Mr. Avonaco?"

Avonaco looked from Roosevelt to Jake as the younger man turned toward him, expectantly. Avonaco removed a long-stemmed pipe from his jacket and began unrolling his tobacco pouch.

"The English word is *skin-walkers*. They are wicked outcasts from many tribes. Men and women who consort with dark spirits."

"Think witches," Roosevelt interjected.

Avonaco lit his pipe before resuming.

"The skin-walker forsakes his ancestors and the ways of his people for unnatural power. They live in the wild lands. They answer to no man. No spirits other than those that dwell in the shadows."

Jake was mesmerized by Avonaco's explanation. His voice was low and his speech deliberate. Avonaco and Roosevelt seemed to genuinely believe the tale the Native was spinning.

Avonaco believing, Jake could understand. It was part of his culture. He had lived with it all of his life. But Roosevelt was an educated man. A practical man. The idea that Roosevelt would entertain such ghost stories as truth went against everything Jake knew about the man. If Jake had learned anything about him during their association, it was that Roosevelt was not a fanciful man.

"What are you saying, Avonaco?" Jake asked,

although he suspected he already deduced the answer. He decided to follow his intuition. "Are you saying that the wolves we are hunting . . . aren't wolves?"

"The skin-walker has the power to become a beast," Avonaco clarified. "A wolf, a coyote or even a fox."

"And you're saying these wolves aren't wolves? They're really people?"

"They were people," Roosevelt clarified. "The way Avonaco tells it, the longer they live as wolves, the harder it is for them to change back into men."

"And you believe all this . . . " Jake searched for the least insulting word in his limited vocabulary. "This . . . superstition?"

"It is only a superstition until you see it with your own eyes," Roosevelt replied.

"And you saw something," Jake concluded.

"A few years back, I was a rancher in these parts, as you know."

Jake nodded as Roosevelt continued, "One night, I was on the porch enjoying a cigar and a wee sip of brandy when I heard an unholy ruckus in the main barn. I got my rifle and went to investigate. I'd had trouble before with thieves on that land and I was eager to catch one of them with their hand in the till. That's what I thought I was stepping into."

Roosevelt paused as he retrieved his cigar and lit it again. He inhaled a lungful of smoke before continuing. "Instead, I found the barn doors open and one of my prized stallions dead and gutted. Blood everywhere and chunks of him all around," he stared into the fire as the memories surged through him, "I've seen a lot of ugliness in my time. I've seen too much bloodshed, watched as good men lay praying and pleading as they died."

Roosevelt looked away from the fire as he fixed his eyes on Jake. It was a haunted gaze.

"But I've never seen a slaughter so savage. Vicious. My mares were still bucking and whinnying. I won't mince words. My short hairs were at full attention. So was my rifle. And that was a good thing."

Roosevelt took a moment to sip his coffee.

"The wolf came out of nowhere. It happened fast. I shot it once. That slowed it down, but it wasn't stopping. I had maybe a couple of seconds to get off another shot and there must have been an angel on my shoulder that night."

"You hit it in the head," Jake concluded.

"No, son," Roosevelt corrected, "My shot went over his head. What I didn't know then was I could have shot it a dozen times, and it would have kept coming. What saved my life was the lamp I was carrying."

"The lamp?"

"The beast leaped and knocked me ass over tea kettle. It was on me a moment later. All I could see were red eyes and fangs. I didn't think. I just swung the lamp and smashed it against the murderous creature. The lamp shattered and the next thing I knew the whole world was on fire. The thing howled as burning oil covered its whole side and half its head. It was an ungodly sight for certain."

"I slipped out from under it, grabbed another oil lamp hanging by the door and hurled it at the flaming monster. It exploded, and then the wolf was fully engulfed. I watched it spin and squeal like a hellhound chasing its tail. It was something out of a nightmare."

"But you killed it," Jake stated.

"I did." Roosevelt confirmed. "That's when the real nightmare started."

Roosevelt paused as he took another long drag from his cigar. Smoke spilled from his mouth as he resumed.

"I watched the thing burn for I don't remember how long and then it collapsed. I thought that was the end of it, but then it started to . . . " he considered his word choice, "change. It was as charred as those embers, but it started growing."

"Growing?"

"The skin stretched and split as it got . . . longer. I heard the cooked flesh tear and bones snap as it turned back into a man right before my eyes. It was burnt to the bone so I couldn't see any features, but it was a man. Make no mistake about that."

Jake leaned away from the fire and rubbed his eyes with his palms. Roosevelt's tale was beyond implausible. It was impossible fiction. The kind of thing boys fabricated as a prank to dupe their unsuspecting friends.

However, Jake could not reconcile the idea that Roosevelt and Avonaco had concocted the story, hired Jake, rode hard for four days in the miserable cold and spent a king's ransom on silver bullets just to have a laugh at his expense. Whether or not it had happened, Roosevelt believed it had. And Avonaco did not strike Jake as the kind of man who would indulge a man's delusions to simply swindle Roosevelt out of a few dollars.

In the Territories, the boxes of bullets alone would have fetched more than most men would earn in a decade. If it was about money, Avonaco would have lit out into the night long ago.

"What did you do?" Jake asked.

"Only thing I could," Roosevelt answered, "I dug a deep hole, buried the remains, polished off the bottle of brandy, went to bed and tried to forget the whole nightmarish encounter. After that, I never spoke a word of the incident. Until I met Avonaco that is."

"And he told you about the skin-walkers?"

"Indeed he did," Roosevelt replied.

"For the sake of argument, let's just say I believe all of this. Why would you seek these things out? Why not leave well enough alone?"

"Because these . . . creatures possess the basest instincts of both man and beast." Roosevelt responded as he exhaled a cloud of smoke, "That means their only function is to kill, eat and breed. Do you understand?"

"I think I do."

"Avonaco tells me their pack, for lack of a better word, is still small, but growing. He also tells me the only way to kill them is with fire or with silver. Fire consumes everything it touches, and according to my Native friend, silver poisons them."

"You can take heads as well," Avonaco added. "No living thing can live without its head."

"That may be true, my friend," Roosevelt acknowledged. "But I'm hoping we don't get near enough for that. Seeing one of those things up close once was enough for this lifetime."

Roosevelt took a swallow of coffee as he nursed his cigar. Several minutes passed with the only interruption of the ensuing silence the popping and crackling of the campfire. Jake studied the silver round as he considered Roosevelt's tale.

Finally, Jake broke the stillness.

"I want to believe you, sir," he began, "but you have to admit, it's a wild tale by any measure."

"It is," Roosevelt agreed.

"But the way I see it, I signed on to hunt wolves," Jake said as he looked up from the rifle round. "And that's still the job. You say I have to hunt them with these," he held up the round to accentuate his point, "then that's what I'll do. Lead or silver, it doesn't matter. They all kill just the same. So no matter what I believe, this will kill them, right?"

Roosevelt and Avonaco shared a mutual glance across the diminishing flames. After a moment, Roosevelt offered a sage nod to Jake.

"Then that means the only thing that's changed is the bullets I'm using," Jake surmised. "After all, dead is dead, and it don't matter how it got that way. Are we good with that?"

Roosevelt crushed the remainder of his cigar beneath his boot and smiled.

"I think we understand each other, Mr. Cutler," Roosevelt stated, "Now, let's discuss tomorrow night."

"What happens tomorrow night, sir?"

Roosevelt's smile widened as he leaned forward. The dancing flames of the campfire were reflected on the lenses of his spectacles.

"Tomorrow night, son," he answered in a low voice, "tomorrow night, we hunt."

Roosevelt had not slept well.

After his discussion with Jake, he had conferred

487

with Avonaco. The Native had been correct. Roosevelt did not favor either of the options the tracker had presented. The two men had debated and deliberated until the fire had reduced itself to ash. As the moon dipped toward the horizon, they came to an agreement, but Roosevelt was still unhappy.

Choosing the lesser of two evils still meant that you were making a bad choice.

Avonaco was of the opinion that the pack was either leading them to a box canyon south of their position, or to a sharp bend in the river to the north. Both locations had the virtue of essentially being dead ends. The canyon would put their backs against a wall. One way in, one way out. The bend in the river was too deep and the current too fast for the horses to attempt swimming, so it was equally as effective in blocking any retreat.

The main difference in the two locations affected the wolves more than it did Roosevelt and his men. The canyon had the benefit of truly trapping the men, but it was narrow, and that meant the wolves would be funneled into what would effectively become a shooting gallery. The river was not nearly as confining and allowed the pack to split and attack from multiple angles. It also allowed multiple possibilities for retreat. Any break in the wolves' ranks was a potential point of egress for Roosevelt and his comrades.

In the end, Roosevelt and Avonaco agreed that the canyon was the better option. Though there was little chance of retreat, it put the wolves at a significant disadvantage when facing firearms. If Jake had time to find higher ground and Avonaco and Roosevelt could entrench themselves, their weapons should do the rest.

He mentally reviewed the conversation as he readied his horse.

"And if they choose the river?" Avonaco had asked.

"They won't," Roosevelt had stated, confidently, "But on the off chance they do, they'll realize their mistake and come running."

"Perhaps," Avonaco sounded unconvinced. "Perhaps not."

"Remember, my friend, they know that we are not just hunting any wolves. We are hunting their kind. They know that we know what they are and I'm confident that they don't want what we know to become common knowledge. They'll seize this opportunity, just as we have."

"And you are certain of this?"

"Not in the least," Roosevelt acquiesced. "But there are certain critical mistakes a leader cannot afford to make and assuming you are smarter than your opponent is at the top of the list."

"You are assuming that they would do what you would do."

"Exactly."

"There is a flaw in your logic, my friend." Avonaco stated in his usual neutral tone.

"And what is that?"

"You are assuming that you are smart." Avonaco deadpanned.

Climbing into the saddle, Roosevelt laughed for the second time as he remembered Avonaco's joke.

Roosevelt had never cared for humorless men. Much of man's limited time in the world was spent in hardship and misery. Working barren soil, fighting wars in places even God himself had abandoned, and living with sickness and loss were routine for most men. Some chose to embrace that bitter truth and allowed it to shape their outlook on the world.

In Roosevelt's opinion, those men went on to become bankers, evangelical pastors and mean drunks. However, those who chose to reject those truths with laughter and love, whether it be for family, an animal, their country, or God, not only saw the world as a place to be relished, they saw it as a place to be bettered. And despite Avonaco's stoic demeanor, he was one of the latter.

Roosevelt knew that the man had suffered much, and still, despite the fact that he medicated his pain with alcohol, he saw the world as something worth protecting. Perhaps it was his spiritual upbringing, or perhaps it was as elementary as the Native needing something to champion, some purpose in life, but regardless, the results were the same.

He was a warrior, and he would stand with Roosevelt no matter the outcome.

Roosevelt trotted his horse over to the others. They were both mounted and waiting.

"Are we ready, boys?" he asked.

Avonaco nodded.

"I'm not sure about ready, sir," Jake said with a wry smile, "but I'm willing. I don't know what's about to happen or how it ends, but it's going to make a helluva story."

"I hope we live to tell it, son."

"Forget about telling it," Jake said as his smile broadened, "I just hope I can find someone who will believe it."

LONE WOLVES

Bloated, dark clouds hung like a shroud over the slush covered plains as they urged their steeds onward. It was a difficult ride exacerbated by the uneven ground and frigid winds. A deep chill had settled into Jake's bones, and he was so famished his stomach was threatening to devour itself. However, their pace showed no sign of slowing, and there was no discussion about stopping for a meal. Or even a piss, for that matter.

As desperately as Jake needed a variety of reliefs, he understood their urgency. They had to be inside the canyon hours before sunset. If they missed that deadline, they would have to camp on the open plain. It would be an indefensible position that would make them short work for the pack. Or as Jake put it to himself . . .

Suicide.

Before departing camp, Jake had loaded both his guns with the newly minted silver ammunition. In addition, he had stocked his belt and pouch with the expensive rounds. He wondered how drastically changing the composition of the projectile would influence its trajectory, but quickly dismissed the thought. It changed nothing. These were the rounds he had to use, and he would have to compensate for any irregularities in the moment.

Ahead, Avonaco was increasing the pace. Jake clucked, cueing his horse into a faster gallop. He had no doubt they would make the canyon before nightfall.

It was what happened once they did that caused his empty stomach to lose its appetite.

The canyon was near. Even though Avonaco was certain that they would reach their destination with daylight to spare, he did not relent in their furious pace. He was in agreement with his colleague's plan, but he had spotted something in the distance that led him to believe that they had less time than Roosevelt had predicted.

A lone wolf.

The sliver of a silhouette had dipped beneath the horizon before the others had noticed it. Avonaco had considered slowing long enough to inform them, but opted against doing so. Roosevelt had been correct. Though the pack had laid their trap at the river, they had left a sentinel behind. Now that lone sentry was beyond their reach, however, it would return. And when it did . . .

It would not be alone.

The craggy walls of the canyon cast long, heavy shadows as the sun receded beyond sight. Outcroppings, boulders and the remains of broken trees once swept along by flash floods had created a maze of minor obstacles that slowed their progress. As they rounded each bend, Roosevelt studied the terrain, searching for the ideal site to stage their ambush.

The lack of suitable locations was proving worrisome.

For his plan to succeed, he needed to position Jake on higher ground in a spot that offered an unobstructed view of the canyon floor. Not only could the kid hit a target on the move at a distance further than most men could see, he could do it quickly and repeatedly. However, none of that mattered if Jake could not see the targets.

In addition, the ground below needed to have multiple covered positions. Boulders, tree trunks, basically anything that would force the wolves to redirect their attacks. He and Avonaco on open ground would be run down in a matter of minutes. They needed to divide the pack's ranks and give Jake as much time as they could afford.

Avonaco had informed Roosevelt and Jake about the lone wolf as soon as they had reached the mouth of the canyon. Roosevelt had only nodded and checked his pocket watch. It had come as no surprise to Roosevelt, as he had suspected the pack would have left a lookout.

He also suspected that the wolves would approach cautiously. He had no way of knowing how much of their human mind they retained in their lupine form, but even the boldest of wolves rarely charged recklessly. They were pack animals, and their tactics reflected that mentality. However once the shooting began, chaos would ensue. Whatever happened, it would be over quickly.

As they rounded another bend, Avonaco's voice broke the silence.

"There."

Roosevelt twisted in his saddle to see his friend's outstretched arm pointing toward the canyon the wall. In the distance ahead, a narrow ledge near the lip of the canyon widened into a rocky platform. It was big enough to accommodate two men.

Roosevelt scanned the ground beneath the outcropping. Several large rocks and a few boulders were strewn along the canyon floor. He had hoped for a narrower passage, but he doubted the terrain beyond that stretch would be any more favorable. He looked upward and saw the clouds had parted; the twinkle of stars emerging with the twilight. He reined in his horse as he consulted his watch.

They were out of time.

"This is it, boys," Roosevelt proclaimed. "Are we ready?"

"Am I ready for the three of us to go to war against a pack of magical man-wolves?" Jake clarified, "I'll never be ready for that, sir."

Avonaco turned his head toward Jake. He wore a queer expression Roosevelt had never seen before, more inscrutable than his usual poker face. After a moment, he turned and addressed Roosevelt.

"What he said," Avonaco announced.

For a split second, both Roosevelt and Jake looked at one another incredulously. Then without warning, they both erupted into laughter. Even Avonaco allowed himself an inkling of a smile.

"Regardless of the outcome, gentlemen," Roosevelt said as his laughter subsided, "it has been a privilege knowing you."

Jake's mirth evaporated as quickly as Avonaco's.

"I think I speak for us both, sir," Jake presumed, "when I say that the privilege is ours."

He looked to Avonaco, who nodded his approval. Roosevelt smiled at them both.

"You know what to do, men," he assured, "We finish this tonight, my friends, and we sleep in our own beds before the week's end. That is our pact. Agreed?"

LONE WOLVES

Both men nodded as the first rays of moonlight penetrated the canyon walls.

"Then let's get to work."

The moon was near its apex and almost full. The shadows within the canyon had shrunk beneath its silver rays and the stars shone brightly above. In addition, the winds had subsided significantly. For Jake, the conditions were as close to optimal as he could expect given the circumstances.

Nothing about the situation was precisely ideal. A daylight confrontation in a more controlled environment would have shifted the advantage to him and his companions, but so would a Gatling gun and a dozen of Roosevelt's fabled Rough Riders. Jake had lost too much money playing poker to learn a simple lesson; you do not play the cards you want, you play the cards you are dealt.

The climb to the ledge had been strenuous but not difficult. Roosevelt had been anxious to get Jake onto his perch as soon as possible, but Jake had a few adjustments to their plan he wanted to implement before he effectively stranded himself. Roosevelt had begrudgingly agreed.

The three men had moved quickly and efficiently as they staged the battleground. Roosevelt and Avonaco had focused their energies on building pyres at the edges of the makeshift arena, and Jake had employed his skills as a trapper to better safeguard the men he would soon leave behind. They were nearing completion when the wind carried the first faint howl from the plains into the canyon.

As Jake situated himself, he watched Avonaco

move from pyre to pyre. As the tracker lit each bundle of deadwood and detritus, the illumination inside the canyon rose. Flickering flames licked at the sky and shadows ebbed and flowed across the stony surfaces of the canyon walls. From Jake's position, it was a mesmerizing sight. On any other occasion, it would have instilled a sense of serenity and wonder. Tonight, it only served to accentuate the surreal nature of their circumstances.

Another howl echoed along the canyon walls. Moments later, another joined it. Then another. Soon, it became a chorus. The pack was close. Despite the chilly air, Jake wiped sweat from his brow.

It won't be long, now, Jake thought.

Jake was not a particularly spiritual man, but he said a simple prayer all the same. Not for himself or for the men below. He prayed for his mother. Her health, her safety and her happiness.

Just in case.

Avonaco listened as the skin-walkers' howling dwindled. The pack would be upon them within the hour. He had lit all twelve pyres and for the moment, the blazes were brilliant. The orange flames and fierce warmth reminded him of an earlier, happier time.

A time when his people would celebrate a successful hunt or a victory against a neighboring tribe. A time when the braves moved from fire to fire, feasting and laughing. It had been an exhilarating time for him and his brothers. A time of triumph. A time of joy.

Now, those times lived only in memory. His brothers and sisters were long dead. Their songs, once offered to the Great Spirit, had fallen silent. Their bones were now dust. He himself had been a ghost for many years, wasting the days until the spirits determined it was finally his time to join his ancestors.

He tossed the torch onto the tinder collected in the center of the makeshift ring. Avonaco and Roosevelt had spent the better part of an hour constructing the central bonfire. The torch vanished inside the crude tower of rotten, desiccated wood and moments later the base began to glow. Soon, it would become a raging conflagration.

Another howl overpowered the pops and sizzles of the emerging inferno. The pack was nearly upon them. As Avonaco retreated to the cover of a boulder, he wondered if tonight would be the night he was reunited with his ancestors. If that was his fate, he had made peace with it. Because if he died tonight, he would not die a drunken, empty shell . . .

He would die a warrior.

Roosevelt watched as Avonaco settled against the side of the half-buried boulder. There was roughly forty feet between the two friends; thirty feet to the canyon walls on either side of them. Considering their current circumstances, it felt as if there were an ocean between them.

Another round of howling echoed around the bend in the canyon. It was now a matter of minutes. Roosevelt's finger curled around the trigger of his Winchester rifle. He had been on the verge of battle many times in his life and one thing never failed to surprise him. When it happened, it happened fast.

When he recounted the events in the years to

follow, he would swear he could hear the smacking of lips and the gnashing of teeth as the pack approached, but that would only be the embellishment of memory. In that moment, he could only hear one thing. Roosevelt had led men into to battle many times, had heard everything from battle cries to quiet sobs, but there was one thing that he never failed to hear.

The beating of his own heart.

Pounding in his chest; blood rushing in his ears. The sound of raw fear. Every nerve in his body thrummed. His spine tingled. Every instinct he had told him to flee. His mind screamed at him to run as fast and as far as he could away from the perverse folly he had orchestrated.

Roosevelt crouched and raised his rifle. A beating heart and a healthy fear of death told him all he needed to know. He was alive.

And he planned to stay that way.

At first, the skin-walkers were indiscernible. Vague shades among the shadows beyond the firelight. Their movements were agitated, but careful. An occasional tentative step accompanied by a snap or snarl.

From his vantage point Jake could see Roosevelt and Avonaco nestled against their respective rocks. Although Avonaco was sighting down his rifle, Jake noticed the tracker had kept his shotgun within arm's reach. Jake had little use for such an inaccurate firearm, but he suspected Avonaco was quite proficient with the thunderous weapon.

On the other hand, Roosevelt held his rifle less like a marksman and more like a gunslinger. Jake had seen the stance before. It was preferred by men who valued speed over accuracy. It was not Jake's tactic of choice, but the man had taken both Kettle Hill and San Juan Hill, so it was also not his place to argue.

Instead, he returned his attention to the wolves.

The skin-walkers were still under the cover of darkness. The ambush was obvious, and even if the fires had not alerted the pack, the men had taken no precautions when it came to their scent. The pack knew what awaited them, and Jake suspected the beasts were simply working up their courage.

As if the creatures' mystical powers extended to mind reading, one of the wolves stretched its snout into the firelight. Jake relaxed his shoulders and gingerly placed the tip of his finger against the trigger of his rifle.

This is it, he thought.

The wolf withdrew its snout. Jake slowly inhaled as he curled his trigger finger. A single bead of sweat ran along his temple onto his cheek.

The moment stretched into an eternity.

Jake's muscles were as tight as a hangman's rope. The wind was drying his eyes and his mouth felt as if it was made of cotton. Holding his position had escalated from a struggle into a battle against his aching body.

The wolf extended its snout, again. Moments later, it took a cautious step into the firelight.

Jake began to exhale.

He squeezed the trigger.

The night exploded into a maelstrom of bristling fur, gnashing teeth, deafening gunfire and howls of rage. The bullet from Jake's rifle shattered the wolf's head as if it were an egg. Blood, brain matter and chunks of bone blossomed in the firelight as the corpse of the now headless wolf pitched forward into the dirt.

The remaining members of the pack wailed as they charged forward. In the firelight, their wide eyes looked utterly demonic. Tendrils of drool whipped in the air around rows of razor sharp teeth as the unnatural creatures sped toward Roosevelt and Avonaco. It was impossible to count how many of the hurtling dark shapes there were, but to Roosevelt it looked as if the gates of Hell had been thrown open and the devil himself was vomiting forth the worst of his charges.

He rose slightly as he fired the rifle. The shot was rewarded with a squeal, but he had no time to confirm the kill. He cocked the lever and fired again. The muzzle flashed. Roosevelt worked the lever and snapped off another shot. That time the crack of the rifle was followed by a nasty yelp, and Roosevelt glimpsed one of the marauding wolves tumble end over end.

The pack was splintering as they closed the distance with frightening speed. Roosevelt changed stances as he tracked the two skin-walkers speeding toward the outer edge of the canyon. They would attempt to flank him from the shadows, and he had no intention of making it easy for them.

Avonaco's first shot had gone wild. He adjusted and fired again. This time the bullet found its mark. The wolf's chest collapsed inward as its momentum caused it to flip unceremoniously into the central fire. A shower of sparks burst skyward as the wolf yowled and thrashed. Avonaco saw none of this; he was already acquiring another target.

It was a large wolf. A male with a shimmering coat of silver and black fur. Avonaco drew a bead as the wicked abomination raced toward him. He had only a few seconds to fire. As Avonaco pulled the trigger, he knew it was a bad shot. The bullet nicked the wolf's hip, but the animal did not take notice. It was less than ten feet from its prey and moving at an unholy speed.

Avonaco attempted to chamber another round, but he knew it was futile. He gripped the rifle with both hands as the skin-walker leaped and—

The bullet whined as it sped over Avonaco's head.

The massive predator pinwheeled in the air as Jake's shot ripped through fur, muscle and bone. A geyser of blood fanned through the night air as the skin-walker's corpse smacked against the boulder and flopped to the ground.

Avonaco wasted no time. He dropped the rifle, snatched the shotgun and turned to face the remaining wolves. Only one remained in the firelight.

The rest had moved into the shadows.

By Jake's estimation, there had been thirteen wolves. Roosevelt had killed one and hobbled another. Avonaco had killed one. Jake had killed five.

Jake tracked the last wolf still near the fire as it raced toward Roosevelt's position. He exhaled and caressed the trigger. Gunfire flared. The skin-walker left a bloody streak across the canyon floor as it tumbled to a stop.

Eight down, five to go, he thought.

Jake rolled onto his side as he re-positioned

himself. His eyes searched the pockets of darkness below him as he sought a target. A brief, brilliant light accompanied by an ear-bursting *boom*, flashed beneath him as Avonaco discharged his shotgun. Jake pivoted toward Roosevelt. He could see that the larger man was on the move. His thick frame moved with remarkable speed as he sprinted toward the next boulder.

Two of the skin-walkers pursued him. They were little more than sleek shadows. Jake settled and drew a bead. He pulled the trigger and cursed beneath his breath as the bullet kicked up dirt inches behind the charging monster.

He readied the rifle and fired again.

The bullet shredded the skin-walker's hind quarters as it crumpled into a whining ball of agony. Jake was already seeking his next target. He spotted the second wolf and sighted down the barrel. It would be on top of Roosevelt within the next few seconds. Jake exhaled and squeezed the trigger.

The rifle issued a dry *click*.

Roosevelt tossed the rifle aside and reached for his Colt revolver as he ran. He had never been a slight man, but at that moment, he regretted neglecting his evening constitutionals. With every step he ran, his belly felt more and more as if it were made of lead rather than flesh. His breathing was coming in harsh bursts and his glasses were fogged with sweat.

He slammed into the enormous rock and immediately spun. The skin-walker's eyes were as large as wagon wheels as it leaped at him. Roosevelt drew his revolver and fanned the hammer.

LONE WOLVES

A barrage of bullets tore through the wolf's throat and torso; the dead weight of its corpse crashed into the ground and rolled to a stop inches from Roosevelt. Gunshots echoed off of the canyon's stone walls as he gulped for air and staggered back into the night.

Avonaco reloaded the shotgun as he searched for the remaining two skin-walkers. He could not see or hear them, but he could feel their presence in the air like coming rain. Pebbles crunched underneath his boots as he cautiously crept toward the edge of the firelight.

The skin-walkers' aggressive assault had failed, but Avonaco was certain that the pack would not retreat. The remaining members would no longer work in tandem. They would divide in an effort to conquer. They would do what they did best. What they were born to do.

They would hunt.

Avonaco moved to the far wall of the canyon. With his back to the wall, that was one less avenue of attack for the skin-walkers, and made him much more visible to Jake—if the young man was still with them.

Jake saw nothing. Both Avonaco and Roosevelt had been swallowed by the shadows, and the skin-walkers were natural nocturnal hunters.

Unnatural nocturnal hunters, actually, Jake reminded himself.

He could discern furtive movements within the shadows below him, but nothing tangible. Nothing he could target. An anxious knot formed in his stomach. He could not shoot what he could not see, and he was trapped on his perch. He was effectively useless.

Roosevelt and Avonaco were on their own.

A low growl issued from the oily darkness ahead of Avonaco. He froze in mid-stride as he peered into the black void. He saw nothing. His hands tightened around the shotgun as he took another step. The growling intensified.

It was a skin-walker, but something was wrong. It had the advantage, but it was not attacking.

It was wounded.

The tracker advanced, slowly. His nerves were wound so tightly his trigger finger was threatening to cramp. Ahead, he could see hints of white glimmering in the night.

Teeth.

He raised his shotgun as he stepped forward. The moonlight outlined the quivering wolf. It was crouched and its fur stood on end. It was a silhouette of pure menace. Something about the situation was wrong. Very wrong.

The wolf was a diversion.

Avonaco spun and fired as the wolf that had been stalking soared toward him. The blast from the shotgun vaporized the attacking beast's head. Blood sprayed from its useless stump of a neck as its dead weight collided with Avonaco. The Native toppled backwards onto the ground as the air escaped his lungs.

The skin-walkers had deceived him. He had emptied both barrels of his shotgun and now he was lying stunned on his back. Warm saliva plopped onto his cheek. He tilted his head backward and looked up into drooling jaws. Hot breath steamed against his exposed flesh. The skin-walker would be the instrument of his death and—

BLAM!

Roosevelt fired once. The wolf collapsed as if it were a marionette with clipped strings. Avonaco looked up to see his friend straightening his spectacles as he approached.

"Laying down on the job already?" Roosevelt quipped as he offered his hand.

"The day has been long," Avonaco responded as Roosevelt pulled him to his feet.

"Close enough," Roosevelt conceded. "Is that all of them?"

"Perhaps."

It was not a howl, it was a shriek. More human than wolf. It was a sound familiar to anyone that had lost someone close to them. The sound of anguish. The sound of rage.

Both men turned as the last skin-walker charged them with the speed of a runaway locomotive.

Roosevelt raised his revolver and fired.

Nothing. The cylinder was empty.

Avonaco discarded his shotgun and unsheathed his knife. It would prove little help, but it was better than his bare hands.

Roosevelt snapped open the revolver's cylinder as he fumbled for a silver round. His fingers were slick with sweat. There was not enough time.

SNAP! CLANG!

Jake's bear trap snapped closed around the skin-walker's leg. Bone shattered; the wolf twisted as it collapsed. It mewled and ground its teeth as it attempted to pull its mutilated leg from the trap. As it writhed, it looked up at Roosevelt and Avonaco with eyes that were nothing more than deep wells of hate.

Roosevelt snapped the cylinder shut as he stepped forward and cocked the hammer.

"Whatever grace you sacrificed in this life," he said softly, "may you earn it in the next."

He pulled the trigger and the night fell silent.

THE GREAT STONE FACE VS. THE GARGOYLES

JEFF STRAND

T HE ENTIRE SIDE of the two-story home toppled over and landed flat on the ground. The only thing saving Buster Keaton from being crushed was an open window, which he passed through with only inches to spare.

He glanced around, confused by what had just happened.

Once again, he'd evaded almost certain death. These types of antics occurred so often that he'd taken to having a film crew follow him around when he tried to do something like build a house, because he knew these sorts of things would happen and he could edit the footage into a financially successful motion picture.

"You should be squished right now!" shouted the horrified cameraman. "Completely squished!"

Buster nodded. Even with an above-average dose of good luck on his side, the house should've at least taken off an ear, yet he was entirely unharmed. And he felt perfectly calm—his heart wasn't racing at all. He should have been having a panic attack and screaming even louder than the cameraman: *"Aaaahhhh!!! I almost died! Did you see that? And now I have to rebuild the whole house!"* But he never panicked. Never broke a sweat. His reaction, invariably, was *"Hmmm, that's odd."* That's why they called him The Great Stone Face.

"Great work, Buster, great work," said the producer, walking over to shake his hand. "One of these days you're going to die on the job, but it didn't happen today, and audiences are going to love it. Did you hear me laughing? Funny, funny stuff. Because you didn't die. Obviously, it would have been less funny if you didn't survive. Or were terribly injured. But you're just fine." He brushed some sawdust off of Buster's shoulder.

Nobody knew that his films were essentially documentaries. The studio would never have been able to get insurance for his productions if they were aware that the death-defying situations were real. Later, he'd concoct a story about how much planning went into the stunt, the sheer precision required to ensure that he was not injured.

Buster Keaton, who "directed" his own movies, was a prolific filmmaker, but he'd estimate that if camera crews had been in the right place at the right time, he could've made ten times as many movies. Once he'd been ice-fishing and the shack broke through the ice. He'd calmly stepped over its roof before it disappeared beneath the surface. The camera crew was still setting up, so this astounding feat was lost. He'd also lost the time he fell off a roof and his landing was cushioned by a wedding cake, the time a vicious dog kept tearing away his clothing without biting him or exposing anything that should not be seen in cinemas, and countless other moments. It was frustrating, but he knew there'd always be another one.

For his next film, Buster had been alerted to a dilapidated gothic mansion. The owner had died under mysterious circumstances and his heirs were happy to let Hollywood use the place until they tore it down to make better use of the land. There had to be plenty of craziness that could happen here.

Everybody arrived early in the morning. "This place is huge," said the lighting director.

One of the cameramen smirked. "That's the definition of a mansion."

The lighting director glared at him. "I'm just saying, is all."

"We're making a silent film. You don't need to say anything."

"All right, all right, no bickering," said the producer. He looked up at the mansion and whistled. "I see lots of potential here already. Check out those gargoyles."

Buster had already checked them out. There were four of them draped over the roof. A lion with wings. A panther with wings. An ape with wings. And a demon with wings. Ironically, the ape was scarier than the demon, but all of them could be put to good use in a story about a hapless man who inherits a big spooky mansion and has two reels' worth of slapstick misadventures.

The camera crew set up and began filming as Buster walked around the perimeter of the mansion, inspecting it in character. He expected one of the gargoyles to come loose, plummet to the ground, and nearly crush him, but they all remained firmly fixed to the roof. There was a rake lying on the ground, tines up, but Buster tried never to consciously create a moment of amusing self-injury. Anyway, stepping on a rake was too easy of a gag. He was better than that.

The crew moved their equipment inside, and Buster walked through the house, room by room. There was a lot of dust in the mansion, and his sneezes created several classic cinema moments, including one where he sneezed so hard that he struck a shelf of valuable heirlooms. Well, they weren't really valuable; it was junk that the heirs hadn't bothered trying to auction off, but for the purposes of this motion picture each of them was priceless. Using all of his appendages, Buster caught each one of them before they could shatter against the wooden floor. That is, except for the last vase, which he would have caught in his porkpie hat if it hadn't ripped through the top. Buster scratched his head at the damage.

At lunchtime, everybody left the mansion and went out to the craft services table that had been set up outside. Buster was extremely happy with the way the shooting day was going and was in the mood to smile, but he didn't dare with so many cameras around. The Great Stone Face didn't smile on camera.

"This is going to be one of your best," said the producer, speaking through a mouthful of ham sandwich. "When that vase ripped through your hat I thought I was going to bust a gut laughing. You're a genius, even if it's all accidental."

Buster shrugged. He never felt like a genius.

"Anyway, I can't wait to see what you come up with for those three gargoyles."

Buster almost smiled at his producer's math error, but when he looked up at the roof, he saw that there were indeed only three gargoyles. The demon one was gone. Where would a giant stone gargoyle go? He assumed that some crew members had removed it, probably to leave in a yet-to-be-explored room so that he'd be hilariously startled. They weren't supposed to do this kind of thing without his direction, and it would be out of character for him to react with shock or terror, but he decided not to say anything. Maybe the gag would play well.

They finished lunch and started to file back into the mansion. Which is when Buster noticed that only the panther gargoyle was still on the roof.

"Weren't there more gargoyles up there before?" asked the producer.

Buster nodded.

"What do you think? Group hallucination?"

Buster shook his head.

"Oh well. It's definitely odd, but what can you do?"

Lunch had been pretty good, but Buster Keaton wasn't the type of person to let a tasty meal distract him from giant stone gargoyles being removed from the roof of a mansion while he sat in the front yard. His crew was efficient—they had to be, since they never knew exactly what mishaps they'd be capturing on film—but they weren't good enough to move heavy gargoyles without him noticing. Even if you assumed that the gargoyles were just sitting up there without being attached to the roof in some way, they would've required machinery or a dozen men to lift. It made no sense.

Unless they weren't really made of stone. They could've been made of something lightweight that was painted to look like stone. If that were the case, yes, a crew member could've swiped them off the roof without calling attention to himself. That made a lot more sense. Buster would quit worrying about it.

He went back inside the mansion. The crew had set up in the main foyer, with the expectation that Buster could find many ways to climb the large staircase with comedic difficulty. He looked at the top of the stairs and froze.

The ape gargoyle was there. He couldn't be sure, but he thought it was in a different position than it had been on the roof.

"Oh, hey, look at that," said the producer. "Maybe when you get to the last step, it would topple over and bounce down the stairs after you as you flee."

That seemed like a fine idea in terms of the movie they were making, but Buster couldn't shake the creeped out feeling that the gargoyle gave him. Even if it was a thin plaster replica that would shatter as soon as it struck the carpeted staircase, Buster still believed that its wings had been placed differently when he saw it on the roof.

He also believed that he just saw it blink.

He also believed that he was watching it breathe.

He also believed that it turned its head to watch him watch it breathe.

"Does anybody else think the gargoyle up there is alive?" asked the producer.

Buster nodded.

The producer shoved him forward. "Then get up there and do battle!"

Buster had no lack of courage, but fighting a supernatural stone gargoyle held little appeal for him. Though he'd been in many, many dangerous situations, none of them had blatantly violated the known rules of the universe. This seemed like a good way to get killed.

"Go on!" said the producer, giving him another shove. "Look at the production values happening up there!"

As Buster opened his mouth to protest, the lion gargoyle crept into view at the top of the staircase. He had allowed himself to possibly consider that the first gargoyle was a puppet created by his extremely talented crew, but no puppet could walk as smoothly as the lion gargoyle just had. No, there were two living stone gargoyles at the top of these stairs, and the only intelligent decision he could make right now was to rapidly exit the mansion and shoot a different film in a safe padded cell.

"The cameras are rolling!" said the producer. "This will be your masterpiece! Charlie Chaplin isn't doing a movie where he fights giant gargoyles! Harold Lloyd would never go up those stairs! You think Fatty Arbuckle could win this war? You're Buster Keaton! Get up there and kick some gargoyle posterior!"

Buster took the first step, then hesitated. This was a terrible idea.

"Do it! It'll be poetic on a level beyond anything ever seen on the silver screen! The Great Stone Face versus creatures of stone! Amazing! You were going to be a legend already, but this cements it! Are they made out of cement? Cement isn't stone, is it?"

Buster felt that his producer was getting sidetracked a bit.

"Doesn't matter," said the producer. "What I'm saying is that even if you die a gruesome death, it'll be worth it! It'll be the most successful studio-produced motion picture in the over thirty years that the medium has existed! I'm not saying that anybody wants you to die, or that you should want to die yourself, but if you *were* able to choose the method of your death, how could there be a better one than going out fighting a gargoyle? It's simply not possible. We could hire every writer in sunny California and ask them to come up with a pitch for how the legendary Buster Keaton should die, and not a single one of them would . . . you know what, I don't want to take it that far; some of those gentlemen are quite talented. All I'm saying is that you fighting a pair of stone gargoyles—well, make that a trio of them now—is a gift from the movie marketing gods."

The demon gargoyle had joined the ape and the lion. Presumably creatures made of stone didn't eat anything (surely they didn't have a digestive tract or anything that would allow them to absorb nutrition) but these three all looked ready to devour him.

Buster didn't much want to do this. But it wasn't simply about big screen immortality. It was about monsters that could potentially go on a killing rampage if he didn't face off with them right now. He'd feel terrible if they left the mansion and killed dozens of innocent civilians, and as Buster Keaton, he was humanity's best chance for that not happening.

He calmly walked up the steps. Behind him, various members of the production crew wished him luck.

The panther gargoyle stepped into view behind the others. Okay, his current situation was now thirty-three percent more dire. Still, if he was confident enough to go up against three gargoyles, he should be confident enough to go up against four of them. He clenched his fists, kept his stone face rigid, and continued walking up the stairs.

"Don't do it!" wailed one of the more cowardly crew members. "You're gonna die! You're gonna die!" Another crew member slapped him and he went silent.

At the top of the stairs, Buster wondered why he'd been so sure that these gargoyles wished to inflict violence. Maybe they were peaceful gargoyles. It wasn't the demon's fault that he'd been carved into something terrifying and blasphemous. Perhaps the hilarious set piece of this movie would be the damage wrought by these oversized beasts when they tried to help him fix up the mansion.

The lion swiped at him. It struck Buster right in the face, knocking him down the stairs.

Buster had learned to take a fall as a young child, when he was part of his father's vaudeville act. Usually these weren't after being hit by the extremely heavy stone arm of a gargoyle, but he remained professional the entire way down. Somebody who wasn't Buster Keaton would have broken at least two arms, three ribs, and one neck, but Buster bounced his way down with nary a bruise. Except for the horrific bruise on his face from the gargoyle slap.

"Makeup!" shouted the producer.

The makeup girl hurried over and applied some pancake makeup to Buster's face to cover the damage. He knew that if he took the time to think about his actions, he'd stay safely at the bottom of the stairs, so he ran back up there.

As he ran, it occurred to him that maybe taking a *little* bit of time to think about his actions would've been appropriate, since he was rushing up there without a weapon or a plan for how to defeat these creatures. "Things will just work out" had resulted in many excellent motion pictures, but this was by far the most dangerous thing he'd ever done, and it might've been helpful to figure out how one might destroy a living gargoyle before confronting four of them head-on.

As he reached the top of the stairs, the ape looked at him with its cold dead eyes (obviously, any eyes made out of stone would be cold and dead, but somehow these were even colder and deader than you'd expect) and then grabbed Buster by the neck. Buster thought the gargoyle was going to pop his head right off, which might or might not have turned out to be an amusing sight gag, depending on the amount of blood.

The gargoyle flung him back down the stairs. Again, Buster was more than equipped to take a tumble down a staircase, but it usually didn't happen when he was airborne first. He crashed to the bottom. He lifted each of his appendages in turn to make sure they weren't broken, while the makeup girl dusted more makeup onto his face.

"That looked like it really hurt," said the producer. "That much pain isn't funny. Audiences like pratfalls but they don't like getting the impression that every bone in your body shattered."

Buster nodded and stood up. He was feeling a bit wobbly. He wobbled almost to the floor, then back up, then almost to the floor again, much to the delight of the crew.

During his fall down the stairs he'd constructed a

plan. Human flesh and bone were not useful against stone . . . but stone was! (Diamond would be even better, but he did not have any giant diamonds available.) He marched back up the stairs, still maintaining his stone face, ready to teach these fiends a valuable lesson about messing with a silent comedy movie star.

The lion took another swipe at him. By this time, the shock of seeing living gargoyles had worn off and Buster was ready. He ducked. He was excellent at ducking, having done it in many of his films. The lion's stone paw struck the ape's wing, knocking off a chunk of it.

The ape looked furious. Unfortunately, its fury was aimed at Buster rather than the lion who'd actually done the damage. It threw a brutal punch. Buster dodged, and the ape punched the panther in the side, leaving a crack.

The gargoyles all attacked at once.

But, though the mansion was spacious, there wasn't enough room at the top of the stairs for four giant gargoyles to be attacking somebody simultaneously. Wings crashed into wings. Paws struck paws. Teeth accidentally snapped down on tails. Pieces of stone flew everywhere.

Buster leapt around, keeping himself from having large chunks of flesh torn from his body. He really hoped the cameras were in focus, because this was the best stunt work of his career. He bounced, jumped, and did flips as the gargoyles knocked pieces off each other. The entire lower jaw of the demon came off.

He heard a creaking sound.

He looked confused, the way movie comedians did when the floor was about to collapse beneath their feet.

When constructing the mansion, nobody had considered the structural integrity that would be necessary to support four giant gargoyles in a violent scuffle. The floor beneath them, along with the entire staircase, came down with a deafening crash that Buster assumed would be represented by a title card reading: Crash!

He sat in a pile of rubble.

The producer applauded. "Well done, well done. This will be your finest cinematic moment! Nobody will believe that . . . " He glanced around. "Uh-oh."

None of the crew members had died, or even been severely injured. The camera equipment had not been so fortunate.

"Well, that's disappointing," said the producer. "Still, at least the gargoyle menace has been vanquished, right Mr. Keaton?"

Buster kept his stone face.

It was decided that since they couldn't prove what had happened, and nobody wanted to be locked in an insane asylum, that they would say nothing. It will forever remain a mystery whether Buster Keaton saved humanity, or if the gargoyles would've just stayed in the mansion and not really done anything to anybody, but his bravery and comedic genius cannot be questioned.

THE RETURN OF THE THIN WHITE DUKE

NEIL GAIMAN

HE WAS THE MONARCH of all he surveyed, even when he stood out on the palace balcony at night listening to reports and he glanced up into the sky at the bitter twinkling clusters and whorls of stars. He ruled the worlds. He had tried for so long to rule wisely, and well, and to be a good monarch, but it is hard to rule, and wisdom can be painful. And it is impossible, he had found, if you rule, to do only good, for you cannot build anything without tearing something down, and even he could not care about every life, every dream, every population of every world.

Bit by bit, moment by moment, death by little death, he ceased to care.

He would not die, for only inferior people died, and he was the inferior of no one.

Time passed. One day, in the deep dungeons, a man with blood on his face looked at the Duke and told him he had become a monster.

The next moment, the man was no more; a footnote in a history book.

The Duke gave this conversation much thought

over the next several days, and eventually he nodded his head. "The traitor was right," he said. "I have become a monster. Ah well. I wonder if any of us set out to be monsters?"

Once, long ago, there had been lovers, but that had been in the dawn days of the Dukedom. Now, in the dusk of the world, with all pleasures available freely (but what we attain with no effort we cannot value), and with no need to deal with any issues of succession (for even the notion that another would one day succeed the Duke bordered upon blasphemy), there were no more lovers, just as there were no challenges. He felt as if he were asleep while his eyes were open and his lips spoke, but there was nothing to wake him.

The day after it had occurred to the Duke that he was now a monster was the Day of Strange Blossoms, celebrated by the wearing of flowers brought to the Ducal Palace from every world and every plane. It was a day that all in the Ducal Palace, which covered a continent, were traditionally merry, and in which they cast off their cares and darknesses, but the Duke was not happy.

"How can you be made happy?" asked the information beetle on his shoulder, there to relay his master's whims and desires to a hundred hundred worlds. "Give the word, Your Grace, and empires will rise and fall to make you smile. Stars will flame novae for your entertainment."

"Perhaps I need a heart," said the Duke.

"I shall have a hundred hundred hearts immediately plucked, ripped, torn, incised, sliced and otherwise removed from the chests of ten thousand perfect specimens of humanity," said the information beetle. "How do you wish them prepared? Shall I alert the chefs or the taxidermists, the surgeons or the sculptors?"

"I need to care about something," said the Duke. "I need to value life. I need to wake."

The beetle chittered and chirrupped on his shoulder; it could access the wisdom of ten thousand worlds, but it could not advise its master when he was in this mood, so it said nothing. It relayed its concern to its predecessors, the older information beetles and scarabs, now sleeping in ornate boxes on a hundred hundred worlds, and the scarabs consulted among themselves with regret, because, in the vastness of time, even this had happened before, and they were prepared to deal with it.

A long-forgotten subroutine from the morning of the worlds was set into motion. The Duke was performing the final ritual of the Day of Strange Blossoms with no expression on his thin face, a man seeing his world as it was and valuing it not at all, when a small winged creature fluttered out from the blossom in which she had been hiding.

"Your Grace," she whispered. "My mistress needs you. Please. You are her only hope."

"Your mistress?" asked the Duke.

"The creature comes from Beyond," clicked the beetle on his shoulder. "From one of the places that does not acknowledge the Ducal Overlordship, from the lands beyond life and death, between being and unbeing. It must have hidden itself inside an imported off-world orchid blossom. Its words are a trap, or a snare. I shall have it destroyed."

"No," said the Duke. "Let it be." He did something

he had not done for many years, and stroked the beetle with a thin white finger. Its green eyes turned black and it chittered into perfect silence.

He cupped the tiny thing in his hands, and walked back to his quarters, while she told him of her wise and noble Queen, and of the giants, each more beautiful than the last, and each more huge and dangerous and more monstrous, who kept her Queen a captive.

And as she spoke, the Duke remembered the days when a lad from the stars had come to World to seek his fortune (for in those days there were fortunes everywhere, just waiting to be found); and in remembering he discovered that his youth was less distant than he had thought. His information beetle lay quiescent upon his shoulder.

"Why did she send you to me?" he asked the little creature. But, her task accomplished, she would speak no more, and in moments she vanished, as instantly and as permanently as a star that had been extinguished upon Ducal order.

He entered his private quarters, and placed the deactivated information beetle in its case beside his bed. In his study, he had his servants bring him a long black case. He opened it himself, and, with a touch, he activated his master advisor. It shook itself, then wriggled up and about his shoulders in viper form, its serpent tail forking into the neural plug at the base of his neck.

The Duke told the serpent what he intended to do.

"This is not wise," said the master advisor, the intelligence and advice of every Ducal advisor in memory available to it, after a moment's examination of precedent.

THE RETURN OF THE THIN WHITE DUKE

"I seek adventure, not wisdom," said the Duke. A ghost of a smile began to play at the edges of his lips; the first smile that his servants had seen in longer than they could remember.

"Then, if you will not be dissuaded, take a battle-steed," said the advisor. It was good advice. The Duke deactivated his master advisor and he sent for the key to the battle-steeds' stable. The key had not been played in a thousand years: its strings were dusty.

There had once been six battle-steeds, one for each of the Lords and Ladies of the Evening. They were brilliant, beautiful, unstoppable, and when the Duke had been forced, with regret, to terminate the career of each of the Rulers of the Evening, he had declined to destroy their battle-steeds, instead placing them where they could be of no danger to the worlds.

The Duke took the key and played an opening arpeggio. The gate opened, and an ink-black, jet-black, coal-black battle-steed strutted out with feline grace. It raised its head and stared at the world with proud eyes.

"Where do we go?" asked the battle-steed. "What do we fight?"

"We go Beyond," said the Duke. "And as to whom we shall fight . . . well, that remains to be seen."

"I can take you anywhere," said the battle-steed. "And I will kill those who try to hurt you."

The Duke clambered onto the battle-steed's back, the cold metal yielding as live flesh between his thighs, and he urged it forward.

A leap and it was racing through the froth and flux of Underspace: together they were tumbling through the madness between the worlds. The Duke laughed, then, where no man could hear him, as they traveled together through Underspace, traveling forever in the Undertime (that is not reckoned against the seconds of a person's life).

"This feels like a trap, of some kind," said the battle-steed, as the space beneath galaxies evaporated about them.

"Yes," said the Duke. "I am sure that it is."

"I have heard of this Queen," said the battle-steed, "or of something like her. She lives between life and death, and calls warriors and heroes and poets and dreamers to their doom."

"That sounds right," said the Duke.

"And when we return to real-space, I would expect an ambush," said the battle-steed.

"That sounds more than probable," said the Duke, as they reached their destination, and erupted out of Underspace back into existence.

The guardians of the palace were as beautiful as the messenger had warned him, and as ferocious, and they were waiting.

"What are you doing?" they called, as they came in for the assault.

"Do you know that strangers are forbidden here? Stay with us. Let us love you. We will devour you with our love."

"I have come to rescue your Queen," he told them.

"Rescue the Queen?" they laughed. "She will have your head on a plate before she looks at you. Many people have come to save her, over the years. Their heads sit on golden plates in her palace. Yours will simply be the freshest."

There were men who looked like fallen angels and

women who looked like demons risen. There were people so beautiful that they would have been all that the Duke had ever desired, had they been human, and they pressed close to him, skin to carapace and flesh against armor, so they could feel the coldness of him, and he could feel the warmth of them.

"Stay with us. Let us love you," they whispered, and they reached out with sharp talons and teeth.

"I do not believe your love will prove to be good for me," said the Duke. One of the women, fair of hair, with eyes of a peculiar translucent blue, reminded him of someone long forgotten, of a lover who had passed out of his life a long time before. He found her name in his mind, and would have called it aloud, to see if she turned, to see if she knew him, but the battle-steed lashed out with sharp claws, and the pale blue eyes were closed forever.

The battle-steed moved fast, like a panther, and each of the guardians fell to the ground, and writhed and was still.

The Duke stood before the Queen's palace. He slipped from his battle-steed to the fresh earth.

"Here, I go on alone," he said. "Wait, and one day I shall return."

"I do not believe you will ever return," said the battle-steed. "I shall wait until time itself is done, if need be. But still, I fear for you."

The Duke touched his lips to the black steel of the steed's head, and bade it farewell. He walked on to rescue the Queen. He remembered a monster who had ruled worlds and who would never die, and he smiled, because he was no longer that man. For the first time since his first youth he had something to lose, and the discovery of that made him young again. His heart began to pound in his chest as he walked through the empty palace, and he laughed out loud.

She was waiting for him, in the place where flowers die. She was everything he had imagined that she would be. Her skirt was simple and white, her cheekbones were high and very dark, her hair was long and the infinitely dark color of a crow's wing.

"I am here to rescue you," he told her.

"You are here to rescue yourself," she corrected him. Her voice was almost a whisper, like the breeze that shook the dead blossoms.

He bowed his head, although she was as tall as he was.

"Three questions," she whispered. "Answer them correctly, and all you desire shall be yours. Fail, and your head will rest forever on a golden dish." Her skin was the brown of the dead rose petals. Her eyes were the dark gold of amber.

"Ask your three questions," he said, with a confidence he did not feel.

The Queen reached out a finger and she ran the tip of it gently along his cheek. The Duke could not remember the last time that anybody had touched him without his permission.

"What is bigger than the universe?" she asked.

"Underspace and Undertime," said the Duke. "For they both include the universe, and also all that is not the universe. But I suspect you seek a more poetic, less accurate answer. The mind, then, for it can hold a universe, but also imagine things that have never been, and are not."

The Queen said nothing.

"Is that right? Is that wrong?" asked the Duke. He wished, momentarily, for the snakelike whisper of his master advisor, unloading, through its neural plug, the accumulated wisdom of his advisors over the years, or even the chitter of his information beetle.

"The second question," said the Queen. "What is greater than a King?"

"Obviously, a Duke," said the Duke. "For all Kings, Popes, Chancellors, Empresses and such serve at and only at my will. But again, I suspect that you are looking for an answer that is less accurate and more imaginative. The mind, again, is greater than a King. Or a Duke. Because, although I am the inferior of nobody, there are those who could imagine a world in which there is something superior to me, and something else again superior to that, and so on. No! Wait! I have the answer. It is from the Great Tree: *Kether,* the Crown, the concept of monarchy, is greater than any King."

The Queen looked at the Duke with amber eyes, and she said, "The final question for you. What can you never take back?"

"My word," said the Duke. "Although, now I come to think of it, once I give my word, sometimes circumstances change and sometimes the worlds themselves change in unfortunate or unexpected ways. From time to time, if it comes to that, my word needs to be modified in accordance with realities. I would say Death, but, truly, if I find myself in need of someone I have previously disposed of, I simply have them reincorporated . . . "

The Queen looked impatient.

"A kiss," said the Duke.

She nodded.

"There is hope for you," said the Queen. "You believe you are my only hope, but, truthfully, I am yours. Your answers were all quite wrong. But the last was not as wrong as the rest of them."

The Duke contemplated losing his head to this woman, and found the prospect less disturbing than he would have expected.

A wind blew through the garden of dead flowers, and the Duke was put in mind of perfumed ghosts.

"Would you like to know the answer?" she asked.

"Answers," he said. "Surely."

"Only one answer, and it is this: the heart," said the Queen. "The heart is greater than the universe, for it can find pity in it for everything in the universe, and the universe itself can feel no pity. The heart is greater than a King, because a heart can know a King for what he is, and still love him. And once you give your heart, you cannot take it back."

"I *said* a kiss," said the Duke.

"It was not as wrong as the other answers," she told him. The wind gusted higher and wilder and for a heartbeat the air was filled with dead petals. Then the wind was gone as suddenly as it appeared, and the broken petals fell to the floor.

"So. I have failed, in the first task you set me. Yet I do not believe my head would look good upon a golden dish," said the Duke. "Or upon any kind of a dish. Give me a task, then, a quest, something I can achieve to show that I am worthy. Let me rescue you from this place."

"I am never the one who needs rescuing," said the Queen. "Your advisors and scarabs and programs are done with you. They sent you here, as they sent those who came before you, long ago, because it is better for you to vanish of your own volition, than for them to kill you in your sleep. And less dangerous." She took his hand in hers. "Come," she said. They walked away from the garden of dead flowers, past the fountains of light, spraying their lights into the void, and into the citadel of song, where perfect voices waited at each turn, sighing and chanting and humming and echoing, although nobody was there to sing.

Beyond the citadel was only mist.

"There," she told him. "We have reached the end of everything, where nothing exists but what we create, by act of will or by desperation. Here in this place I can speak freely. It is only us, now." She looked into his eyes. "You do not have to die. You can stay with me. You will be happy to have finally found happiness, a heart, and the value of existence. And I will love you."

The Duke looked at her with a flash of puzzled anger. "I asked to care. I asked for something to care about. I asked for a heart."

"And they have given you all you asked for. But you cannot be their monarch and have those things. So you cannot return."

"I . . . I asked them to make this happen," said the Duke. He no longer looked angry. The mists at the edge of that place were pale, and they hurt the Duke's eyes when he stared at them too deeply or too long.

The ground began to shake, as if beneath the footsteps of a giant.

"Is anything true here?" asked the Duke. "Is anything permanent?"

"Everything is true," said the Queen. "The giant comes. And it will kill you, unless you defeat it."

530

"How many times have you been through this?" asked the Duke. "How many heads have wound up on golden dishes?"

"Nobody's head has ever wound up on a golden platter," she said. "I am not programmed to kill them. They battle for me and they win me and they stay with me, until they close their eyes for the last time. They are content to stay, or I make them content. But you . . . you need your discontent, don't you?"

He hesitated. Then he nodded.

She put her arms around him and kissed him, slowly and gently. The kiss, once given, could not be taken back.

"So now, I will fight the giant and save you?"

"It is what happens."

He looked at her. He looked down at himself, at his engraved armor, at his weapons. "I am no coward. I have never walked away from a fight. I cannot return, but I will not be content to stay here with you. So, I will wait here, and I will let the giant kill me."

She looked alarmed. "Stay with me. Stay."

The Duke looked behind him, into the blank whiteness. "What lies out there?" he asked. "What is beyond the mist?"

"You would run?" she asked. "You would leave me?"

"I will walk," he said. "And I will not walk away. But I will walk towards. I wanted a heart. What is on the other side of that mist?"

She shook her head. "Beyond the mist is *Malkuth*: the Kingdom. But it does not exist unless you make it so. It becomes as you create it. If you dare to walk into the mist, then you will build a world or you will cease

531

to exist entirely. And you can do this thing. I do not know what will happen, except for this: if you walk away from me you can never return."

He heard a pounding still, but was no longer certain that it was the feet of a giant. It felt more like the beat, beat, beat of his own heart.

He turned towards the mist, before he could change his mind, and he walked into the nothingness, cold and clammy against his skin. With each step he felt himself becoming less. His neural plugs died, and gave him no new information, until even his name and his status were lost to him.

He was not certain if he was seeking a place or making one. But he remembered dark skin and her amber eyes. He remembered the stars—there would be stars where he was going, he decided. There must be stars.

He pressed on. He suspected he had once been wearing armor, but he felt the damp mist on his face, and on his neck, and he shivered in his thin coat against the cold night air.

He stumbled, his foot glancing against the curb.

Then he pulled himself upright, and peered at the blurred streetlights through the fog. A car drove close—too close—and vanished past him, the red rear lights staining the mist crimson.

My old manor, he thought, fondly, and that was followed by a moment of pure puzzlement, at the idea of Beckenham as his old anything. He'd only just moved there. It was somewhere to use as a base. Somewhere to escape from. Surely, that was the point?

But the idea, of a man running away (a lord or a duke, perhaps, he thought, and liked the way it felt in his head), hovered and hung in his mind, like the beginning of a song.

"I'd rather write a something song than rule the world," he said aloud, tasting the words in his mouth. He rested his guitar case against a wall, put his hand in the pocket of his duffel coat, found a pencil stub and a shilling notebook, and wrote them down. He'd find a good two-syllable word for the *something* soon enough, he hoped.

Then he pushed his way into the pub. The warm, beery atmosphere embraced him as he walked inside. The low fuss and grumble of pub conversation. Somebody called his name, and he waved a pale hand at them, pointed to his wristwatch and then to the stairs. Cigarette smoke gave the air a faint blue sheen. He coughed, once, deep in his chest, and craved a cigarette of his own.

Up the stairs with the threadbare red carpeting, holding his guitar case like a weapon, whatever had been in his mind before he turned the corner into the High Street evaporating with each step. He paused in the dark corridor before opening the door to the pub's upstairs room. From the buzz of small talk and the clink of glasses, he knew there were already a handful of people waiting and working. Someone was tuning a guitar.

Monster? thought the young man. *That's got two syllables.*

He turned the word around in his mind several times before he decided that he could find something better, something bigger, something more fitting for the world he intended to conquer, and, with only a momentary regret, he let it go forever, and walked inside.

THE END?

The end?

Not quite . . .

Dive into more Tales from the Darkest Depths:

Novels:

The Mourner's Cradle: A Widow's Journey by Tommy B. Smith

House of Sighs (with sequel novella) by Aaron Dries

Beyond Night by Eric S. Brown and Steven L. Shrewsbury

The Third Twin: A Dark Psychological Thriller by Darren Speegle

Aletheia: A Supernatural Thriller by J.S. Breukelaar

Beatrice Beecham's Cryptic Crypt: A Supernatural Adventure/Mystery Novel by Dave Jeffery

Where the Dead Go to Die by Mark Allan Gunnells and Aaron Dries

Sarah Killian: Serial Killer (For Hire!) by Mark Sheldon

The Final Cut by Jasper Bark

Blackwater Val by William Gorman

Pretty Little Dead Girls: A Novel of Murder and Whimsy by Mercedes M. Yardley

Nameless: The Darkness Comes by Mercedes M. Yardley

Novellas:
A Season in Hell by Kenneth W. Cain
Quiet Places: A Novella of Cosmic Folk Horror by Jasper Bark
The Final Reconciliation by Todd Keisling
Run to Ground by Jasper Bark
Apocalyptic Montessa and Nuclear Lulu: A Tale of Atomic Love by Mercedes M. Yardley
Wind Chill by Patrick Rutigliano
Little Dead Red by Mercedes M. Yardley
Sleeper(s) by Paul Kane
Stuck On You by Jasper Bark

Anthologies:
Welcome to The Show, edited by Doug Murano
Lost Highways: Dark Fictions From the Road, edited by D. Alexander Ward
C.H.U.D. Lives!—A Tribute Anthology
Tales from The Lake Vol.4: The Horror Anthology, edited by Ben Eads
Behold! Oddities, Curiosities and Undefinable Wonders, edited by Doug Murano
Twice Upon an Apocalypse: Lovecraftian Fairy Tales, edited by Rachel Kenley and Scott T. Goudsward
Tales from The Lake Vol.3, edited by Monique Snyman
Gutted: Beautiful Horror Stories, edited by Doug Murano and D. Alexander Ward
Tales from The Lake Vol.2, edited by Joe Mynhardt, Emma Audsley, and RJ Cavender
Children of the Grave

No Mercy: Dark Poems by Alessandro Manzetti
Eden Underground: Poetry of Darkness by Alessandro Manzetti

If you've ever thought of becoming an author, we'd also like to recommend these non-fiction titles:

The Dead Stage: The Journey from Page to Stage by Dan Weatherer
Where Nightmares Come From: The Art of Storytelling in the Horror Genre, edited by Joe Mynhardt and Eugene Johnson
Horror 101: The Way Forward, edited by Joe Mynhardt and Emma Audsley
Horror 201: The Silver Scream Vol.1 and *Vol.2*, edited by Joe Mynhardt and Emma Audsley
Modern Mythmakers: 35 interviews with Horror and Science Fiction Writers and Filmmakers by Michael McCarty
Writers On Writing: An Author's Guide Volumes 1,2,3, and 4, edited by Joe Mynhardt. Now also available in a Kindle and paperback omnibus.

Or check out other Crystal Lake Publishing books for more Tales from the Darkest Depths.

ABOUT THE AUTHORS

Kevin J. Anderson is the author of 140 novels, 56 of which have appeared on national or international bestseller lists; he has over 23 million books in print in thirty languages. Anderson has coauthored fourteen books in the DUNE saga with Brian Herbert, over 50 books for Lucasfilm in the Star Wars universe. He has written for the *X-Files*, *Star Trek*, *Batman* and *Superman*, and many other popular franchises. For his solo work, he's written the epic SF series, The Saga of Seven Suns, a sweeping nautical fantasy trilogy, "Terra Incognita," accompanied by two progressive rock CDs (which he wrote and produced), and alternate history novels *Captain Nemo* and *The Martian War*, featuring Jules Verne and H.G. Wells, respectively. He has written two steampunk novels, Clockwork Angels and Clockwork Lives, with legendary drummer and lyricist Neil Peart from the band Rush. He also created the popular humorous horror series featuring Dan Shamble, Zombie P.I., and has written eight high-tech thrillers with Colonel Doug Beason.

Michael Bailey is the multi-award-winning author of *Palindrome Hannah*, *Phoenix Rose*, and *Psychotropic Dragon* (novels), *Scales and Petals,* and *Inkblots and Blood Spots* (short story/poetry collections), *Enso* (a children's book), and the editor of *Pellucid Lunacy*, *Qualia Nous*, *The Library of the Dead*, and the *Chiral Mad* anthologies published by Written Backwards. He is also an editor for Dark Regions Press, where he has created dark science fiction projects like *You, Human*. He is currently at work on a science fiction thriller, *Seen in Distant Stars*, and a new fiction collection, *The Impossible Weight of Life*.

Jessica Marie Baumgartner is the award winning author of *The Golden Rule*, and *Embracing Entropy*, as well as *My Family Is Different*. She is a current member of the Missouri Writers Guild. Her articles and stories have been featured in a wide variety of publications including: *The Society of Misfit Stories*, *FrostFire Worlds*, *Outposts of Beyond*, *The Horror Zine*, and many more. Check her out at www.jessicamariebaumgartner.com

Mort Castle, deemed a "horror doyen" by Publishers Weekly, has won three Bram Stoker Awards®, two Black Quills, a Golden Bot, and has been nominated for an Audie, the International Horror Guild Award, the Shirley Jackson Award, and the Pushcart Prize. He's edited or authored 17 books; his recent or forthcoming titles include: *New Moon on the Water*; *Writer's Digest Annotated Classics: Dracula*; and the 2016 Leapfrog Fiction contest winner *Knowing When to Die*. More than 600 Castle authored "shorter works," stories, articles, poems, and comics have appeared in periodicals and anthologies, including *Twilight Zone*, *Bombay Gin*, *Poe's Lighthouse*, and *Tales of the Batman*. Castle teaches fiction writing at Columbia College Chicago and has presented writing workshops and seminars throughout North America.

Richard Chizmar is a *New York Times, USA Today, Wall Street Journal, Washington Post*, Amazon, and *Publishers Weekly* bestselling author.

He is the co-author (with Stephen King) of the bestselling novella, *Gwendy's Button Box* and the founder/publisher of *Cemetery Dance* magazine and the Cemetery Dance Publications book imprint. He has edited more than 35 anthologies and his fiction has appeared in dozens of publications, including multiple editions of *Ellery Queen's Mystery Magazine* and The Year's 25 Finest Crime and Mystery Stories. He has won two World Fantasy awards, four International Horror Guild awards, and the HWA's Board of Trustee's award.

Chizmar (in collaboration with Johnathon Schaech) has also written screenplays and teleplays for United Artists, Sony Screen Gems, Lions Gate, Showtime, NBC, and many other companies. He has adapted the works of many bestselling authors including Stephen King, Peter Straub, and Bentley Little.

Chizmar is also the creator/writer of Stephen King Revisited, and his third short story collection, *A Long December*, was published in 2016 by Subterranean Press. With Brian Freeman, Chizmar is co-editor of the acclaimed *Dark Screams* horror anthology series published by Random House imprint, Hydra.

Chizmar's work has been translated into many languages throughout the world, and he has appeared at numerous conferences as a writing instructor, guest speaker, panelist, and guest of honor.

Please visit the author's website at www.Richardchizmar.com

Neil Gaiman makes things up and writes them down. Which takes us from comics (like *Sand-man*) to novels (like *Anansi Boys* and *American Gods*) to short stories (some are collected in *Smoke and Mirrors*) and to occasionally movies (like Dave McKean's *Mirrormask* or the *Neverwhwere* TV series, or my own short film *A Short Film about John Bolton.*)

In his spare time he reads and sleeps and eats and tries to keep the blog at www.neilgaiman.com more or less up to date.

Christopher Golden is the *New York Times* bestselling, Bram Stoker Award-winning author of such novels as *Of Saints and Shadows*, *The Myth Hunters*, *The Boys Are Back in Town*, and *Strangewood*. He has co-written three illustrated novels with Mike Mignola, the first of which, *Baltimore, or, The Steadfast Tin Soldier and the Vampire*, was the launching pad for the Eisner Award-nominated comic book series, *Baltimore*. He is currently working on a graphic novel trilogy in collaboration with Charlaine Harris entitled *Cemetery Girl*. His novels *Snowblind* and *Tin Men* will be released in 2014.Golden was born and raised in Massachusetts, where he still lives with his family. His original novels have been published in more than fourteen languages in countries around the world. Please visit him at www.christophergolden.com

Michael Paul Gonzalez is the author of the novels *Angel Falls* and *Miss Massacre's Guide to Murder and Vengeance*. His newest creation is the audio drama podcast *Larkspur Underground*, a serialized horror story. A member of the Horror Writers Association, his short stories have appeared in print and online, including *Drive-In Creature Feature*, *Gothic Fantasy: Chilling Horror Stories*, *Lost Signals*, *Seven Scribes—Beyond Ourselves*, *18 Wheels of Horror*, the *Booked Podcast Anthology*, HeavyMetal.com, and the

Appalachian Undead Anthology. He resides in Los Angeles, a place full of wonders and monsters far stranger than any that live in the imagination. You can visit him online at www.MichaelPaulGonzalez.com.

Eugene Johnson is a writer and Bram Stoker nominated editor who has written and edited in various genres. His anthology *Appalachian Undead*, co-edited with Jason Sizemore, was selected by FearNet as one of the best books of 2012. Eugene's articles and stories have been published by award winning Apex publishing, The Zombiefeed, Evil Jester Press, Warrior Sparrow Press and more. Eugene also appeared in *Dread Stare*, a political theme horror anthology from Thunder Dome Press. Eugene's anthology, *Drive-in Creature Feature*, pays homage to monster movies, features New York Times best-selling authors Clive Barker, Joe R. Lansdale, Christopher Golden, Jonathan Maberry and many more. He was nominated for the Bram Stoker award for *Where Nightmares Come From: The Art Of Storytelling In The Horror Genre* along with his co-editor Joe Mynhardt.

As a filmmaker, Eugene Johnson worked on various movies, including the upcoming *Requiem*, starring Tony Todd and directed by Paul Moore. His short film *Leftovers*, a collaboration with director Paul Moore, was featured at the Screamfest film festival in Los Angeles as well as Dragon Con.

Eugene is currently developing fun projects at EJP. He spends his time working on several projects including *Brave*, a horror anthology honoring people with disabilities; the *Fantastic Tales of Terror* anthology; and his children's book series, Life Lessons with Lil Monsters. Eugene is currently a member of the

Horror Writers Association. He resides in West Virginia with his fiancé, daughter, and two sons.

From the day she was born, **Jess Landry** has always been attracted to the stranger things in life. Her fondest childhood memories include getting nightmares from the *Goosebumps* books, watching *The Hilarious House of Frightenstein*, and reiterating to her parents that there was absolutely nothing wrong with her mental state.

Since picking up a pen a few years ago, Jess's fiction has appeared in anthologies such as Crystal Lake Publishing's Where Nightmares Come From, Unnerving's *Alligators in the Sewers*, Stitched Smile's *Primogen: The Origins of Monsters*, DFPs *Killing It Softly*, and April Moon Books' *Ill-Considered Expeditions*, as well as online with SpeckLit and EGM Shorts.

She currently works as Managing Editor for JournalStone and its imprint, Trepidatio Publishing, where her goal is to publish diverse stories from diverse writers. An active member of the HWA, Jess has volunteered as Head Compiler for the Bram Stoker Awards since 2015, and has most recently taken on the role of Membership Coordinator.

You can visit her on the interwebs at her sad-looking website, jesslandry.com, though your best bet at finding her is on Facebook and Twitter (facebook.com/jesslandry28 and twitter.com/jesslandry28), where she often posts cat memes and references Jurassic Park.

Joe R. Lansdaleis the author of 48 novels and over 20 short story collections. He has written and sold a number of screenplays, has had his plays adapted for stage. His work has been adapted to film; *Bubba Ho-Tep* and *Cold in July* among them. His best-known novels, the Hap and Leonard series has been adapted for television with Lansdale as co-executive producer with Lowell Northrop under the title, *HAP AND LEONARD*. He has also edited or co-edited numerous anthologies.

Vince Liaguno is the Bram Stoker Award-winning editor of *Unspeakable Horror: From the Shadows of the Closet* (Dark Scribe Press 2008), an anthology of queer horror fiction, which he co-edited with Chad Helder. His debut novel, 2006's *The Literary Six*, was a tribute to the slasher films of the 80's and won an Independent Publisher Award (IPPY) for Horror and was named a finalist in *ForeWord Magazine's* Book of the Year Awards in the Gay/Lesbian Fiction category.

More recently, he edited *Butcher Knives and Body Counts* (Dark Scribe Press, 2011)—a collection of essays on the formula, frights, and fun of the slasher film—as well as the second volume in the *Unspeakable Horror* series, subtitled *Abominations of Desire* (Evil Jester Press, 2017). He's currently at work on his second novel.

He currently resides on the eastern end of Long Island, New York, where he is a licensed nursing home administrator by day and a writer, anthologist, and pop culture enthusiast by night. He is a member (and former Secretary) of the Horror Writers Association (HWA) and a member of the National Book Critics Circle (NBCC).

Author Website: www.VinceLiaguno.com

Bentley Little writes Horror. Not Dark fantasy. Not Thrillers. Not suspense. Bentley Little was born in

Arizona. He received a BA in Communications and an MA in English and Comparative Literature from California State University. He currently lives in Fullerton, California with his wife and son. He also writes under the pseudonym 'Phillip Emmons'.

Jonathan Maberry is a New York Times bestselling author, 5-time Bram Stoker Award-winner, and comic book writer. His vampire apocalypse book series, V-WARS, is in production as a Netflix original series, starring Ian Somerhalder (*Lost, Vampire Diaries*) and will debut in early 2019. He writes in multiple genres including suspense, thriller, horror, science fiction, fantasy, and action; and he writes for adults, teens and middle grade. His works include the Joe Ledger thrillers, *Glimpse,* the Rot & Ruin series, the Dead of Night series, *The Wolfman, X-Files Origins: Devil's Advocate, Mars One*, and many others. Several of his works are in development for film and TV. He is the editor of high-profile anthologies including *The X-Files, Aliens: Bug Hunt, Out of Tune, New Scary Stories to Tell in the Dark, Baker Street Irregulars, Nights of the Living Dead,* and others. His comics include *Black Panther: Doomwar, The Punisher: Naked Kills,* and *Bad Blood.* He lives in Del Mar, California.

Find him online at www.jonathanmaberry.com.

Elizabeth Massie is a Bram Stoker Award and Scribe Award-winning author of novels, short fiction, media tie-ins, poetry, and nonfiction. Her works include *Sineater, Hell Gate, Desper Hollow, Wire Mesh Mothers, Welcome Back to the Night, Twisted Branch* (under the pseudonym Chris Blaine), *Homeplace, Naked On the Edge, Afraid, Sundown, The Fear*

Report, The Tudors: King Takes Queen, The Tudors: Thy Will Be Done, Dark Shadows: Dreams of the Dark (co-authored with Mark Rainey), *Homegrown, Night Benedictions, Versailles, Buffy the Vampire Slayer: Power of Persuasion,* the Ameri-Scares series of spooky novels for middle grade readers, the Young Founders series of historical novels for young adults, the Silver Slut superhero adventure series, and more. Massie spends her spare time knitting, geocaching, and staring mindlessly into space. She lives in the Shenandoah Valley with her husband, illustrator and theremin-player Cortney Skinner.

Paul Moore is a filmmaker who has written and directed four feature films, most recently *Keepsake* and *Requiem.* He is also the co-owner of the movie production studio *Blind Tiger Filmworks,* and his first short story *Spoiled* was published in the well-received anthology *Appalachian Undead.* It was a very rewarding experience and he is happy to follow that effort with *Things,* an homage to both the spirit of B-movie alien invasion films and several of the films that inspired him to pursue a career in filmmaking. He also appeared in *Dread State* and *Where Nightmares Come From.*

Lisa Morton is a screenwriter, author of non-fiction books, award-winning prose writer, and Halloween expert whose work was described by the American Library Association's *Readers' Advisory Guide to Horror* as "consistently dark, unsettling, and frightening." Her most recent releases include *Ghosts: A Haunted History* and the short story collection *Cemetery Dance Select: Lisa Morton.* Lisa lives in the San Fernando Valley and online at www.lisamorton.com.

John Palisano has a pair of books with Samhain Publishing, *Dust of the Dead*, and *Ghost Heart*. *Nerves* is available through Bad Moon. *Starlight Drive: Four Halloween Tales* was released in time for Halloween, and his first short fiction collection *All That Withers* is available from Cycatrix press, celebrating over a decade of short story highlights. *Night of 1,000 Beasts* is coming soon. He won the Bram Stoker Award in short fiction in 2016 for "Happy Joe's Rest Stop." More short stories have appeared in anthologies from Cemetery Dance, PS Publishing, Independent Legions, DarkFuse, Crystal Lake, Terror Tales, Lovecraft eZine, Horror Library, Bizarro Pulp, Written Backwards, Dark Continents, Big Time Books, McFarland Press, Darkscribe, Dark House, Omnium Gatherum, and more. His non-fiction pieces have appeared in *Blumhouse*, *Fangoria* and *Dark Discoveries* magazines.

He is currently serving as the Vice President of the Horror Writers Association. Say 'hi' to John at: www.johnpalisano.com and http://www.amazon.com/author/johnpalisano and www.facebook.com/johnpalisano and www.twitter.com/johnpalisano

Luke Spooner is a freelance illustrator from the South of England. At 'Carrion House' he creates dark, melancholy and macabre illustrations and designs for a variety of projects and publishers, big and small, young and old.

Jeff Strand is the four-time Bram Stoker Award-nominated author of over forty books, including *Pressure*, *Dweller*, and *Bring Her Back*. His website is www.JeffStrand.com.

Perhaps best known for his chilling performance as "Candyman," the charismatic 6' 5" actor **Tony Todd** as consistently turned in compelling performances since his debut in the fantasy film *Sleepwalk* (1986). Born in Washington, D.C., Todd spent two years on a scholarship at the University of Connecticut, which, in turn, led to a scholarship from the renowned Eugene O'Neill National Theatre Institute. It proved to be the foundation for intense stints at the Hartman Conservatory in Stamford, Connecticut and the Trinity Square Repertory Theatre Conservatory in Providence, Rhode Island. Todd appeared in dozens of classical and many experimental plays, yet still managed to find time to teach playwriting to high school students in the Hartford public school system.

Todd's extensive credits exemplify his versatility. They include such film classics as *The Rock* (1996), *The Crow* (1994), *Lean on Me* (1989), *Bird* (1988), *Night of the Living Dead* (1990), *Final Destination* (2000), the multiple Academy Award winning Oliver Stone film *Platoon* (1986) and *Le secret* (2000), which was nominated and screened at the Cannes Film Festival. Todd's film career also includes the independent film *Silence* (2002) and *Final Destination 2* (2003). He has had prominent guest starring roles in numerous critically-acclaimed television series, including recurring on Boston Public (2000), For the People (2002) and The District (2000), as well as NYPD Blue (1993), Smallville (2001), Law & Order (1990), Crossing Jordan (2001), Homicide: Life on the Street (1993) and The X-Files (1993). Todd recurred on three incarnations of Star Trek and guest starred on Xena: Warrior Princess (1995) and episodes of CSI: Miami and Andromeda. His television movies include starring roles in *True*

Women (1997), *Black Fox* (1995), *Butter* (1998), *Ivory Hunters* (1990), *Babylon 5: A Call to Arms* (1999) and *Control Factor* (2003).

Todd's considerable theatre credits include the world premiere of award-winning playwright August Wilson's *King Hedley II*, where he originated the title role in Pittsburgh, Seattle and Boston. Variety commented: "Todd's King Hedley dominates the stage. A sour-faced mix of rage and resolve, anger and vulnerability. Todd's Hedley was a memorable tour-de-force even on opening." He also received a coveted Helen Hayes nomination for his performance in Athol Fugard's *The Captain's Tiger at La Jolla*, the Manhattan Theatre Club and the Kennedy Center. Other theatre credits include *Les Blancs*, *Playboy of the West Indies*, *Othello*, *Zooman and the Sign*, award-winning playwright Keith Glover's *Dark Paradise*, *Aida* (on Broadway), and most recently, *Levee James* for the prestigious Eugene O'Neill Playwrights Conference and The New Dramatist Guild.

Bev Vincent is the author of some 80 short stories, including appearances in *Alfred Hitchcock's Mystery Magazine*, *Ellery Queen's Mystery Magazine* and two MWA anthologies. His work has been nominated for the Bram Stoker Award (twice), the Edgar (for *The Stephen King Illustrated Companion*) and the ITW Thriller Award, and he was the 2010 winner of the Al Blanchard Award. He is a contributing editor of *Cemetery Dance* magazine, where his Stephen King: News from the Dead Zone column has appeared since 2001. His most recent book is *The Dark Tower Companion*. He lurks around various corners of the internet including Twitter (@BevVincent), his book review blog (OnyxReviews.com) and website (bevvincent.com). In the "real world," he lives in Texas, where he is trying to ignore the news while working on a novel.

Tim Waggoner has published close to forty novels and three collections of short stories. He writes original dark fantasy and horror, as well as media tie-ins, and his articles on writing have appeared in numerous publications. He's won a Bram Stoker Award, been a finalist for the Shirley Jackson Award and the Scribe Award, and his fiction has received numerous Honorable Mentions in volumes of Best Horror of the Year. He's also a full-time tenured professor who teaches creative writing and composition at Sinclair College in Dayton, Ohio.

David Wellington got his start serializing his zombie story *Monster Island* online in 2003. Since then he has written more than twenty novels, including the 13 Bullets series, the Jim Chapel thrillers, the standalone novel *Positive*, and most recently a science fiction trilogy beginning with *Forsaken Skies* (as D. Nolan Clark). He has also worked in video games, comic books and other media. He lives in New York City.

Stephanie M. Wytovich is an American poet, novelist, and essayist. Her work has been showcased in numerous anthologies such as *Gutted: Beautiful Horror Stories, Shadows Over Main Street: An Anthology of Small-Town Lovecraftian Terror, Year's Best Hardcore Horror: Volume 2, The Best Horror of the Year: Volume 8*, as well as many others.

Wytovich is the Poetry Editor for Raw Dog Screaming Press, an adjunct at Western Connecticut State University and Point Park University, and a mentor to authors with Crystal Lake Publishing. She is a member of the Science Fiction Poetry Association, an active member of the Horror Writers Association, and a graduate of Seton Hill University's MFA program for Writing Popular Fiction. Her Bram Stoker Award-winning poetry collection, *Brothel*, earned a home with Raw Dog Screaming Press alongside *Hysteria: A Collection of Madness*, *Mourning Jewelry*, and *An Exorcism of Angels*. Her debut novel, *The Eighth*, is published with Dark Regions Press.

Her next poetry collection, *Sheet Music to My Acoustic Nightmare*, is scheduled to be released late 2017 from Raw Dog Screaming Press.

Follow Wytovich at http://www.stephaniewytovich.com/ and on twitter @JustAfterSunset.

Mercedes M. Yardley is a dark fantasist who wears poisonous flowers in her hair. She is the author of Pretty *Little Dead Girls, Nameless*, and the Bram Stoker Award-winning *Little Dead Red*. Mercedes lives in Las Vegas and can be reached at www.abrokenlaptop.com.

Hi readers,

It makes our day to know you reached the end of our book. Thank you so much. This is why we do what we do every single day.

Whether you found the book good or great, we'd love to hear what you thought. Please take a moment to leave a review on Amazon, Goodreads, or anywhere else readers visit. Reviews go a long way to helping a book sell, and will help us to continue publishing quality books. You can also share a photo of yourself holding this book with the hashtag #IGotMyCLPBook!

Thank you again for taking the time to journey with Crystal Lake Publishing.

We are also on . . .

Website:
www.crystallakepub.com

Be sure to sign up for our newsletter and receive two free eBooks: http://eepurl.com/xfuKP

Books:
http://www.crystallakepub.com/book-table/

Twitter:
https://twitter.com/crystallakepub

Facebook:
https://www.facebook.com/Crystallakepublishing/

Instagram:
https://www.instagram.com/crystal_lake_publishin
g/

Patreon:
https://www.patreon.com/CLP

Or check out other Crystal Lake Publishing books for more Tales from the Darkest Depths. You can also subscribe to Crystal Lake Classics where you'll receive fortnightly info on all our books, starting all the way back at the beginning, with personal notes on every release. Or follow us on Patreon for behind the scenes access.

With unmatched success since 2012, Crystal Lake Publishing has quickly become one of the world's leading indie publishers of Mystery, Thriller, and Suspense books with a Dark Fiction edge.

Crystal Lake Publishing puts integrity, honor, and respect at the forefront of our operations.

We strive for each book and outreach program that's launched to not only entertain and touch or comment on issues that affect our readers, but also to strengthen and support the Dark Fiction field and its authors.

Not only do we publish authors who are legends in the field and as hardworking as us, but we look for men and women who care about their readers and fellow human beings. We only publish the very best Dark Fiction, and look forward to launching many new careers.

We strive to know each and every one of our

readers while building personal relationships with our authors, reviewers, bloggers, podcasters, bookstores, and libraries.

Crystal Lake Publishing is and will always be a beacon of what passion and dedication, combined with overwhelming teamwork and respect, can accomplish: unique fiction you can't find anywhere else.

We do not just publish books, we present you worlds within your world, doors within your mind from talented authors who sacrifice so much for a moment of your time.

This is what we believe in. What we stand for. This will be our legacy.

Welcome to Crystal Lake Publishing.

THANK YOU FOR PURCHASING THIS BOOK

14738410R00313

Made in the USA
Lexington, KY
09 November 2018